Of Shepherds

A Novel

by J. R. Cicero

TO GARTH (G-MAN) INFANTINO,
MAY GOD BLESS YOU WITH A
LOVING FAMILY AND MANY YEARS
OF HAPPINESS! YOUR FORMER
CO-WORKER,
Joseph R. Cicero
1-16-2002

AmErica House
Baltimore

First printing

ISBN: 1-58851-614-8
PUBLISHED BY AMERICA HOUSE BOOK PUBLISHERS
www.publishamerica.com
Baltimore

Printed in the United States of America

To my wife,
Betti,
for her unwavering support

and to my father,
Ray,
for the quiet stick-to-itiveness that he fostered in me.

PROLOGUE

"… But we had to celebrate and rejoice! This brother of yours was dead, and has come back to life. He was lost, and is found."

– Luke 15:1

PART ONE

Chapter 1

I hovered over Tom, as did his waiting spirit. His mutterings of faith told me he wasn't the "Doubting Thomas" penned on his pocket flap. I was his gatekeeper—assigned by God and the Marine Corps to usher his soul from this earth—yet I questioned my fitness for the role. As a man of the cloth, though, I couldn't let this young soldier down.

It didn't take a trained eye to see that he wouldn't make it, the doctor's glance confirming it as he inserted the chest tube. A "priority one" chopper was called to whisk Tom away, but I knew the Doc was following the script ... not for Tom, but for Lenny, his black partner. As the morphine took hold, Tom's thoughts, which should have been of loved ones, were instead of angry comrades. He kept mumbling that he didn't want his buddies to be mad at him.

"I did what I could, Chaplain," said Lenny. "I put that cigarette wrapper over his chest ... like they taught us in boot camp. He'll make it, won't he?"

Tom's chest heaved, his words mixed with blood: an all-too-familiar gurgling. "Tell Matt." Tom halted, his tongue dry and neck muscles straining. "Tell him ... and the others ... I'm sorry. Tell them!"

I clasped his dog tags and eyed the crimson chest tube as he repeated his plea. The tags were covered with blood and mud, but the lettering appeared as I rubbed my thumb over the shiny metal. He was Roman Catholic, and my priestly duty was to administer Last Rites. Doc McGurty, a cigarette clinging to his lower lip, poked his head through the tarpaulin flap and twirled his finger to signal the chopper's arrival. I waved him off. No words were necessary—we'd been through this scene before. When life could be given, the Doc's desires would prevail, but when death was certain, my will had to be done. For this Marine, only seconds in this purgatory remained.

When Tom groped at my leg, I was stunned by his viselike grip. His

eyes were glazed, his breathing shallow. "Tell Matt and the others …
I didn't mean it. Please!"

I pried his hand from my leg, then turned to Lenny. "Is he religious?
Tell me, man!"

"I've heard him flappin', Reverend. Especially when the mortars
was comin' in. I think he was prayin', but he never said the Lord's
name."

Tom was too far gone to offer consent. I traced the cross on his
soiled forehead, my thumb passing over a childhood scar. There was no
time for a "Litany of the Saints," as the incoming mortars—their
accuracy confirmed by my calibrated ear—meant that triage would
soon overflow. Pressing my palm to his head, I said, "I commend you,
Brother Thomas, to Almighty God, and entrust you to your Creator.
May you return to Him who formed you from the dust of the earth …
May you see your Redeemer face to face and enjoy forever the vision
of God."

"Amen," quivered Lenny's voice.

Tom's torso shuddered as his soul wrestled free. He wasn't more
than nineteen, yet he was already at heaven's gate. This asinine war had
snuffed another life. Throughout, the VC mortars kept pounding the
airstrip's steel plates, like a drum roll at a public execution.

I closed his eyelids, then dabbed the oil of the sick on his palms and
crossed his forearms. His hands were cool, his fingernails encrusted
with earth and blood. He wore no wedding band, only a high-school
ring—Class of '67 emblazoned beside the stone. There'd be wailing in
his household tomorrow, but at least no bride or fatherless child would
be among the mourning. The tears running down Lenny's cheeks told
a timeless tale: the color of a man's skin meant nothing in combat.

"You were close, huh?"

"Like brothers, Reverend." He closed his eyes, then lowered his
head.

"What was he sorry about? What happened on that hill?"

"He took some cash from the R&R kitty. Just borrowed it. Honest."

"Who's this fella Matt? Is he the banker or what?"

"Nah. He was just sore when Tom didn't pay back the money. But
Tom didn't have it 'cause he'd sent it to his girl in Ohio. They were
fixin' to get married."

"You'll tell Matt what Tom said, right? They'll patch you up, pin a Purple Heart on your chest, and you'll be back on that hill in a couple days." His eyes filled with fear.

"There's more. Tommy ran and hid in the elephant grass in the last firefight. Matt was plenty pissed and …"

"Who the hell is this Matt, anyway?"

"Just a dirt-eatin' grunt, like the rest of us. His name is Garrison."

"Garrison, you said?"

"Yeah."

Two faces flashed through my mind: Julie, who I loved, and Matt Garrison, who'd pulled me, drunk and stoned, from a burning auto wreck. He lied, claiming to be the driver, to protect me from the law and my Bishop.

"What's he look like? Where's he from?" I asked in rapid fire.

"He's white. From Pennsylvania … some town near a big lake. He's got a college degree, but he ain't no officer. I figure he's hidin' something."

"Describe him," I blurted. Could this somehow be the man who'd saved my life?

"Average lookin'. Brown eyes and dark hair. Nothin' special. Well, he's got a scar on his hand. Like it got burned or something."

"Which hand, Lenny?"

"His left, Sir. I'm pretty sure."

For God's sake! This was my Matt! Why was he in this rat-infested corner of the world? Why Vietnam? Why Khe Sanh?

"He's OK? Right, Lenny? I mean, has he been wounded?"

"He's fine, Reverend. Like everybody on 881 South, he's been livin' like a rat and prayin' that Charlie don't blow us away."

"I know this Matt. I'm sure of it."

"He ain't said nothin' about knowing a priest."

I grinned. Considering how I'd treated him, it was little wonder.

"Looks like I'm going to visit your hilltop real soon." It was Friday, January 19, 1968 and if I whined enough, I could hop a chopper on Sunday for a mountaintop service. I'd stuff my saddlebags with chocolate-coated gee dunks and a few beers, and then make a triumphant descent onto Matt's turf.

"When you go, Reverend, be sure to hold a prayer service for

Tommy. It's easy to feel close to God on that hill, especially when the clouds come rollin' in."

"How many men are up there?"

"Three hundred. We've got India and two platoons of Mike Company. We're all with the 3/26. Your buddy's in India."

What could three hundred guys do on a hill? It was then I remembered my history lessons of the Spartan's defense at the Thermopylae Pass. While the corpsman dressed Lenny's leg, a commotion erupted outside the Charlie-Med tent. An evacuee from one of the hillposts was shouting, but it wasn't Matt. I should've attended to him, but I was focused on Lenny.

"Why man that hill? What do you guys hope to accomplish?" I'd seen enough movies to know to hold the high ground, but this seemed an exercise in futility. We were dying for a plateau comprised of coffee groves, trout streams, and twelve-foot-tall elephant grass—real estate not worth the lives of men ten thousand miles from home.

"The CO says that if we weren't there then the North Vietnamese would set up shop. Give 'em a few mortar tubes, maybe some artillery and anti-aircraft guns, and Charlie would make life miserable for your base camp. On a clear day, you can look right down the throat of your runway—it'd be a turkey shoot, Reverend. Trust me."

His explanation made sense, but I wanted the global picture, not a microscopic viewpoint. I'd marched in enough anti-war rallies to know not to accept the Establishment line.

"I've been up there a month. Some Christmas present, huh, Reverend? It's an eerie place. Being above the clouds makes ya feel like you're in God's country—that's what the 881 means, we're 881 meters above sea level. Just like Moses, we come down from that mountain lookin' for sinners; come night, though, we head back home to the faithful. We ain't throwin' no tablets, though, Reverend. Just grenades, napalm, and anything else we get our hands on. Last month we patrolled all the way to Laos. We may not've wandered as long as Moses did, but we sure felt as lonely. I was scared. Scared shitless. Know what I mean?"

He smiled with satisfaction at his biblical allusion.

"What was going down when you and Tommy got hit?"

"We were searchin' for some radio gear and code cards that a recon team lost last Wednesday. The boss says if Charlie gets hold of 'em, he'll play hell with our communications."

"So you got the cards. Was Matt on the patrol, too?"

"No to both. Our point man and Charlie's was shootin' it out—High Noon style. Coop would've been proud. I was blazin' away with my M-60, mowin' down elephant grass like a machine. Then the Second Louie said to lay low and let the 81mm mortars do the dirty work. That's when Tommy got it. He was runnin' away, Reverend. Everybody was plum scared—Tommy just more so than the rest of us."

I squeezed Lenny's wrist and dabbed his forehead with a washcloth.

"Lots of things scare me. Even the trees, what's left of 'em, are full of ghoulish globs of melted plastic from the napalm. Just last week, we was diggin' a trench-line when we fell into a pit of dead VC. I've never touched a rotting body before, Reverend—the smell had us heavin' our guts. The Louie said they died in last spring's hill fights; plenty of our guys bought it there just tryin' to unjam their M-16. We're stuck, though, with them pieces of shit, 'cause the Louie says that's what the Corps issued us. Damn brass."

"Ditto."

Lenny was near exhaustion. "Where's Tommy, Reverend?"

I'd positioned myself to block his view of Tom. "They've taken him to Graves Registration, Lenny. You want him cleaned up before we send him home, don't you?" The veins in his neck bulged as he sat up.

"I ain't done talkin' to him, Reverend. You hear?"

Corpsman Suscheck, responding to my anxious nod, injected Lenny with a sedative while I talked him down. Only my promise to accompany him back to Hill 881 would quiet him.

The overhead light swung lazily, like a man in a noose, from the rumble of incoming. I left Lenny mumbling about how he'd "… make it right with Matt and the others." Doc McGurty stood resting against a pyramid of sandbags. I raised two fingers to my lips and he lit me a smoke, his bloodstained finger leaving an imprint on the wrapper.

"Dammit, Andy. You know the drill. I gotta get that Marine to Graves Registration."

I'd taken the liberty of returning Tom's body to Lenny's side. "Ah, come on, Gurt. What's the harm in giving the guy some time with his dead buddy?"

"We've hashed out this shit before. That's my world in there, my little chapel and sacristy. Christ! You were so glued to that black that I couldn't examine his wound."

He was flapping his arms like a penguin. I thought sure the cigarette would fly from his mouth, but it clung to his lower lip. I grinned. "Not to worry, Doc. It's only a flesh wound. I'm gonna personally escort him back to 881 South this Sunday." He smiled and I patted his bony shoulder, admonishing him to get off his ass and tend to his flock.

The shelling had halted, so I stood erect, helmet in hand and back arched, to bask in the sun's rays. I adjusted my flak jacket so it wouldn't chafe, then headed south toward the trash dump. Like a turtle hiding in his shell, I planted my piss pot on my head and snugged the chinstrap. Colonel Lowell, the base CO, had ordered all hands to hunker down, wear their helmets and jackets, sleep and eat with their weapons, keep their water cans filled, and lay lots of concertina wire. Yet the more we dug in, the greater our casualties.

I hated the wire. It rustled and chimed in the wind. Like a boa, it coiled itself around our camp. I couldn't decide whether it kept the enemy out or us in. It was ugly, strewn with razors and barbs, and surrounded by a maze of foot-traps. God help those who'd scale it, and we who looked to it for protection.

The trash dump soon came into view, its odor foul. Missing, however, were the Montagnard tribesmen. There'd be a hundred sifting our waste on a normal day, poking around for treasures to eat or to barter on the black market, but only a handful were present. Something was in the wind, in the elephant grass that swayed before its breath. The absence of the Bru Montagnards was a bell-ringing, whistle-blowing heads-up that something was wrong.

Speculation accompanied our recent killing of five senior NVA officers. God rest their souls, I thought, but take no pity on their cause. Clad in green fatigues and Ho Chi Minh sandals, they were gunned down while reconnoitering our camp—all but one, that is. Wounded, he cut the shoulder straps of the others and dragged himself and their dispatch cases into the jungle. What alarmed us was the size of one of their dead. He was big and looked Chinese, and our old-timers recalled what their hordes did to us in Korea. Our medical staff examined the corpse but it gave up no secrets, leaving our rumor mill to churn out a yellow scare.

I booted a clump of red clay and watched as it tumbled through a patch of ground-hugging fog. At 1500 feet, the haze rolled in like the evening tide. Standing in this mist was like standing at heaven's gate, only these clouds could swallow me up—could lead me to stumble into an unseen trench or shell hole. I scratched my armpit, curling my nose at the BO, then fingered the letter from Julie that lay tucked in my breast pocket. God, I was thankful for mail call. Too often it was an orphan to the four-B's: bombs, bullets, bandages, and beans. In exchange for this foursome, we placed our dead in body bags and mailed them home—where the brass and politicians spouted eulogies over their flag-draped caskets.

I removed Julie's crumpled communication. I had cared for it like an intelligence officer would the enemy's battle plan, like an immigrant his green card. It was my link to the world. When I wrote her I was filled with passion, but my words were measured because I was married to the Church. The loneliness was oppressive, but I couldn't open a window to vent it without closing the door on my celibate life. I read her letter aloud.

Dearest Andrew,

Do I bore you with my drivel? I hope not. I need someone who'll listen and care. You've always been that someone. Since Faith was born, Dan has become impossible. He's caught up in his own world, and I'm disgusted with his pothead ways. I had so many dreams when I finished college, but all that changed when I got pregnant.

I should've had an abortion, but I didn't want to anger you. Carrying Faith was a physical hell, and marrying Dan has been an emotional one. I'm in a pickle, and I pray I haven't ruined my life. Somehow, I'll get out of this mess.

Before I got married I felt like a damsel in distress, and I let Dan's false chivalry sweep me off my feet. It didn't help that my parents freaked out at the thought of my being an unwed mother. Now I'm afflicted with breast feedings, neighbors' gawking, and a husband (provider?) who squanders our money traveling to peace marches and buying dope.

Remember Matt, the classmate I dated in college? I still think of him, just like I do you. I should've told you of the troubles we had, but I didn't want to come off as an airhead who was more interested in her carnal instincts than the anti-war movement. I just didn't want to disappoint you. Well, enough of my grumbling about the men in my life. I'm sure your hands are full with the men in your life—your flock of wayward Marines.

I don't like what I hear about Khe Sanh. It may be blasphemous but I'll say it anyway—your asshole Bishop had no right ordering you off to Nam! You may be married to the Church, but she's a bitch. You deserve better. Much better.

Please take care and know that I miss and love you—platonically, if that's what your Bishop has to hear.

I'll write again soon.

Yours Forever, Julie

I returned the letter to my pocket, smiling. *She's right, my Bishop is an asshole.* "I miss you, too, Julie," I uttered.

She was a 60s campus radical—determined to champion the rights of women, blacks, American Indians, and draftees fleeing to Canada. I remember how her delicate fingers gripped a bullhorn to proclaim her brand of fire and brimstone. Her message was as convincing as any delivered from my pulpit and soaked up by believers hungrier than those in my fold. Give her a cause and she could persuade any group to see the injustice. Damn, what a firebrand!

She talked of Matt, but did he know that she was a wife, a mother, and hurting? *Better that he focuses on his own suffering,* I thought, *or he might not live to see her again.* Lord willing, my prodigal son would return to her waiting arms. Before I could nurture that reassuring thought, the klaxon wailed a warning, and the Montagnards scurried for cover. The incoming slammed the terrain like hailstones on a tin roof—like meteorites against our lunar-looking landscape—and I dove into a trench. Thank God for those spotters on 881 South. Maybe Matt's eyes and ears were alerting us to the VC's incoming? Maybe he was my guardian angel and I his wayward son. I smiled at that thought.

The dirt kept flying, fist-sized clumps clobbering my body. I was in a fetal position when a helmet with a gaping hole landed beside me.

Taped to its camouflage cover—below the inscription "I love you, Mom!"—was a short-timer's calendar with twelve of thirteen months X'ed out. He had just three lousy weeks left of C-rats, jungle rot, and anti-malaria pills. I sprang up. There, beside a smoking crater, lay his mangled body.

Any other branch of the service and his hell would've been 365 days, but the Grunts, the Leathernecks, the Jarheads, did the shit detail—a thirteen-month tour. He should've been home a week ago. Instead, he was another statistic for the bean-counting brass; another battle cry for the anti-war protesters; another mother's heart broken. God, I hated this war!

While I knelt in prayer over him, they collected his remains. The Colonel's messenger, winded and panting, suddenly appeared and motioned for me. I traced the cross on the dead man's forehead and slowly lifted my frame.

"Colonel Lowell wants to see you, Sir."

I sighed. "Let's go, Corporal." As we half-crouched, half-jogged, I noticed the movie schedule tucked beneath the messenger's arm. "Say, what flicks do we have? Any *Gunsmoke*?" He passed me the clipboard and I slowed to read it. "*Murderer's Row*? *One Spy Too Many*? Are they making Khe Sanh documentaries already?"

"Beats me, Sir. But I'm gonna find some popcorn and take them all in."

Lowell's command bunker—its windows peering above the sandbags like the eyes of a Peeping Tom—was a cramped structure built by the Special Forces in '64 and designated as our Combat Operations Center. It had one sought-after feature though: concrete walls. Next to the Seabee's 'Alamo Hilton,' it was the best damn bunker in town. Dave Lowell was Roman Catholic, though not outwardly devout. Yet I felt certain that combat would chip away at him, like the ten plagues did the pharaoh. He was attentive to my pastoral needs, however, and that was all a priest could ask of a commanding officer.

When I entered the bunker, Lowell lifted his gaze from the map table. His eyes were dark and sunken, and signaled resolve. "Good seeing you, Andy. It's been a few days."

"Since the regimental briefing last Saturday, Colonel. I thought of

17

dropping in for a martini and some macadamia nuts, but the natives have been restless." We exchanged smiles—his wooden.

"You're one of my senior chaplains. At least one of the battle-hardened. The men look up to you, and so do I."

With modesty I nodded and removed my helmet, thumbing the cross attached to its cloth cover that I had fashioned from flechette spikes—miniature winged darts that were packed into our beehive artillery rounds.

"There are plenty of rumors flyin', but let me give you the straight poop, Padre. We've got recon aircraft crisscrossing the heavens around the clock. We've got high-speed, high-resolution photos of every square-inch of terrain within thirty miles. We've got planes sniffing the air with electrochemical analyzers that are supposed to home in on the VC's sweat and piss. We've even got seismic and acoustic sensors planted around this hellhole to detect enemy movements—real Batman stuff. Damn things are so hush-hush that they're operated by Air Force pukes from a plane circling overhead twenty-four hours a day. And you know what? I still don't know where the bastards are."

I could feel his frustration.

"You know, Andy, the Intelligence boys say there are twenty thousand NVA out there—that's bigger than the town I grew up in. And we've got five thousand men. I can see and touch our boys, but not the gooks. I know them sons-of-bitches are out there. I can smell their fish heads and rice, but I can't do a blessed thing. Every time I send out a recon team, they need emergency extraction. Every time I lob a shell, Charlie returns it. It's a damn cat-and-mouse game. You wanna know, though, what sends a chill from my ass-end to the crown of my head?"

I leaned closer.

"The similarities between this place and Dienbienphu. General Giap wants a repeat of the licking he gave the French in '54. I won't let that shit happen, Andy ... not on my watch. That old slope-head has met his match." He stroked his handlebar mustache, then ground the heels of his palms into his eye sockets.

"What about reinforcements, Colonel? Better yet, can't we break out?"

"I can barely supply the troops I've got. And break out to where? Shy of massing like honeybees on Co Roc Mountain, this base camp is our best hope. What irks me is that the Intel boys say the 325C and 304 NVA divisions are massed against us. Have you been reading your history books, Andy? The 325th are the ones who bloodied our nose in last spring's hill fights, and the 304th is a veteran of Dienbienphu. Now you know why I've got bags under my eyes."

"OK, so why be here at all? What good can come of ..."

"Spare me the sermon, Padre. We've been over this before. This ain't a democracy. We're here because somebody ordered it. Pure and simple."

"Yeah, but what's the gain? We're just white knuckling it for the enjoyment of the brass. Westmoreland just wants a showpiece battle so he can return home a conquering hero. Why are we the guinea pigs ..."

"Hey! We're here. My job is to save asses and kill Viet Cong. Yours is to save souls. OK?"

"I just don't get it. It's all such a waste."

"I'm a bird colonel, Matte, and I can't figure shit out either. One thing's for sure: what you and I think doesn't amount to a dunghill. I get more unwanted advice from visiting brass than you can shake your dick at. The bastards even count the rolls of shit paper we use. But I'd rather be part of the solution here than sitting behind a desk in Washington as part of the problem. Actually, I'd rather be at Howard Johnson's sharing some hot soup and tea with you. These C-rats are giving me the squirts."

We laughed aloud.

"So why did you call me, Colonel? You know I can't help with the tactical situation."

His eyes searched mine. "But you can help with the men. I'm concerned about their morale as this standoff drags on. We may be cornered here for months. Or maybe the bastards will attack tomorrow ... or poison our water. But whatever goes down, I want the men to have spiritual comfort. I want you and the other chaplains to roam amongst them like a cowpoke does his herd. Sing 'em lullabies if you have to, but do your level best to keep 'em calm. No stampedes, got it? And whatever you do, Andy, don't assemble in groups larger than five."

"Aye, aye, Colonel."

"You brief the other chaplains; I'm not as comfortable with them.

Be my emissary—my eyes, my ears. OK, Andy?"

"You have my promise, Sir."

"And dummy up about those sensors, and especially about the water. God help me if the brass found out I was disclosing Top Secret info to a mackerel-snapper. OK, One-Nine?"

"Not to worry. Before I shove off, Skipper, can I get your consent to take a hop to 881 South this Sunday? I've got an old friendship to renew and a promise to keep to a wounded Marine."

"Well, at least it ain't a broad. Those souls up there could use some spiritual reinforcement, too. Be sure to OK it with your boss—and I don't mean the guy upstairs. And don't get your six o'clock position shot off."

"Will do." I turned, fastening my chinstrap, when his palm touched my shoulder.

"Before you leave, Andy—Father—how about hearing an old man's confession?"

I tried not to look thunderstruck, but in my five months with him, he'd never received a sacrament. I motioned to the radio operator to give us a wide berth, then I sat atop a sandbag mound in a darkened corner and placed my forest-green stole around my neck. Dave approached, as though on hallowed ground, and knelt. He confessed his sins, and I gave him the absolution the rite afforded. I dispensed with the penance and he understood why—he was serving it now. In the coming hours, many would be called to atone for their sins. Men would fight this battle, but its outcome was preordained by their Supreme Commander—by Abba, our Father.

Chapter 2

In one hand I gripped my crucifix like a miner's pick and, in the other, my ammo box of bread and wine like a lunch pail. I had just celebrated a worship service with four grungy bunker rats and was hunched over in a half-sprint, weaving toward my quarters—my hooch. Firefights and air strikes had been going down on Hill 881 North since 1000 hours, with shrill, high-speed, high-explosive combat shattering my solemn service. I downed a C-rat of chicken and rice, scooped a palm full of consecrated hosts into my pocket tin, then hustled for the airstrip. From that vantage, I could determine if the battle had spilled over to Matt's encampment on 881S.

When I arrived, I was immediately enlisted to help off-load the wounded from choppers. I should've abandoned my lunch to the rats—the men's wounds were ghastly. Some were crying for their mothers, while others lay glassy-eyed in shock. Our 155mm Howitzers were deafening as they hurled their ninety-five pound rounds into the 881N ridgeline, some five miles away. My mind was racing round a track with no entry or exit point. Though I tried, I couldn't forget Lowell's brief of the night before.

After loading the last ambulance, I made for the command bunker. The place was a stew of voices, odors, and bodies. A Tower of Babel. Lowell and his staff, like a team of maskless surgeons, huddled over the map table. The Communications Officer spotted my helmet and took pity on me. When he finished his brief, my armpits were wet.

India Company, Matt's company, had launched a reconnaissance-in-force toward the 881N hilltop. Lowell had flown in a hundred men to hold 881S, while India's skipper led the assault. Their task was simple: probe for NVA and find the missing code cards and radio gear that Lenny spoke of. The radio traffic made it clear India was taking it on the chin. A medevac chopper, strafed by machine gun fire, had been downed, and a platoon leader had been killed. His radioman, a lance corporal, was now in charge. Awarded a field promotion, this boot-camper was giving a blow-by-blow account akin to the one describing the crash of the Hindenberg. India Company's commander had summoned A-4 Skyhawks to his rescue, but their greeting card—a boiling, churning, oozing mass of napalm—proved anemic.

The base radio blurted out a call. Off the eastern end of the airstrip, under the nose of Bravo Company's 2nd Platoon, an enemy soldier—white flag in one hand and AK-47 in the other—had surrendered. Lowell seemed annoyed, his mind focused on 881N's engagement, but then the airwaves crackled with the news that the captive was an officer. The bunker became silent. NVA officers didn't surrender (Chieu Hoi)! The Colonel barked an order for the 17th Interrogation-Translation Team to report any info of military value on the captive, then he rejoined the frantic radio chatter.

I opted out, as every crack of the radio made me edgier, but once outside the Howitzer blasts, with their haze of cordite, assaulted me. I ran, dodging shell craters and hurdling sandbags—gripping my trouser pocket where I kept my large metal crucifix—as I dashed for C-Med.

The place was tense yet still, awaiting the wounded to arrive. Only the body of a black Marine, lying on a gurney with his boots removed, was in view. We removed him to a sheet-metal shack called Graves Registration, where we cleaned his face and wound. A single sniper's round had found its mark, the steel-jacketed bullet leaving a clean entry and exit. *At least his body would return home intact,* I thought. We tucked him into an olive-drab body bag, its plastic liner moist from his fleeing body heat, then I offered a canned prayer. My mind couldn't grasp the indignity.

I raced back to the command bunker, as though it was a scrap yard magnet and I was a chunk of iron. *What would I do if Matt were dead? How would I tell Julie? Did she know that he was in Nam?* I needed him alive! Without him, Julie's affections would be aimed at me, and I knew I couldn't withstand that barrage. The commotion inside had intensified. India's CO was demanding more air support. Lowell, obviously preoccupied, remained huddled with a gunnery sergeant from the Interrogation-Translation Team. The squint of Lowell's eyes and his puckered lips signaled bad news. He rose and we came face to face.

"Why aren't you with the wounded, Chaplain?"

"Trust me, no wounded are being neglected."

"Let's hope not."

"I'm worried, though, about my buddy on 881 South. When this dust settles, I need to know his fate."

"Yeah, well, the dust is settling, Padre. I ordered Daniels, India's CO, to withdraw. I want that ragtag bunch to live to fight another day."

"How many casualties, Colonel? Their names?"

"What? I can't even get a chopper in there. We'll do what it takes to get our dead and wounded out. 'Semper Fidelis' won't be a casualty of this skirmish—not on my watch!"

"But how long before you'll have the casualty report? The names?"

"Christ Almighty! Right now, it's four KIA and twenty-five plus wounded. Daniels must have run smack-dab into an NVA battalion."

"And the deserter?"

"There you go again. Do you suppose I could brief Tomko before you? After all, I do work for the General."

"How can I be your eyes and ears with the other chaplains, with the men, if you don't keep me informed?"

"All right, Chaplain Patterson, General Wannabe Patterson. But if you spill any of this before I give you the high sign, we'll be exchanging some unpleasant words."

His eyes sparkled, and he crouched.

"This gook deserter is a gold mine! I can't believe a Lieutenant knows so much." He was karate chopping his palm as he spoke. "His name is La Thanh Tonc and he's been with the North Vietnamese Army fourteen years. You believe that? Fourteen years and only a First Louie? He claims that the hardships of battle and family separation aren't worth it. Sound familiar, Andy? I've heard that sorry-ass complaint before."

"Yeah, yeah, Colonel."

"I'll say this, though. If what this rice-eating, apple-knocking, pig fucker spouts is gospel—if he's not a plant—then we're in deep shit. That's why I ordered Daniels out of the lion's den." He smirked.

"What're you going to do with him?"

"That's up to the Intel boys. God! What this guy knows ought to have those pencil necks at headquarters changing their skivvies."

Lowell paused, training his eyes on the butt-strewn floor, then he smartly about-faced. That command presence I admired—that his subordinates respected and feared—suddenly cloaked him. He was like Superman bursting from a phone booth.

"Major, secure the O-Club and all movie houses. Pass the word: this base and all the hill posts are on red alert! Gunny, hop a chopper to Lang Vei and brief those boys on the deserter. Anyone who's disappointed at not having a Purple Heart should find comfort in this news—we're in for some combat, gentlemen. Write home to mama and reconcile your sins with the good Padre here. We'll have a regimental briefing in thirty minutes."

He marched out—either for a snort or to take a booming shit. I turned to leave but the Ops Boss was holding a staff brief, so I stayed. In minute detail, the deserter had revealed the enemy's battle plan: an all-out attack was scheduled for half-past midnight—a no-holds-barred blitzkrieg worthy of a Nazi field marshal. The NVA would target Matt's outpost first, then Hill 861, and finally our base camp. It was an 'I' Corp coup-de-main, a blood lust, and we were its intended victims. I turned, my stomach churning, and made a dash for the shitter.

The outward signs of the red alert, like flies at the garbage dump, were everywhere: sandbags being stuffed and stacked, shovels flinging earth to contour trenches, water barrels and canteens being filled, rifles sighted and test fired, artillery registered and re-registered, and men, their mouths dry, nestled in foxholes with binoculars pressed to their blackened cheeks. Marines, like helmeted ballerinas, tiptoed around and through the barbed wire to fasten trip flares and set Claymore mines. The bow was strung. All that remained was to let go our quiver.

I took to visiting bunkers, distributing sanctified hosts and wine, and pausing often to hear confessions. I set aside my own angst to fortify their needs, issuing brick and mortar to those whose spiritual foundation seemed ready to crumble. Photos of loved ones, along with yarns of family, friends, and the girl next door helped relieve the tensions. It was nearing midnight when I returned to my hooch, my mind and body spent. I tried napping, but the deserter's account wouldn't let me. As troubling as Lowell's revelations were the night before, they relied on military intelligence, on guesstimates. The deserter's information, however, was different. He had much to lose and little to gain by his treason. So why would he compound his misery by lying to his captors?

I kept visualizing the 325C and 304th NVA divisions at our doorstep, fulfilling Santayana's prophesy that, "Those who cannot remember the past are condemned to repeat it." Our Intel boys could catalog facts and figures, but could they see beyond their arrogance to the parallels between Dienbienphu and Khe Sanh? I tossed restlessly in my bunk, wind gusts ruffling the canvas door flaps as if a spirit had entered. Had I goat's blood, I would've smeared it over every doorway to ward the Angel of Death away. In and out of sleep, I lurched at each machine gun burst as our men cleared their weapons and made ready their emotions.

I woke abruptly at 0200 hours, my candle casting an eerie pall on the dirt walls. There was heavy automatic weapons and mortar fire to the northwest, so I hustled outside. Hill 861 was lit like a Roman candle. I pissed into the artillery tube outside my hooch, then dragged on a half-smoked butt while assessing the uneasy calm over our camp. For now, Hill 881S was a dark stump against the sky. Returning to my bunk, I surrendered to fatigue. Moments later, a savage explosion jarred my teeth, showering dirt from the overhead and tumbling my candle to the deck. I ran to the doorway, where another explosion sent me cartwheeling backwards as though I was made of papier-mâché. I crawled back to the entranceway and was bathed in a red glow. Our fuel dump was ablaze and red pop-up flares ripped through the smoke-congested sky. Clouds of teargas—CS gas—seared my eyes as I pawed the floor for my gas mask. "God help me," I muttered.

I stood up, but another blast pulled my legs from beneath me. I cowered under my desk, praying aloud, as heavy metal objects struck the roof. *If it's God's will that I meet Him, then let it be done now,* I thought, *before I choke on my own phlegm.* Fearing entombment, I ran, and soon tumbled into a pit of smoldering LAW canisters and recoilless rifle rounds. I thrashed, like red ants were nipping at me, then sprang to my feet. Tripping again and again, I fell headlong into the Charlie-Med bunker.

"Whaddaya doing, Marine? This shit hole is mine!"

"Just trying to survive," I blurted.

He wheeled about. "Oh, sorry, Chaplain ... I wasn't expecting company."

"B-52 strike?" I gasped, laboring from the CS gas.

25

"Nope. The VC blew the lid off the ammo dump. Doesn't Charlie know that the 4th of July is months away? Our ammo is strewn about like confetti."

"I gotta get to C-Med, Sailor. Must be an army of wounded there."

"Better you than me, Chaplain. I'm staying put. I've seen arty rounds bowl our guys over like they were duckpins."

"God bless us all. And pray for rain to douse your hotheaded neighbors." I pointed to a large pocket of smoking arty rounds, clustered like hot coals, then watched his eyes widen.

"Holy shit! I'm outta here, too!"

He soon vanished into the mist, while I lunged ahead and through the triage door flap like a drunk ejected from a bar. I dunked a towel in a water trough and held it over my nose and mouth. Wounded were everywhere, some hyperventilating from fear or respiratory distress. Several needed to piss, so helmets, like offertory baskets, were passed around and filled. None were dying, so I decided to make for Lowell's command bunker.

I sprinted across the scarred landscape, hurdling craters and rubble, and finally laid eyes his bunker. I entered to what looked like a pagan rite—the explosions had destroyed the generator and the place was alight with candles. Ghoulish shapes pranced about the walls. It was déjà vu—like the pot parties I frequented with Julie—but without the incense and rock music. Our drumbeat was the VC incoming and the lyrics the crackling radio net, but the odors of cordite, burning rubber, and armpits were no match for the cinnamon and peppermint of yesteryear.

The radio traffic from Khe Sanh Village had everyone edgy; we were like cheerleaders at a seesawing gridiron match. I kept hearing, "Go Strammer. Go! Kick some ass! Take some names!" Eventually, I realized that Strammer was leading a charge—counterpunching as the NVA backpedaled. He and his men were candidates for a Distinguished Service Cross or a Silver Star, and, if they were lucky, it wouldn't have to be awarded posthumously. This contest, however, was only a scrimmage for the championship match to come.

A beam of sunlight streamed through a porthole, and I suddenly became the object of stares. I felt like a curtain had been raised and I was center stage to the hoots and hollers of a band of drunken sailors.

I thought maybe I'd wet myself, until I noticed that flechette spikes were stuck in my flak jacket. Miniature arrows, like clove buds on an Easter ham, had skewered my chest area.

"Say, Father, stay clear of that beehive arty, or we'll be nominating you for sainthood. Yeah … and tell Cupid to save his arrows for us studs allowed to bed down the women."

Laughter erupted—even Lowell joined in. I looked like a pincushion. I made an exaggerated sign of the cross, then about-faced into the open air. Between cigarettes, I plucked the spikes and pocketed them as souvenirs.

I headed for the 1/26 Bravo Company lines, certain that the explosions of the adjacent ammo dump had given them a dose of humble pie. Its 2nd Platoon area was a wasteland of collapsed bunkers, shredded tarpaulin, and smoking ordnance. Instead of being stockpile for enemy destruction, the dump had become a belching volcano—a self-inflicted, spurting wound. Secondary explosions had ripped open fifty-five gallon drums of CS gas, spewing its witch's brew everywhere. Pockets of the gas collected in bunkers and trenches, sending Marines scampering for the open air and the threat of a sniper's round.

Entering the Bravo company bunker, a hovel built by the "Green Beanies," I collided with its commander. Our masks butted together, and our breathing sounded like that of snorting bulls.

"Take off, Chaplain!" barked Penski as he waved his massive forearms. "This powder keg could blow any second or the Dac Cong might overrun us … you know, like my wife's bridge club at a Christmas sale."

We smiled and removed our masks. He was a salty dog, a chaw of tobacco frequently packed beside his molars to accent his puffy jowls.

"What the Lord has in store for us, Skipper, may make Sodom and Gomorrah look like Romper Room. Can I help your men?"

"Yeah. Take this handgun and hole up in your hooch. If those slant-eyed devils rush you, let 'em have it."

I pulled out my metal crucifix. "This is all the protection I'll need."

He shook his head and spit. I grinned and took off. I'd come to Nam to bring life, not take it. Penski knew that chaplains didn't tote firearms. The one thing that made this nightmare tolerable was that I could claim to be a noncombatant. I wore the uniform and insignia of a Marine Corps Captain, I saluted and was saluted, I polished my boots and brass, and said, "Sir" and "No, Sir," but that was all a game. I wasn't a warrior, but a mediator—a lamb, not a lion. I had no aspirations other than the slogan penned by Grunts on their flak jackets: "Eat the Apple; Fuck the Corps!"

I could just make out the sawtooth contour of Penski's trenchline when an explosion yanked my legs from under me. My ears rang, and my mask was torn from my face. Then the odor of burning sandbags, doused with fuel to keep the rats from nesting in them, struck me. The stench pushed me back into the bunker, where Penski and I landed atop one another like linemen scrambling for a ball. Suddenly the crack of dry timber and the groan of a sagging beam stormed our senses. With no time to run, we curled. The roof settled, but held. A layer of red earth, like powdered snow, blanketed us.

"That was no arty round, Padre. That's plastique! The ammo dump is full of it. Another jolt like that and they won't need to dig a hole to bury us in."

"Pull back, Skipper," I pleaded.

"Not without orders, Skypilot. I ain't bailing out without a single enemy round being fired. What sort of candy-ass do you take me for?" Tobacco juice dribbled down his chin, as though he'd sprouted a Fu Mann Chu mustache.

"Dammit, Penski! God helps those who help themselves. Clear out now!"

"Clear out to where, Chaplain?"

I scooted along on my ass until my mouth was in Penski's ear. "God help you, Skipper, if you throw away these men's lives. If Lowell were here, he'd tell you the same."

His soiled face betrayed a glint of uncertainty, then his eyes glared. The Marine Hymn was pounding in his brain—there was no room at the inn for my message.

"We'll be Charlie's Welcome Wagon. He'll know the fury of the Corps. We'll fight and die if we have to, but we'll do it like Marines!"

I squeezed his wrist. "God be with you and the men," I said and headed toward Lowell's bunker. I knew Matt's company would embrace the same madness; the peer pressures aroused by combat were

28

an awesome force. Matt was my ward, my battle hymn, and my prayer was that we'd meet before events swept us both away.

It was nearly 0800 hours, time for Sunday worship service, but there was nowhere to hold it. I wandered like a stray dog, scouting for an undisturbed parcel to erect an altar and consecrate the bread and wine. Troops passed by as if in a dream. In and out of the gassy mists they charged, as though entering and exiting a gateway draped in chiffon. Some were close enough to touch—I felt the rush of air as they passed—but nobody seemed to notice me. As they whisked by I mumbled, "God be with you. God keep you." None of it made sense, but it was Sunday and offerings had to be made. Nothing appeared as it had. Nothing smelled as it should. Nothing tasted as bitter as the winds of our impending defeat.

My eyes were watery slits when Lowell's command post came into view. I dunked my head in a barrel of water and bobbed up, pinching my nostril to blow my nose. The detonation of ordnance outside gave way to the mayhem of radio chatter inside—whatever was happening beyond the concertina wire dominated the conversations inside. Men second-guessing men and machines, second-guessing each other and the wisdom of their plan. The confusion, I learned, was centered on Khe Sanh Village.

Lowell spun about, and the men fell silent. He shifted his weight and narrowed his glance. "I want choppers. Now! Only Americans get picked up. The SV troops and government types can walk. Nobody that ain't got a Stars and Stripes tattooed on his ass or a patch of hair on his chest is to get out first. Got that, Major?"

"Yes, Sir!"

Lowell turned to my anxious face. It wasn't in his character to be indifferent to civilians, to let them perish on the battlefield, but then nothing in his look conveyed a sense of normalcy. I stepped forward, slowly at first.

"That's far enough, Chaplain Patterson. I don't wanna hear your bleeding-heart bullshit. The village is doomed. Right now, it's Yanks first! Marines first! Got that?"

For several days we'd been evacuating villagers in groups of fifty aboard C-130s. His anguish was now focused on the Bru Montagnards and how Charlie would treat them.

29

"Look, Colonel, I think …" His palm shot up like a traffic cop.

"I want to save souls, too. But for now, they've gotta be American souls. Every chopper I've got is for medevac or gunfire support. This isn't a spiritual operation, Chaplain." He wet his lips, then moved closer and lowered his well-defined jaw.

"I don't have the resources, Padre. It's that simple. We're in deep shit here. Real deep!" He spoke in a whisper, like his confession of the night before. "It'll be dark soon, Andy. Our ammo is ninety-five percent depleted. I can't get cargo in because the pilots—even the gung-ho ones—refuse to fly through that anti-aircraft fire. And for the few flights that I can beg, borrow, or steal, I gotta divert all my artillery to suppressing the VC's anti-air. I've got half the usual runway length, no landing lights, and Hill 861 is screaming for troop replacements. Dammit, man! I can't be all things to all people."

"You're doing your level best, Dave. Everybody knows that."

He winced, as though a kidney stone was on the move. "And to compound things, I've got a thousand-plus civilians huddled outside the gates. Now how bad is it out there, if they think this hellhole is a good refuge?"

"Why not let them gather in our trenches?"

"You don't understand, Andy. I can't let a Trojan Horse in. One gook looks the same as the next. It's the Bru situation that's killing me. That damn 'I' Corp commander, General Lam, won't evacuate them. The idiot knows I've got Bru manning the FOB-3 portion of this base. What does he think those men will do when their own people are used as human shields by the VC?"

"Ignore that shithead and corral 'em all in a hold area, then …"

"No way! I can't be their deliverer, nor do I have the men to guard them. Those gates stay padlocked. For once, watch over the ninety-nine … instead of searching for that lone stray."

I took a deep breath. *Turn the other cheek,* I reminded myself.

"So what's our next move, Colonel? Do we break out or fight?"

"Didn't you hear anything I said last night, Andy? There's no breaking out, and only the VC want to break in."

"Can't General Tomko send a ground force to rescue us?"

"Ah, Andy. Please. You've been watching too many John Wayne movies. Tomko doesn't have a magic wand. We're all stumbling in the dark, and only Giap knows where the light switch is. He's the grandmaster at this game, and he isn't telegraphing his next move. Hell! Just today, I had to blow up Howard Johnson's to keep Giap's bastards from overrunning the village. Next thing you know, I'll be calling in B-52 strikes on this bunker. When that shit happens you'll know he's got me in checkmate."

"We can't let them take the village! What about the children and elderly? And the nuns at the Catholic school? You'll be branded a Pontius Pilate." He closed his bloodshot eyes. If Khe Sanh was to be another Titanic, then I wanted the women and children in the lifeboats first.

"Try to understand, Chaplain. This isn't a Boy Scout maneuver. Those are real soldiers out there, with real guns and bullets, and real ambitions of capturing this place with you and me in it. I dutifully scoff when reporters bring it up, but those camera-toting devils are right. The VC mean to make this another Dienbienphu!"

Those close by stood silent. Lowell's head ratcheted left and then right to inventory the believers and disbelievers. He'd uttered the D word, and there was no taking it back. Others thought it, but to hear the CO say it was the crossing of the Rubicon.

"Now you know why I asked you to hear my confession."

My spine tingled. The somber faces in the bunker, the heart and soul of the camp's resolve, were testimony to Lowell's slip. *But was it a slip,* I wondered, *or a calculated move to root out complacency?* For fifty-six days, the Vietnamese had laid siege to the French garrison at Dienbienphu. A supposedly invincible French army against a rag-tag, sandal-footed foe. In the end the cheese-eaters yielded to Giap, nicknaming him "Volcano Under the Snow." Wasn't Vo Nguyen Giap the same field marshal today that he was fourteen years ago? History seemed ready to repeat itself, and Matt and I were caught in the maelstrom—caught in a net from which even the small fish couldn't escape.

I left thinking that the fate of our army and Giap's had been preordained; that all this strife had occurred before; that many would return to ashes—Matt and I among them. I needed to make my peace with Matt, to apologize for having pushed him down the wrong path. So what if that path was strewn with my good intentions? Divine providence had seen fit to place me here to atone for my sins against him. As I broke into a trot for C-Med, I knew we were on a parallel course with the French—a collision course with Giap.

Triage was stacked with wounded and dying, and soon after arriving a relentless barrage of VC rockets and mortars shook me to my spiritual foundation. As the incoming accelerated, I assumed a fetal position, clutching Julie's letter as I coiled tighter. Tears flowed as the CS gas slithered along the floor. Then a familiar cry resounded: "Corpsman up! Corpsman up!"

I pressed my helmet to my head and shook, praying—as Christ had in the Garden of Gethsemane—that the Almighty would deliver Matt and me from our crucifixion at the hands of Giap.

Chapter 3

I woke to the smell of feet and stale blood. Five wounded lay crammed in my hooch. Wearing only my boxer shorts and helmet, I leaped over their bodies and made for the shitter. I plopped down on a cutoff fifty-five-gallon drum, its wooden seat wet from the dew, and let go with a grunt. A gentle breeze sent tear gas crystals, stirred up by the ammo clearance teams, my way. That—together with the cauldron of shit and fuel oil below—sent me hustling back to my bunker.

My overnight visitors, battered by flying ordnance from the erupting ammo dump, were stretching their bruised limbs and brushing the dirt from their fatigues. My charge was to herd them at first light to Charlie-Med for further examination. I watched with alarm as one Marine rolled over, his muscles painfully stiff, to expose a cluster of blood-soaked tissues. I quickly hoisted him atop my shoulders, and moments later we entered triage.

"Hey! Over here, Corpsman! He's got a head wound. There's blood everywhere." I unfurled him on a gurney and waited anxiously for the medic's assessment.

"Oh, he's OK, Chaplain." He turned to resume his duties.

"What do you mean? My hooch is littered with blood-soaked tissues."

The corpsman shook his head. "I don't doubt it, Padre—but that's not his blood. His buddy took a chunk of shrapnel that tore off his arm, and this fella here hauled him in using a fireman's carry. He must've used those tissues to mop himself up."

I stood wide-eyed. "Did his buddy make it?"

"What do you think we're running here? A field-training camp for med school dropouts?"

He pointed to a darkened corner, where a spaghetti work of IV tubes hung, like Spanish Moss, over a body in a mummy wrap. I approached, then halted. "Ah, no! Penski, why you? Jesus, Mary, and Joseph."

His torso was heavily bandaged and a stump, like a sawed-off limb of white birch, was all that remained of his right arm. Just hours before I had squeezed the wrist attached to that arm. With his tour over in a few days, would he be forever asking himself if he should've heeded my advice? *I should have kept my mouth shut,* I thought. I left, awed by what a man could do when motivated by love—the corporal that carried Penski to Charlie-Med had done it on a busted leg.

I spotted Lt. Colonel Whiley, my battalion commander, and headed his way. "Colonel. Sir." He turned, fatigue in his eyes. I saluted, but he didn't return it. His eyes roved from my forehead to my chin and back again, his lower jaw sliding side to side.

"What the … you all right, Reverend? You got chickenpox or something?"

I swept my palm over my face. To my surprise, it was riddled with tiny welts and scabs.

"Now don't pick 'em, Son. Didn't they teach you anything in the seminary?"

My befuddlement eased when I realized that minute particles of shrapnel had peppered me during the ammo dump explosions. First the flechette spikes and now this. *How many lives did I have?*

"Guess I'll skip shaving, Colonel. That way I'll fit right in with that bunch on 881 South."

"What's that, Chaplain?" He had one ear cocked toward some automatic weapons fire near the runway.

"I need to visit 881S pronto."

"Why today, Captain? Your station is here, not roaming these hills." His arm swept the gray horizon to make his point.

"An old friend's in trouble."

"There wasn't any action on 881 South last night. Make the trip another time. OK?" He turned toward the small arms fire erupting near the runway.

He didn't understand! This wasn't a reunion of drinking buddies. This was my link to the past, my road to repentance, and maybe Julie's bridge to a new life. "Colonel! Sir. I don't ask for favors, you know that. But I need a chopper hop to 881 South *today*. If we can shuttle reporters here, there, and everywhere, then we can damn sure ferry one priest to minister to the needs of a lost soul."

His nose twitched, but he was preoccupied with the distant gunfire.

If I were any other junior officer, he'd have booted my ass up and down the trenchline. His eyes softened and he cleared his throat.

"OK, Andy. But you be damn sure to make it a one-day affair. And remember, there are others up there in need of your spiritual support. Some of those men will be going home in a body bag." He wheeled about and headed toward the runway, while I mulled over his remark.

Once in my hooch, I gingerly washed my face, stuffed candy bars and beer into my ammo box, and made for the tarmac—where I paced the helo pad like an expectant father. Matt may not have been my flesh and blood, but his path in life was largely due to our symbiotic relationship—with me the parasite and he the host. As the fog lifted, the VC incoming arrived. I cradled my olive-drab ammo box, its sides painted with a white cross, then pressed down on my helmet and trotted for the chopper—its huge blades slowly whirling, black exhaust spewing. The cargo master radioed the pilot, then the craft shook as we lurched upward.

I strained to keep the base in view. Huge rubber fuel bladders, soon looking like miniature pillows, were scattered about the landing zones. On both sides of the steel-plated runway were unexploded rounds and men could be seen scurrying from hole to hole, smoke from incoming mortars shadowing their movements. Sporadic tracer bursts from the jungle cover produced a stream of green light as the VC raked the landing field and surrounding bunkers. We churned through a dense cloudbank, while my eyes searched for Matt's sky-high fortress.

Crates with medical markings were stacked in the chopper, a pallet of plastic water jugs shuddering with the helo's vibration. The slim crew chief sported a jet-black flight helmet, yellow lightning bolts like horns emblazoned on its sides. I motioned to him and he squatted beside me.

"How much water do you transport a day?" I pointed to the shimmering pallet. He glanced over, and then a disgusted look crossed his face.

"Son of a bitch!" He hopped up, shaking his fist. "The cocksuckers did it again."

He kept jabbing his finger toward the pallet. I stared, mystified. Then I saw the stream of water trailing out the cargo gate.

"The fucksticks put a round through our belly," he shouted. "Now we're pissing in the clouds."

We banked sharply and the crew chief grabbed the overhead walk-line. I pressed my nose to the glass just as a dogbone-shaped ridgeline appeared. It was 881 South all right, as I'd seen the aerial photos. The landing zone officer fanned his arms briskly, and the pilot responded with a corkscrewing descent. We settled with a thud, and the cargo hatch opened like a drawbridge. I leaped out and fell flat on my face, my boot lodged in a rut left by an earlier chopper's landing gear. My clumsiness was immediately rewarded when two VC rockets bracketed the LZ, hurling shrapnel. I turned to see the crew chief and cargo master shouting into their headsets, then the chopper choked to life. As I made for the trenchline, the helo's engines snorted and it sprang from the pad like a lineman at the center's snap. The chopper circled overhead, as though on a leash, while Marine small arms and rocket launchers laid into the VC from the hill's northern trenches.

The helo reappeared and made a steep descent, as though gliding down the handrail of a spiral staircase. When the gear touched its jaw flopped open, and a dozen trench apes scrambled to off-load the supplies. The shouts of "Corpsman up!" competed with the thwomp of the blades and muzzle blasts. The faceless pilot waited momentarily, engines revving, as three wounded were hurled into the ship. *God, I hope Matt isn't among them,* I thought. Its appetite satisfied, the engines came alive.

As the helo's din subsided, the Doppler effect of inbound Huey choppers could be heard overhead. I anxiously wormed my way along the trenchline, examining the wounded. They deserved my prayers, my support, but I was focused on locating Matt. A corpsman was winding a dressing around a soldier's head, and, as the bandage turned crimson, he wound faster. The man's face was unrecognizable, so I examined his hand. Not Matt—missing was the burn scar he'd suffered when rescuing me from that fiery car crash. I dropped his limp arm like a hot-handled skillet, then moved to the next casualty.

Three Hueys were on final approach. The Helo Support Team (HST) coached them down as the hill's defenders poured on the small arms and grenades from the northern trenches. The choppers were queued up and, like skateless carhops, the HSTs shuttled from one to the next, filling them with human cargo—the drama played out in body language and hand signals. The first Huey peeled off, then the second, while the third bucked like a mustang as its pilot awaited the "Go" signal from his crew chief.

Enemy tracers from the vicinity of Hill 881N sliced overhead, but missed their mark. Then I realized Charlie's game: the VC wanted our wounded alive; wanted them to carry the message that destruction awaited the base defenders, purposely leaving behind the ones who'd died—who'd made the supreme sacrifice—to bear the indignity of rotting until the next flight out. I continued scouring the LZ perimeter, examining weary, frightened faces, until I met a heavyset chief corpsman, his walrus-like mustache soaked with condensation.

"What brings you to the war, Captain?" He crossed his arms, his look dispassionate.

"I'm looking for Matt Garrison. Can you help me?" He eyeballed me as I had the wounded—now he was the inspector and I was the side of beef—then he focused on the cross sewn on my left lapel. I'd seen that look before—it was the contempt only a nonbeliever could muster.

"You'll have to see one of the officers. I don't know any Garrison." He pointed to a knoll and added, "Maybe your sight-seeing tour should include those five KIAs." He then walked off.

Rebuked or not, I couldn't pray over those dead. I had to find my lost lamb. Not until I saw Matt—alive if the Lord willed it or dead if the VC engineered it—could I offer a devotion. The five dead lay equally spaced, their faces trained skyward. I thanked the Lord that Matt wasn't among them, then knelt beside one and closed his eyelids; dust from the helo wash had already settled on his eyeballs. His face was unblemished except for a pimple. Not a whisker, only peach fuzz. They were young … innocent … unfulfilled. I shook my head, then walked toward the pennant fluttering above the command post.

Inside were three officers crouched over a map. A captain squinted at my helmet, straining, it appeared, to determine what its cross was constructed from. In gangly strides he closed the gap, then gave me a snappy salute.

"Chaplain Patterson, I presume." His hand enveloped mine like a Venus Flytrap. His eyes were raven black, and his two front teeth slightly gapped. He looked my age, though combat had robbed him of boyish features. He had one attribute, though, that eluded his troops and me—he was clean-shaven.

"That's me, Skipper." The other officers never looked up, the map holding their attention like a Playboy centerfold.

"Good! We could use some spiritual uplifting. Some of that old-time religion if you've got it, Chaplain."

I nodded. As my eyes adjusted to the dim light, I read the name stitched above his breast pocket. So this was Daniels, the same hard-charging commander whose voice boomed across the airwaves two days earlier to argue for reinforcements and air strikes. His appearance was refined, not gruff as I expected. Faceless voices and orders barked in the heat of battle often created the image that those giving the commands were larger than life—understandable, since their decisions could give or take it.

"I need to return before nightfall, OK?"

"Don't bank on that, Chaplain. I lost five men when that rocket barrage greeted your arrival. Any more casualties, and there won't be room at the inn when your hop arrives."

"I'm counting on your luck changing, Skipper. Mine, too. I'm here to find an old friend."

"Forgive me if I don't help you look … but I've got a recon mission to plan. One other thing, Chaplain. Don't hold worship services for more than five men at a time. Not that five is our unlucky number, but I can't have some Alvin York of a gook take out half my command while you're giving them a sermon on this mount."

He flashed a wily smile and I left. I had faces to see, worship services to celebrate, and confessions to hear. Somewhere in this mishmash of foxholes and wire entrapments was Matt—my pot of gold at the end of the rainbow. I crouched in a quickstep and peered into each man's face. Some were expressionless and haunting, others timid, but most had eyes that looked through a man … eyes fixed in a thousand-yard stare.

Many of the men were sleeping in fetal positions, their mouths open, helmets askew, and drool running down their chin. Every other man jack was cuddling his weapon, like an infant would its rattle. Finally, I encountered a lanky private who knew Matt's whereabouts. He directed me to a trenchline along the southern edge of the crest and I ran upright, crossing the open terrain just as a mortar punctured the landscape. I ate dirt and coiled for the sister round. Two ugly ones arrived, and a shower of earth and smoke enveloped me. My hands quickly inventoried my body—no parts were missing—so I rose and I sprinted on.

"Arty up! Arty up, Marine!" roared a voice from my right flank, and I hit the ground again.

When I looked up, I saw an officer toting binoculars and racing about a 105mm Howitzer battery, stabbing the air with his finger. "Wake up, Soldier! That's a fuckin' gook mortar tube out there in that fuckin' crater! Get the motherfuckers! Get the motherfuckers, now!" He kept screaming and hopping about, like he was riding a pogo stick.

Within seconds the Howitzer was blasting away, its shockwaves rippling through my body. Smoke and cordite strung my eyes and nose, while shell casings clanged in a heap. A chorus rose from the trenchline, "Yahoo! Git 'em arty! Waste the fuckers!"

I scrambled for the trenches, knowing the return fire, like an echo, would arrive any moment. I leaped beside a black Marine, landing squarely atop his sleeping companion, who stirred wildly. "What the hell …?"

He stopped mid-breath. He was Matt to me, but was I Andy to him? His widening eyes and dangling chin were confirmation enough. He lunged to embrace me. He reeked of body odor, but his welling tears and trembling jaw overrode my sense of smell. He touched my cross made of flechette spikes, dabbed the scabs on my cheeks, then thumbed the cloth cross sewn on my lapel.

"You're not hallucinating, Matt. It's me." I rubbed his cheeks with my palms, smudging the corners of his mustache.

"I can't believe it. How the devil did you get here? And an officer and a gentlemen, to boot."

"Yeah, yeah. Look at you, you chump. You're a college grad. You're 'O' material, too." I pointed up and down the gouged earth, then added, "But you had to make a statement and be a trench rat."

"I figured you'd be in a cozy stateside rectory sipping altar wine, eating surf and turf, and pinching some young nun's ass."

"Watch your mouth, Corporal," I said. "Not only are you addressing an officer but a man of the cloth! A duly-appointed messenger of the Bishop and the Almighty."

The black fellow beside him must not have seen my accompanying grin, because he put a grip on Matt's shoulder and gave it a tug. "Yeah, Garrison, watch your mouth. You're talkin' to a preacher, dipstick. Didn't your mama teach you better? Or do you even know who she is?"

"Whaddaya gonna do? Call me a dumb honkey, Eddie? You don't hear me calling you a dumb nigger, now do you?"

"Yeah, well, this dumb nigger is gonna have a piece of your white ass, Sailor. You best bow when you're talking to me and genuflect when addressing the good reverend here."

"Ah, go fuck yourself," said Matt, then he grinned at me.

I was ready to lunge between them, but Eddie turned away, mumbling something about "shithead honkeys." I quickly cupped my hand over Matt's mouth to stifle a retort, then the Howitzer boomed again and we both winced.

"So what's it all about, Father Andy? Why are you here in this God-forsaken armpit?"

"My Bishop wasn't exactly pleased with my anti-war activities. Said I was too outspoken. Heaven help a priest who condemns war. He was a chaplain in the big one—WWII. You know, the war to end all wars. He told me I needed a battlefield education, a little baptism by fire. I think he honestly expects me to chant, 'My country, right or wrong.'"

"But why the Corps? Are you sure you didn't get drafted or dropped on your head?"

I paused to collect myself. The cordite had brought tears to my eyes, conveniently masking my emotions. Between the cannons and Matt's questions, my mind was spinning. I sniveled, then said, "Like you, I had to answer a higher calling. I wanted to see what this 'Military Action' shit was all about. And what better way than to become a Jarhead? Ya see," I gripped my helmet with both hands and twisted, "I can screw my piss pot on with the best of 'em."

"However you got here, Andy, I'm damn glad to see ya. But why Khe Sanh? Why not Saigon where they wear civvies and shack up with their Suzie Wongs?"

An image of Julie flashed into my mind, then that crazy gunner started hooting and hollering in a war dance around his Howitzer. "We

40

got the motherfuckers! We got 'em! Did you see their fuckin' shit fly with that last round?! Fuck you, gook!"

Matt and I frowned, our thoughts a communion of disgust.

"Well, Khe Sanh wasn't always under siege. This can be a beautiful countryside, one of Mother Nature's vestal virgins. That is, until a stratofortress rapes the landscape, or napalm deflowers the tree line, or a defoliant strips away the greenery. Then you realize what a piss-ass war this is."

"As fine a homily as you've ever given, Padre. I'll betcha if the Lord gave this planet an enema, He'd bury the hose right in this plateau. You know, there's plenty of scuttlebutt about a 'siege.' You best clear out today. Those slant-eyed mothers begged off last night, but I'm scared shitless they'll come knocking tonight. Get your rocks off in the confessional, pass the hat for that monopoly money they pay us, then hyaku on the next chopper."

"One thing I can tell ya, Matt. The brass are anxious for this canker sore to be a set piece battle. You know, a toe-to-toe slugfest with the NVA to see who blinks first. I just hope this isn't another Dienbienphu." We lit another smoke and stared at a bank of low-moving clouds.

"They're like the Angel of Death. I don't like it, Andy. Know something else? I don't like the mention of Dienbienphu. I don't want any part of some textbook battle. Let the brass find another guinea pig! Some other fuckin' canary in a cage for their mining expeditions."

"How about joining me for a worship service? I'd feel a lot better knowing you were at peace with the Lord."

"Have you forgotten, Padre? I'm your Prodigal Son. I don't do worship services, confessions, sacraments, or windows."

I squinted disapprovingly. "Enough with the chin music. I gotta be about my Father's business ... if you'll allow me some poetic license. After all, I didn't fly through that gunfire to see only you."

His lip quivered and I suddenly realized I'd hurt his feelings. His black buddy could throw stones—they were trenchmates—but a twinge of suspicion still separated Matt and me. I didn't want to abandon him, but it was time to follow Whiley's orders and tend to the others. I promised him, though, that I'd return in plenty of time before the chopper arrived.

41

With a lukewarm smile I hugged him, holding back my emotions. I was being silly, though, as I should've been big enough to open up to him as others had to me. I gently tilted his helmet, traced the cross on his gritty, strap-reddened forehead, then rose before the lump in my throat choked me. *Damn!*—I suddenly remembered Lenny. He couldn't accompany me because his leg wound had become infected. Before his medevac to Phu Bai Hospital, though, he'd made me promise to tell Matt about Tommy. There was no going back on that tearful pledge.

"You know, Matt, there *is* something special I came to tell you. Tommy McAndrews died last Friday." A calm, like a descending dove, came over him.

"Yeah, we heard. Bad news travels fast. He was good people, but a kid in so many ways. We busted his chops a lot … even called him 'Doubting Thomas.' He was always questioning things: whether he'd make it home; whether his girl could handle their separation; whether he could scrounge the money for his wedding and honeymoon. Funny thing, though, he didn't question this shitty war. Maybe it was bliss, or his sly way of refuting his nickname. Whatever it was, I wake up and crash every day thinking how screwed-up this war is. But not Tommy."

"He recently made an R&R, didn't he?"

"Yeah. He went to Pearl last month to see his fiancée. We badgered him to go to Bangkok to get some poontang, but he was determined to see the little woman. Come to think of it, her love was the only other thing he never questioned."

"There's no rhyme or reason to this madness. I'm a religious man, right? I'm supposed to separate truth from fiction, distinguish good from evil, admonish sinners and praise do-gooders. But everything here is ass backwards. I'm losing track of what's what and who's who. I need to get home … before I lose all my marbles."

"Just don't make the trip in a body bag. OK, Andy?"

As I'd done for him, he traced a cross on my forehead. *If I left now would I see him again? What undisclosed price had he paid for my arrogance?* It was all so confusing.

"You know, Tommy left this earth asking for your forgiveness. His final words were for you, not his fiancée. I couldn't comfort him. It wasn't until after he'd died that I discovered he was talking about you. That's one hell of a power to have over another man."

"Why was he sorry, Andy?"

"He'd taken some money from your R&R kitty. Little more than putting his hand in the cookie jar. Funny, isn't it? A man—more correctly a boy—is poised to meet his Maker, and all he can think about is a penny-ante debt to his shipmates."

"He wanted to surprise his girl with an engagement ring. Shit! We'd have given him the damn money. You mean he died thinking that we thought he stole it?"

When I nodded, his face paled and his Adam's apple bobbed. He worked his grungy fingertips into his forehead, then raked them through his glistening hair.

"For the love of God, Andy, the money didn't matter. All any of us wanted was for Tommy to enjoy himself … to get away from this hellhole. We knew he had it and we all agreed to say nothing—to just give him some time. Damn this fuckin' war!"

There was nothing more to add. "God be with you, Matt. God be with us both."

I scrambled out of the trench, not looking back, and began to visit with the other men. To the man, this grubby-looking collection of Marines—our country's youth, its flower—wanted only to enjoy the American dream. Instead, they were being led down the garden path to fight and die in a faraway land. They sought life's simple pleasures: to complete their education, pursue a job, rekindle a love affair, bounce a child on their knee, caress a loved one, pet a faithful dog, step outside and not fret a sniper's round, enjoy a slow passage into middle age, and to live long and prosper and die in their sleep.

Prayer and contrition flowed freely from these conscripts, helping me to mend souls and steel resolves—a holy man's true calling. Thankfully, there were light-hearted moments: men chuckling when fun was poked at their looks, grinning at photos of playful sweethearts or recounting tales of their children's pranks. From laughter came mental displacement. Maybe it lasted only a few heartbeats, but it was a welcome tonic.

By 1500 hours I had returned to Daniels' command post, where I found him pacing while his radioman, headset on, scribbled on a clipboard.

43

"Good to see you, Padre. Find your buddy?" He had shed his earlier detachment.

"Yes, indeed, Skipper. Met my old friend, comforted some new ones, dodged the incoming, and shared lunch with a returning patrol." I paused, but he said nothing. "How bad has it been up here? A lot of the men were sacked out and missed the worship services."

"Don't take this personal, Chaplain, but I didn't announce your coming. I didn't want to disappoint the men if you couldn't make it … and, yes, many of them are exhausted. Charlie bypassed us last night, but a stay of execution can be worse than the hangman's noose. I told them to stand down until nightfall, then the waiting game can start again."

He made it sound like it was bad luck not to have been attacked. I shared the uniform, but not the mindset of a Marine combat officer.

"Things will get better. I promise to return in February to bless the men's throats—the Feast of Saint Blasé, you know. Promise me, though, that you'll tell them I'm coming. OK?"

"You're always welcome, Chaplain. Try to understand … both of my companies were at one-hundred-percent alert since yesterday morning when your base was rocketed. They were bushed."

"You were wise then to stand down, Captain. These Grunts are a haggard-looking lot."

He chuckled. "Looked in a mirror lately, Chaplain? Washing and shaving is a luxury around here, same as sleep, but neither our water rations or the VC will oblige."

"If it's any consolation, the crew at Khe Sanh is just as scraggly."

He unclasped his canteen and took a gulp. "You see, Padre, water is key. An army may march on its stomach, but without the water to wash it down, you choke to death. We allot two canteens per man per day. It takes a whole bird to quench the thirst of my 400 men, and choppers make easy targets. I'd rather save the birds for medevacs and bullets. If I work the men during daylight, they drink more. It's simple arithmetic. Besides, the VC are night owls. When they come, it'll be by the light of the moon. Just once …" He glanced at his watch. "Ah, enough of my bellyaching, one-nine."

"Thanks for the school call, Captain. A man in my station doesn't always see the 'why' in things as much as the 'who' or 'what' that's affected."

My tribute was genuine. So long as Daniels put his men first, I wouldn't sit in judgment. In my role as a noncombatant, I let myself believe that warfare was orchestrated by geriatric warriors moving miniature battleships and toy divisions over map tables. To hear a man my age talking tactics served to remind me of my lost youth.

"Is the chopper on for 1600, Skipper?"

"Negative. It just lifted off from the base camp. You'd best hustle. That's no Sunday driver in that bird. He won't loiter with the welcome committee he'll get."

"But I planned to rendezvous with my buddy." My tone was a mix of disappointment and exasperation.

"That chopper is inbound now! And I've got five other riders besides you that wanna go home. Remember?"

He hurled me a tomahawk chop salute, which I feebly returned. *Dammit!* I wanted to talk more with Matt. As I darkened the doorway, an explosion rocked the bunker. I steadied myself and heard someone yell, "Corpsman, up!" I dog-paddled through the smoke to a heap of limbs and flesh. I knelt briefly, but the 'whomp' of the chopper's blades broke my concentration.

I ran for the LZ, helping a pair of wounded carry a stretcher along the way. The roar of the H-34 Sea Horse helicopter was deafening as it sat on the deck, like a sprinter awaiting the starter's gun. Immediately the VC mortars began to impact and the craft lurched. The pilot had heard a gun all right. He lifted off and banked violently to the right. Acrid-smelling clouds from the 120mm mortars were washed into our faces by the chopper's downdraft, yet my hearing followed the helo's overspeeding engines. Suddenly, I heard the thud of hollow metal and whirling steel slamming into the jungle floor, then it was silent. I peered into the eyes of the wounded. A round whistled in, spraying us with grapefruit-sized clumps of earth. As I brushed the faces of the stretcher bound, the cry for a corpsman erupted, leaving those already injured afraid of being bumped and left behind.

The HST shouted, "Standby! Standby!" as he circled the trenchline like an Indian rain dancer. Then he leaped beside me and dropped to one knee. "Those fuckers got Harold!" Like a jack-in-the-box he stuck his head up and screamed, "You motherfucking gooks!"

His face was contorted, his crooked lower teeth protruding. Spit trickled from his mouth as he shouted a refrain, tears streaming. He was squarely in my face, and I touched the sinewy blood splattered on his neckline. I was about to call for a corpsman when he grabbed my hand and turned it palm up.

"That's Harold, Reverend. He ain't got no head. He ain't got no head, I tell you." He dropped to both knees and sobbed.

"He's with the Lord, Son. You've gotta get a grip. We need you, Private. I need you!"

"But Harold was our Chief Corpsman, Father. Lots of guys owe it all to him. It's not right, I tell ya. It's not ..."

He wept, his frame trembling as I stroked the nape of his neck, while I quietly admonished myself for having judged the Chief during our earlier encounter.

Suddenly, the boy's head popped up. "Chopper inbound!" he blurted.

Duty had won out. Wide-eyed, he exclaimed, "I gotta finish Harold's work. I gotta get these wounded home!" In an instant, he was centered in the LZ, in the VC's bull's-eye, scanning skyward as the eggbeater blades of a camouflaged Sea Knight whipped up the dirt. The wounded smiled, nearly as much white showing from their teeth as their bandages. Our deux ex machina had arrived.

Not since the Bishop told me I was going to Nam, or that winter's night a year ago when Julie broke me down, were my prayers so intense. Both had tested my vows. He, my love for the church—her, my celibacy. Why now, on this hilltop, was I being racked by self-doubt? *Let go, Satan,* I thought. *Release me, Lord, from this inferno and from Julie's grip.*

"Go! Go! Go!"

The chorus was like the answer to my prayer. The Private waved us toward the chopper's tailgate, and we sprinted to the beat of the bracketing mortars. The engines choked, coughed, then revved to an ear-splitting pitch. With the polished handle of a stretcher in one hand and my ammo box in the other, I leaped inside the chopper.

Immediately the hatch shut, darkness everywhere. We sprang upward and to the right, pitching and rolling like a cork in a speedboat's wake. Thank God! We'd slipped through the VC's noose just as the hangman tripped the trapdoor. I sat in a jump seat, cradling my ammo box, as the pilot steadied the craft and our forward movement accelerated. Moments later the crew chief roared, "Standby," and my body stiffened. I gulped saliva, fighting back the urge to vomit. Out the porthole, columns of smoke, like pillars of Greek ruins, dotted the tarmac of the Khe Sanh base camp as the mortars registered our arrival.

We descended rapidly and I watched as men threw themselves into trenches. The Hail Marys flowed from my lips and a bead of sweat clung to the tip of my nose. I felt a jolt as the landing gear settled, then light streamed in. Someone hollered, "Go! Go!," but my legs wouldn't budge. Nothing but my lips could move. Then a hand gripped my collar, tugged, and I somersaulted down the ramp.

Hands grappled my arms and waistline, dragging me to an earthen ledge. There I slid down its steep wall and collapsed, vomiting violently into a muddy hollow left by a boot print. I shook, certain that dirt would be shoveled over me.

Chapter 4

A centipede crawled atop the vomit puddled beside my hands—*at least something would benefit from my disgorge,* I thought. I stood, a cool breeze fanning my face, and unlatched my chinstrap. As my piss pot tumbled over the lip of the trench, I was awed by a blade of sunlight piercing the cloud-cover. Whiter than a marble column, it moved gracefully across the landscape like a silent tornado.

I had entered the priesthood thinking I could provide counsel, inspired sermons, and, through my deeds, a tireless display of the Lord's good news. In short, that I'd be a contemporary Solomon. I had prostrated myself before my Bishop and God, accepting the anointing oil on my head and palms like a groom accepts his bride's ring. Now I wondered if the church—in accepting my vows—had erected a pillar on a sandbar. I knew the honeymoon was over, but I wasn't ready for a divorce.

I had assumed, at home and now under fire, that I could perform my pastoral deeds and still maintain a comfortable distance from my flock. I wanted to be a weekend messenger, devoting myself to those who only fed on a hebdomadal schedule. Trouble was, I could no more perform spiritual healing by remote control than a surgeon could wield his scalpel from the golf course. Now I was fighting for my clerical life, with no support system to fall back on—no rectory to hide in, no sedan to whisk me away, no lay clothes in which to masquerade. I'd lost my rose-colored glasses. No longer could I ignore the bleats of my flock. I had become one of the very sheep I was sworn to protect, with no shepherd to chase away the self-doubt that was devouring me.

My call to serve Matt and Julie was a stark reminder that I had to regain my priestly course. During my Holy War against social injustice, I had my Pastor's broad shoulders to cry on and my Bishop's paternal ear to bend. Once wise to my shortcomings, though, they sent me to the doghouse—a true sheepdog's house. As my mentors, they knew that only through a baptism by bullets and repentant men could I know my life's work.

I felt it my solemn duty to rekindle Matt and Julie's romance, but for now my immediate task was to shepherd my flock of Marines. I grabbed a swatch of canvas and blew my nose like a trumpet. My head seemed to finally clear and with it my walls of uncertainty had tumbled down. I closed my eyes as the sun's soothing rays, like a hummingbird in flight, hovered over me. Like Saul when struck down by the light, I succumbed to the voice of the Lord. As the rays renewed me, I drifted into sleep. Not until my batteries were recharged and my spiritual engine tuned did I want to stir.

Sometime later I was awakened by a gaggle of inbound choppers. Groggy, I stood atop a mound of sandbags for the best vantage. Like geese in flight, the helos were in a V-shaped formation. Dozens—no, hundreds!—of fresh troops spilled onto the tarmac and moved swiftly for cover. They were like a tag team partner to an exhausted wrestler. But Lowell said we couldn't supply the troops we had. So why the reinforcements?

As darkness fell, I returned to my hooch, learning along the way that the helos had transported the 1st Battalion of the 9th Marines. Throughout the evening a test of our two armies' wills continued as B-52s dropped their payloads while the NVA flung their rockets and mortars. It was a tussle of David-and-Goliath proportions. Frequently, a brilliant orange-red flash of napalm lit the sky as it broiled the landscape beneath it. Our camp, meanwhile, was being reduced to shambles—remnants of tents, sandbags, and fatigues blew about with the shifting winds. We'd become tattered soldiers in a tattered world—everything and everyone was defiled.

∞

The days unfolded, and we cleaned up from our savage party, our Night of the Long Knives. Everyone's ears were tuned for incoming, with conversations abruptly halted at the sound of the VC's whistling messengers. Whenever a chopper was inbound from 881S, I made for Charlie-Med, fearful that Matt was its "priority" cargo. Each morning I knelt beside my bunk, brushed the dirt and insects from its covers, and prayed for his safety. I tried to revisit his hilltop—a Twilight Zone four miles away—but the weather shackled me to Khe Sanh. Like brothers separated by an impassable ravine, all we could hope was that the smoke rising from the other's encampment was from the hearth, and not the roof.

My link to Matt became our klaxon. Its wail, which warned of VC incoming, gave us a precious eight seconds to leap into the nearest hole. When a lookout on 881S spotted a puff of smoke or heard a rocket's trajectory—its sound like that of a chipmunk scurrying through dry leaves—he'd send a radio alert. I often thought of Matt as being my lookout. With each howl of the klaxon I'd see him in my mind's eye, then I'd touch Julie's letter that I kept in my breast pocket. She and Matt were joined by events, by hardships, and each was destined—if my dream could be realized—to release the other. These shipwrecked souls didn't have to drift apart; all they needed was some navigational aid from me.

Mail hadn't arrived for days, so I contented myself with re-reading Julie's letters and nibbling crumbs from a tin of Christmas cookies she'd sent. Even my Bishop had sent me a care package. For months, the image of his flowing robes, mitered head, and arthritic grip on his Crosier set my teeth to grinding. I had come, however, to see his wisdom in sending me here. Just as God had admonished Jonah when he shirked his duties, so my Bishop had admonished me. If I couldn't handle this exile, then I knew I didn't have the mettle to resist Julie and renew my vows.

I watched intently as a rat circled my boots, its head bobbing. Our mutual purpose was to survive the VC's barrages. Only the klaxon gave me the edge. I nudged the rodent aside and climbed out of the hole, probably the tenth one I'd leaped into this damp day, and left the buck-toothed beast foraging on a can of C-rats. When I entered my bunker, I scanned the desktop for mail. Instead, I saw a pair of dented Hamm's beer cans rested on the corner—Colonel Whiley's calling card. "Have can, will travel," we called him. Like Saint Nick, he gleefully doled them out to the tune of one can per man every other day. I stashed them under my bunk, so I could be a good host when visitors dropped in. I was thankful, though, for the candle lighting. Otherwise, my guests would've seen the gnaw marks made on the cans by the voracious rats.

Matt had no beer—just getting water to his outpost was challenge enough. Half a canteen per day, a galley slave's portion, had become the hill ration. To increase the allowance would increase the helo downings. Sleeping by day and working by night was their routine. Captain Daniels' school call was hitting home now.

My preoccupation with water influenced my behavior. Though I gulped a gallon a day, I was careful not to let it dribble down my chin. I shaved with it—Whiley demanded it of his officers—but I didn't bathe in it. Only when removing bloodstains or during the ritual cleansing of my hands for the offertory did water touch my skin. If Matt could survive without it, then I'd do likewise to cement our bond. Water became our fixation. On the hill posts it was its scarcity, at the Khe Sanh Base Camp it was its purity.

No airships could have navigated the cloud cover or the VC's gauntlet to sustain our flow of water. Cut off our water, and we'd have to break out. Break out, and we'd be fodder for the VC's sausage machine. Siege warfare dictated that the VC poison our water supply, that they pinch the artery tight. Oddly enough, they chose not to. I admired them for that. Those who lived off the land, who took their bounty from its scarred landscape, refused to deal it a final defacing blow—even in war, it would seem that some things remained sacred.

A week had passed since my reunion with Matt, and I settled down to visit with an officer of Delta Company 1/26. We shared C-rats—combat-individual-canned rations for those unfamiliar with the jargon—and exchanged tales. He was a wise First Louie named Spanner, whom the Seabees affectionately called "Wrench." His men respected him, and he tactfully scolded me when I voiced my anti-war convictions. Try as I did to refute his hawkish ways, he'd stealthily guide me back to the realization that some evils in life were necessary. As a celibate priest, I understood that all too well.

I was Spanner's diary, something of Delta Company's collective memory. They shared their thoughts with me, not only because of my collar, but because they believed that I would survive this hellhole. I was a repository for their fears and hopes, a safety deposit box to be opened by their estate when the bell tolled for them. It was our unwritten contract that if they died, I would be the messenger to inform their loved ones.

Spanner was a consummate storyteller, and I'd sit, like a child at his grandfather's knee, as he spun his tributes to men and machines. When he spoke, my thoughts flitted to and from Matt's perils like a butterfly navigating a flower patch. Only by absorbing and appreciating this knowledge could I properly minister to a foot soldier's needs. Spanner's wisdom was born of toe-to-toe combat, and today he recounted his platoon's sweep of a plateau near our water point. From his recollections, I learned these truths:

Blood rushes through arteries like white water, while eyes betray the terror and uncertainty of sheep being led to slaughter. Sights and sounds and smells bring every instinct to red alert; the rustling of the elephant grass or the snapping of a twig affording milliseconds in which to avoid an ambush. For many, trigger fingers will squeeze and magazines will empty before the mind analyzes the threat ... or sees the foe. Load, shoot, aim will be their mantra.

They'll watch as the muscles of their prey twitch after the mind is dead, watch gaping wounds that are bloodless and shallow flow crimson, and hear the dying plead and beg. They'll gag at the sweet smells of burning flesh and hair, and collapse exhausted, eyes glazed, after adrenaline, nature's amphetamine, has coursed through their veins.

The death of a rival will bring celebration and posturing, while the passing of a comrade will leave hate and a profound sense of loss. All this they'll come to know in a blink of an eye and, for some, it'll be a lesson they didn't survive.

Only by witnessing violent and unpredictable death, explained Spanner, could men realize the value of life. It was an argument opposed to the commandants I had vowed to keep and teach.

My role as a peacemaker was soon tested when the North Vietnamese launched their Tet Offensive—Thursday, February 1, 1968. Tet was the Vietnamese celebration of Homecoming and Thanksgiving, which ended the Year of the Goat and rang in the Year of the Monkey. After listening to the AFRTS broadcasts, I thought for sure we'd rang in the Year of the Sheep. Something ugly was in the air, and nobody knew if we were up or downwind from its wrath.

The onset of Tet proved quiet for Khe Sanh and the hill posts, time that we spent anticipating the worst and hoping for the best. Weapons were checked and rechecked, and grenades, their pins straightened, were piled in pyramids—a mound of salvation for us, a volcano of destruction for the VC. But neither rockets nor hordes assaulted our camp, leaving us with only the fog as our constant companion. Like a dog it heeled at our ankles and brushed our calves, swirling in and out of trenches like an uninvited guest.

The ground rumbled as our high-flying B-52s spewed bombs along an ever-shrinking circle. As the noose tightened around Charlie's neck, our camp breathed easier. Our once-scenic view, however, was changing as these airborne earthmovers stripped away the tree line. The countryside was becoming a churning sea of red earth and uprooted greens, with us an island in the middle. God help those under the flight path of these invisible birds. Hawks by day, owls by night—their tons of explosives ripped the landscape to its bedrock.

Added to our high-tech war machine were Mini and Micro 'Arclight' strikes—the simultaneous detonation of high-explosive artillery over a confined area—annihilating anything beneath their umbrella of pulsing light, shrapnel, and concussions. The Pentagon had devised a weapon of mass destruction whose signature was not a mushroom cloud. Our troops cheered wildly whenever this orchestra of death played, leaping up to shout ovations of "Screw you, Charlie!" and "Tell Hanoi Rose and Jane you love it!" I'd have chieu hoi-ed (surrendered) had I been on the receiving end of an arclight.

On February 3, I unwrapped the long stem candles the Bishop sent me at Christmas. I crossed them like a pair of scissors, then bound them with red ribbon. It was the Feast of Saint Blasé, revered for having healed a boy choking on a fishbone, and I traveled about the camp commemorating his miracle by blessing the throats of the men. What had us choking, though, was no fishbone:

The fog was choking our hopes. It left us groping about and cursing the darkness rather than lighting a candle that the VC might target. This gray soup held our supply and medevac flights hostage—flights that delivered troops, whisked away casualties, spirited home the lucky ones, ferried the news reporters, and hauled the beans, bacon, and bandages that filled our stomachs and patched our wounds. Most of all, it held hostage the mail!

We choked on the sounds of war. From bombs detonating ... klaxons screaming ... helos whining ... jets streaking ... machine guns bursting ... artillery blasting ... sniper rounds whistling ... mortars popping ... non-comms barking ... loudspeakers blaring propaganda ... the stroke of the trench digger's shovel ... the timpani roll of a B-52 strike ... the thump of a VC rocket impacting a mountain of sandbags ... the crack of dry roof timbers ... the groan of a soldier with dysentery ... the shout of "Corpsman, up!" ... the gurgle in a dying man's breath.

We choked on the smells of war. From plumes of CS gas ... rubbish fires ... belching diesel generators ... garbage dumps ... decaying flesh ... urine, vomit, farts, feet, fungus, sour breath, crotch rot, and diarrhea ... 55-gallon drums of petroleum and excrement ... cordite ... moldy canvas ... fermenting fatigues purple with blood ... rancid C-rats ... decomposing rodents ... socks, shirts, and underwear ... and the fear that oozed from our pores.

I crawled out of a hole, having dodged a mortar, and stood eyeing Hill 881 South. The summit's immersion in clouds had kept me from blessing the throats of Daniels' men. Matt's hilltop had become a Mount Calvary—a Golgotha—where innocent and guilty alike were meeting their end.

I began to see my pastoral role more plainly: I was here to point the way for those heading on high. I was a gatekeeper, an usher in a theater of horrors, who collected their ticket stub and permitted them to pass. But I wasn't going to let Matt through! I needed Julie to focus her love on him, not me. Finding Matt had launched my priestly renewal. I felt good about our triangle. A rich harvest could come from the seeds I planted in this soil, and, once they sprouted, I'd work hard to see that no forbidden fruit touched the lips of my Adam and Eve.

Content with my matchmaker's plan, I approached a Marine who was sitting on his piss pot and shining his boots. An incongruous sight. His whistling gave a serene, almost surreal, quality to the moment. He was oblivious to my movements, tapping his heel and humming in sync to a Beatles ballad that boomed from a neighbor's foxhole.

"Say, Corporal. Corporal!" He looked up. "What dance are you prepping for?"

"Ah, just gettin' spruced up for the trip home, Sir. I shipped over for six months. Stupid, huh? Well, now I'm gonna get my payback and take a thirty-day leave. I'm goin' home to some real food, a warm, dry bed and my woman Rita. You know, Reverend," he said, with wonderment in his eyes, "I might even propose to her." He smiled, exposing a gold tooth, then returned to chewing his gum and buffing his boot. *He wouldn't need me as his gatekeeper,* I thought.

"Enjoy yourself and … tie the knot with Rita, if she'll have you." He grinned and inspected his boot.

As I walked away, I heard the whistle of an incoming rocket. I leaped into a shell hole as a hail of earth showered my backside. When I uncoiled, a boot had landed beside me, its toe glistening. I jumped up, but the Corporal was gone. The rocket had hit smack-dab where he was sitting, the music or his inner bliss having drowned out its flight. Two Grunts ran to the smoking crater, but nothing was left. Nothing! I examined the boot, then mumbled a prayer. Weak-kneed, I handed the boot to his staff sergeant.

"He was going home today, Chaplain. Why him?"

"He is home, Staff Sergeant," I offered with a sigh. It was a lame and, yet, profound reply. To the nonbeliever it was tripe, but to the believer …

"I'll see that his personal effects get home, Chaplain. We'll find some remains. His family won't mourn over an empty casket."

"Let me keep the boot, Sergeant. His girl would want it—maybe it'll comfort her to know he was polishing it for her."

With that I cradled the boot and returned to my hooch. I found a strange attachment to the boondocker. Why not his helmet or dog tags or some other article of a soldier's gear? Yet … what better remembrance of a Grunt than his weathered boot? Its skin was lacerated and its tongue moldy, but the toe came alive when struck by the light from my candle.

I decided to hold onto it until I saw Matt again. The boot would remind me of the precipice he walked. I would cherish it as a talisman until our separation was over. Once I knew Matt was safe and his future with Julie charted, I'd ship the boot to the Corporal's sweetheart. If Rita were here, she'd understand. Matt was to me what that Corporal was to her. I would hold a vigil until his return, or his passing.

Chapter 5

February wore on and we burrowed in like moles.

I'd been bunker-hopping through the night, ministering to those who slept by day, when I entered Lowell's command bunker for some Khe Sanh coffee—shaken, not stirred, as we liked to say. It was just after midnight on February 7. As I sipped the brew, I heard that the Lang Vei Special Forces camp was under attack. Lowell was pacing—clearly, no news was bad news.

The radio crackled, and a voice shouted, "Tanks! Tanks!" I looked quizzically toward Lowell, thinking I'd heard "Yanks," but his stony face, jaw muscles knotted like golf balls, said otherwise. Our silent exchange reaffirmed the loneliness of command.

"Radioman. Advise Lang Vei that it's a 'Negative' on the relief force," snapped Lowell. Instantly, we heard a static-laced reply.

"Khe Sanh Base! Tanks in the wire! Repeat, tanks in the wire! Need…"

The plea halted. Everyone looked at Lowell, and he pursed his lips. "I said *no* reinforcements! You people have a short memory. We rehearsed a relief two months ago. It took a rifle company nineteen hours to cover the five miles to Lang Vei … and in broad daylight. This isn't a fucking cavalry charge! Those Green Berets know the score—and so should you." He stared down the group, then faded into the shadows.

"Khe Sanh Base," the voice was rapid and shrill. "Charlie has flame-throwers. Repeat, flame-throwers! Request …"

Silence followed, and Lowell shrank deeper into his thoughts. The radio choked to life again, and with it came Lang Vei's CO. With calm he called for artillery on his own position. We'd forsaken a cause, a friend, and, like a Judas, given Lang Vei the kiss of death. A flash suddenly lit the bunker as a camera shutter tripped open, then closed. I was startled, but Lowell, the focal point of the shot, was unshaken. As he emerged from the shadows, the reporter backpedaled.

"Move on," Lowell said without a trace of malice. Resting his palm on the man's shoulder, he added, "There's no call for you or your Pulitzer prize-winning camera to get swept away in the tide. If a plane comes, get on it. You hear me? And tell your press club buddies to do likewise." He offered the advice as a father would counsel a son. As Travis did at the Alamo, Lowell wanted the civilians out of harm's way.

We paced like expectant fathers, the radio appeals like the wails of a newborn—we, however, were witnessing life's passing. Shortly after 0300 hours, Lang Vei's commander made a final transmission. The silence was oppressive, and the men glanced toward me as though I could answer the riddle. My thoughts were a mosaic of guilt and relief: guilt at being alive, relief that their cries had ceased. God, how I hated this war!

I rose slowly, stepping into a light bulb's harsh glare, hands clasped, and recited the Lord's Prayer. Many joined in. Then I removed my pocket-sized Psalm book, paused, and opened to the dog-eared page of the 23rd Psalm. The words flowed:

The Lord is my Shepherd; I shall not want. He maketh me to lie down in green pastures; he leadeth me beside the still waters ... Yea, though I walk through the valley of the shadow of death, I will fear no evil; for thou art with me ... Thou preparest a table before me in the presence of mine enemies; thou anointist my head with oil; my cup runneth over ....

I knew by the tranquility, the eye of the hurricane wherein we stood, that the men had gathered peace from its dispatch. I stowed the book and left. Clouds with dark underbellies sped across the moonlit sky, like greyhounds chasing a hare. Given time and the tradewinds, I knew they would pass over Julie. Given more time, and Matt's cooperation, they might one day accompany a mail flight that would tell me of her swan song for our love.

I was resting on my bunk, reflecting, when the mortars started pounding. The sprinkle became a shower, then a torrent as hundreds fell. I surveyed the damage at dawn, brushed the soil from the toe of the Corporal's boot, emptied my bladder, and plodded back to Lowell's commander bunker. Instead of arriving to a wake for Lang Vei, I entered another funeral march: Hill 64 had been overrun and a portion of 861A captured. Giap was playing Russian roulette with our hill posts, and 881S might well be his next target.

We dumped everything on the attackers: artillery from Camp Carroll, the Rock Pile, Hill 881S, Hill 558, and from our heavy guns at the Khe Sanh Base Camp, but the bastards, even those wounded, kept charging. The scuttlebutt was that the VC had become a drug-crazed pack of suicidal maniacs—our scouts had found syringes and chemicals, thought to be speed, on their corpses. Combine dope with adrenaline, and the chaos of battle, and the result was a berserker's cry.

I left the command bunker, thinking I would toss my guts, after hearing that three hundred had perished at Lang Vei; two dozen Green Berets presumed dead among them. I breathed in the chill morning air and quaked. *Six thousand against twenty thousand. Six against twenty.* I kept tossing those lopsided figures about in my head. I should have visited C-Med, but I collapsed instead on my bunk and cradled the Corporal's boot, bawling.

෴

A fortnight had passed since my visit with Matt. Another week of incoming, casualties, sniper fire, food shortages, rats, and a ceiling of zero-zero visibility that clogged our airborne lifeline. The beast, our war machine, needed to be fed, but, without its diet of bombs, bullets, and bandages, it was on its knees. Even when visibility was good elsewhere, the runway remained shrouded, its steel plates a magnet for clouds and fog. No matter how sophisticated our guidance systems, aircraft couldn't land. Forced to approach through a corridor of tracers, many fell victim. Our long metal runway had become a double-edged sword.

I prayed for the aircrews and for Matt; he was my lifeline to the future, while they were our lifeline today. Like the men defending the base, the aircraft supplying it were worn and battered. Bullet holes scarred every wing and fuselage, and more tires were shot out in midair than were blown on the jagged runway plating. The duel was relentless. To complicate matters, the base's landmarks had been blown away or sunk underground. Our mountains had become molehills, our living quarters anthills. Everyone and everything had gone subterranean.

We'd become a boot hill of demolished equipment—mounds of earth, like freshly filled graves, scattered everywhere. It must've been an eerie panorama for the pilots as they descended through the cloud cover. God, how I hated this war!

Thankfully, a silver lining in these clouds emerged: a resurgence of faith. When I first arrived, my worship services were poorly attended. It wasn't that the men were godless, only that they felt the need to display a macho behavior. Now, with the battle going badly, the chaplains found their flocks growing. Those who'd been indifferent were now anxious for our arrival. The transformation was exhilarating, and when the chaplains huddled, our only lament was that fear, not brotherly love, had motivated it.

Still, I marveled at a handful of nonbelievers—the branches that would bear no fruit. They were the whiskery Bluto types who embraced the cigar-chomping, blood-lusting bravado nurtured by Hollywood's filmmakers. One burly sergeant, on occasion, would shadow me as I made my rounds. If I glanced in his direction he'd grin like the Cheshire Cat, then turn away. If I moved toward him, he'd vanish into some nondescript bunker. His one identifiable feature was his helmet, which sported a cluster of sprigs that fanned from its netting like a peacock's tail feathers. He appeared the sort to clench a bayonet between his teeth and crawl through the booby-trapped jungle on a one-man search and destroy mission.

Charlie's ceaseless incoming had put a halt to my celebrating daily Mass. Too often, the chalice had been torn from my grip, spilling Christ's Body and Blood onto the red earth. I resorted to consecrating the gifts in my hooch, then setting out with my ammo box full to deliver the good news. I'd become a spiritual newspaper boy, anxious to increase my circulation whenever possible. If a host were undelivered, I'd fret over the parishioner's whereabouts. An absence was often a reminder that injury and death were only milliseconds away. Then I'd hurry to C-Med or Graves Registration where, if the worst were confirmed, I'd anoint their bodies. Every farewell was painful but some, after weeks of friendship, brought spasms of tears. Once entombed in the dark green bag, we stacked the corpses head to toe.

The bell could toll for anyone and, dog collar or not, I was no less vulnerable. Though some viewed my noncombatant status with envy, I shared the same mud holes, failings, and trepidation they did. Saint Matthew's thoughts frequented mine: "You cannot know the day your Lord is coming ... The Son of Man is coming at the time you least expect."

By mid-February, the C-130s were banned from landing, and the generals resorted to parachute drops. Trouble was, they reminded us of the French efforts to supply their crumbling defenses at Dienbienphu. It was exhilarating to watch the chutes blossom and their cargo drift into our laps, but to see a payload wander beyond the camp's perimeter was unbearable. If it carried mail or medical supplies, we'd muster a patrol to fetch it. If it carried beans, bacon, bullets, or bombs and night was approaching, we'd summon our jets to destroy it. Like kids with their noses pressed to the candy store glass, we savored every morsel these descending mushrooms provided.

As the casualties mounted, our focus turned to bunker material. By late February one in ten men had been wounded or killed. Wood became our deliverance. With a posture like Christ, men hunched under the beams they carried to shore up their bunkers. Not just any wood would do, however. It had to be dry and stout or it would snap under the weight of the sandbags or the jab of a mortar. The trees surrounding our base camp weren't up to the challenge. They were too green, splintered, or so riddled with shrapnel that a chain saw would foul on the first cut. We'd have been better off unleashing our saws on a stand in the Petrified Forest than to try and harvest this plateau's timber.

Like pioneers erecting a cabin before the first snow, we rushed to reinforce our bunkers. Burrowing deeper was the only way to save ourselves from the gravedigger's shovel. Bartering wood became a brisk business. Just let a sturdy beam show up and troops would descend on it like jackals. Eventually, the men resorted to stealing metal runway strips. It seemed incongruous to dismantle our lifeline, but the strips were perfect for reinforcing our roofs. Simply put, dead men didn't need supplies.

Nothing remained snug or secure for long, including our dead. We stacked them in a temporary morgue, and twice we dug them out from an avalanche of dirt. The earth seemed determined to claim her dead. For the VC it didn't matter whether their potter's field was north or south of the DMZ—either way, their dead were being buried in Vietnamese soil.

The VC's internment proved temporary, too, as our skybound onslaught exhumed their bodies. Westmoreland's cascade of B-52s—code named "Niagara"—rounded jagged peaks until our vista lost its definition. Trees were splintered like seedlings under a hiker's boot, while rivers were diverted from their ancient routes. Operation Niagara delivered thousands of tons of bombs; pouring them from the bellies of our stratofortresses, as though these giant birds had been disemboweled in flight. *How could Charlie take this beating and still blacken our eyes daily?*

My morale would ebb and flow. I talked myself up and down, and, by day's end, I was exhausted. I felt I was suffering from multiple personalities, and frequently talked aloud to myself. I was a one-man debate team, championing both the affirmative and negative argument. I wanted out so badly that "doing the deed"—the dirty deed of a self-inflicted wound—frequently entered my mind. I resisted only because I had to cement Matt's future to Julie's. So long as her letters piled up in my pockets and not his, my priesthood was in jeopardy. She was too much of a temptation, too much a lost sheep for me to ignore. I knew I wouldn't abandon her unless it was into the arms of Matt.

The VC's shelling reduced us to knee-hugging, dirt-eating cretins. A Private with a five-string guitar summed it up when he sang the popular ballad:

Where have all the flowers gone?
Long time passing.
Where have all the flowers gone?
Long time ago.
Where have all the flowers gone?
Gone to young girls every one.
When will they ever learn?
When will they ever learn?

Where have all the young girls gone?
Long time passing.
Where have all the young girls gone?

Long time ago.
Where have all the young girls gone?
Gone to young men every one.
When will they ever learn?
When will they ever learn?

Where have all the young men gone?
Long time passing.
Where have all the young men gone?
Long time ago.
Where have all the young men gone?
Gone to soldiers every one.
When will they ever learn?
When will they ever learn?

Where have all the soldiers gone?
Long time passing.
Where have all the soldiers gone?
Long time ago.
Where have all the soldiers gone?
Gone to graveyards every one.
When will they ever learn?
When will they ever learn?

Boom boxes were silenced in deference to this roving minstrel. Had the generals seen this Music Man's gift for moving minds and hearts, they'd have transferred him out for fear he'd subvert our warlike stance. I could envision a serpentine column of troops following him, like a Pied Piper, to the stillness of the DMZ. Once there, this army of flower children could lock arms and chant anti-war slogans in a massive sit-down strike. Not surprisingly, his guitar came up missing. My manner of protesting the war was to blow off the regimental briefings and drift, like the cargo parachutes that delivered them, into a three-pack-a-day cigarette habit. Maybe it was a death wish, or maybe I'd hit bottom, but either way I inhaled deeply and regularly.

The events of February 25 turned my stomach. A Marine patrol, twenty-nine strong, set out south in search of a VC mortar position that had been hammering their lines. Their mission was planned to a gnat's ass—the squad had plenty of firepower and would travel a line-of-sight route so artillery could defend them instantly. Nonetheless, they were caught in a fierce ambush and picked off like ripe grapes on a vine. A fifty-man relief stormed to their rescue, only to be pinned down by small arms and mortar fire, leaving Lowell no resort but to retreat. It was high-stakes gambling, another spin of Giap's Russian roulette wheel, and we'd lost our shirts.

I had positioned myself at C-Med, waiting for the patrol's casualties, but none arrived. Before the morning was over a grim toll had been tallied: 1 KIA, 21 WIA, and 25 MIA. We knew that many of the missing were dead, while pleading radio calls told us that others lay dying. It was an unthinkable breech of Marine Corps tradition to leave a dead or dying comrade on the field of battle. "Semper Fidelis" (always faithful) meant everything. When told we'd left our dead, I knew how dire our situation had become. A smothering wake gripped the regiment. For days men stared through binoculars toward a point some 700 meters away, but only the elephant grass moved on that killing field. The memory of our uncollected dead—like a splinter hidden in soft flesh—left a howling pain whenever their names were mentioned. Knowing Matt might face the same fate upset me all the more.

Those fortunate enough to return from that aborted mission reported a looming threat: NVA trenches. They were snaking toward our gates, their zigzagging course a few hundred yards shy of our perimeter. At night, we observed lanterns bobbing, as these diggers boldly walked the trenches. B-52s churned up the soil and trees, hurling them skyward, but it didn't matter. Charlie just kept burrowing, and we kept sweating. Sooner or later, it would be a hand-to-hand bloodbath.

∞

I stood motionless, watching the VC's lanterns—their intermittent glows like fireflies on a summer's night. It was the evening of the 28th, Ash Wednesday. Suddenly, a figure appeared and I blurted out the call sign. I repeated it, but heard no password in reply. Then a soldier sprang from behind a mound and fell at my feet. I thought a sniper's bullet had hit him, until his grip tightened around my leg. He sobbed, and I squatted to a helmet crowned with sprigs and the odor of cigars. My phantom had revealed himself!

"I don't want to die, Father!" His hold became viselike. "I know it's gonna happen! All my platoon is gone."

He shook so violently that my heel tapped.

"Sweet Jesus, don't take me away. Help me get home, Father? Please!"

I removed his helmet and could just make out his short-timer's calendar. He had months to go. His coarse exterior had been a ruse— the "MOM AND DAD FOREVER" penned inside his piss pot confirmed it.

"I'm scared too, Son. Plenty scared. The Lord knows that we're hurting. Will you join me in a prayer?" We knelt facing an opening in the clouds. He sniveled, and I placed my arm around his shoulder. Through the sky's peephole we watched the stars and prayed.

"Father, You are holy indeed and all creation rightfully gives You praise. Let Your spirit come down upon this Sergeant and me and help us to see the wisdom of Your ways. Spare us from this hell of man's making and keep us whole in body and spirit, and deliver us unscathed into the arms of our loved ones. We ask this through Jesus Christ, Your Son, who lives and reigns with You forever and ever."

"Amen."

"Remember, Sergeant," I added, tugging him closer, "God so loved the world that He gave us His only begotten Son. Believe in Him, and He'll protect you."

Without warning, a mortar barrage moved toward us, like a stomping child with a temper, but we remained kneeling. The footsteps became louder as the mortars sidestepped us, peppering our bodies with earth. A beam of moonlight bathed the camp and we looked at one another; me with satisfaction for his spiritual rescue, him with the knowledge he had a new master to serve. The tears streamed down his face, cutting channels through his dirty cheeks. The branch I thought was barren had bore fruit.

We rose and embraced. I blessed his forehead with my tin of ashes, saying, "Remember, you are dust and to dust you will return." At that moment the clouds, like shutters, closed. Our audience with the

Almighty had concluded, leaving only the diggers' lanterns twinkling in the darkness.

Chapter 6

Sadie Hawkins Day began like any other. Leap year, Bissextile year, Intercalary year—whatever name chosen—was a cruel joke to play on a Marine. To a Grunt already screwed and tattooed for a thirteen-month tour, leap year's extra day only added insult to injury.

Our spirits had been lifted by a morning mail drop. I listened to a pair of sleeveless Grunts huddled over a *Pacific Stars and Stripes* (known as 'Read and Wipes' because of our toilet paper shortage) as they discussed Father Walt. So I squatted to read the headlines. There, in large print, was an excerpt from a February 27 commentary by Walter Cronkite. Before a TV audience of millions, he peered into his crystal ball and predicted the war's outcome. We knew the verdict, but to have it proclaimed by a media icon was a wake-up call for every armchair warrior. I read it aloud while the two nodded in agreement:

To say that we are closer to victory today is to believe, in the face of the evidence, the optimists who have been wrong in the past. It seems now more certain than ever that the bloody experience of Vietnam is to end in a stalemate.

Many of the lifers scoffed at Cronkite, but that only increased his believability. To my way of thinking, the career types had squandered their credibility by playing games with body counts—Charlie's and ours. I was disgusted and wanted to flag the brass with "Maggie's Drawers," but it was pointless to tell the emperors they had no clothes.

Searching for an escape, I re-read the letter I'd just received from Julie:

My Dearest Andrew,
    Well, I did it! It's 2 AM, zero two-hundred hours as you guys say, and the adrenaline is pulsing through my veins. I finally mustered the courage to tell my deadbeat husband to hit the road. The house reeked of pot. Then the ass got blitzed on downers and beer and toppled Faith's bassinet with her in it.

The bastard! I threw him out and if I have to I'll sleep with a club at my side.

Ever since Tet he's gotten uglier and uglier, just like the damn war. He's verbally abusive and ignores Faith. Last weekend he skipped town for a demonstration in DC with my last $20. I shoved him out the door without a toothbrush and cursed him up and down the hallway. God only knows what the neighbors thought.

This marriage was a colossal mistake. Why didn't I listen to you? Now I'm penniless with no one but Faith. Maybe I should pull up stakes and return to Titusville. My parents will take me back, though I dread hearing my mother say, "I told you so." Dad will understand, I think, but Mom still has raw nerve endings from my decision to keep Faith and marry Dan. The bum! Christ, I can sure foul things up!

I wish Matthew were here. Hell, I wish you were here! I treated him so shabbily. I didn't tell you, but we were lovers. Here I go again. I'm no saint, that's apparent, but why I burden you with long-distance confessions, I'll never know. Maybe it's so I don't have to grovel when you dole out the penance. Isn't what I've done a mortal sin? I mean, if I died today I'd go to hell. Right? Ah, it's all so depressing. Now I know how Matt felt when I dumped on him. I was so certain of all the great things I'd do and I hen-pecked him unmercifully. You know—about his grades, his views on social issues, his stance on the war. Who am I to judge anybody, anyway?

I wouldn't tell this to another soul, but Matt had a bout of impotence and I berated him up and down for it. Yours truly, the liberated woman, was so damn sure he was being a male chauvinist pig. God, the things I called him were terrible. By the time I'd educated myself to his problem, it was too late. We'd graduated, and I was seeing Dan. But it was you I really wanted to see.

I worry about you a lot. Khe Sanh is in the headlines everyday. Whenever I see a TV spot, I freeze in the hopes of getting a glimpse of you. I get physically ill at the casualties from Tet. The carnage! The destruction! My God, I can't believe the stupidity of our leaders.

Please come home soon, but above all, safely. I worry that this war will change you in some ugly way—make you harder, less caring. Call it womanly intuition or a nanny syndrome. Whatever. But just understand that it won't be a hero's welcome when you and the others return. People don't want this war. And knowing that you've only got a few months left makes me more uptight than ever. You've been beating the odds, and we both know it. Don't you dare re-up or I'll board a flight and drag you home myself.

I'll close with a silent prayer for you and the thousands stuck in that fort. Please don't despair. God and I love you! The candle is burning in my window.

Love, Julie

PS: I sent more cookies to fatten you up for the homecoming!

Her words would enter my thoughts throughout the day. I was glad she'd left Dan and excited that her affections for Matt ran deep. She'd married to ease her parents' anguish over her becoming a single mother, but marrying a pot-head college dropout six years her senior was a lousy bet. When she told me she was pregnant, I urged her to settle down, but I meant it with respect to her lifestyle, not her marital status.

Julie was such a free spirit in college, a love child running wild. She was always caught up in some cause celebre. Our first encounter was at a civil rights rally in the fall of '66. I had paused to read the placards. Instead, she captured my interest as she clasped the bullhorn and exhorted the crowd to indignation. Her dark hair cascaded down her shoulders and stroked her backside like a whisk. Sporting tight jeans and a pullover sweater that clung to her every curve, she could've been a bunny at a Playboy Club. It's no wonder I succumbed to her charms that winter's night a year ago.

ఴ

It was late morning when I spotted a Huey, its outline like a tadpole, making a beeline approach from the northwest. Coming full bore from

Hill 881 South, I knew it was a medevac. The ambulance had just off-loaded when I got to Charlie-Med, so I cupped a mask to my face and entered the OR. Two corpsmen were attending to a black soldier: one was unwinding a head dressing while the other unlaced his boots. Their pace told me he was dead. I examined his dog tags. His name was Edward Jackson III. Though he wasn't Catholic, I knew he was a Christian by the Latin cross that graced his neckline. My focus shifted to the medics hovering over his partner, who'd been hit in the stomach.

I hesitated to look, hating abdominal wounds for the agony they wrought. Then, as clearly as Julie's written words had rung in my thoughts, I heard Matt shout, "How's Eddie? He's OK, right? I love you, Eddie ..."

I leaped to his side. Seeing the terror in my eyes, Doc McGurty calmly stated, "He'll make it, Padre."

I gripped Matt's hand, dabbed his forehead with a towel, and murmured in his ear, "It's me. Father Andy, Matt."

He was under the influence of morphine, his eyes rolling. "Where's Eddie?" he gasped.

The Doc motioned for me to get out, saying, "We've got business to attend to here, Reverend."

I inched aside.

"No shit, Andy. He'll make it. Now beat it!"

I backpedaled through the canvas flap. As I exited, I heard Gurt say, "Let's put him under. Standby with six units of whole blood. And get Eddie to Graves Registration. I need some elbow room."

I paced, praying that the Lord hadn't brought Matt and me to this crossroads only to send us in opposite directions. I chain-smoked and watched as the stratus clouds began to blot out the sun. The fog also arrived, and the two enveloped our camp in a gray body bag. If the Doc were right, Matt's next stop would be the hospital at Phu Bai. I knew, however, that our zero-zero visibility would thwart his evacuation. For once, this pea soup would aid our reunion.

I passed the time by prepping Eddie's body for the journey home. While inventorying his personal effects I came upon an unsealed envelope addressed to Matt. I hesitated, then read its contents:

Dear Brother,

I don't know how to say this, so I'm using a letter. It's the coward in me, but I love you too much to tell you face-to-face. In two weeks I'm shipping out. My sorry ass has been in Charlie's gunsights for over a year, and now it's time to bail. Until we met I was one miserable Marine who didn't understand this war or his own conscience, but you helped me see things clearer.

I've been tortured by my homosexuality since my daddy kicked me out three years ago. I know your dad didn't understand you either, but at least we found some peace together. Being your partner has meant a lot to me. You let me be myself and not run from who I am.

Where I'll go when I get stateside is anybody's guess—I sure as shit won't go home, though. They'll never accept me. I won't try to keep in touch, least not right away. Put me out of your thoughts, 'cause you can do better than me. I know that you're still unsure of who you are. I've crossed that bridge, and know who I am. Now you've got to make that same journey, alone. Having me around would only cloud your vision, just like this damn fog that creeps around our sorry asses all day. Whatever you do, don't live a lie. I've done that, and it's hell.

So this is good-bye, my brother. I love you! I'll never forget you. Do what's right by your own head. Don't let anyone twist your arm. You don't have to love only women to be a man. You just got to love. You're one hellava man, Matt Garrison!

Your Brother, Eddie

Jesus! What Matt's stepsister, Janice, had said was true! Yet he and Julie were lovers? *Ah, this thing with Eddie was an aberration ... combat fatigue run amuck. Hell, this whole letter could be a fabrication, some trip into Eddie's fantasies.* What matters is how Matt feels about Julie. Nothing else! Judging him by this letter would be craziness. Let Julie be the judge. Let her set Matt and me free. I folded the letter and placed it in my pocket.

Three hours later a corpsman summoned me to Matt's side, where I stood counting the IV tubes dangling above his bandaged torso. He lay still, as though awaiting a puppeteer to stir him to life. I made a

71

cross with my thumb over his forehead, lips, and heart, then clasped my hands in prayer. My hopes were so tied to him.

The afternoon, and his IV bottles, drained away. My stomach growled with hunger and my lungs ached for a smoke, but I stayed by his side like a dog guarding his fallen master. Matt would awake to my face and, if the VC made it necessary, I would shield his body with mine. Suddenly, Corpsman Suscheck burst in to announce a red alert. I felt sure this was the VC ground assault we'd been expecting. I asked him to help me load Matt on a stretcher, then we heaped flak jackets over him and made a dash for my hooch, like a rickshaw in rush-hour traffic. We placed him on my bunk, checked his vitals, then Suscheck darted out flashing a thumbs-up.

I lit candles and returned to my vigil—my heart pounding as fast as the flames flickered—and strained to hear small-arms fire that would signal an assault. Matt soon stirred and moaned, awaking to the tremors of a mortar barrage.

"Where's Eddie? My glasses? Where … where am I?"

I had carelessly left his eyeglasses in C-Med. I put my face near his and rested my palms on his shoulders. "It's me, Matt. Andy! You're in my hooch. The Doc says you'll be OK."

"Where's Eddie? I gotta talk to Eddie."

I wanted to lie—to tell him Eddie was in C-Med getting patched up—but his pleas persisted. If I was to win him over to Julie, then I had to release him from Eddie's grip.

"There's nothing we can do for him. Do you understand me, Matt? Maybe if we said a prayer …"

"What? No. He was with me on the chopper. He was right at my side. He can't be …"

Tears flowed, dripping from his earlobes, then he abruptly regained his composure and felt about his body with his hands, grimacing when his stomach muscles moved. Relief was evident when he'd completed his inventory.

"You've got a nasty shrapnel wound in your side. The base is on red alert, and the fog has everything socked-in."

"Eddie saved my life. He must've heard it coming. He threw himself at me, and we hit the ground together. I kept yelling for him to get off

… but he didn't move. The next thing I remember is the 'thwop' of a chopper's blades."

"When did all this happen?"

"At colors."

"That was nine hours ago! You've been out ever since."

"How did Eddie die? When? Tell me."

"Head wound. He never regained consciousness. My prayers for him were too late. He died on the flight in."

"Did he suffer? I wanna know, Andy."

"Isn't it enough to know that he died saving you? Let it go, Matt. He's at peace in his world, and you should try to be at peace in yours." His chest heaved spasmodically and he unleashed more tears. I dabbed his cheeks and helped blow his nose.

"Damn VC! The bastards didn't let us raise the stripes before the incoming started. We always had twenty-one seconds after the bugle sounded—not a second more—before the 120s would start impacting. Fuckin' Charlie! We should've had more time."

He struggled with his words.

"You see, Andy, we'd hide in a trench. You know, the one in the saddle between our two ends of the hill. We called the place No-Man's Land. At 0800 we'd bolt for a radio antenna rigged to be a flagpole; they called us the salt and pepper team. Like clockwork the mortars would pop just as we cleared the trench. But not today. I didn't hear shit. We ran up the colors and jumped back to salute. That's when Eddie tackled me. Our twenty-one seconds weren't over … the clock was still running. Fuckin' gooks!"

He motioned for the canteen, but was too weak to hold it. I cradled his head and trickled water into his gaping mouth.

"I can't get enough of the stuff," he gasped. "We had to stretch ponchos out to catch the rain, then huddle around to pour it down our throats. I haven't seen a razor, bath, or toothbrush in weeks."

"Yeah, I can see … and smell. So what? This whole camp has buffalo breath, crotch rot, and the squirts." A smile stretched his chapped lips. "How long did you know Eddie?"

"Two months, but that's an eternity in a God-forsaken place like 881. I knew him better than any other man I've known."

It hurt that he felt he knew so little about me.

"He had a way with people—before you knew it, you were spilling your guts to him. But he never made judgments or belittled anyone. He'd have made a good minister."

Did he say that to get back at me?

"I wish I'd met him. He sounds like a fellow after my own heart."

"You did, don't you remember? He was the black guy in the trench with me. You know, the one I called a 'nigger.' All that claptrap was just for shits and giggles. He liked to play mind games, especially around officers. You being a priest just doubled his fun."

I found myself admiring Eddie. Not only did he save Matt's life, but he reminded me to be less uptight with mine.

"What a clown. After colors and the incoming, he'd dive into our foxhole and raise a long pole with 'Maggie's Drawers' tacked to it. Then he'd wave that bitch like it was the checkered flag at the Indy 500. The gooks didn't have the foggiest what that fuckin' red flag meant. Only a Grunt could appreciate that prank. Charlie must've thought we were headcases."

"Some fruit juice? I've been saving it for a special occasion."

"Nah. Just water."

I poured it till it ran from the corners of his mouth.

"Whoa! My tank is full. We got our water from helos dropping cargo nets. But the way those jugs burst, you'd have thought we were having a water balloon fight. Then some whiz kid got the idea of stuffing 105mm shell casings with plastic water bags so they'd survive the drop. Wish I'd have thought of it … but then the sort of suggestions I would've made wouldn't sit well with the brass."

Breathless, he coughed up a wad of phlegm and spit it into a canvas swatch.

"Look, Matt, take a rest. We can talk later."

"Nope. I'll be on a flight to Phu Bai later. Or is that FUBAR, old man? The way this fuckin' war is going we might not see each other again." I couldn't disagree with his logic.

"OK. Let's talk. And what better place than in the comfort of my lavish hooch?" *My confessional,* I thought, as I swept my arms to draw attention to my quarters.

"Not bad for a pot-smoking, anti-war activist with a hard-on for the Establishment. The brass must've figured you out by now. You haven't got 'em completely buffaloed with that dog collar, have ya?"

I snickered. At least his mind was off Eddie.

"Wanna hear something funny? We'd use those 105mm shell casings for crappers and piss tubes. We'd fill them suckers to the brim, then put their lock tops on and roll the sons of bitches down the hill." He chuckled and winced. "Imagine the look on Charlie's face when he opened up one of them babies. Priceless, huh?"

He hacked, and I passed him another swatch of canvas to spit in.

"I'll take that juice now. My throat smarts. Last time I saw juice, we were pouring it over a mortar tube."

I gave him a puzzled look.

"Earlier this month we were helping those Jarheads on 861 Alpha repel a VC attack. You know, our good neighbor policy. Well, we had three mortar tubes going nonstop. I mean, nonstop! Damn things got so hot they practically glowed. First we used water, then, when it ran out, we hit the juice." He began giggling. "When that ran out, we pulled out our cranks and started pissing. What a hissing stench!" He was roaring now. "And then … and then good old Eddie says … he says … we oughta … we oughta … jack-off on the tubes. Blow our loads while blowing Charlie to kingdom come. What a fuckin' clown!"

I grinned, and he settled back. Then an anxious look crossed his face.

"I've gotta take a wizz bad! My teeth are floating."

I helped him roll on his side, then held a coffee tin I'd saved for such occasions. He nearly filled it to the rim. I was relieved, too, as there was no trace of blood in his urine.

"Why not nod and get caught up on your dreams of home and the girl you left behind? I'll check on the alert and your medevac."

"No. I … I don't want to be alone if fighting starts. The chopper will come when it comes. They'll know where to find me."

"You've gotta be anxious to get home," I said in an envious tone. Yet I knew there wouldn't be any flights out tonight. The only flight I wanted to launch was his fantasy of Julie.

"There ain't shit to go back to, old buddy."

"You been smoking loco weed, or are you in love with suds shack Suzie Wong?" He smiled, but we both knew he'd been eating dirt, not pussy. "You've got your family. And there must be someone special?

75

I thought every Jarhead had a girl back home."

Grim-faced, he said, "I got the word two weeks ago that Dad died. Collapsed from a massive heart attack."

My jaw fell. Why hadn't I thought sooner to ask about his family? "Ah, Matt. If only I'd known. I could've offered a Mass in his memory. Why didn't you go back? You could've taken emergency leave."

"When I got the word it all seemed so final ... the events so distant. I'd lost my chance at a reconciliation. You know what my Mom always said, 'Send the flowers while I'm living, not when I'm dead.' Didn't seem right to put a helo crew at risk to send me home for someone already dead. One thing eats at me, though, like it ate at Tommy."

"What's that?"

"Knowing my Dad died thinking I was sore at him."

Matt seemed miles away.

"I haven't heard from my Mom since the funeral. I'm sure she wanted me there in full dress uniform. The old man was big on pomp and ceremony. He always wanted a military send-off. It may sound goofy, Andy, but I've come to view that hill as my home. At least there people cared about me ... especially Eddie."

"That's a hellava place to call home. And you can't really believe that your family doesn't care. Your Mom is probably up nights, pacing and worrying herself sick. Khe Sanh is front-page news back in the States."

"Yeah, well ... she's strong. She knew the Major and I weren't on the best of terms. As for my stepsisters—if I were Cinderella, they'd be Drizella and Anastasia. You wouldn't believe the backstabbing those misfits could dish out. I wanted out of that house so bad I traded my pumpkin coach for a C-130 and my glass slippers for some smelly boondockers."

Matt's color was peaked. His pain medication was wearing off.

"OK. So the women in your life can be a pain in the ass. But isn't there someone special? I know you didn't spend four years at college wearing out library cards."

"Sure. Just because I feel at home on that hill doesn't mean I only want to hang around guys." He looked timorous. "I dated a girl named Julie. I thought we had something special ... until she yanked the plug.

But that's in the past. She got knocked-up and married some peacenik twice her age."

I was worried he'd pass out, so I poked my head out the canvas flap and hollered for Suscheck. Instantly a dark figure catapulted from a shell crater. He pulled Matt's empty IVs, propped him up for an excruciating throat-clearing exercise, then gave him a hypo in the hip.

"He'll be comfortable now, Chaplain. A bit woozy, but out of pain. I'll be in that rathole a little longer if you need me."

"Thanks. If it gets nasty out there, duck in here." Suscheck smiled, his white teeth and eyes contrasting sharply against his black face paint.

"Give me that piss can again, will ya, Andy?" When he'd finished he took a long draw from the canteen.

"Tell me about Julie," I said.

He threw his head back, his chin jutting skyward, and stared at a point deep in space. "She's a real independent sort. Into every cause you could imagine. Don't you remember her? You met her when you were a seminarian. She and I were in college together."

I should be confessing to him, I thought. I knew they'd dated, but it wasn't until Julie's last letter that I realized they'd been lovers. She'd kept it so hush-hush from me. He was the neutron and I the proton, and Julie our nucleus, but the time had arrived for me to free myself from her orbit.

"Andy, wake up there! You remember her, right?"

"Yeah, but describe her anyway."

"OK, here goes. It's as though she's in my dream. Flowing dark hair held snug by a wine-colored headband, draping over grapefruit-sized breasts. A slim waistline with two dimples at the small of her back, and just a twinge of stomach muscle. She's coming in clearer now. A curvaceous ass as taut as a rice bag. Hips that filled her blue jeans as snug as any sandbag I've stuffed. Long legs with just the right muscle tone, and ankles smaller than your wrists. I can almost touch her, Andy! Spindly fingers with manicured nails. Skin color like a peach and body hair just as soft. I'm touching her now, Padre! Subtle cheekbones. Ears pale from the shadow cast by her hair, with lobes graced by simple gold rings. Thick eyebrows that hint of joining one another and petite nostrils that flare when she's angry. Eyes … oh, how they could penetrate. And those lips! Full and moist and always colored. She's kissing me now, Padre! Ya hear? She could give one hellava lip-lock. And in more places than one, old buddy. Ah, what a woman!"

I almost yelled, "Enough! Enough!" Either he'd rehearsed that oration or he was enchanted.

"Wake up there, Andy. Now you remember her. Right?"

"Whoa! You took my breath away, Sailor."

"She had her faults, mind you, but nothing a photographer could capture. She could be single-minded … downright stubborn … and we quarreled like alley cats about the war. So when she dumped me, I joined the Corps—as much to spite her as to impress my Dad. Now he's pushing up daisies, she's married and living in suburbia, and I'm shit out of luck—stuck in this armpit and praying that some gook doesn't entomb me with a rocket. Sorry, Andy … at least this armpit is shaved and deodorized."

He chuckled, his chest rattling like a loose cage.

"Doesn't sound like you're being fair to the 'woman' in your life … or should I say the 'women' in your life."

"Look, you didn't have to live with 'em. With Julie it was endless crusading for this cause or that. She loved bashing the Establishment … and me. And my mother … God love her … just didn't know when to lift her thumb off of my backside. And my stepsisters … Christ! … they kept busy making me look bad in Dad's eyes. They sunk my battleship at every turn."

"That summer I was a Deacon I didn't see any dark intrigue." I was baiting him.

"You've gotta short memory! I ought to visit your confessional sometime. Your idea of being a sinner would render me a saint. Remember Janice, my freckle-faced little stepsister? Well, she had the old man convinced I was … queer. Next thing I know, he's reading me the riot act. Shit! Vipers are kinder to their prey than those two were to me."

"Now why would your Dad believe such a fairy tale? No pun intended." I knew the details, as Janice had written me with the story; she never had a kind word for anyone except her sister. Somehow, she'd gotten it into her head that Matt was a bad seed. I think she was jealous that he lived with his real father, while hers had abandoned them long ago. She wanted to control Matt and, failing at that, to discredit him. She quit writing me when I told her as much.

"I was just being me, Andy. That was enough to tick-off the old man."

I knew his conscience and the painkiller would work to my advantage. So I took a swipe at him. "Oh, so you *were* acting queer?" His head turned abruptly toward me, his eyes glassy.

"I make mistakes. Who doesn't? Sometimes … I get myself into stupid situations."

"What are you saying?"

"I did something dumb. OK?"

The pieces were fitting, but I wanted him to complete the puzzle. "Uh-huh, I'm listening. I can wear a dog collar or not." Seconds passed, and I felt dirty for being so manipulative. He sighed and turned his head in my direction.

"I was at my five-year high school reunion and drank too much." He paused, then continued. "I ended up in the backseat of a car with an old classmate … a guy. And Janice saw me. She blabbed big time to my Dad. Man, what a donnybrook." I paced slowly, but stayed within his field of vision. "Well, the guy had come out of the closet—I guess everybody at the dance knew it but me. I was coming off a nasty break-up with Julie and my head was … I mean … I couldn't find a decent job and all, and …"

"Yeah?"

"Shit … I let the dude blow me! OK? I don't know why. It just happened," he blurted in a single volley of breath. His face was flushed as he wondered if our friendship had suffered a mortal blow. He must've been thinking of me more as a comrade than a priest. Either way, I gave his disclosure an inner and outer shrug. We all had something to hide. Even I'd gotten too close to a fellow seminarian a few years earlier.

"I see." I tried not to sound judgmental.

"So, the old man gave me both barrels. I mean, I'd never seen him that torqued off."

"Knowing your Dad, I can just imagine."

"I got dragged to the verbal woodshed, big time. Even my stepmother didn't defend me. The chill in the house was so bone-numbing that I had to get out. Between wanting to snub Julie and prove my manliness to Dad, I enlisted in the Corps. So here I am, seven months and seven times seventy-thousand rounds later, in your makeshift confessional spilling my guts—literally and figuratively. And you wonder why I've got a hard-on for my stepsisters!"

Relief settled over his face, and his body relaxed; he'd been fighting the sedative. I watched as tranquility enveloped him, and he drifted to sleep. I briefed Suscheck on Matt's condition and suggested that he crash, too. Then I lit a cigarette and lounged outside. Large pockets of fog roamed past like herds of buffalo. I welcomed their stampede. Without them, Matt and I would've been reduced to frantic bits of conversation while we scurried from foxhole to foxhole in a dash for a medevac chopper. What wasn't welcome, though, was the odor of decaying flesh. The twenty-five Marines we'd abandoned four days earlier were rotting, and no amount of garbage at the dump could mask the scent.

Darkness was total. I leaned against the sandbags and lit another smoke. The rats sensed my presence and chittered wildly within the crevices separating the bags. I amused myself by recalling one corporal's tale of feeding them peanut butter laced with C4, a plastique explosive. The goofball thought the vermin would explode. Instead, the explosive made the rats so thirsty that they drank themselves to death and rotted amongst the sandbags. God, what a stench.

Butts had accumulated at my feet when I heard Matt moan. I lit up, entered, and shoved the weed between his dry lips. He relieved himself, again without a trace of blood. But several hours had passed since he'd been wounded, and the pain was setting in with a vengeance. I checked his stomach wrap, then sat beside him, hoping to continue our conversation.

Into the early morning we chewed the fat and I understood, even encouraged, the anger and bewilderment he felt. He arrived in Nam a gung-ho believer, certain Julie was mistaken and that his father would cheer him on. Like me, though, he'd had his share of battlefield school calls. Now he realized that none of us would return heroes—that many would return to the jeers and sneers of our countrymen. What did the glory matter now, he wondered. His dad was gone, and Julie had married another.

I'd been self-centered in thinking that our base camp was taking the brunt of the punishment. It was Matt's hardships, like Spanner's chronicle of toe-to-toe combat, that I'd do well not to forget. I sat hoping that Matt's hilltop ordeal wouldn't shadow him, swallow him, when he returned home. Today his wounds needed a medical nurse, but tomorrow's might need a nurse skilled in emotional healing. All the more reason, I concluded, that Julie should pick up where this stinking war left off.

Matt and I had seen combat up close and personal. We'd come to understand that the unseen traumas—those not requiring a battle dressing—were the real wounds of this conflict. Julie's concern for my mental state was justified. She had seen men return to a heroless welcome, to the catcalls of "Murderer" and "Baby-killer." At least I had my noncombatant's status to help me reconcile the madness. Matt's ghosts, though, might not be as timid. I feared that wherever he went or whatever he did, he'd be plagued by Nam. Yet, I felt sure that Julie could change all that. Her kiss, I believed, would transform him into her sweet prince.

Julie's letter spoke fondly of her association with Matt, when the ugliness of life was their collective naïveté. Someone other than a protective stepmother or a mean-spirited stepsister should greet him on his return, and Julie was that someone! All that was needed was some tinkering under the hood, and I felt certain that God had anointed me the mechanic that would troubleshoot their romantic engines. Like Christ, Matt had suffered forty days under siege in a wasteland. He'd been tempted by the devil, experiencing firsthand his handiwork, and had fasted from life's pleasures. He'd survived these trials, and now Julie was the angel appointed to minister to his needs. It was time for him to return to her; time for him to forget Eddie and recapture a woman's love.

Matt slept comfortably through the remaining night; Suscheck saw to that. I woke often to check his condition, eventually taking advantage of my restlessness to roam among the bunkers. Since the red alert had just been lifted, those who normally slept at night were awake. I returned before dawn and just as Matt was waking. The ache in his side had become acute, and his groan, like a lion's, practically ruffled the door flap of my lair. I comforted him with water, the coffee tin, and a moist towel on his forehead. He had a low-grade fever, though his eyes and speech were clear, and we shared a smoke as though it was Colombian Red.

"You'll be out of here today. We'll put you on an express for Phu Bai, then you'll be homeward bound. You're history, man!"

"Bullshit. I'll be back in two months." His voice broke, obstructed by phlegm.

"Listen up. You're going home, Laddie. Stateside home! Back to the land of the burger and shake. The Doc says you'll need some reconstructive surgery, so I suggested they take the skin graft from your flapping tongue or, better yet, from that expanding forehead of yours."

"Even better, from my cock, old boy. That's where the excess is."

"Dream on! You're a needle dick from pumpkin crick."

"Shit! Were you peeking while I was asleep?"

"Well, I had to find something to get Julie interested in you. Between your looks and that nasty disposition, how will you ever get that woman's attention?"

"Don't blow your pencil lead on that cause, Andy. Besides, she already knows I pack a Genoa salami for a middle leg. They don't call me the human tripod for nothing!"

"Hallucinating, huh? Look, why don't you stick that big dick out and pen Julie a note?" My eyes searched his for a twinge of interest.

"Nice roofing job, Andy," he uttered as he stared skyward. "Maybe you could help me build my little sugar shack someday."

"Yeah, but who's gonna share it with you?"

"You don't have a woman and you manage OK. You can stay in your plush rectory, and I'll bury myself in a backwoods cabin with my dog and a shed full of Stroh's beer."

"Why not add Julie to that equation? You and she and a hound would make a fine threesome. Even a priest has a housekeeper."

"Julie's not the housecleaning kind, old buddy ... though I wouldn't mind hearing from her. Ah, what the fuck am I saying? The woman's married with a kid. She already has her threesome."

From his side of the fence, she appeared contented and happily skipping barefoot through a meadow of clover. He didn't see the quicksand she was mired in.

"Then write her in care of her parents. Let them decide whether to forward it or not." The hour for his medevac was approaching, and my plan seemed stalled.

"Nah."

"I'll make it easy for ya. I'll pen a letter and you sign it. You'll be stateside soon. What better time than now to plant the seed?"

"Gee, I don't know, Andy. This is all happening too fast. How do I even know she cares? It would be better if I just …"

"I've got a pen and paper. I'll be your secretary, your mouthpiece. It'll just take a minute." Two corpsmen entered with a stretcher. In seconds they checked his dressing and gave him another shot. The chief corpsman said that the evac chopper would arrive in ten minutes and that he'd given Matt a full dose of morphine for the buggy ride to follow. I told him I had to have five more minutes—that it was a matter of spiritual importance that demanded my attention.

I buried my face squarely in Matt's. "Let's go, Marine! Julie is waiting. Today is the first day of the rest of your life."

"What? Whaddaya peddling? What's this gonna cost me?"

He was justified in chiding my motives, as long ago his Dad and I had formed an unholy alliance to steer him into college and away from a technical school. My thoughts today, however, clung to Julie's written words and to the love I felt sure she wanted to rekindle.

"Won't even cost you a stamp, Matt. Uncle Sam will pick up the postage. You're in a combat zone, remember? Come on now! Those corpsmen are itching to set you free—this letter will set both you and Julie free." *Set me free,* I thought.

"I'm fuzzy … real fuzzy. I can't think of any words. You write something, Andy. You're better with words. I'll sign it. Just keep it simple."

I had a premonition, a priestly intuition, it would go down like this, so I had penned a letter during the night. I attached the last sheet to a clipboard, then held it to the light and read aloud the closing paragraph. It was straight from our hearts.

… As I lie here wounded, to the sounds of shell bursts and men's hurried bootsteps, my thoughts are of you. I'm tired of this war! I don't want to cause you trouble, but I think of you and your baby often. I regret not being the man in your life, of not being the father to that child. I guess I have many regrets. Write

me if you can, but I'll understand if you don't. The weeks ahead will be difficult, but if I knew your thoughts were with me, it would help my recovery. I miss you and only wish that things had been different.

    Love, Matthew

"Here, sign this. Then we can get it and you on your separate ways." I held the clipboard in front of his face and put the pen in his hand. The morphine was taking hold.

"What's this 'love' shit? The woman will think I'm … I'm some starstruck sailor."

He slurred his words, and I tensed up at seeing the corpsman's hand part the canvas flap. Matt had to sign it. A forgery wouldn't do.

"You sure about this? I mean … what … what if her old man reads it, then …?"

"Trust me, Matt. Just sign. There's no fine print. Give yourself and Julie a break—put this damn war behind you. Let her know she's the rock you want to build your future on. Please, do it for both of us." I whispered the last line. He held his breath and signed, the burn scar on his hand wrinkling as he clinched the pen. I scrawled a postscript to say that the letter was in my hand because of his wounds, then I quickly sealed the envelope, addressing it directly to her.

We hoisted Matt onto the stretcher, then fast-stepped it toward the airstrip. A few incoming peppered the eastern sector, but nothing heavy fell. We huddled in a trench with eight other Marines, who were yuckin' it up about the wine, women, and song they had planned for their R&R. They'd beat the odds, but they knew they had one last spin of the revolver's cylinder before they could claim victory. The high stakes of Giap's game were etched on their brows and on the dry lips they tried to wet.

I stuffed Matt's letter into a mailbag. A descending C-123 Provider, its engines howling with power adjustments, poked a wingtip through the cloud cover. The VC small-arms fire was intense and the plane's descent steep. Streams of automatic fire crossed one another, twisting and knotting themselves, but the craft escaped the gauntlet, touched down, and raced to a hold area where it shit pallets out its ass end—then it positioned itself for takeoff. The eight men, each gripping a mailbag, made a fifty-yard dash that felt like five hundred. They leaped headlong into the plane as though being swallowed by a whale, a whale anxious to dive back into the safety of the clouds. The Provider's jet-boosted engines came alive with a funnel of flame and I knelt breathless as the VC's gunfire erupted—their tracers gracefully spraying the underbelly of the clouds.

An H-34 Sea Horse chopper jabbed its nose through the gray mist, drowning out the fleeing Provider. The Helo Support Team gave us the standby signal and I looked at Matt's pale face; he'd opened his eyes to slits, as though his radar had been activated by the blade-slapping rhythm that his HST blood danced to.

A machine gun burped, and white puffs followed the helo's movements as the mortars registered him in. The H-34, like a gooney bird, made a bouncing touchdown, and our dash began. We panted, puffed, and grunted. I held onto Matt's stretcher like it was a wheelbarrow full of sanctified hosts. We arrived at the craft's dark throat, its cargo master pointing anxiously toward the mortars as they moved up the tarmac. The walking wounded lunged into the helo's bay, leaving only their white field dressings visible.

I ripped off my flak jacket and yelled for Suscheck to do the same. I positioned both jackets on the helo's deck, then we hoisted Matt's stretcher atop them. We butted another stretcher up to his, then the cargo master shouted into his mike and the craft lurched. I could just make out Matt's faint smile as I stumbled out the hatch and onto the ground.

With its mouth clamped shut the engines roared to life. The debris whipped up by the downdraft pummeled our bodies, and Suscheck and I skedaddled for the trenchline. I popped up like a prairie dog and scanned the skyline—proud at having launched my lonesome dove. For forty days I'd weathered this storm, this siege, and now I prayed that Matt would return to Julie, not me.

"They made it! They both made it!" I shouted. My deliverance from Julie lay wounded on one craft, his letter of reconciliation bundled snuggly in the other.

I motioned for Suscheck to stay put, then I hurried to C-Med to retrieve two flak jackets. He readily accepted my apology for commandeering his body armor, as he understood my love for Matt. We strolled toward the hospital tent where he fingered the pocket of his jacket, chuckled, and said, "You owe me a pack of smokes, Reverend. And a matching pen and pencil set."

"It's a deal. Come on over to my hooch. Who knows," I said with a broad grin, "maybe I can find us a couple of brews to christen our new vestments."

He rushed to check triage, promising to catch up with me. I paused to light a smoke, walked a few paces, then instinctively buckled my knees when I heard the incoming mortar. The arc of its flight told my ear it had C-Med squarely in its path. I hollered wildly, but Suscheck exited the tent into the blast. I ran to his side, where he lay in a twisted heap. I whirled about in anger—his leg was missing, half his face gone—then I knelt and wept. I removed the Camels from my hip pocket and a small bronze crucifix from the other, tucking the pack into his vest pocket and resting the crucifix on his blackened forehead. Others arrived, and they, too, knelt. Soon, they silently collected his remains.

I walked heartsick toward my hooch and there, resting serenely against the sandbags, was an upright boot. Suscheck's foot was cinched within its leather walls. I loosened the laces and tugged on the sock. His foot glided out with a sucking sound, then dangled heavily inside its cotton sack. His big toe, dirt under its nail, protruded from a hole in the sock. I ran with it to C-Med, holding it out like a lantern to illuminate my way. Trembling, I handed it a sobbing corpsman. Then I threw up.

Now I had two boots. Two left boots. One toe shiny, the other dull. I packaged the shiny-toed one with a note to Rita and mailed it that day. My vigil for Matt had ended. His fate had been in God's hands, and, when the Almighty delivered him into my care, I charted the one course I hoped his soul cried out for. I felt sure that Matt and Julie would thank me one day. She was the best port for him in this storm. She would calm the turbulent waters he sailed, as he would hers. In time they'd form a catamaran of love that could pilot any squall.

I slept soundly that afternoon, a weight having been lifted from my chest. I could once more tend to the ninety-nine. A mortar barrage awoke me to that task—the familiar shout of "Corpsman, up!" lifting me from my stupor. The plea seemed louder, as no other calling competed for my thoughts. I grabbed my cross and ammo box and made for Charlie-Med. My little war, my temporary hell, had resumed its pace.

Once more I was adrift in the breakwaters of warfare, only this time my precious cargo had been safely stowed on land. All that remained was for me to save myself. Like Matt, it was time that I revisited an old flame—the Church. I had drifted from her embrace, at times been impotent in her presence, but all that could change. I, too, was a Prodigal Son for having sinned against my spiritual father and against my calling.

I decided to write my Bishop, telling him of my love for the Church. I knew I could one day find a parish near Matt and Julie and watch as their bond grew. My destiny was to keep my lost sheep from straying again. That was a good shepherd's role. My role. I'd keep Suscheck's boot as a bridge with my past. Its leather was dull and lacerated, like my spirits before finding Matt, but it—like me—could be restored. Its renaissance would mirror mine. I fell to my knees, thanking the Lord for having sent me to this war.

PART TWO

Chapter 7

Staring at the ceiling, twisting the coarse bedspread in my palms, I tried to accept that my forty-year existence had come to this miserable end. I accepted my mortality—I'd planned my burial and paid my life insurance—yet I'd failed to protect my son from an early grave. I was haunted by the knowledge that I'd wasted my life and had to stand by helpless as my son's life came to a premature end. Surviving a son is a father's worst nightmare.

I kept asking myself what I could've done differently. Nobody has a say in entering this world, but we cling, often naively, to the belief that family will comfort us on the way out. A father shouldn't have to think that his family wouldn't mourn his death. The irony was that I'd planted my family's seed with love, nurturing it for years, only to trample it with my reckless behavior. For months, more correctly years, my mistakes had broiled me under a hot sun of guilt. Now, as I woke from a drunken stupor, I had to wrestle once more with these ugly recriminations.

Lusts had brought my world crashing down, and, as I lay naked in bed, I felt helpless to overcome them. I didn't have time, though, to be disgusted with myself. I had to focus on business affairs, and not my crumbling home-life. Still, the atmosphere surrounding me was painfully familiar. This wasn't my hotel room, nor was the person sleeping beside me my wife. It felt like I was back in Nam, deep in the jungle, listening for a twig to snap or a leaf to crumple—waiting breathlessly to be ambushed by the VC.

A pulse of amber light streamed through the window—my only porthole to the outside world—flashing eerie shadows on the wall. This clash between light and darkness muddled my head further. I sat up and examined the walls and ceiling—dingy and paint-chipped, the overhead light missing its bulb. This room was like a bamboo cage, with me the prisoner and my partner the guard. As my anxiety grew, I could smell my armpits. I wanted to run, but I couldn't risk waking my companion.

I edged toward the corner of the mattress, watching the body beside me that was tangled in the sheets. My head suddenly began spinning like I was trapped in a whirlpool. I sat in a trance until the swirling images passed. Without my glasses, though, everything was a blur. My head thumped as though I'd been in a brawl, pulsing in rhythm with that amber light. It would've been convenient to blame my aches on a thug, but it was boozing and my craving for flesh that had brought it on. I'd bargained for a conquest when I left home, but I'd forgotten just how nagging my conscience could be when the alcohol wore off.

Once on my feet, I hobbled across the mangy carpet toward the light. I waddled, my ass end sore. Neighbors and coworkers had taken notice of my recent weight loss, but their comments only fueled my thoughts of Robert, my son. Though I was under Doc Golden's orders to shed the pounds or risk a coronary—my father's premature death made that risk real—the hidden reason for my weight loss was my depression over Robert.

Tiptoeing, arms outstretched, I stumbled about to find my eyeglasses. I hastily put them on, hoping my clumsiness hadn't awakened my partner. Seeing no movement, I began collecting my clothes. Partially dressed, I stood beside the window. The shade, yellowed and cracked along the edges and stripped of its drawstring, rustled lightly against my thigh as the stale city air parted the curtain. The scent of garbage was offensive, but nothing like the odors in Nam, nothing like the stench of a corpse. The street noises—sirens wailing, horns honking, cats fighting—were like an urban war zone.

Some eighteen years had passed since Nam, yet it was hard for me to forget it. I'd conditioned myself, however, to blot out certain memories. I probably looked like a daydreamer to some, to others a blank-eyed mountain man, but it was my survival technique to overcome the horrors of the war. This morning, however, I couldn't blot out the argument I had had with Faith, my stepdaughter. It wasn't so much our words, but her pleas on Robert's behalf. Her whining reminded me of how her affections had smothered him—keeping me isolated from his love. She had undermined my relationship with him just as my stepsister, Janice, had done to the bond I wanted with my father. *Bitches!* I thought.

Suddenly a squad car sped by, its engine racing and exhaust

howling—red and blue lights flashing—and my desire to escape the room was reignited. First, I needed to see the source of that amber light. I parted the curtain and peered through the nicotine-stained glass. There, perched atop a tavern sign, swaying gently in the breeze, sputtered a neon bulb spelling the word "Vacancy." Shit! Another flophouse—the second one this month.

Sunrise was approaching, and so was my business meeting. I'd been sent to recover a lost account from the Powertrain Corporation, and the prospect of entering that corporate lion's den was making me nervous. I felt my job was hanging in the balance. I needed more time to prepare for this boardroom skirmish, more time to lay wire and set mines. Most of all, I needed a clear head.

It was crazy to tackle this "Mission Impossible" alone. I wasn't in the fast lane, nor was my boss grooming me for the management team. To flap and flail, then fail, was all that SOB wanted to see me do. White-shirted wannabe executives—like gravestones at a national cemetery—dotted my workplace. They'd lounge about in smoke-filled conference rooms, listening to others yap about charts and graphs, while I was shackled to "the trenches." My mission to resurrect this business account was a fantasy. I was nothing more than meat on a hook, waiting for the executive hounds to rip at my flesh.

After collecting my things, I inspected my wallet. Money wasn't so much my concern, but my credit cards and driver's license held my identity. Matt was as far as I wanted to go in revealing myself. One-nighters were no places for formal introductions. "Slam, bam, thank you ma'am," was the conventional wisdom and today—Wednesday May 7, 1986—was no different from any other. I still had a family, a mortgage, and bills out the ying-yang. The last thing I needed or wanted was a lover cruising the streets with my name and address. Thankfully, my inventory found everything intact. *My anonymity was secure,* I thought. Why I cared, when my marriage was on the rocks, made little sense. I hadn't had sex with Julie in ages. To make matters worse, I doubted she'd been faithful to me. I shook my head—this train of thought was getting me nowhere.

I eased into an armchair, hoping to settle my stomach, but a hot flash ripped through me—sending a tingling sensation through my scalp. I felt and smelled like shit. I needed a toilet but only a corner sink, its basin stained and faucet dripping, was available. I straddled it and drained my bladder down its metal throat. I needed a drink, but there was no cup. I considered slurping water from my palm, like my dog from his dish, but making good my escape was priority one.

As I dressed, I shoved my arm through my shirt sleeve, popping a cufflink and toppling the shade off a floor lamp. I froze, my heart thumping, but only a fly buzzing overhead could be heard. *To hell with the cufflink,* I thought. After all, it was a gift from Julie. Dressed, but missing my underwear, I walked to the bedside. The mattress, its corner stained, was lumpy, and had left my back and neck stiff. Soon a wave of amber light illuminated the room and my partner stirred.

"You're an idiot," I hissed. After all the promises I'd made to Eddie's memory. There, sprawled before me, was a man, whose shoulder had wisps of hair and a heart-shaped tattoo. Swearing on a Bible and on Eddie's headstone had done nothing to curb my appetite. A panic began to creep in, as though an ugly intruder had jammed his foot inside my door.

When the adrenaline subsided I ached to take a shit, but the bathroom was down the hall. Lifting my smokes from the nightstand, I examined my partner's muscular frame. His body was alluring. For years I told myself that my estrangement from Julie had driven me to a road job, but taking men as lovers was the real reason for my frequent business travels.

"No," I murmured. I couldn't—I wouldn't!—unleash my passions while sober. As a teenager I'd tested my sexuality without the aid of booze, but that was youthful curiosity talking. In Nam, where there'd been no alcohol, I found Eddie, but he was someone special. It took a VC mortar to end that relationship. No, whiskey courage had become my signature. I'd rather live a lie than reveal myself—to come out of the closet would be the deathblow to my fragile existence.

I opened the door, the hinge squealing, and a wedge of light flooded the room, casting my long shadow across the floor while a mirror on the far wall framed my reflection. I paused to view my portrait ... I felt like Dorian Gray. I tried to recall my lover's name, telling myself if he woke I'd wave good-bye, disarming him with a nonchalant farewell. *Let him think I'd planned it all—that he was the victim, not me.* Just once, I wanted to feel good the morning after. But he kept on snoring.

I hoped his asshole burned like mine, then he'd remember who his lover was.

I walked down the dimly lit corridor, its carpet matted and burnt by cigarette ashes. Turning the corner I encountered a stranger and instantly I knew what his glance meant. I wanted to scream "No!" but my smoldering lust wouldn't let go. His quiet disposition was probably in sharp contrast to a few hours ago, when alcohol had unmasked his inhibitions. I could smell the beer oozing from his pores and feel the blood surging through my groin. His need, like the one building in me, was consuming. As we passed our shoulders brushed, and he halted.

"Where's the bathroom, friend? I've suddenly got some business to do."

We looked at one another, our thoughts an unholy communion. Like two race car drivers with headlights glaring, we sped hypnotized toward one another.

"It's that way and to the right," I answered.

He pulled out a cigarette and fumbled for a light. Not once did his eyes leave mine. Then the sizzle of the match-head broke my trance. Through the film of smoke that obscured his face, he said, "Be kind, won't you … and show me the way?"

What a play on words. He knew exactly what and who was going down. More to the point, he knew I knew it. *If you want me, skip the gamesmanship and get to the point.* My breathing had become as shallow as my thoughts, but I still couldn't take the lead.

"I'll make the trip worth your while, friend."

That was it! He'd pushed the right button. Had I gone berserk? Here I was, another nameless face at my side, hustling to a john for a blowjob. Passing by my room, I heard a muffled cough. Christ, he was up! Swiftly my companion moved ahead and opened the commode door, hooking his fingers in my coat pocket to keep me in tow, and then he peered left and right, like a point man on patrol. As he motioned for me to enter, I heard the door hinge to my room squeal. I jerked free and rushed down the hallway, capturing a glimpse of my lover's face as he poked his head out the door. His sharp nose, bushy eyebrows, and square, whiskery jaw were branded in my memory, while my backside was branded in his. I rounded the corner just as my bathroom lover grumbled, "What the hell's your …?"

I slowed on the dimly lit stairway, where a cocktail of odors assaulted my nose. I dodged a wet spot, then paused on the landing to catch my breath. I coughed and hurled a hocker on the floor, straightened my sports jacket, then assumed an unruffled air as I entered the lobby. I looked in vain for a water fountain, then scrambled out the doorway.

The predawn air was thick, the cloud cover signaling rain. The skies were like those around Hill 881S, and I found myself wishing once more for a full canteen of water. I wandered the sidewalk in search of a landmark, but no street signs were recognizable—they'd been ripped down or spray-painted. I lit a Camel and the flame, like a muzzle flash, momentarily blinded me. Traffic was increasing, its headlights winding up the roadway like a string of sparkling diamonds.

I turned toward a glass storefront to knot my tie when a screech of tires arose. I flinched, but no impact followed—no hollow thud, no explosion of glass, no hissing steam. Only a horn blast and the jeer, "You asshole! Get the fuck off the road!" Engines revved, tires squealed, and the shouts faded as the traffic resumed its pace. I knotted my tie and took stock of the pawnshop's window display. Whether a craving for flesh, drugs, booze, or gambling, these keepsakes had been surrendered because others were weak, too. Their company, however, was small consolation.

A yellow cab's reflection appeared in the plate glass and I spun about, waving. The driver halted and lowered his window. I told him the Ramada Inn on Nott Street and, with a glance at his wristwatch and a flip of his cigar ashes, he replied, "Schenectady?" I nodded and he grinned.

His ruddy complexion, Mets ball cap, and ulcerated nose suited his bulging eyes and pudgy jowls. He could've been J. Edgar Hoover's twin brother. I took a drag on my Camel, cast the butt down a sewer grate, then slid into the rear seat. I asked him the time and he answered, "Six-twenty, pal." Then he threw the meter handle down and gunned it.

He stared at me in the rearview mirror, then wheezed, hacked, and mumbled some comment about my being his last fare. I was about to say something when the cabbie made an abrupt U-turn. As he accelerated, we passed beneath that pulsing amber sign. Beyond the curtain and the raised shade was my lover's silhouette. *Who was he?* I wondered. *And did he feel as dirty as I did?*

I sat motionless. The ride was long and the scenery unfamiliar. I soon became alarmed, my breadbasket swirling with butterflies, at the realization that I'd spent the night in Albany. I remembered sitting at a barstool in my Schenectady hotel pouring down the drinks. *Man, those Manhattans registered a direct hit! No "Maggie's Drawers" last night,* I thought. My reason for parking my ass in the crosshairs of the hard stuff didn't take a detective to solve. With my home-life, I felt entitled to pickle myself.

"Your granddaughter?" I asked, glancing at the photo clipped to his sun visor.

"My daughter, pal."

"How old is she?" I asked, thinking he looked too old to be her dad.

"Dorothy will be seven in August."

"Kindergarten … no, first grade, right?" My voice shot up to counter his frown.

"Yep, and at the head of her class. That gal is goin' places."

"Good for her. How are the schools around here?"

He smiled, his stubby fingers scratching his pockmarked neck. "Nothing like the old days, pal. That's for sure! Hell, back then you didn't have dope, punk rock, or silly-ass rules about spanking pupils. Nowadays these kids dress like gypsies, can't spell their own damn names, smoke pot in study hall, and every other broad is knocked-up. Know what I mean? The whole thing's gone to shit in a handbag."

I nodded.

"And another thing, pal. This squirrelly school board is a bunch of wild-eyed faggots. All they do is vote for teacher raises and jack up our taxes. Don't these idiots know that us working stiffs ain't got that kind of dough? With the GE laying off, the tax base around here is shit. Ain't nobody gonna make a living flipping burgers."

He held up the morning paper, its headline announcing a layoff at the General Electric plant.

"And another thing. Why don't they get rid of those touchy-feely, grab-ass courses, cut them bozos on the administrative staff, and get back to the three R's? Know what I mean?"

Now you're talking! I'd seen my own kids steamrollered by the system. Julie wanted them to attend Catholic school, but I'd argued against paying the tuition. At times, I felt uneasy with that decision—particularly when Andy challenged us to give the kids religious training—but cuddling up to the Church made me squeamish. Institutional religion and a steady diet of Andy wooing me to Mass weren't my idea of salvation.

"Say," I interjected, "where do you send your little girl?"

"Saint Luke's. Catholic school, you know. Nuns, religion, and they don't spare the rod. The kids even wear uniforms. That's the way school oughta be. Know what I mean?"

"Good choice," I murmured, my tone reflective. How was it this bonehead had the brains to do what I didn't? Graduating from college hadn't done shit for my intellect. I should've gone to trade school, instead of allowing myself to be bullied into college by Andy and my dad.

When the cabbie relaxed and began humming, I closed my eyes and let my thoughts drift back to when I was a zit-faced teen. It was 1963, and I'd just graduated from Lincoln High—an average student with average dreams who hadn't a clue what to do with his average life. Then I met Andrew Patterson, a seminarian assigned to our neighborhood parish. His counter-culture ways were refreshing. Given his hard-on for authority, though, it didn't compute that he'd accept the rigid lifestyle of the priesthood, let alone the prohibition of taking a bride. For a time I thought he was gay, but that wasn't my attraction to him. Somehow, I felt that if I understood his personality, then I could better understand my own.

I always felt that once he strapped on that dog collar he'd be hard pressed to conform. Time proved me right, because his radical thinking quickly got him into hot water. He was the spiritual equivalent of the squeaky wheel, and his no-nonsense Bishop greased him plenty. Why he didn't resign is a mystery to me. He seemed better suited to be a car salesman or game show host, yet he had substance—anyone who'd survived Nam was no Milquetoast. Like it or not, our tour at Khe Sanh had forged a lifetime bond.

It was convenient to blame Andy for my entering college, but neither he nor my old man had put a gun to my head. I just didn't have the guts—the conviction—to hose down the flame they lit under my ass. They argued that I should forego technical school for the prestige of a four-year degree. Andy, in typical fashion, spouted Scripture to make me feel inadequate. He used chapter and verse from the New Testament—from "Brother Luke," as he liked to say—and hurled it at me during a Sunday sermon. I didn't see it then, but his pontificating about the "Prodigal Son" was a left-handed salute to me.

Suddenly the cabbie hit the brake, and the seatbelt forced the air from my lungs. He righted himself and barked, "Jesus Christ! You dumb ass. Get the hell off the road!" All I saw was the taillights of a yellow sports car. We accelerated ahead, and I left behind, too, my youthful recollections. My head had cleared some, and I was thankful for having spent the night elsewhere. *What if I'd met a business associate while in my stupor? Then what?* The risks I took were crazy, but I needed a man's love as much as I wanted my son's love. Both were a part of me, one a weakness, the other a strength.

The cab pitched and I swayed side to side. The narrow roadway, cratered like the Khe Sanh terrain, was an obstacle course of potholes from the preceding winter. The cabbie gave me a final jolt as he bounced over the speed bumps, then came to a halt. Tipping his ball cap, he collected his fare. He smiled like a contented bulldog, gave me a two-finger salute, then sped off—his day ending, mine beginning. I paused to draw in the morning air, inhaling and exhaling with a seafarer's rhythm, then tallied the wad I'd spent. *This trip would require some creative expense accounting if corporate America was to underwrite my gay life.* My adopted hometown of Titusville, however, was simply too small a community for me to risk taking a lover.

I sought the best of both worlds—the sense of belonging that typified small-town America, along with the reckless lifestyle that a big city offered. I liked to think of myself as a high-wire walker whose fall could be broken by a soft landing in the Titusville valley. But instead of being a showstopper under the big top, I'd become an organ grinder with a monkey on my back.

When I entered the hotel lobby, the chlorine vapor from the swimming pool momentarily reminded me of the CS gas that clung to the Khe Sanh plateau. The pool was still and inviting, but my meeting was less than ninety minutes away. The desk clerk politely ignored my unkempt appearance and informed me that I had no messages. I wanted to hear from Julie with an update on Robert, but that would've meant getting the third degree for not being at the hotel last night. I entered the elevator, the doors opening and shutting like a camera shutter, then exited to a welcome soda machine. I fed change down the slot, gulped a Coke, then lost a mouthful through my nose as the carbonation struck my palate. I used my tie to dry my face and proceeded down the hallway.

I greeted a passerby, his demeanor and dress decidedly different from my earlier suitor, but I wasn't one to be fooled by appearances. I'd been lured to parties where gays masqueraded as everything from Wall Street brokers to longshoremen. For a wallflower gay, the test was to read the eyes and gestures of would-be lovers without displaying the swagger the activists enjoyed. Always guessing, always on guard, always shackled to a code of concealment … that was the lot of a closet homosexual. That was my lot.

Once in my room I collapsed on the bed, but soon the wake-up buzzer sounded and I leaped to deactivate it. *Why not an angelic voice instead of the klaxon's wail as a reveille call?* I loitered under the shower, soaping down twice—wishing this ritual scrubbing could cleanse me of my sin. I stood and examined myself. Lovemaking could be a rough and tumble affair, but this go-around I'd avoided any tears or snares. I spit out mouthful after mouthful of hot water and then shaved using the bar soap as my lather.

Sags, bags, and a double chin stared back at me as I stood naked before the floor-length mirror. Rubbery folds of skin from the shrapnel wound in my left side dated me to the Vietnam War. My recent weight loss was welcome, but it had an uneven appearance. I was slimmer in the cheeks, legs, and around the chest, but my belly seemed distended, like that of a poster child for a starving nation. My mustache was salt and pepper, the hair around my temples so thick the barber layered it, while my forehead—except for a single patch of hair—had reached the crown of my head. My mama, God rest her soul, would say that I should accept my baldness as a badge of manhood. She didn't know that I'd been testing that manhood since puberty, and that I'd come to prefer the love of another man.

I combed my hair, splashed on after-shave, dried my ears, took a booming shit, then donned my business suit for the coming skirmish.

I mussed the bed sheets so they'd look used, put a tip on the nightstand, fetched my weathered briefcase, then exited as quietly as I'd entered. I marched down the hall, determined to outdistance the anxieties that nipped at my heels.

For the moment, there were no wet spots to dodge, doorways to avoid, or foul odors to attack my nostrils. Absent, too, was that pulsing amber light to remind me of my dual personality. As my pace quickened, all I could see was the vision of my son, Robert, wasting away, bedridden with AIDS.

Chapter 8

I entered the hotel restaurant and sat at a corner table, determined to have a breakfast dripping with cholesterol. Julie rejected such tastes and was a nag about my eating habits. At a hundred and twenty pounds, she ate like a sparrow and scorned my meat-and-potatoes mentality. With her, each bite had to be chewed a precise number of times. *Nonsense.* Food wasn't for fondling. In Nam we learned to gobble our C-rats before a mortar round took it away. *Doctor's orders and heart attacks be damned!* I knew that coronary disease, the "family curse" as my dad called it, would take me out. His father and brother had died of it, along with my old man at age forty-nine. My curse, though, defied a clinical cure. Instead of clogged arteries, my ailment nibbled away at my mind and spirit.

"May I take your order, Sir?" The waitress's question halted my moody recollections.

Without looking at the menu, I rattled off the images in my head and lit a Camel. I'd quit smoking once, just before marrying Julie in 1968. Our whirlwind courtship and her pleas had convinced me to abandon the weed. I tried to rid myself of the damn things in Nam, but everybody in that shithole, Andy included, smoked. He'd busted my balls about it in college—but between his Bishop and Khe Sanh—he'd gotten hooked, too. Since then, he's never uttered a word about the nasty habit. That might've been the only time I'd gotten the last laugh on him. *Some laugh,* I thought, as I hacked in my napkin.

When the food arrived I waded in, pausing to savor the coffee, but after a few mouthfuls my appetite waned, my stomach churning. I spent my remaining time scanning the men, calculating that one in ten was gay. I wondered which of them was wrestling with the after-morning-effects of having slept with another man. None of them looked my way, but then it was early to be planning the evening's conquests.

I tipped modestly and made for the lobby, where the chlorine gas from the pool still lingered. Though I enjoyed swimming, I avoided going shirtless because of my shrapnel scar—a trophy I wasn't anxious to display or explain. I rubbed my side, fingering the ripples of leathery skin, and thought of Eddie. His death gave me life, but I hadn't bargained for how Andy wanted me to live it—or, for that matter, how Julie and her daughter, Faith, would make me live it.

By design, my business trips were solo affairs. Only once did Julie accompany me, and we ended up arguing because of her protests that I favored Robert over Faith. She had a chip on her shoulder where Faith was concerned, which, undoubtedly, had a lot to do with the girl being conceived out of wedlock. That wouldn't arouse much attention today, but it was scandalous in 1967. Titusville was simply too small to keep such a gossip-mongering event under wraps. To her credit, though, she made it plain that she'd carry and keep the baby.

Julie, like Andy, was a scrapper, and both were cut from the same anti-Establishment cloth. That was a tolerable, almost admirable, condition. That is, until she hoisted religion as a banner. It was tough enough coping with my sexuality, but Julie's religious fanaticism served to further unravel our marriage, just as Robert's illness was undoing my sanity. What made it a feeding frenzy was that Julie's spiritualism and Robert's AIDS fueled one another, leading her to frame his disease in biblical terms. *Ah, this train of thought was getting me nowhere.*

While a group of Japanese businessmen paraded single file into a van, I made for my rental car. The skyline was a collection of low-flying gray clouds. *Let it rain,* I thought, as I turned the key and headed for the Powertrain plant. After Nam, I vowed never to complain about rain again. I followed my chicken-scratched directions to Powertrain's headquarters, barely arriving on time. From the outside, the plant was unimpressive—dull red brick with double-hung windows. The cash they could've spent on glitter, though, was funneled into paychecks and bonuses for their workforce. Their employees took a keen interest in their product and in the company's stock, and they didn't take kindly to our supplying them with shitty equipment.

Powertrain wasn't a huge account but my boss, Ron Evans, was sensitive to their harsh criticism, which prompted my visit. I was sent to pull our chestnuts out of the fire, and all because our Marketing Team had made promises that Engineering couldn't keep. *Christ*

Almighty! Maybe that vanload of slant eyes was headed here to sell the same equipment I was hoping to rescue. I signed in with the receptionist, then inspected the trim of my clothes in the doorway glass. What I couldn't see, though, was whether my eyes were bloodshot.

"Good morning, Matt," boomed Dave Webber's deep voice. I reeled about and extended my hand. "I'm Dave," he added with a toothy grin. "Good to meet you at last."

His steely gaze confirmed my belief that he was a force to be reckoned with. "Thanks and good morning," I replied with a wary smile.

"How was the trip?" By now he'd crossed his arms, standing tall like a cigar store Indian.

"Ah, the usual delays. Traffic is hell around here, but I got a decent night's sleep."

Thankfully, he didn't scrutinize my eyes. Dave was a strapping fellow, and we'd had our share of spirited exchanges. As my counterpart, he handled the technical end of the Powertrain purchases. I was taken aback, though, by the mismatch between his face and voice. I had figured him to be a big guy, but I didn't expect his boyish features, cow eyes, and "Dennis the Menace" cowlick. I quietly followed him, without the benefit of small talk or a stop at the coffee machine.

When I entered the conference room my anxiety mounted. Sitting upright, their hands folded, was a stern-faced duo. A brief round of introductions with handshakes and mechanical smiles ensued, then I unlatched my briefcase and settled into an overstuffed chair. The pair wore long-sleeved white shirts, with starched collars and cuffs, and dark-striped ties—the corporate look. Along with Dave was Ed Powers, Purchasing Manager, who had knobby knuckles, huge hands, and slicked-back hair. At his side, eyes darting, was Jake Williams, Sales Manager, who'd been shouldering the brunt of their customer's complaints about our equipment.

Our relief valves hadn't lived up to our marketing hype, and Powertrain was facing some costly field changes. These shock troops wasted little time in asking me what our Engineering and Quality Control departments were doing to correct the problem, which led me to think they were extending an olive branch. I was reciting our stock and trade QC homily when the oak door fanned open and a rather heavyset man ambled in. His nose and cheeks were beet red, his forehead shining, and he swung his arms like a lowland gorilla. The others tried to appear indifferent, but the inflection in their voices betrayed their interest. He listened intently, never speaking, while the others jockeyed to impress him. It was soon apparent that I was the ping-pong ball, they the paddles, and he the silent referee.

Powers abruptly said, "We purchased over a half-million dollars in equipment from Bentley Valves last year. If we're to continue doing business, we want you to pay for the field changes, including our Product Service costs."

My boss, Evans, had labeled this as a technical bout, giving me no license to make financial concessions. Now I knew why I disliked the bastard! He'd send someone on a mission with all the responsibility but no authority. *I'd have fragged the SOB in a heartbeat,* I thought, *if he had been my platoon commander in Nam.* I had to show some teeth … even if I was a paper tiger.

"I'll need the figures." My words were authoritative, even if my charter wasn't.

"We only have an approximation, you understand," said Williams.

"But I'd estimate the engineering backcharges alone will exceed thirty thousand," interjected Dave. The three nodded simultaneously.

I sank deeper in my chair. That sum exceeded my salary and old man Taylor, Bentley's President, would wring it out of my hide if I agreed to their terms.

"May I have until tomorrow to decide?" I stammered. All eyes shifted toward the referee in the corner, while I stared ahead to a nicely framed photo of a groundbreaking ceremony that hung on the wall. Someone looked familiar in the picture, but my concentration was broken when their eyes snapped back at me.

"Are you saying that Bentley Valve won't agree to this arrangement?" The challenge came from Powers, whose lips quivered with anticipation for the kill.

"No, no! I just need time to study your request."

William's face flushed and I squirmed.

"Let me see if I understand. Your company requests a meeting, then they send a rep who's reluctant to make an equitable settlement."

William's tone was measured, but anger flashed in his eyes. God, my hot flash just wouldn't stop!

I raised my hand and shook my head. "That's not what I said. I'm simply asking for time to think this through before ..."

"Don't you think you should've done that before you arrived?" snapped Williams. "What did you think we'd want? To give Bentley a slap on the wrist while they made more empty promises? No way, Mr. Garrison. We want compensation for your company's fuck-up! And we want your agreement to it today."

My temples throbbed and my glasses slid down my nose. I looked to Dave, but he lowered his eyes. I'd been set up, sandbagged by associates and outgunned by opponents. I arrived a paraplegic and was leaving a quadriplegic. This whole trip was a farce, nothing but a gesture to save an account already written off by Bentley's bean counters. *I oughta accept their demands and put Bentley's old man on the hotseat . . . but he'd just get the last laugh when I got my pink slip.* With a cotton mouth I responded, "May I call my office?"

Williams looked to the corner, then said, "Certainly. We're not trying to be unreasonable, Mr. Garrison."

"We won't reconvene, however." Those were the first words uttered from the referee in the corner. Like a field commander, he had remained above the skirmish, shaping the strategy and leaving the tactics to others. Now he was giving the marching orders. He added, "We'll wait here, Mr. Garrison, while Dave escorts you. Please return within fifteen minutes."

I nodded and rose. A gun was at my head, the round chambered, and the hammer cocked. When we left, I asked Dave who the watchdog in the corner was. He apologized for the lack of an introduction, explaining the old man wanted it that way. I felt faint at his words.

"For Christ's sake, Dave, you never hinted your president would be at the meeting!" Now I suddenly recognized the face in that wall photo.

"That's the way McFadden operates. Sorry, Matt, but there was no heads-up I could've given you." Dave looked genuinely flustered and I saw no point in protesting further.

We passed a restroom, and I motioned for Dave to wait. I hurried to the stall and let go. "Damn diarrhea," I muttered. I splashed water on my face, finger-combed my hair, then rushed to rejoin Dave. He directed me to a cubical, where I punched in Bentley's switchboard number.

"Is Ron Evans there? This is Matt calling from New York." My fingertips drummed the tabletop as I stared at my watch. Nearly ten minutes had passed.

"I'm sorry, Matt, but Mr. Evans is nowhere to be found."

"What do you mean, 'nowhere to be found'? Page him, Carol. This is important!"

"I did, but there's no reply. I can try Mr. Gramm?"

"OK, but please hurry."

"I'm paging him, Matt ... but he's not answering either." I swallowed repeatedly, but the lump in my throat wouldn't move.

"Look, Carol, try to raise Mathers, OK? I've got my tit in a wringer and ..." I abruptly halted. A short silence followed. "Excuse my language, Carol."

"I'm sorry, Matt, but Mr. Mathers is out of town. Is there anyone else who could help you?"

I lowered my head, raking my fingertips over my forehead. "No. I gotta go, Carol. If you see Evans in the next few minutes have him call me at Powertrain, OK?" Without waiting for her acknowledgment, I hung up.

Dave stuck his head in and tapped his wristwatch. I rose like I was carrying an eighty-pound field pack. When the conference room door came into view I thought once more of my lover of a few hours ago. I wanted to run, just as I had then, but there was no escape. My fifteen minutes were up. McFadden and his "yes-men" were seated as before, and I steadied myself for their volley. It came like clockwork—just like those chilly mornings on 881S when Charlie's mortars greeted our flag raising—only now I didn't have Eddie to shield me.

"Well, Mr. Garrison?" The old man's voice was steady. He knew that I now knew who he was.

"Well, Sir, I was unable to contact my management and since I wasn't given carte blanche to negotiate I'd like to have until tomorrow to respond."

"No," hurled McFadden.

"We've been generous to the extreme with Bentley," said Williams. "We're pulling the plug on this marriage and filing for divorce."

It was over; I felt mortally wounded. My parting request, more a plea, was that they not notify my management. I wanted to be the messenger, even if my shithead boss knew the likely outcome. I should've seen this set-up coming when Evans grinned and told me I was bound for Schenectady—all I saw, though, was a chance to escape Julie and cruise the bars.

I stood beside Dave, certain that this was our first and last meeting. "I wish things had gone differently," he said.

"Me, too. It's an ill wind that blows no good, right? Well, right now I'm twisting slowly in that wind ... the noose tightening with every turn."

"I'm sorry. I wanted to warn you of our hard-line stance, but I couldn't risk my job."

I bit my tongue. "I understand, Dave." Then I exited through the double glass doors, cursing under my breath. *Did it ever occur to him that I'd lose my job? Dog-eat-dog ... just like in Nam.* When the shit flew back then, I knew I couldn't rely on anyone but myself—anyone, that is, but Eddie. I had to go halfway around the world to find a true friend, only to see him get blown away and me get roped into marriage. "Damn you, Andy!" I said aloud.

Free of the building, I stopped to view the gray cloud cover. I felt I was standing on the ocean floor looking up at the underbelly of some huge freighter's hull. It was springtime, the snow had fallen on the daffodils, and a thunderstorm was brewing. The wind mussed my hair and tugged, like a purse-snatcher, at the folder sandwiched beneath my arm. A damp chill, one that slices through the skin and brings a tear to the eye, was in the air. Mother Nature was aroused from her winter nap, and, like a lustful woman, her breathing was husky and her scent strong.

I sat motionless, staring, clasping the car wheel and pondering my estrangement from Julie. No marital contentment, let alone bliss, existed to help me ward off my gay cravings. I'd lost my battle with the demon inside me and that, coupled with my scorn for Faith, had alienated me from Robert. I thought I'd married Julie for love, but it was really from loneliness. She was down, just as I was after Nam, and rebounding from a bad marriage. Her husband was an aging flower child; a long-haired gypsy incapable of a long-term commitment. I laughed at their decision to name the baby Faith, as though the child could restore what was missing from their lives.

I reclined the driver's seat and watched the raindrops strike the windshield. A gust of wind buffeted the car, whistling through the window seals. I was in no hurry, though, as my flight wasn't until the next morning. I had envisioned my meeting dragging on through the day, with me pulling off an eleventh-hour victory. Now, I'd probably end up being canned. For a guy my age, there were no jobs in a rustbelt town like Titusville, Pennsylvania. The cascading rain soon became a torrent. I sighed and closed my eyes, letting it lull me to sleep.

I awakened to the blast of a noon whistle. People, many holding umbrellas, were streaming from the Powertrain plant, some leaping puddles with Olympic strides. *Just like Nam,* I thought, only these folks were taking cover from Mother Nature and not Charlie's incoming. The windshield was fogged up, so I sat patiently with the defroster on. When the exodus subsided, I eased onto the roadway like a funeral director leading a caravan of mourners.

I captured a glimpse of the General Electric logo, its monogram towering above the skyline. I thought of Schenectady's sweeter times, its romantic postwar boom, a time when neighborhood grocery stores, shops, and taverns were crammed with the rank and file. Families, futures, and fortunes—some three generations strong—had been nurtured by that manufacturing plant. Sons and daughters—like their fathers, mothers, uncles and aunts before—had sunk their roots in this community. The soil that nourished them was made of brick, mortar, and smoke stacks—a monument to Yankee ingenuity. Now that earth had become barren. Swarms of people, whose worker-bee ethic had created the wealth, were being swept aside by cheap foreign labor and the fast-buck philosophy of CEOs who fancied themselves the queen bees. Now sons and daughters—unlike their fathers, mothers, uncles and aunts before—were left to litter the bars, unemployment lines, and crack houses. So little of it made sense to me.

Spotting a convenience store, I stopped and purchased two six-packs. I plopped behind the wheel and gulped down a can. It brought a glaze to my eyes, froth to my lips, and a tingle to my nose. I needed that drink! No sooner was it down than I raised another, then sheepishly lowered it when I saw that someone was watching me. I spent the afternoon in my hotel room, and both the beer and my bladder were flowing. After a particularly wobbly visit to the head, I stood before the mirror and stuck out my tongue—my throat was red and white scallops ringed my tongue where it made contact with my molars. I felt a second wind coming on, though, so I left to check the mail. The lobby was awash in red hues, as though I was looking through bloodshot eyes, and even the desk clerk was wearing red, her crimson hair and rosy complexion accented by a maroon sweater.

"May I help you, Sir?" I stood admiring her. She possessed an innocence I could never recapture. "Sir? Can I be of assistance?" The break in her voice awakened me.

"Yes. Are there any messages for Garrison in 321?" She turned, hair sweeping her shoulders, then stood on her tiptoes to retrieve something.

"Here you go, Mr. Garrison. Anything else?" I scanned the notes, then realized she was hanging on my next word.

"No ... no. Thanks." One note was from Julie and the other, just minutes old, was from Ron Evans. I couldn't handle my boss, but there was no ignoring Julie if I wanted an update on Robert. Just one more beer, I calculated, and I'll be ready for her grief.

Early bloomers in business suits were watering down in the lounge, which was lit like a cave. Without delay I ordered, chugging the schnapps and washing it down with a swallow of beer, then I noticed a bowl of peanuts atop the bar. As I reached out, a hairy hand, with a turquoise pinky ring, clasped mine. The palm was warm, its grip steady. My instinct was to pull away, but I turned to see the sharp nose and bushy eyebrows of my Albany lover. My adrenaline was pumping.

I gaped at his smile, recalling how my lips met his. I was surging with anticipation. Yet, I felt I'd drunk too much to handle a scene and too little to be uninhibited. My eyes searched his, then moved down his neckline to his open shirt and chest hair. I eased back onto my stool, embarrassed at having forgotten his name.

"I didn't think you'd be here so early," he said. I raised my beer for another mouthful. "You sure bolted early. Why the rush, Matt?"

His casual manner had me wondering just how much of my sorry guts I'd spilled. Damn booze! The stuff was great transporting me there, but once I arrived I was helpless to recall the events that followed.

"I had an early morning meeting." I spoke into my glass like it was a microphone.

"Must've been *real* early, Matt."

Dammit! I couldn't remember his name. "I'd have left earlier had I known I was in Albany." I turned back toward the long mirror that stretched the length of the bar. My reflection was captured between two bottles of scotch, as though my head was a gong and the bottles the mallets. A brief silence passed.

"Don't be sore, Matt. Let me buy you a drink."

I was certain our first encounter had started in the same innocent fashion. I downed my beer, wiped the foam from my mustached lip, and turned to my suitor. "Look, I have to go. I've got a family matter that can't keep."

He assumed a contrite, almost conciliatory, air and settled onto the adjacent stool. "Don't think I'm bullshitting here, but I rarely do this sort of thing. This is my first trip away from home in a long time … and I guess I let myself go."

"Yeah, I know exactly where you're coming from." My resistance was crumbling. "But, I really have to be on my way, uh …?"

"Mike is my name. Can't you stay awhile longer?"

His introduction was like a father greeting a confused son—*a Prodigal Son,* I thought. Just like Eddie's soothing voice when he talked me through a rocket barrage. Another time, another place, another set of rules, and I might've adopted Mike as I had Eddie. I suddenly felt that my early morning escape from him was unnecessary. Maybe it was his shoulder tattoo that scared me, but even I had a tattoo—a small Marine Corps seal inked on my forearm during a drunken R&R in Hong Kong. I understood the battle that Mike was waging.

"No, I gotta go, Mike. I've got a problem on the home front to attend to." I hoisted myself up like a tired warrior and slipped a tip in the barkeep's cup.

"Can I see you tonight?" His eyes were like a lost pup.

I gestured farewell and said, "My flight leaves in a few hours." I didn't look back, preferring to remember him as a whining pup rather than a snarling challenger to my willpower.

Back in my room, I felt chilled and my fingertips and toes were icy cold. I answered my persistent diarrhea, then sat and stroked my feet across the carpet. Finally, with a deep breath, I dialed home.

"Hello," Faith answered. Her voice was cheerful, almost upbeat, as though she were expecting a call from one of her boyfriends.

"I have a message here to call Mom. Put her on." A pause elapsed and I added, "Come on, Faith! I'm calling long distance."

"Wait," she said and laid down the receiver.

She was clearly still upset over the argument we'd had—she could only be forgiving where Robert was concerned. She had a guard dog mentality toward him, while he followed her around like she was his seeing-eye dog. I felt she was always hiding something from me, and I resented it. Particularly her ceaseless effort to build an impenetrable barrier, her Great Wall, between Robert and me—just as Janice had erected between my father and me some twenty years earlier.

"Matt! Why didn't you call sooner?"

"I didn't get your message until just now. How's Robert?"

"It'd be nice if you asked about me. When are you coming home?"

"Tomorrow. Now what's up that you had to send me a message?"

"Why tomorrow? Your business must be finished by now."

"We can discuss that later. How is Robert?"

"Faith told me how you two argued. You know she adores Robert, so why do you torment her?" I rolled my eyes and grit my teeth, gripping the receiver like it was a dumbbell.

"Our disagreement doesn't concern you. She's old enough to answer for herself."

"What do you mean it's not *my* concern? She's *my* daughter! You're forever mistreating her. The Lord will judge you harshly one day for the way you abuse her."

My mind raced, then settled. *Surely she didn't know or she'd have been on the next flight here.*

"Look, the sooner you see the flaws in your precious little diamond, the better off we'll all be."

"That's the devil talking. She's a good girl! She cares for her family, especially Robert, and wouldn't do anything to hurt us." Her voice broke, but the avalanche of hurts she'd inflicted on me smothered my sympathy. *Who was Julie trying to kid, anyway? Faith was always distant from me, both by blood and temperament. If she hadn't been so*

*busy with bleeding-heart causes, Bible thumping, and charming Andy,
she might've given Faith more attention. None of that, though, gave
Faith the right to take Robert from me. She was no better than Janice
and deserved ...* "Matt! Are you still there?"

"I don't want to discuss Faith. It's all goddamn lies. I wanna know
what's going on with my son."

"Your language is abominable! And he's *my* son, too! No wonder
you swear like you do. You never attend Mass or receive the
sacraments from Father Patterson or ..."

"Enough, woman. Enough! Tell me about Robert or I ... I swear to
Almighty God I'll make Faith's life a living hell. Oh, and I'll confess
to Andy all right. Wouldn't he love to hear about your drinking and ..."

She began to sob, then Faith interrupted. "I don't know why you two
are fighting again. And I don't really care, but ... but for Robert's sake,
you should come home. Doctor Golden admitted him to the hospital
this morning for observation. It's nothing life-threatening, but he's
weak and needs to see you." Faith's voice cracked.

I rested my chin on my chest, my eyes shut, and let go a deep sigh.

"Mom's upset, and so am I. We want you ... you to stop ignoring
Robert. He needs to see you. He needs to know you care." She was
sniffling throughout.

Did she really think I didn't care? That I didn't love him? I just
made the fatherly mistake of wanting him to be what I wasn't. Didn't
other dads do the same? Now he'd never be the things I wanted ... nor
the things he wanted. He'd leave this world with only a tombstone to
mark his passing. For months, it would seem, I'd been mourning my
losses more than his. As my head cleared, I realized that Faith, for
once, was championing Robert's needs and not her own.

"It's late, and the weather is too stormy to catch a flight. Tell your
mother I'll be home tomorrow afternoon. And, yes, I'll go to see
Robert. I promise."

"Good! I gotta go now."

I rolled back on the bed, tears welling. I slipped off my glasses and
bawled, my chest heaving as the tears streamed down my cheeks. I
wanted to call Andy, but I couldn't muster the courage. Instead, I
curled beneath the bedspread and buried my head under the pillow.
Sometime later, the phone rang and it took awhile to realize it wasn't

part of my dream. I groped for the receiver and uttered a raspy, "Hello." Instantly, I heard a click. Was Mike checking up on me? Maybe he knew that my story about the flight home was a lie. I hobbled out of bed, the ball of my left foot sore with arthritis, and took aim at the toilet bowl. A glass of water was at my lips when I heard a tap on the door.

I froze, the glass wedged between my forefinger and thumb. Visions, like the lights on a movie marquee, flashed through my head. It had to be Mike. Unless … it was Dave from Powertrain. Maybe he'd come with the news that McFadden had a change of heart! My thoughts became a whirlwind of heroics. I pictured myself making a triumphant return to work, my boss forced to publicly congratulate me. That I'd rescued the Powertrain account would be my claim to fame—kill the fatted calf and prepare a feast for my return! I was consumed by the pageantry when the tap became a knuckle-busting rap.

I set the glass down, my heart pounding so hard my temples throbbed.

"Matt! I know you're in there. Open up."

I couldn't stand another moment of uncertainty, another moment of impending doom.

"Who is it?" I replied and pressed my ear to the door.

"It's me, Mike. Open up!"

I stared at the shiny doorknob. My promise to Eddie's memory was again in jeopardy, if not in shambles. I unlatched the bolt … I was no match for this opponent. My day had been littered with defeats—battles joined and lost, victories imagined and squashed—with surrender my only choice. Once more I was being swept out to sea by a remorseless undertow: my lust for another man's body.

Chapter 9

Lying naked beside Mike, I knew how hopeless my situation had become. The things I should've held dear just couldn't compete with my craving for another man. I was repeatedly being pushed and shoved beyond the boundaries of what I wanted to be: someone who could look in the mirror and not vomit. Any dream I once had to project a "Father Knows Best" image was in ruin. I rolled over and clawed the air for my beer—the can now warm—while Mike lay still under the sheets, asleep. The solitude was comforting, though not my conscience.

My wristwatch, crystal scratched and leather band worn, told me it was time for network news. The *Titusville Gazette,* my hometown paper, was fine if I wanted to know the train length of Susie Shortcake's wedding gown, or who had bagged a buck during hunting season, but for national news I turned to the tube. Mike stirred, muttering something. *Did his dream include me?* I wondered. I sat on the bed corner and tuned in CBS, where anchorman Dan Rather opened his broadcast with a story on AIDS. The media frequently portrayed victims of the virus as gays or IV drug users whose homes were urban centers of sin and decay. Yet other places—small and out of the mainstream—were afflicted, too. Network camera crews might not visit Titusville, but the news of Robert's illness would spread soon enough.

Rather reported on the experimental drug AZT, which I knew was Azidothymidine. Although it wasn't a Magic Bullet, it should've been made more available to the suffering. The Establishment, it seemed, was more concerned with covering their asses if the drug didn't work. Fuckstick bureaucrats! It's doubtful, though, that Robert would've taken AZT. From the beginning he seemed willing to accept the virus as the victor. I wanted him to fight, to rally every molecule in his body and mind for the struggle ahead, but he chose not to. I was angry at his surrender, but it never meant I didn't care. I'd heard and read plenty about AIDS, yet I couldn't bring myself to admit to how Robert had

117

contracted it. It was so futile to probe the mind of a mass murderer. What purpose was there in understanding the mechanics of the destruction if I was powerless to halt it?

Suddenly, a loud and annoying TV commercial roused Mike. He sat up, stretching his arms and twisting his torso, then he rolled his neck to work out the kinks. He was well built, in his mid-thirties, with veins like vines that branched up his forearms.

"News already?" he uttered through a yawn. "Woo, last night must've worn us out. Eh?" He stretched again, then added, "How long have you been up?"

"Just a few minutes. I've been watching the tube and daydreaming."

"Say, hand me a brew." I passed him a can, knowing the complaint to follow. "Christ, it's warm! I'll run for some cubes. These beers can chill in the sink while we're in the shower."

Shower? It hadn't crossed my mind. Mike, wearing my bathrobe, left the room and quickly reentered, shaking the ice bucket like an oversized maraca. He dumped the cubes and cans into the sink, ran the tap to make a slurry, then stripped down. He was like a Greek god, and I forced myself not to look below his waistline.

"Hot shower, anyone?"

"I wouldn't be much fun." I turned back toward the TV.

"Want to talk about it?" He wrapped a towel around his hips and sat cross-legged on the adjacent bed, like an Indian chief awaiting the return of a peace pipe.

"Nothing's going my way. Nothing. Today, for instance, my boss sent me on this no-win mission—a make-or-break for my job—and I fell on my sword. Not because I didn't know what to do, but because the SOB didn't give me the authority to do it." Mike's head nodded in agreement, though I knew he understood nothing of my true anguish.

"I see why you booked this morning. That meeting had you worried, huh?"

"It's not just the job … it's my family. I feel like I'm being boiled slowly in oil. My wife and I are miles apart and, to top it off, I think she's seeing another guy. Worse yet, she's hooked on religion. She's become a Jesus freak … a real Jonestown cult-type. And Faith—that's my stepdaughter—she spends her time driving a wedge between my son and me. She's got this hold over him that I can't seem to break.

And now that he's ill, she's just sinking her claws in deeper."

"Ill?"

"Well, ya see … he has an incurable disease. It's only a matter of time and …" I turned away. "I feel so helpless. I love my boy and only wanted the best for him." Mike put his arm around me. "Yeah, and if you're wondering, I wanted him to be straight, too."

"Oh, come on, he's not like us. Lightning doesn't strike twice in the same place."

"I want to believe that, but coming from such bad stock …"

"How old is he?"

"Sixteen. Christ, I was fourteen when I had my first man! And twenty-five years later, I still don't know who I am." I felt every bit as baffled as my words implied.

"But why would you think he's gay? Did he tell you or did you catch him or … what?"

"No, I didn't catch him or I'd have kicked the …" My angry tone was spontaneous, without calculation. *What would I really have done?* I wondered. My dad felt he raised me proper, yet look at the result. My situation as a youth wasn't so unlike Robert's—I, too, had to look on while my stepsister ruled supreme. Damn women! They were either domineering like my mother, unpredictable like Julie, or control freaks like Faith and Janice.

"Matt, what are you thinking there? That maybe he's not gay after all?"

"I *know* he's following in my footsteps," I proclaimed, slicing the air with my open hand.

"It sounds to me like you're being too harsh. Maybe because you love him so much, you're concentrating on the one thing you fear most. You know, seeing something that isn't there."

"I'm not hallucinating. I tell you the boy is gay, and it's tearing my insides out!" He lifted his hand from my thigh and cracked his knuckles.

"OK! So he's queer. I just wish you had more than a hunch to go by."

"Don't use that word 'queer.' Please. I can still hear my classmates calling me that."

"Well, what's different today? Aren't you accusing your son without all the facts?"

I stammered, biting my lip, then decided to go with the truth in the hope it could set me free.

"Wouldn't you accuse your son if he had AIDS? Well, dammit, that's what he's dying from! The gay plague ... the gay cancer! What other conclusion is there?" Mike said nothing, staring into space as though assessing his risk. I waited, almost defiantly, for a volley of ignorant questions.

"God bless. I'm sorry ... for you and for your boy, Matt. I never figured he had a life-threatening disease. AIDS is like ... like a modern day plague." His voice trailed off. I knew I'd befriended a man whose thoughts were in harmony with mine. *He really was like Eddie.*

"Funny you'd frame it that way. That's been my thinking all along. Being a gay makes me feel like I'm under the spell of some dark and sinister force. But, you know, there's no walking away from it ... or from AIDS. I've got to sit by, bound and gagged, while my boy is dragged to the gallows."

Mike squeezed my shoulders. "That's an awesome weight to be carrying around. Hey, look, I've got an idea. Let's have another beer, take that shower, then I know of a place where there's a party. It'll take your mind off your troubles." I looked into his dark, brown eyes and nodded.

An emotional letdown followed our steamy shower. Except for my time spent with Eddie, my customary reaction to lovemaking was to tumble from a peak of ecstasy into a valley of despair. My only consolation was in the self-doubts that followed. So long as they continued, I would cling to the notion that I could one day go straight.

"This party will be just the ticket." He handed me a beer, and we popped the tops in unison. "Here's to us, Matthew, and the good times to come."

I took a gulp, my throat burning as the bubbles burst against its walls. We dressed hurriedly, as though late for our own wedding, and made for the door.

"You got your things, Mike?" I didn't want to give him any excuse to return with me to the room.

"Yep. Let's hit it, partner. This bash will start with a bang and fizzle early."

I stashed the beer under my coat, and we quietly left through a side exit. I wheeled from the parking lot, bottoming the car on a speed bump as Mike motioned for me to turn right.

As though reading my mind, he said, "Not to worry, Matt. It's not far."

The cloud cover had broken enough for me to see the sun setting in a monstrous ball of reddish hues. Smiling, I recalled that ditty my Mom would recite: "Red sky at night, sailor's delight; red sky at morning, sailor take warning." The prospect of sunshine for the flight home was a welcome thought.

"What's that, Mike? Looks like a campus over there."

"It is. That's Union College." *I thought he said he wasn't familiar with the area.*

"We're not off to some college party, are we? My head's not ready for that."

"No, no! These folks are just middle-aged hippies. Your garden variety 'Me' crowd."

"You know, I'm really not sure why I'm going with you. I've already done my share of partying today." I squeezed his hand.

"Oh, I bet you could rally for an encore, Matthew. Why should I be the only one to enjoy your company?" I couldn't believe that he thought I'd want another partner.

"Tomorrow is a big day, and I haven't slept well in two nights."

"You worry too much, Matt. Trust me! Slow down now and make a right onto Wendell ... and we're at our destiny." I squinted, as much to acknowledge his silly comment as to avoid the streetlight's glare. "Park anywhere," he added.

I jockeyed the car into an opening and sat with the engine idling. Mike placed his hand atop mine and entwined our fingers—giving them a squeeze, then a pat.

"Not to worry, Friend. This interlude will be good for you."

I stopped by a huge tree and fumbled with my fly, then hosed down its trunk while admiring its octopus-like roots. *If only this hulk could talk,* I thought. After my Powertrain fiasco, I felt a definite kinship with the abuse this tree was taking. I caught up with Mike, and we stood in

121

front of a two-story house as the bay window reverberated with the music's bass beat.

"You sure this ain't a college party? It sounds rowdy ... and motorcycles in the driveway."

Mike grinned, then rapped on the door. A head blotted out the amber light streaming through the door's single pane, then the lace curtain parted to unveil a gaunt, wide-eyed face with a short-cropped beard and a headband. Mike wrapped his arm around me and pulled me to his side.

"Ah, we'll be a having a fine time tonight, laddie," he spouted with a Scottish brogue.

As the door opened, the music struck me full force. The lanky man, his eyes scanning me like search radar, greeted us.

"Eh, so you made it after all, huh, Mike? This your buddy?"

The smell of pot was everywhere. His hairy chest, partially covered with a tie-dye tank top, heaved with laughter at something Mike said. He seemed indifferent to me, so I walked toward the kitchen. When I glanced back, Mike was gesturing toward me. *What trust was he betraying?* I wondered.

"Hey, you're a new face." I turned to see an attractive brunette squatting at the open refrigerator, shuffling bottles and cans about.

Childlike, I pointed my index finger to my chest, answering, "Me? Why, I'm Matt. I came with Mike over there." I motioned toward the front door, but Mike was out of sight. "I'm from out of town, and he asked me to tag along."

"So, you don't know Mike? I mean, he usually doesn't show up with a companion."

Usually? Companion? I told myself not to become paranoid. After all, not every stand of elephant grass hid a VC sniper. She obviously knew Mike and rightfully concluded that we were lovers. He hadn't said, and I never asked, if he'd come out of the closet. Christ! I suddenly realized I knew *nothing* about him.

"Well, we met yesterday. And when our paths crossed again today, he asked if I wanted to party some more."

I cringed. Before I could qualify my comment, she muttered, "I see." Her arms were crammed with bottles, so she tilted her head and twisted her braless torso in the direction of the music. "Come on." I followed, wondering why I was so uptight that she knew I was gay.

The riveting beat of Sixty's rock-and-roll had a sound that only my generation understood—tried-and-true protest music, vintage anti-war stuff. I enjoyed it now, but eighteen years ago I'd have smashed the album and kicked in the speakers. Returning from Nam—shot-up, depressed, and without a hero's welcome—left me with a huge chip on my shoulder.

"Hey, there's Mike's friend. Come on over, man."

The invitation came from one of three muscular-looking fellows nestled on a sofa. I passed through an archway, like traveling through a time portal, and breezed into a pastel-colored room. A dozen people were scattered about, a handful huddled around a joint, and, while the stereo belted out another Sixty's standard, I flooded my throat with beer. It was a Golden Oldie album, where the groups changed swiftly . and with them the party's mood. Smoke clung to the ceiling and was slowly descending to eye level. The three men, one brandishing an unlit joint under his nose like a Cuban cigar, motioned for me to join them.

"Come on, Matt," said the tallest of the trio. "Let's Bogart this number."

How did he know my name? Ah, what the heck. I took three strides, then plopped down on the sofa, my forearms wedged between my legs. Immediately the joint was in front of my lips, smoke spiraling from its red embers. The tall one held it as I took a drag, then I snorted a column of smoke as he passed it beneath my nose. Within moments I was one with the music, its earthy beat standing my neck hairs on end. I tingled all over, and my eyes were like watery canals as I slugged down some vino from a passing wineskin. Then the munchies hit, so I scooped up a few hors d'oeuvres from a passing tray.

"Say, Matt, let's fire up another."

The hairy-chested one fumbled in his pant pocket for papers, then produced a nickel bag. I followed the three into a dimly lit bedroom, where I stood gaping at my reflections in a collection of ceiling and wall mirrors. Someone ignited a tape player and we blew another joint, then I plopped down, shit-faced, into an overstuffed armchair.

"Hey, let's really get high!" came the tall fellow's challenge as he pointed to a dresser. There, beside it, stood the stockiest of the three, busily sculpting powder ridges on its glass top. He pulled a crisp bill from his wallet and deftly rolled it. He exhaled then leaned into a ridge, vacuuming up the grains with the bill lodged in one nostril and his jeweled pinky pinching the other.

"Nose candy, Matt. Let's do some!"

Within seconds I was poised over a seam, smirking at the thought of what a sneeze might do and watching as the others glided about. Halfway through the vein of coke I reeled back, my nose hairs so clogged I had to breathe through my mouth. God, what a rush! I'd never felt anything like it.

We began laughing hysterically. I shimmied up to the tallest, slurring my words as I asked, "And how did you know my name? And who are you?" He just kept gyrating to the music. The dope was cramming my head into unfamiliar places—places I'd enjoyed in college, but now in my unstable world seemed threatening. Their laughter continued until I noticed that they were eyeing me up and down. A whisper gave way to a nod, then a snicker, and finally the tallest spoke.

"Let's get naked and party, Matt. Jerry and Art here feel confined with their clothes on. As for me ... I always party better in the flesh."

He turned to watch as the other two peeled off their shirts, momentarily helping one to unzip his trousers. Once they were naked, the tallest one undressed and rolled his hips erotically, pointing his cock at me.

"Join me, Matt. I'm lonely over here."

Either I participated or ... or what? One was already going down on the other, his head bobbing while his mate mumbled words of encouragement. I rounded the foot of the bed and edged toward the doorway. "I gotta make a head call or my bladder will bust!" Before I could take another step, the tall one grabbed my forearm and gave me a foxlike smile, his glistening teeth framed by a Fu Manchu mustache and goatee.

"You wouldn't be walking out, would ya? We thought you came for a good time. At least, that's what Mike said."

The other shoe had dropped—like a VC rocket landing in my lap. My head was in a spin, my hand tingling from his vise-like grip. Suddenly the music stopped, and all I could hear was moaning and a giggle from the direction of Jerry and Art.

124

"Look, I don't know what you think, but …"

"We think you're sweet meat. Fresh meat. Queer meat!" blurted the tallest. "And we want to have you!"

"I'm going to find Mike," I said.

"He's gone. He said to show you a good time, and that's what we aim to do." His grip tightened, then he spun me around by my belt and the others tore at my clothes. Buttons popped, but I couldn't form the words to cry out.

Within seconds I was naked, lying face-up on the bed, the tallest licking me while the others knelt on my outstretched arms and slapped my face with their dicks. Suddenly a heavy-handed jolt flipped me over, and one of them crawled beneath me to swallow my cock. I felt a pair of callused hands spread open my ass, then he shoved his prick home. I lunged forward, but the third man had squatted in front of me. He was on his knees, trying to ram his cock into my mouth. I turned away, but he grabbed my ears and twisted my head. I tried to diminish the thrusts to my rear-end, but with each lurch I made that bastard below me dug his teeth in deeper. Immobile and crouched on all fours, I finally submitted.

Within minutes it was over—the one to my front had come on my face and was rubbing it through my hair. As they laughed uproariously it was clear I was only an interlude in their orgy. Their promise to Mike—my Judas—had been fulfilled.

"Feeling better, Matt? See, I told you we'd show you a good time," declared the tallest as he towered over a line of coke. "Next time, let yourself go. Triple your pleasure, not your pain. We know you're quite a performer, mano a mano. Eh, brother?"

I couldn't trust anyone—not family, friends, business associates, or lovers. Every inch of turf, no matter how green and lush it looked, was booby-trapped. As they assembled around the dresser giggling, I frantically dressed. I wanted to hurl obscenities, but my asshole was on fire. I opened the door and the light struck the mirrors. The music, once deafening, had ceased. I stepped into the hallway light, my eyes squinting. As I closed the door the tall one's laugh echoed in the hall. "And don't let it hit you in the fuckin' ass, man." They all broke out laughing.

I walked to the kitchen where I scrubbed my face. Only the skipping phonograph needle broke the eerie silence. *Mike wasn't shitting,* I thought, *when he said this party would end early.* I exited swiftly. I wanted to toss in a torch, yelling "Fire!" at the top of my lungs, then hide in the bushes and club those SOBs as they sprinted out. But I was too scared to do anything but run.

My car stood out like a shimmering oasis and I jogged, stiff-legged, my key in hand. My nose was a runny mess and my rear-end felt like it had been smeared with turpentine. The drive back seemed ungodly long, the cocaine confusing my mental clock. My paranoia ebbed and flowed at the most trivial occurrences, and a panic immediately set in when a squad car or a tailgater appeared. My bubble had been shattered. I had left Titusville feeling estranged, but now I felt desperate to return. I needed to anchor myself against my runaway emotions. Just perching on my porch swing, listening to it squeal as my eyes wandered up and down Main Street, would be soothing enough. I had to get home!

I turned wildly into the hotel driveway, grimacing with pain when the car bounced abruptly over an unmarked speed bump. I wheeled into a space, suddenly realizing that I was unaware that the radio had been blaring all the way, then I sat and cried. In all my drunken larks, I'd never been attacked. God Almighty, and to think I had told Mike about Robert! I felt like I'd violated my own son, the one thing that still held value for me.

My bladder was bursting, so I sprang from the car and flooded the pavement, watching as my frothy puddle merged with the water from the afternoon rains. I blew my nose and tucked in my shirttail, noting that I'd lost my underwear again. I shuffled through the lobby, my appearance convincing me not to check for messages. After all, Julie wouldn't have called again so soon ... *unless Robert was in trouble.* I wheeled about and made for the front desk.

"Any messages for Garrison? I'm in 321."

A well-groomed young man looked up, focusing momentarily on my hairline. When he turned away, I finger-combed my hair. "No, Mr. Garrison. Do you want me to wake you if someone calls?" I paused, not knowing how to answer.

"I really need my sleep. Don't wake me unless my wife, Julie, or my daughter, Faith, calls. OK?"

"Let me see, Julie or Faith," he whispered as he jotted down their names. Looking up he added, "Faith. That's my fiancée's name." Our eyes met, and he handed me a flier with the breakfast special. A favor for a favor, I thought, as I toyed with giving him some advice about women. Then I realized how crazy it was to think I could counsel anyone.

I stood facing the same soda machine where, not eighteen hours earlier, I had promised myself I'd do better—that I'd keep my pledge to Eddie's memory. Now look at me! I'd graduated from booze to drugs. It was one thing to misread Mike, but I should've been savvy enough to see through his tattooed bullies. Once I was back inside my hotel room I double-bolted the door. Two beers were bobbing in the sink, tiny cubes still glistening in the frigid bath, and I made short work of one. When the second was drained my emotions were in a stampede. For some time now I had questioned my worth as a husband and as a father—now my worth as a human being was being challenged. Somebody had to need or want me. Somebody? Otherwise, I was just a worthless object to be discarded atop life's rubbish heap. Faith had said that Robert needed me, but did he want me? Was there an ember left to reignite, or had I doused them all with my ridiculous behavior?

I needed to talk to Andrew, but I was afraid he'd be a tyrant. Yet if I approached him as a priest, he might give some bearing to my spinning compass. I clamped the receiver in my moist palm. *Should I call? What will I say?* His words could bite and tear ... or soothe and heal. I needed the side he showed me in Nam—not the side that mocked me as a Prodigal Son.

It was after eleven, but I knew that Andy often took in the late-night talk shows. He was nocturnal by habit, turning in early only on the eve of Sunday Masses. With each ring my anxiety mounted, then he answered, "Saint Titus Rectory, Father Andrew speaking." I closed my eyes, clung to my hopes, and tried to speak calmly.

"Andy, this is Matt. I'm calling long distance. Can we talk for a minute?"

"Matt! Why so late?" His speech seemed labored—he was probably drinking—and I immediately questioned the wisdom in calling him.

"I'm in Schenectady, you know. Julie is supposed to pick me up at the airport tomorrow, but we had something of a disagreement this evening."

"Yeah, I spoke with her earlier. She called to tell me about Robert being admitted and mentioned your 'disagreement.'"

Damn! Just once I wanted him to hear my side before hers. "Trust me. She had it coming. The woman is impossible!"

"You know how upset she gets over Robert. She just loses her head—and understandably so—at the threat of losing him."

"Yeah, but what about me? He's my son, too. And she doesn't help matters by throwing Faith up to me all the time … like that little trollop was Mother Mary and I was Lucifer. She knows I can't stand her playing one kid against the other."

Andy sighed. "Look, I know this situation with Robert is running you down, but the hell you suffered in Nam has prepared you better than anything Julie has experienced. You've seen the thin line between life and death, and you've seen those you love get wasted. So give her the benefit of the doubt. Don't forget, she was there for you when you returned from Nam a basket case."

There he goes again, acting as her self-proclaimed defense attorney. At least Julie had Faith to lean on. Christ, I had no one! "Andy, look, I'm really fried. I want to talk but … maybe not over the phone. I was calling to ask if you'd pick me up at the Erie airport tomorrow morning. After our tiff, I doubt that Julie and I could sit in the same car together."

"'Tiff,' huh? Well, what time does the flight arrive?"

"Eleven-thirty. Come on, you know I wouldn't ask unless the creek was rising. Please?"

"It'll be inconvenient, but not impossible. I have a meeting with the principal, but I'll reschedule it. I suppose you also want me to tell Julie? Sure you don't want to use the ride to resolve some of your differences?"

"No way! The chill would frost the windows. I'd end up jumping out, or she'd run the damn thing into a tree. Besides, I was hoping that you and I could chat on the ride home. You know, a confession of sorts but without the curtain."

"OK, Matt, but I hope you're contemplating some kind of reconciliation with Julie. If for no other reason, do it for Robert. I just want this rift to end and the wounds to heal."

"I can't make any promises right now."

"Get some sleep then and try not to dwell on Robert. It looks like a flu bug jumped him, but he's managing as well as can be expected." His tone left me feeling empty, helpless.

"Whatever you say, Andy. And don't forget to call Julie. You're sure about Robert? I'm really ..."

"We'll discuss it all tomorrow."

"OK. Good night." I held the receiver hoping for a response, but it went dead.

Exhaustion, like a wall of water I had tried to outrun, struck me full force. Undressing, I rolled beneath the covers, sandwiching my head between the pillows. Tomorrow would stretch my emotional fiber to its limits. I shivered with the chills, but my restlessness subsided and I soon drifted to sleep.

Chapter 10

It hurt to swallow—my tongue was raw and my throat sore—but at least I was alive. Sweat soaked my sheets, and my shoulders were cold. I lay motionless, thinking my rape had been a nightmare and that I'd wake to a loving wife, a healthy son, and a job with a future. The darkness gave aid to my dreamlike state, but just as I began to drift back under my bowel started churning. Reality set in, and I hobbled to the bathroom to answer its call.

Returning to bed, I tried to recapture my dream. Failing at that as I had so many things, I parted the drapes and lay staring upward. Soon the morning sunlight struck the textured ceiling, making it look like an ocean's whitecaps from high above. I sighed. All I had to do was collect my thoughts and belongings, then board the plane for home. My homelife might be in shambles, but at least there I knew the rules I had to play by.

I tallied my defeats on an imaginary scoreboard. Every time at bat I had struck out—whether it was Ron deceiving me, Dave abandoning me, Julie berating me, Faith hating me, Mike betraying me, or Andy scolding me. If only someone cared. I didn't need to be understood, just loved …

As swiftly as the sun's rays had reached my room, the realization struck me that Robert was that person. He was my savior, my shepherd. He could be as soothing as the sun's rays and just as accessible. He was the true center of my elliptical orbit—my salvation—my medevac to the peace of mind I so desperately wanted. As father and son we had too much in common, too much to lose, and too little time to waste. It was so obvious. I'd go to Robert and ask, plead if necessary, for his forgiveness. For months, I had been his judge and jury, ignoring the pleas of others to comfort him. How was it that a boy of sixteen could handle the certainty of death, while his combat-hardened father cowered in its presence? Instead of treating him as a precious gift, I'd been a spoiled brat—tossing aside my lollipop for the ants to eat.

My destructive ways had had a systematic, though unconscious, air about them. Even ignoring Robert was a part of that mosaic. Yet I felt as though my bickering with Julie and Faith had left me nowhere to turn but to the bottle … or to another man. Even if I lost my job over this trip, I'd at least have Robert. My throat tightened at the thought of the AIDS consuming his body. He'd fallen prey to a plague that was neither airborne nor transmitted by innocent contact, and no amount of denial could prevent its victims from being branded gay. Contract it, and you were a leper. It was a global morality play, and for Julie its only plausible explanation was to blame it on the wrath of God.

I'd been punishing Robert and myself for his illness, acting as though I wanted to join in his fate. It was oddly comforting to know that a partnership of misery existed between us, one that would link us together in another time and place: heaven to some, limbo to others, but not the hell we shared today. Once in that paradise, I'd be all those things I wanted to be while he'd be all I prayed he'd be. No, I couldn't let him die—as my dad and Tommy McAndrews had—thinking that I was angry with him.

Before leaving the hotel room, I placed a generous tip on the night stand. It was a self-serving ritual that gave me a sense of value, if not redemption, when I struggled with my conscience over using my business travel to pursue my homosexuality. I checked out and stood in the chill morning air to clear my head. It was a brilliant day, just as Mom's jingle had forecast. As I wheeled from the lot, I slowed for each speed bump. The traffic was forgiving and soon I arrived at the Albany County Airport, where I ditched my rental car and made for the ticket counter to get my seat assignment.

When my flight was called I swiftly boarded, fastening my seatbelt with anticipation. The plane accelerated rapidly, lifted off, and the captain banked the bird lazily to the right and turned off the No Smoking lamp. The cars below soon became minute, their passage snail-paced; mammoth buildings were like Monopoly pieces setting atop some huge green- and jaundice-colored quilt, the roadways like loose threads winding through the fabric. I bid a silent and final farewell to those who were watching our vapor trail, then I sat back and lit up.

Soon the drone of the engines subsided and the plane leveled off.

The attendants, like sidewalk vendors, busily moved the beverage cart down the aisle. I ordered a Bloody Mary and sipped it, examining my smooth palms with their shallow wrinkles. I would've preferred to make a living with my hands, but missteps had pigeonholed me in a desk job. And now I was too old and too much in debt to undo that error. *But I'd reform my ways toward Robert,* I thought, *before they too became an irrevocable error.*

My chief failing was that I couldn't say, "No." Too often I was trying to satisfy someone else. Yet when I championed my own interests—to muster some self-esteem—Robert had unwittingly been caught in the crossfire: me on one side and Julie and Faith on the other. Hah! The idea that I had self-esteem was laughable. My father kept mine in check, while my mother, God love her, labored to compensate. No matter how reasoned my argument, my dad would dismiss it if it didn't coincide with how he thought the puzzle pieces should fit. He was a military man and, like the starched khaki shirts he wore, there was no room for surface defects. Around me, he was a disciplinarian who never displayed affection. Trouble was, he didn't treat my stepsisters the same.

I summoned the stewardess, who descended on me like a nurse would a patient in intensive care. "May I have a refill?"

She smiled and quickly placed a can of mix and a tiny vodka bottle on my tray. "There you go. Call if you need anything else." She beamed, closing her delicate fingers around the money I placed in the hollow of her hand.

My thoughts returned to my father or, more correctly, to the father I wish he had been. As the only boy, I was expected to shoulder responsibility and exude leadership—especially when he was away. He'd coolly remind me that duty, honor, and country transcended his fatherly role and that I was The Man of the House when he was gone. I was hungry for his company, but his long-distance phone calls had been the table scraps of my youth. Being The Man of the House, however, proved impossible given my mother's domineering ways. That's why Andy was so appealing: he was attentive to my needs.

Though he was less demanding, Andy could be just as condescending as my dad. With rugged good looks and a build to match, it remained a mystery to me why he chose the priesthood. I could picture him chasing women on the beach or wooing them at singles' bars easier than I could see him studying scripture and Church doctrine into the wee hours. He had the air of an Ivy Leaguer, the humor of a cab driver, the listening skills of a bartender, and the gab of an auctioneer. He could be pious when events warranted, but, like a novice mountain climber, he had to struggle to reach those peaks. That was the side of him I understood—that inner conflict, that repression of one personality over another. For a time I questioned his sexual orientation, but I was never willing to reveal myself to him, never willing to believe that we could be anything more than friends.

His world was like a sanctuary with picture windows and a bolted door. Everyone could observe him through the glass, but only a few gained entry. And once inside, what they had seen through the glass seemed to be the reverse of what was real. Like me, he wanted to be special, to be looked up to and revered, but we both had mentors who saw through us. For me it was Andy himself, while for him it was his Bishop.

The flight attendant reappeared, her voice deep, to ask if I'd finished my drink. Her eyes—brown, almost cow-like—met mine, and a concern, an attraction, I thought, was relayed.

"Will you be laying over in Pittsburgh?" I asked.

"No. I'm bound for Erie."

"Is it the 10:55 departure?" She nodded yes, and my eyes were like a child who'd spied his shiny new bike beside the Christmas tree. "Well, then we can talk again."

Though she said nothing, I sensed a willingness. My mind sprinted in several directions, a fantasy of wining and dining her, then I sighed and reminded myself to accept my homosexuality. I busied myself with mock discourses on how I'd sidestep her invitation to enjoy more than a drink, then I closed my heavy eyelids. I slept, undisturbed, until the landing gear deployed with a thud. The plane, as though wounded in flight, was rolling and yawing. Wisps of cloud buffeted the wing and within seconds the tires impacted, the captain easing the nose down to the roar of reverse thrusters and groaning brakes.

Lumbering like a seal on the beach, we taxied to our gate. I sat calmly watching the baggage handlers, thankful I had only carry-on luggage, then I positioned myself at the end of the line, hoping to chat with her. I wanted to reaffirm that I still had her in my crosshairs, even if Andy's presence would make it impossible to squeeze the trigger. Her businesslike farewell, however, told me that the older attendant standing beside her was a supervisor.

From a lookout post in the airport lounge, I nursed a beer and watched the bustling throng. Gone were the kids with freaky hair, headbands, sandals, and backpacks. Gone, too—like the Vietnam-bound Jarheads who toted their gear to defend the Establishment—were the legions of hippies toting placards and bullhorns to defend their anti-Establishment ways. I missed that dichotomy. The sameness of the Eighty's made for dull viewing and headlines. As college students, my generation was a lucky breed—mustangs free to roam. Kids today wanted to be Wall Street brokers or fast-track executives. Owning a Porsche, a high-rise condo, a yacht club membership, or a personal locker at an exclusive spa was their badge of honor. Nobody seemed to have the time for social issues. The Peace Corps—"What the hell is that?" they'd ask.

Their schooling lacked values and their upbringing the sting of the rod. Whether social awareness or mistrust of the Establishment, today's kids lacked both. They'd taken the thinking of the "Me" generation to the "Me-Only" level, and the only counter-culture sentiment surviving this social bleaching was an occasional demonstration at a nuclear power plant—not exactly an acid-popping revolutionary agenda. Into this vacuum the AIDS virus, like a tenon in a mortise, fit nicely. Just as music and drugs was my generation's signature, herpes and AIDS had become theirs.

Another Vietnam was what this generation needed. They'd become too complacent. Social flab plagued today's youth. The war certainly didn't do shit for the fifty-eight thousand who came home in a body bag, but it did galvanize the thinking of young and old alike. Looking at the airport crowds, I wondered who among them had shared in the misery that was Nam. My memories of that gritty 881S hilltop—riddled with craters that never healed and me, like a flea, leaping from sore to sore to dodge the incoming—slowly gave way to the warfare I had waged in my head.

I thought of Tommy McAndrews, our platoon's Doubting Thomas, who wasted his dying breath worrying about the silly R&R kitty. That was the bond, though, that combat forged: men came before machines, friendships before self, reality before dreams, and mail call was more welcome than a woman in heat. I thought of Hank who took a shell fragment in the head. He should've made it, but the medevac couldn't get through the fog. I recalled how I stood on the LZ screaming encouragement to the pilot as the chopper descended through the pea soup, only to run low on fuel and pull out. As the whop of the blades dimmed, so did Hank's life. When they came the next day to pick him up, the hurt I felt at loading his body bag aboard the chopper was immeasurable. *No, we didn't need another Vietnam. What we needed was a cure for AIDS!*

I stopped musing before my emotional elevator hit bottom. I finished my drink, then swam with the other fishes to my departure gate. As the cabin door closed I spotted the flight attendant and listened intently as she offered a greeting. Within minutes we rolled across the tarmac, the captain hurling the DC-9 into the brilliant morning sky. The flight was brief, the plane barely leveling off before it started a descent. We banked and the city of Erie, Pennsylvania was suddenly sprawled before me. The crook-fingered peninsula and icy blue-green lake were to one side and the city's industrial smokestacks on the other. As we descended, I busied myself with sighting landmarks—nostalgically recalling that Erie had been Julie's and my newlywed home. After the other passengers departed, I paused at the doorway as though I were expecting trumpeters to announce my arrival. Instead, I felt silly when an unfamiliar stewardess gave me a quizzical look.

"Can I help you, Sir? Did you misplace something?"

"Where's the other attendant? I had something to ask her."

"Sorry, Sir, but Cathy had to deplane early."

"Is she in the terminal?"

She looked at me like I was a lecherous fart. "She didn't confide in me, Sir." Translation: if it wasn't her business then it sure as hell wasn't mine.

I blushed as I stepped onto the telescoping ramp. My peach-complexioned goddess had probably thwarted many an advance in the same manner. I steadied myself against a hot flash, my earlobes afire, then passed through the terminal doors. There, not ten paces away, stood Andrew ... his air detached. He wore his dog collar, and his wire rim glasses instead of contacts. It was a red flag—he was on a Holy Crusade and wanted the visual effects of his vocation to optimize the impact.

Andy was tall and barrel-chested, though understandably paunchier around the waistline than in his youth. His ramrod back and iron cross shoulders seemed more typical of a pass receiver than a man of the cloth. He'd avoided the gray temples customary to our age group and, with or without the collar, he could turn a female's eye. I caught his attention, then strode to his side, feeling a bit uneasy with my 911 call of the night before.

"Well, I'm impressed, Matt. The flight was on time. Was your trip pleasant?"

"What? You know it was a bust. I had as much luck as Christ did on Good Friday."

"I meant your flight home. Was it relaxing?" He looked mildly exasperated and I blushed.

"Sorry … guess I'm a bit defensive. How about a quick drink? It'll relax us both."

"Our time should be spend spiriting you back to the wife and kids." He said it as though he had never needed a drink, as though Julie was a haggard housewife slaving over a hot stove, snot-nosed kids tugging at her apron, while she waited for her deadbeat husband to return from the local gin mill.

"Ooo-Kay. Look, did you happen to see a redheaded flight attendant get off that plane? I wanted to ask her something."

"No, but I'm sure it can keep. Shouldn't your mind be elsewhere?"

I had endured his bouts of self-pity, so why couldn't he give me the benefit of the doubt? "OK! I get the message. But can't I serve two masters once in a while, too?"

He glared at me, almost through me, with those iridescent blue eyes. His ears reddened as his look went from quizzical to sullen. "You might feel like the victim in all this, Matt, but I think your misfortunes are largely of your own making." I wanted to lash back, but I wouldn't argue publicly with a holy man. "By your own admissions, you've been squabbling with Julie and Faith, leaving your homelife in shambles because you won't seek a reconciliation. Bury the hatchet, man! No one faults you for Robert's AIDS, but they are upset at your refusal to comfort him." I half expected him to make a sign of the cross to accent his tongue-lashing, but he looked away. I didn't know where the theatrics ended and the sincerity began.

"Look, I didn't say it last night, but I do plan to make it all up to Robert."

Andy turned back, his stare like a welder's torch. "What about Julie and Faith?"

I nervously shuffled my feet and scanned the thinning crowd.

"Let's leave that alone for now. Huh, Matt?"

I hoisted my bag and followed him to his black sedan. He swiftly negotiated the pothole-ridden 12th Street business district, then spun his big Oldsmobile south onto I-79. It was plain he drove in a fog; a glance at the butt-strewn ashtray confirmed his addiction was alive and well. I broke out my Camels and he accepted one. Smoking had an uncanny way of thawing the ice and, if nothing else, it gave me something to do with my idle hands.

"I could use a jolt. This is one arena where we're equals, Matt. We both have a fondness for cancer sticks. I admit, I was surprised a couple of years ago when you started smoking again."

"Not one of my brighter moves, huh?"

Faith was the one who had driven me back to the weed, but I'd gotten even … plenty of times. We both took long, slow drags and the car soon filled with a fog that rivaled Khe Sanh.

"Remember the fog in Nam, Andy?—how it clung to every blade of grass, every shell hole, every rat-infested trench. I still chuckle at your tale about holding a prayer service to ward off that 'Fog of Satan' so our supplies could get through. All I can see is a bunch of guys dancing around with shaved heads, tambourines, and togas."

He grinned, rolling the cigarette in his tobacco-stained fingertips. "It seems like yesterday. I worried about you a lot … just like today. Death was always stalking you. We shared something then—more than the same uniform or piss tube. Our fates were interwoven, you know what I mean? You're here today in part because of me, and I'm here because of you. The Lord works in mysterious ways. We're proof of it."

I looked intently at Andy. It seemed he wanted to express his deeper feelings toward me, but would they be admiration or scorn, I wondered. *Maybe this ride would do us both good,* I thought.

"That day started quiet enough, Matt, until I saw that medevac chopper bee-lining it from 881 South. I'd become quite a cynic where our casualty reports were concerned. Remember how guys were spreading peanut butter on their toes so the rats would bite 'em … or popping a round into their foot for a ticket to some clean sheets at Phu Bai? But something told me that the casualties aboard that chopper were the Real McCoy."

"Yeah, but those head cases you mentioned were a small lot. I mean, we were going through hell and …"

"Now don't get defensive. All of us were whacked out from taking it on the chin. I'm only recalling that morning when you and Eddie were brought in on the meat wagon. Besides, you know you fellas were dropping like flies to battle fatigue. For Christ's sake, that goddamn siege raged on for seventy-seven days! Who in his right mind wouldn't have been foaming at the mouth?"

It wasn't like him to take the Lord's name in vain, let alone to discuss Vietnam. He'd long ago erected a bamboo curtain that nobody, not even Robert, could penetrate. We glided off the interstate and onto a two-lane road heading southeast. Andy gunned the engine, and we resumed our radar-busting speed. He was silent, deep in thought. I didn't know whether he was rehearsing Sunday's homily or the dressing down that he planned for me. His face, though, was etched with strain, and his hands gripped the wheel like he was riding a roller coaster.

"Well, Andy, you gotta admit one thing. Not everything that went down in Nam was bad. After all, it was the perfect backdrop for you to get Julie and me back together. Our paths would've never crossed, otherwise." My remark struck me like a two-by-four. Good intentions aside, Andy had nailed me to a cross of his own making—and now he wanted me to drink vinegar by making up to Julie and Faith.

"Yes, and look at the monster I set loose. I really believed that you two had something special, a love that could stand the test of time, but all you do now is fight. I went from being a matchmaker to being a referee."

"We got married because we wanted to, and if we've drifted apart it's because we did it to ourselves. You didn't cause us to fall in or out of love, now did you?" He seemed agitated.

"You see, Matt," he said, raising his index finger to make the point, "I couldn't have discouraged Julie from getting involved in the Church. Just the contrary, I felt it was my duty as a good shepherd. But now I realize how her involvement has contributed to the rift. If only she'd been less zealous … if only I'd only been less encouraging … you two might not have grown so far apart."

Was he confessing to me or to himself? "It's too late for finger-pointing. Besides, we both know how Julie goes off the deep end. Trust me, the woman thrives on mayhem."

"Aren't you overstating it?"

"Not at all. It's natural that she'd tackle religion with the same spaced-out fervor … fanaticism … that she did her other causes. All you did was push the right buttons."

Our drive took us through the tiny borough of Centerville. The huge valley we passed just west of the town was the crowning panorama of our trip. There, nestled in the thick woods, were small cabins and, atop a crest, a single red farmhouse silhouetted against the skyline, a battery of grain silos on either side. Whether it was fish to be caught or game to be hunted, this was God's country. I pictured myself snuggled in amongst the timber, owls hooting and crickets chirping, just whiling away the hours in my tiny log cabin. Throw in a storage shed of beer and my boy to help split firewood, and my prayers would've been answered.

A calm seemed to settle over Andy, as though this sleepy hollow had transferred its tranquility to him. Titusville was fast approaching, however, and little of substance had passed between us. Until he quit relying on Julie to be my character witness, he'd never come to know the real me. *But, then, did I really want him to know me?*

"Anything special going on tonight, Andy? Any dinner plans or evening activities?" I wanted to ask him to accompany me to the hospital, to lengthen my pole should my vault to Robert's side prove difficult.

"I've got an ailing parishioner to visit at the hospital, then I'm off to the funeral home to conduct a vigil for Ruth Kaylor. I doubt you're aware of it, but the old spinster died the morning you left. All that money, good looks and health to boot, and she squandered it. What a crazy world!"

We barreled past Saint Catharine's pine tree-strewn cemetery where Julie's parents were buried. Saint Titus Church was just a mile ahead, and I hadn't told Andy that I wasn't ready to go home.

"Look, Andy, don't drop me off at the house. I've got some business at Bentleys to attend to."

"What do you mean? What about Robert?" He motioned with his thumb, as though hitchhiking, toward the trunk, then added, "And what about the bags? You don't want to haul those home from work, do you?"

"I need to brief my boss. You know this trip was a piece of dogshit, but he doesn't. I don't want that sword dangling over my head when I see Robert."

He nodded reluctantly, then wheeled down a side street toward the Bentley plant.

"Say, how about joining me later to see Robert? You'll be at the hospital anyway."

"No, Matthew, you have to do this thing yourself. I'm concerned, though, that you're letting business interfere. You're not getting cold feet, are you?" That patronizing air of his was resurfacing.

"Look, Andrew, I told you this trip was a bust. I gotta let my boss, even if he is a flaming asshole, know the outcome. He pays the freight, so I owe him a debrief. OK?"

"All right, but don't forget that you need to iron out your differences with the women of the household. I thought that was the topic for this ride. Remember the confession you promised last night? Well, I'm still waiting!" He glided to a stop just short of Bentley's entrance.

I knew he wanted to hear me catalog my faults, as if Julie hadn't already given him an earful. No doubt she had poisoned him, planting and nurturing the seed of suspicion that I was the one having the affair. Like she really had a clue. My Little Red Hen . . . my little cheating wench . . . my little conniving twatt! So what if he thought I was seeing another woman. I wasn't coming out of the closet for anyone, even if it would prove Julie a damn liar.

"My head's not there right now. Besides, how do I know you'd be an impartial listener? Seems like you're forever taking the girls' side against me."

"That's not fair. I've always had your best interests at heart and …"

141

"Bullshit! Just once, give *me* the benefit of the doubt and not Julie. I'm fed up with all this 'Poor Julie' and 'Poor Faith' crap! You think you know them, but you don't know squat. You defend them as though I was a battering husband and ... and ... and an abusive father." Flashbacks of my confrontations with Faith pulsed through my mind.

"Hold on there, Matt."

"That's what you're really thinking, isn't it? I just know it is."

"You're just upset ... what with Robert and all ... but you'll see things clearer when you've rested up and ..."

"Don't patronize me, Padre!—Chaplain Patterson!—Sky Pilot extraordinaire! Fuck this charade! I see things plenty clear already." I stared into his widening eyes. "And I don't like any of it. Including you! You're always passing out advice ... freebies from your Tree of Knowledge and Good. Trouble is, I'm the one who lives to regret it. You're the serpent and Julie's my Eve, and now you want me to swallow more of your gibberish and go belly-up to those bitches. Well, I'm not buying your bilge. Do you hear me?"

"What are you saying? You sound like some jealous ... crazed ..."

"Cat got your tongue, Padre, or, should I say, your fangs? I'll tell you what I sound like." I was stabbing my thumb into my chest so hard it hurt. "An irate father and a pussy-whipped husband who's fed up with a certain priest butting his goddamn nose into my personal business. Julie was mine until you and your silly-ass pulpit took her away. You weren't satisfied with that, so you took her away from Faith and Robert, too. Now look at the mess my family is in!"

Andy's chin drooped, and he turned away. His Achilles heel was exposed, and I wanted to slash to the bone.

"I might have salvaged my marriage and my place as a father if you hadn't been so damn quick to judge me unfit ... if you hadn't been so fuckin' gung-ho to dump on me when I was down and out."

"So that's it. Get rid of Andy ... get rid of the messenger ... and then you can put Humpty-Dumpty back together again."

"No way, Patterson!—Sky King Patterson! You're not gonna turn the tables on me. I've had it with your claptrap. Stay out of my life ... away from my family ... and ..." My voice cracked and tears flooded my eyes.

"Fuck the bags! And fuck you! Fuck everybody!" I slammed his car door and stormed up the flower-lined walkway, where I stood beside the Bentley logo that was chiseled deep on a granite obelisk. I felt like I was standing beside a tombstone, mourning the death of a loved one. I turned to see Andy lift his head from the wheel and put the car in gear. As he inched forward, I shot him the finger. "Why shouldn't you feel the pain, too?" I blurted out.

I steadied myself against a hot flash, then charged through the Bentley lobby and down the hallway toward Evans' office. I would have my say today—first with Patterson, now Evans, then Julie, and finally with that damnable Faith! I'd save her for last. Before I saw Robert, my tormentors would see that I'd shed my sheep's clothing and become a wolf.

Chapter 11

I halted in the corridor and broke into a coughing spasm. I leaned against the cinderblock wall, its surface cool and comforting, then pressed my forehead to its touch. I wanted to charge into my boss's office, but I knew I wouldn't last a minute if I didn't answer my bowel. I hurried to the john and planted myself in the end stall. Seconds later I heard leather soles scuffing the ceramic tile, running water, and a voice I'd grown to detest.

"Frank, my man! How goes the fight?"

"SOS, Ron. Hey, I heard you sent Matt to Powertrain yesterday."

I held my breath. God, I wanted to shit.

"Yeah, a little damage-control exercise. I don't expect any miracles, though."

"Well, Garrison can handle it. He's pretty squared-away."

"I know you like playing Santa at the office party, Frank, but aren't you being just a bit generous?"

I was aching to let go, but if they knew they had company they'd dummy up.

"Why send him then? Wasn't there someone else qualified to go?"

"Sure, but I'm not wasting anyone else's time to revive that corpse. You heard the old man say he wasn't throwing good money after bad. With Garrison piloting the rescue plane, it's doubtful we threw any good money away."

"So sending him was a ploy? I sure hope he knew what he was getting into. Well, he's an ex-Marine … a Nam vet … he can manage it."

"Yeah … sure, Santa." Half of me wanted to reach in the toilet bowl and grab a handful to smear over his jowls, while the other half was withering with embarrassment.

"Let me get this straight. You sent Matt into that hornet's nest without a fly swatter, without even a facemask? God Almighty! I guess I'm glad I don't work for you."

"Well, Frank, if I thought it would've influenced the battle, I'd have armed him. But that would've been pointless since we'd already lost the war. Besides, you know the old man wanted Garrison on this trip. I made myself scarce yesterday, just to see if he could pull off an upset."

"Sounds like Matt deserves a Purple Heart. I gotta go. I'll see you at the Production meeting."

The place emptied and I finished my business, then growled like a grizzly to clear my sore throat. Just thinking about Evans made me see red, but hearing that the old man had singled me out for the trip was unsettling. *Was he trying to take me out, too?* I wondered.

I stood in front of Evans' wood-stained door, his name prominently displayed on a brass plate. I wanted to kick it down in true John Wayne fashion, but I knocked, acknowledged his secretary with a polite greeting, then darkened his inner office doorway. He quickly rose from his high-backed chair and circled his oversized desk.

"Matt! Funny thing … your arriving just now, that is. Not two minutes ago I was jawing with Frank Dalton about the short straw you drew in getting this Powertrain assignment. He said you deserve a Purple Heart. Some character that Frank, huh?"

"Yeah, he's a riot. But he's right about the medal. I'm bloodier than a self-flagellating fanatic, only I had some help this time."

He leaned against the corner of his desk and folded his arms, peering out the tinted window to its view of a tulip-filled garden court. "Look, Matt, I appreciate that this trip wasn't pleasant, but …"

"Stop right there. You're damn right this trip 'wasn't pleasant!' Where do you get off sending me into a lion's den like that? What did you think those meat-eaters wanted? To serve me coffee and doughnuts and chat about the rising cost of cornflakes in Iowa? Like shit! Those bastards wanted my head on a platter—and you served it up in fine style." I tried to wet my lips, but I had no spit.

"Come on! You knew it wouldn't be a cake walk."

"Maybe so, but you never prepared me for a warranty battle. You said this would be a technical discussion, but they didn't want engineering advice. They wanted retrofit money, lots of it, and a blood oath from me that Bentley would pay the freight. With the ground rules you set, my hands were tied. The whole thing was a clusterfuck!"

146

"Aren't you overstating it? Powertrain was just testing your mettle. Sounds to me like you came off a Milquetoast." Perspiration was trickling down my underarms.

"You don't know what the hell you're talking about … you weren't there! But McFadden was … and big as life."

Evans pursed his lips and rolled his eyes. "Great! So Powertrain's president got to see Bentley with its tail between its legs. That'll make the old man happy."

"Bentley didn't grovel. I did! And I don't give a flying fuck what the old man thinks. Why weren't you standing by the phone yesterday? I called, even had Carol page you. You should've been my point man … not bringing up the rear."

"Now wait a minute."

"Bullshit! You wait. You knew damn well I'd be ambushed. Don't you have any loyalties? Christ, in Nam your own men would've fragged your ass and pissed on your corpse!"

"Oh, don't start belching up Nam jargon to play on my sympathies. I know you're a Purple-hearted vet, but I also know you've got a chip on your shoulder the size of Manhattan. I pay you to think on your feet. You're a foot soldier, Garrison. Remember? So, if you got 'stuck in the trenches,' like you bellyache so often to the others, then wise up to the fact that the other guy ain't firing rock salt … or should I say saltpeter?"

I blinked wildly. "It wasn't the other guy's fire I was ducking. It was yours!"

He paced, unaccustomed to being challenged.

"I could have you fired, Garrison!"

That was it. The fuckstick had dropped the other shoe.

"Yeah, but you won't. You think I'd go down like a lamb? Think again! I'd go kicking and screaming … and take you with me. I've got enough dirt on you to send you to the corporate cleaners. You know, little things like vendor kickbacks, deceptive pricing, material substitutions, etcetera. Don't forget, smart-ass, I know where the skeletons are. You try to take me out and I'm gonna draw blood. And lots of it!" God, if he could only hear my stomach churning. I could've dropped on all fours and heaved my guts, but if he saw my rifle jam he'd rip at me like a hyena.

"What makes you so sure you're right?" His question had a ring of childlike inquisitiveness.

"Because five minutes ago I was sittin' on the shitter listening to you pound your chest and flap your gums to Santa Claus. Remember? Now Frank—being the Bible-thumping, straight-shootin' Christian that he is—would recount the conversation without sanitizing the facts. You sure like to strut like a peacock."

He settled into his chair and gazed longingly out the window. Then he whirled about and rested his feet on the desktop. "Look, Matt, you've got plenty of vacation coming. Why not take some time off and recharge your batteries? Everybody needs a little R&R. I'll fix it so it looks like you're on vacation, but it'll really be compensatory time. Just a little bookkeeping drill ... some of that wheeling and dealing you think I'm so good at. Whaddaya say?"

His offer was disarming, but he was a lousy actor—fear, not benevolence, motivated him. I formed a toothless smile, not wanting to gloat over the canary I'd just swallowed.

"I take it you're interested then? And there's another plum ripe for the picking, but I can't discuss it just now. Trust me, though. I think you'll find it attractive."

I nearly burst out laughing. Trust me? *Go fuck yourself,* I thought. Evans knew he'd been beat, just as I knew that he wasn't the real threat any more than Andy was. The women in my life were the real enemy—a two-headed, fire-breathing dragon that needed slaying—and I was primed to wield the sword. Either their heads or mine would be served up on my shield.

"OK, Ron. I'll take that offer. Now, what about Powertrain?"

"What about 'em?"

"Don't you want to be briefed?"

"Nah. I know the bottom-line."

I glared. "It's just like you to assume the worst. Whenever I'm involved you're ..."

He fluttered his palms. "No, no, no. Ease up. It's not like that at all. After you called yesterday I phoned Dave Webber at Powertrain."

"Yeah, but I asked them, Dave in particular, to keep quiet until I returned. I had a gentlemen's agreement. You mean Webber spilled his guts to you? Fuck!"

"Now don't get worked up again. This is business, Matt. You can't expect Webber or any of those yokels to be tight-lipped. After all, I'm your manager ... I have a right to know." He was shrewdly reminding me of our roles—he was Gleason and I was Quinn—and that if I wasn't cautious the requiem would sound for my Bentley career.

"One thing, though, before I shove off."

Evans sat up, attentive, and folded his hands. "Yes?"

"Why did the old man want me to make this trip? I heard you mention it to Santa."

"That's tied to that plum I spoke of. Look, I'm not at liberty to discuss it. You'll just have to trust me. Now get home to mama and the kids. I'll call you next week."

I gave him a conciliatory nod, made an about-face of military proportions, and left. I considered collecting some folders from my desk, but the water fountain chatter that my unexplained absence would stir up convinced me that it was better to head for the lobby.

"Trust me, the asshole says! I should've punched his lights out," I spouted as I exited the building.

It was sunshiny when I set out for home. The hills surrounding Titusville were a lush green, intermittently dotted by scenic homes. Spring, it seemed, had finally arrived—when things dormant awake and mask the dead of winter. My awakening to my role as a father was also budding and anxious to flower. Finally, I felt I'd begun to hack away, machete swinging, at the deadwood that had cluttered my path to Robert.

Several minutes into my march, with fatigue gnawing at my stride, I stopped near Burgess Park to gaze up the hillside. Two months ago the toboggan run had been alive with kids, and soon family picnics and reunions would rouse the pavilion from its winter nap. One cheerful time flowed into another and I yearned to find my niche in that continuum. For too long I'd been in a state of emotional hibernation, my love for Robert dormant while my love for myself thrived. Now I was alive to my role as a parent and determined to die to my selfish lifestyle.

As I walked further, a doughnut-shaped pond came into view—in its center an island with a solitary pine that stood tall like a quill in an inkwell. The towering tree, its bottom limbs missing, looked almost

149

like a coconut palm. Its branches shaded, at least at noontime, a patch
of turf where adults could flee from their rat race or children could
fashion a hideaway for their dreams. The thought of escaping to that
island prompted me to plant one foot on the lawn and the other on the
sidewalk. I rocked back and forth, undecided, until an ambulance's
siren reminded me of my destination.

Glancing back, I recalled my outings to the park with Julie and the
kids—crayfish, frogs, and fearless squirrels their companions. We'd
ride the corkscrew slide, scale the cargo net, twist on the Jungle Gym,
and glide high on the swings to catch a glimpse of those swimming in
the nearby community pool. When the snow fell, we'd drag our sleds
up the hill for the dash down. In my Currier and Ives dreamscape,
nothing was as welcome as newly fallen snow. Long ago, my marriage
had been like that snow, until Faith saw fit to trample it with her
muddy boots. I paused to peer up the hill to the university dorm that
stood atop a knoll, then I shook my head. My hopes for Robert were
scuttled. He'd never grow up, let alone attend college.

Two doors from my walkway I halted. The bay window, where Julie
often sat, was nearly in view. I checked the straightness of my clothes,
finger combed my hair, and then proceeded to our front gate. There I
stood and examined the aging fence pickets that Robert and I had
painted, and that now mirrored his health. As the steps creaked under
my weight, our collie, Shamrock, announced my arrival. Where fate
would take me was anybody's guess, but one thing was for certain: the
next time I walked this path Robert would welcome me, even if the
women did not.

Once inside, I became the center of Shamrock's leaps and flogging
tail, but when Julie arrived the dog retreated to his bed pillow.

"So, you decided to grace us after all. Andrew dropped off your bags
and said you were at the office. Couldn't that have waited? Even Andy
was at a loss for words to explain your behavior."

"Andy at a loss for words? That'll be the day. Didn't he tell you I
had to brief my boss?"

"Why did you tell Andy I wouldn't pick you up at the airport? I
don't like him knowing our business."

"What? Now that's a beauty coming from you! You run to him with every ache and pain, whether it's physical, mental or …" I knew if I didn't settle down I'd blow a cork.

"Yes, I confide in him. He's a priest! But I don't tell him every detail of our relationship."

"What relationship? We haven't had relations in months. Or is that years? You spill your guts enough as it is. When I called Patterson last night he already knew we'd argued. So what did you do? Run to the confessional, the phone, or get your bullhorn and march around the rectory?"

"Oh, shush! Andrew knows some of our family secrets. Don't forget, he was the first person we told when we learned that Robert had AIDS."

"Ah, that was then, this is now! I'll wager he has plenty of secrets of his own. Probably even uses you as a sounding board—as his lay confessor. After all, you gotta be a saint to put up with the likes of me. Right?"

"All this talk of Andy is giving me a headache. Can't we change the subject?"

"I'm getting a bite to eat." I soon began frying some eggs and a slab of ham. A sandwich would have tamed my hunger, but it carried no aroma to raise her antennae or ignite her distaste for my eating habits. As I sat down to eat, a creak in the floorboard announced her arrival.

"You know what Doctor Golden would say if he saw you. Just because you've lost weight doesn't mean you can ignore your diet." She busied herself fixing tea while I chewed aloud.

"Tea, Matt?" she asked tersely, implying that I stop munching and wash it down.

"Nah, but I'll take some milk."

"You shouldn't drink milk. How about some juice instead?"

"Whole milk, OK? Real milk for real food, or do I have to get it myself?" She stood silently at the sink, stirring her tea in a mechanical fashion. I slid my chair back and grabbed a beer, along with a snack cake from my cupboard stash. When I popped the can, she slammed her cup down.

"Go ahead and kill yourself. That seems to be the one thing you can do well. But I'm not going to stand here and watch." She flung the tea into the sink and stormed up the stairs.

I rose, intending to follow her, but then I spotted Faith coming up the alleyway. She was strutting along with a methodical, cadenced pace that accentuated her hips. At eighteen she had blossomed—too much for Julie's prudish ways, but not for the young men who swarmed about her. She was now squarely in my sights. Through her, I could get to Julie.

The kitchen door fanned open with youthful exuberance, and Faith's hum of a pop tune momentarily filled the room. Upon seeing me, though, she halted and stopped the swing of the door. Our thoughts collided—mine of disgust, hers of contempt. The alarm in her hazel eyes said it all. I measured it, understood it, relished it. She began to backpedal when that old defiant nature emerged. She paused, straddling the doorjamb—her spindly fingers never leaving the doorknob. *The silly nymph!*

"Come on in. I'm not going to bite. And close the door. It's not that warm out." Neither a greeting nor a rebuke, just the mild admonishment a teenager of her temperament needed. Her torso was short, her breasts full, and her legs long in the thigh. Her face and skin color were Julie's, but the curl of her hair, eye color, and cheekbones were her father's. Julie and I could have produced better stock, but she unilaterally declared that two kids were her limit. So I had a vasectomy after Robert's birth, which served to satisfy her fervor for zero population growth.

"Come in, come in," I said with sweeping arm movements, dispersing my cigarette smoke. "I thought you'd be at the gift shop." She'd taken a cashier's job after high school to "find herself." Julie wanted her to bound off to college, but I was glad to save the money. Besides, she was no more college material than my stepsister, Janice, who had dropped out of community college after one semester.

"Where's Mom? Isn't she home?"

I said nothing and raised the beer to my lips. My drinking intimidating enough, but smoking in the kitchen, a violation of Julie's house rules, made Faith visibly uneasy. I commended myself for bullying her without having raised my voice. She called aloud for her mother, but when it went unanswered she slowly slid her fanny down the door stile, coming to rest on her skintight, stonewashed jeans.

Her knees were tucked under her chin, her arms clasped around

152

them like bookends. Her wrists were adorned with silver bracelets, her red nail polish contrasting with her willowy fingers and pale, hairless skin. I knew she wouldn't sit near me, but something kept her from leaving the room.

"So tell me, what have you been doing today?" I asked, twisting the top off another beer bottle. I flung the cap onto the countertop, where it reverberated like a coin in a tin bowl. I was on my feet now, a little wobbly and holding back my bladder.

"Well, I wanted to see Robert, so I took some time off from work. It was such a nice day and ..."

"Yeah. And how is he?" She had captured my interests, but they were divided—her on the front burner, Robert on the back, one at a boil, the other a simmer.

"Don't know."

"Whaddaya mean?"

"He was out for some sort of tests, so I left him a note saying I'd stopped by."

"Well, did you ask the nurse if he was all right? What sort of tests were they doing?" A vision of Robert being whisked to intensive care with tubes dangling and hospital codes blaring seared my mind. "Why didn't you call home to tell us what was going on?"

"The hospital would do that if it was serious. It's nothing to get excited over."

My face flushed, and I swallowed more beer. One side of me was analyzing an array of images: needles poking Robert, monitors pinging like sonar, and doctors probing his ashen flesh; my other side was looking for an opening with Faith, a way to grind her into submission. When my focus swung to Faith, I upended the bottle.

"Did you tell your brother I'd visit him?"

"Yeah, I told him last night after you called. He was thrilled!"

"Thrilled, you say? Good! What about you? Are you thrilled that I'm seeing Robert?" I teetered, then steadied myself against the kitchen counter.

"Sure. If it makes Rob happy, why not?"

"I'll tell you why not. Because I'm cutting in on your turf. You've been his mother hen and Girl Friday for as long as I can remember, but that's all going to change. Now it's my turn to have him, and there's not a thing you can do about it!" I inched forward, confident I'd win not only this skirmish but the war and all its spoils.

"What makes you think Robert will shut me out? You can't just … just push a button and sweep me aside." She rose to her feet and paced, careful to keep her distance. Her heels clicked the ceramic tile like a metronome, and her figure swayed gracefully.

"You'll get your wake-up call today, little lady. Get ready to smell the coffee, because when I see Robert he's going to embrace me … his father, and reject you … his half-sister. Or have you forgotten? Blood runs thicker than water." She spun about, teeth glistening, fists raised.

My anger swelled when I thought of how she'd made a slave of Robert, torturing me and denying him my love. Now she'd feel the sting of the whip and the weight of the yoke she'd chained me to. It was my turn to be lord and master, my turn to rule again! I moved forward slowly, my eyes never leaving hers.

"You're going to get what's coming to you, young lady."

"Father, don't …" Her lips quivered. Would she struggle or accept her "destiny" as Mike had portrayed it to me the night before?

I reached behind her and curled her flowing hair around my fist, then tugged. I watched as the veins in her neck pulsed. She winced, but made no sound. I pressed her body to mine and planted my lips on hers. Her teeth were clenched, so I shoved my fist, like a piston, into her midsection. She gasped, and I plunged my tongue into her mouth. She squirmed, but I coiled around her. Suddenly, she let go a grunt and thrust her knee into my crotch. My eyes bulged and I doubled over. A gut-retching pain enveloped me and I fell on all fours, then I collapsed, gagging.

"Bastard! You sick bastard!" Her kicks were like a club on my backside. She kept cursing as I curled into a fetal position. A spasm of coughing and hacking overcame me, and I thought I'd vomit. Stars swirled before my eyes, then a charley horse gripped my groin. I rolled onto my belly and arched my spine, then pulled myself up by the leg of a stool. Drool, like strands of liquified glass, ran from my lower lip. Half-sprawled, half-sitting, I looked up to see Faith holding a large kitchen knife. She gripped it with both hands, like the plunger of a butter churn, and her knuckles were white.

I waited for her to lunge. I'd seen men bayoneted and heard the gurgle of blood as it mixed with their breath. *Was this how it would end for me?* She held her stance and panted, ringlets of moist hair draping her forehead. Her face was contorted, her lips pressed to a fine line, her brow creased.

"You think … you think you can take me again." Her voice was husky, gasping. "I told myself you'd never … never destroy me again! For too many years I've let your filthy hands touch me … your breath gag me … but not anymore. Do you hear me?! You'll never rape me again!"

Sweat beaded on my face, a drop falling from my forehead. All I wanted was to have Robert. I wouldn't have tried to control her if she hadn't decided to control him. I just couldn't seem to win him over without somehow eliminating her.

"You've treated me like dirt. You were kinder to the dog than to me. You're so damn sure my life has been spent stealing Rob from you. Wake up, you jackass! He was always there … only you were too damn busy … too damn set in your ways … too damn stupid to see his heart was breaking. But I wasn't! He needed me, and I needed him. That's all we ever had in common—you made sure of that. And you call yourself our father, our provider. The only thing you ever provided me or Rob was pain."

Her words were like a sedative. I had trained myself—deluded myself—into becoming a predator: one moment the hunter, the next the hunted. I understood that now, and the destruction that accompanied it. I couldn't undo the past, but there was still time to comfort Robert. He was my last chance in this world to give rather than to take. The fury in her eyes momentarily dimmed, then she glowered as though struck by an unsaid truth.

"I know how your mind works. You think Robbie is gay because he has AIDS. If that's true, it's because you made him that way … because you turned your back on him … because you led him to it."

My head was spinning. Did she know of my secret life? I couldn't comprehend the thought before she bore in again.

"You'd be gay, too, and dying with AIDS if your dad had treated you like you treated Rob. Why weren't you here when he needed you? You made him what he is! You and you alone. I just tried to fill the hole you left. And you've punished me enough for that. Now look what's become of him … and of you." Her breathing was labored, her body trembling.

She'd said it all—I knew it, she knew it. Faith stood over me, tears streaming. We were prisoners of our own wants: mine to love and be loved by Robert— maybe hers, at one time, to have been loved by me. She softened her glare. She'd driven her pick deep, striking the emotional pay dirt that had eluded her for years. She dropped the knife with a thud and ran from the room. What started as a whimper grew into uncontrolled bawling. She careened off the banister and scaled the stairs on all fours. I struggled to my feet, fighting back the urge to vomit.

I stood above the knife and thought of falling on its gleaming point—but I had to live on for Robert. I set it on the counter as though it were a priceless antique. I rinsed my face and mouth in cold water, tucked in my shirt, and finger-combed my hair. As I reached for the doorknob, I heard someone descending the staircase. If it was Faith, I had nothing to say. If it was Julie, I had nothing to confess. Faith had done me a service when she told Robert I would visit him. His need, now my need, could no longer go unanswered. I opened the kitchen door to a welcome rush of cool spring air, while the footsteps approaching from behind hammered the tile floor. I never looked back.

Julie's shrill voice stabbed the air. "Why do you torment her? Why? Just go and never …"

I kept walking. I wanted to stop and admire a budding tulip, but with Robert ahead and Julie behind I felt pulled and pushed along. I turned up the alleyway, knowing the back streets would hasten my arrival at Robert's bedside. When the kitchen door slammed and the wind chimes rattled, I knew another curtain had been drawn, another act concluded. I had closed a dark chapter in my life and was hurrying to open a bright new one.

I moved briskly through the back lanes, huffing and puffing toward the hospital. The blue road signs with their letter H heightened my urgency. I was fatigued, my knees rubbery, but my stride was driven. The public park in front of the hospital was crammed with playful kids, parents, and grandparents—life's uplifting cycle was on display only a few feet from an institution devoted to facilitating its beginning and easing its end. Their laughter buoyed my spirits, and the sun's warm rays relaxed my tense neck muscles. Just a few yards now separated me from my son, from my spoils. I picked up my pace, training my eyes on the double-glass entranceway doors. Near breathless, I entered the lobby and obtained the room number from the receptionist, then I bought Robert his favorite soft drink. Soon I was standing outside his doorway, straightening my shirt and wiping my brow.

At the touch of my fingertips, the huge door glided open. I stood in awe, like Dorothy had upon seeing the Land of Oz. Only this world was colorless, antiseptic, and strewn with tubes and IV bags—not flowering vines and multicolored blooms. No smiling little people or good witch greeted me, only the silent pictures on the TV tube and the hum of the IV dispenser. Feeling like the captain of a sinking ship I stood motionless beside Robert as he slept. His peace was my peace, his dreams my dreams, and we shared the silence as he renewed his strength and I mustered mine. I slumped into an armchair, my sights trained on the ravaged young man. An army of thoughts marched through my head. He was my heir, my reward, my punishment, my love, and now a reflection of my life. All those things and my savior, too.

My thoughts of him, like those of a dying man's life, flashed before me. From when I first saw his newborn face, to his crying at having fallen from his bike, to his shy grin when he handed me his first report card, to his ungainly stride as he rounded third base in Little League, to the wisps of hair on his chin that signaled his manhood, to the first time I dangled the car keys before his eyes, to the bewilderment in those eyes at learning his body had been invaded by AIDS. He hadn't lived nearly enough. Time, it seemed, had passed by like a fleet of racing warships; where once a mighty armada had steamed, now only a faint column of smoke marked its trail over the horizon. So it was with Robert.

He stirred and I leaped to my feet, wiping the tears from my cheeks. I wanted his first sight to be my smiling face. I hoped he'd gather strength from me, yet it was all an act. I would've rather lay cuddling him in bed, but I knew my first task was to regain his trust. Difficult as it would be, I'd wait patiently for his embrace. Just so it was a short time in coming . . . just so when it arrived it was everything my heart and soul desired.

"Dad!" he exclaimed in a strained voice, a thin smile on his pallid lips. His head dropped back onto his pillow and I leaned over him. I raised his head, my eyes not leaving his, and fluffed his pillow. That thin smile returned, and he mumbled something. I hung on his every breath, but I had to get right in his face to understand his words.

"I knew you'd come, Dad. I knew it. I knew ..."

"Don't talk now, Son. Just rest. I'll be right here."

"I knew you'd come," he whispered again. "Even if Faith hadn't told me, I knew." His breathing was labored and I gently squeezed his bony shoulder and stroked his hair.

"Not now, Son. We'll talk later. I'll stay by your side. Forever, if that's where you want me."

His chapped lips parted to unveil a toothy grin, his braces glistening under the sunlight that filled the room. He had accepted me. Time was now our enemy—no more battles with family, friends, or myself. My war was with the clock and the virus's march through his body. Our destinies were intertwined, and I'd stay with him until the end. Like Dorothy, I was home, and home was where I wanted to be. No, I'd never, ever leave it again!

PART THREE

Chapter 12

Faith stood with Robert beside the still waters of the pond, their minds bubbling with adolescent thoughts. They were in the springtime of their lives, watching with excitement as nature ushered in summer. Storm clouds, however, were forming on their horizons—their father's mercurial temperament saw to that. Matt's breath blew warm and cozy for Robert, a gentle South Sea's breeze, but for Faith it was a blast of Arctic air. For his son, no ransom would've been too great; for his stepdaughter, he would've paid no bounty to her kidnapper. Robert saw his dad's disaffection toward Faith, but dismissed it as the natural detachment a father might feel for his stepdaughter.

Robert adored his sister, and so long as his father didn't challenge that love he wouldn't have to choose between them. At twelve, he wasn't ready for such decision-making, and Matt had wisely not forced it upon him. He had, however, forced it upon his sister. The hand that stroked Robert's hair was gruff and invading when it touched Faith. She was the dark side of Matt's life, Robert the bright. As brother and sister they illuminated each other's world, so neither was cast into total darkness.

"I'm nervous, Robbie. Part of me is anxious, the other scared."

"I'd be more scared of going to college, Sis. That's when you don't know anybody and you're miles from home. Don't worry about high school, though. The boys will be falling all over you, then I'll be the one who's nervous."

Her spindly hand squeezed his, and they strolled closer to the pond. They stood on the bank where weeds interspersed with ferns, and Robert squatted to pick up a piece of litter that fouled the waterline. The island that they played on, that they fantasized being shipwrecked on, loomed a few feet away. Its solitary pine, with a trunk like a main mast and drooping limbs like topsails, towered over them. Its roots, like theirs, were firmly planted in this valley's soil. Unlike the tree, however, they swayed not from the wind but from their parents' shifting emotions, with Faith nearly snapping under the weight of her father's yoke. They'd learned that their Neverland had a Captain Hook, their Eden a serpent. They'd also learned to hold firmly to one another.

"Mom says you're serving Mass tomorrow with the new Pastor. Who knows, maybe I'll come and watch. I'm tired of Mom always lecturing me about blowing off church."

"That would be a first, Sis. Not since I was baptized has the family, Father Andrew included, been in church together."

"Only this time you'll be pouring water over his hands instead of him pouring it over your round-ball head." She giggled while Robert visibly displayed his excitement.

"Well, Sis, starting high school makes you nervous … and serving this Mass does the same to me. The only good thing is that I'll be done in an hour."

"Yeah, but then you'll get to hear Dad's critique."

"Thanks for reminding me. It's bad enough trying to satisfy him in baseball. It doesn't matter how hard I try, he just keeps telling me to do better. He doesn't understand … to me it's just a game."

"He doesn't understand you? I'd have better luck talking to that rock over there than getting through to Dad." She flung a pebble at a huge boulder jutting above the waterline, admonishing herself for having missed the image of Matt that she'd mentally painted on its gray face.

"Know what's really neat, Sis? Father Andrew was with Dad in Vietnam. Mom says he was there when Dad got shot up, and that he helped load him on the medevac helicopter. I betcha he's got lots of war stories."

"Probably. Anyway, I haven't seen Mom this excited in a long time. It'll be weird having someone around that Mom and Dad both like."

"I just wanna hear his stories about Nam. Suppose he killed any gooks?"

"Oh, priests don't carry guns, silly. Mom said his only weapons were his cross, a rosary, and his wits. She says he needed more than that, though, to protect himself once he got back home."

"Whaddaya mean?"

"According to Mom, he gets into trouble wherever he goes … his strong social convictions she says. You know, like civil rights and women's rights. That's probably why Dad doesn't talk about him. He's a stiff about such things. To him everything is either 'salt or pepper.'"

"Just so Father Andrew tells me all the gory stuff about Nam. I want to know what it's like to get shot at and see dead bodies and have jets dropping bombs around you and …"

A gleaming sports car rumbled into the nearby lot, and a tall, well-built man with sunglasses and dark wavy hair emerged. He spotted the Garrison kids and strode toward them. He knew them from their photos, but would they recognize him, he wondered. His neatly trimmed and graying beard gave him the look of a contemporary prophet, disguising him from his clean-shaven photo that Julie displayed in the china hutch.

"Sooo, this must be Robert. And you, my fair lady, can be none other than Faith."

He advanced and they hesitated, Robert stepping behind Faith. Then Faith saw the gold cross emblazoned on the front plate of his sleek car. Looking into his iridescent blue eyes, soft and without malice, she remembered a snapshot she'd seen in her mother's purse.

"Remember what Dad said about talking to strangers, Sis," Robert whispered, virtually concealed by her budding frame.

"Hush, silly. That's just Dad's way of keeping us from making new friends." She smiled at the would-be stranger, both to acknowledge his identity and to excuse her brother's childishness.

"It's good to be cautious of strangers," he said. "Only I'm no stranger, kids."

"Are you my dad's boss?" asked Robert.

Faith silently admired his car and his physique. She could see why her mother spoke fondly of him; she could see the contrasts between him and her father.

"Not exactly, Son. Though I must admit, I've been his boss on and off over the years. Only he refuses to accept it." When Robert looked puzzled, Andrew knew it was time to end the charade. "OK, I surrender. I'm Father Patterson, kids. Call me Father Andy, OK? Just so we become fast friends."

Robert leaped from Faith's shadow and put a squeeze on Andy's waistline. Rarely a week went by that his mother didn't spin a loving yarn about Andy's challenges, past and present, and how he'd triumphed over the odds. So pristine was this man's image that Robert instantly felt closer to him than to his own father and, had he been older and more perceptive, he would've seen that Andy had more favor in his mother's eyes than his dad did.

"So tell me, Robert, what keeps a lad like you occupied? Is it school work? Sports? Or is there a girl in your life?"

Robert blushed. Sports were something he did for his dad and, as for girls, he had no time for their games. To him, all they did was tease and taunt.

Andy took stock of Robert, smiling at his ungainly features. His feet were big, his legs knock-kneed, his chest flat and arms limp. Given Matt's love of sports—as a spectator, that is—Andy suspected that Robert was pushed to be what he wasn't. The boy's next words confirmed it.

"Fishing is what I like. And reading comic books. Dad wants me to play baseball, but I like my special fishing hole along the creek. I mean, baseball is OK, but it's …"

"Well, I know that whatever you pursue, Rob, you'll do well at it. I'd like to see one of your prize catches broiling in my oven soon." Andrew grinned, pinching Robert's cheek and patting his shoulder.

"And you, young lady, are no doubt high-school bound. Is it Venango Christian High?" Andrew knew the answer, but he wanted to gauge her response. Would it be one of disappointment or indifference?

"Titusville High, Father. We've never really talked, at least seriously, about my going to a Catholic school. Mom probably wouldn't mind, but Dad … he'd never agree. Long ago he told Mom he wasn't spending his hard-earned money on some Bible-thumping school." She said it matter-of-factly, resigned to Matt having his way.

"Yes, sirree, that's your dad. Not much has changed since you were in grade school, huh?" He frowned to exaggerate his comment. "If I'm smart … and judging by your contented glow … I'd best leave well enough alone here. I'm sure you'll have a great time at Titusville High."

Andy couldn't help but notice her blossoming into womanhood. Her legs were a little stout, but her slim ankles, neckline, and budding breasts foreshadowed a graceful figure. He sized up her attributes—crediting them to her mother—and her faults, which were few, he blamed on her father. In Andy's eyes, her mother's seed was superior to that of her biological father. *If Julie would only teach her how to apply make-up,* he thought, *then a real diamond could emerge.* Behind that thick eyeshadow was a woman in waiting, and Andy knew she'd be turning heads and breaking hearts.

"So, will I see you both at Mass tomorrow?"

Robert piped up to say that he was his altar boy while Faith sheepishly and silently stroked the turf with the toe of her sneaker. Andy knew from Julie's letters that Faith was rebellious, and he relished the challenge of bringing this lamb into the fold. He loosened his collar in response to the sun's rays, then removed his sports jacket. Faith looked away, not wanting Andy to see that she was admiring him.

"Maybe you'll have a different attitude toward attending church now that I'm here. And if you accept that dare, here's another." She peered up, inquisitive. "How about getting your dad to join you? It's been a long time since I had his attention for one of my homilies."

He wanted to hug her, but hesitated. At fourteen, she was already so much like Julie.

"Well, kids, I'm off to the rectory."

"But I wanted to ask you about Nam, Father. Mom says you and Dad were in combat together, and I've got a bunch of …"

"That'll have to keep, Rob. One day soon I'll fill you in on all the gory details. That's a promise, champ."

"Ah, OK."

Father Patterson bid them farewell, reminding them both to obey their parents or he'd bring down the wrath of God. Then he strode off like a drill instructor under review. He lurched his vehicle from the lot, and Faith's senses followed the car's throaty roar as Andy shifted gears up Main Street.

"Wasn't he neat, Sis? And to think he saved Dad's life! I can't wait till he tells me about Nam!"

"Get your needle off Vietnam, will ya? It's not like he volunteered to go there. His boss told him to go."

"What boss?"

"His Bishop, silly. Everybody has to answer to someone. Now for me, I like his views on women's rights and the environment." Her tribute flew over Robert's head, leaving her frustrated. At fourteen she was in limbo, neither a child nor an adult, but anxious nonetheless for a friendship with Andy—something she could never have with her father. Her fluster subsided, though, when she saw a classmate approaching.

"Hey, Sis, don't you want to finish our game? And what about …?" His words were lost on her. He wanted to follow her, to be a part of her social life, but that would've meant languishing in the shadows and listening to giddy tales of boys.

Though Robert and Faith had parted, they wheeled in unison to observe their father as he drove into the parking lot. Instinctively, like birds in flight that abruptly alter course, they knew the winds were about to shift. Faith thought it wiser to look immersed in her friend, and so she strolled away without looking back. Robert, however, waited stoically for his dad to arrive.

As Matt closed the gap he held up a baseball bat and glove, like a warrior would his sword and shield, and Robert sighed. His challenge, as always, was to rise to manhood in his father's eyes—to become a gladiator under his trainer's watchful gaze. *Why,* he wondered, *couldn't he just cling to Faith's side like their dog did to his father's heel?* He might not always feel a part of his sister's world, but eating her table scraps was better than trying to jump through the hoops his dad demanded.

"Come on, Son, we've got practicing to do. You've got a game this afternoon, remember?"

Matt never looked toward Faith. Good riddance, he thought. Her voluntary departure was better than his barking a gruff command that she leave. Martyring her in Robert's eyes, as Matt knew, would only strengthen her influence over him.

"I wish your sister wouldn't drag you off like that."

"Yeah, Dad, but …"

"Women! They don't understand us guys where sports are concerned. Huh, Son?"

He lobbed the glove to Robert, who fumbled it, then he hit a grounder that struck his shin. Robert winced and dropped his mitt to rub out the ache, then he followed his father toward the nearby ball field.

"Hey, Dad, did you know that Father Andy was just here?"

"Oh, yeah. And what did the padre have to say?" Matt knew from

Julie's chatter and her haste to bake a welcome cake that Andrew had arrived.

"Not much, but he seems like a nice guy. Drives a really fancy car, too!"

"Well, don't believe everything your mother says. She tends to exaggerate where Father Patterson is concerned."

"Yeah, but he did save your life. Right? So you two gotta be close. You know, like blood brothers."

Matt gave a cagey smile. He knew it was pointless to try to dispel the myths that Julie had created and nurtured. He knew, too, that if he didn't laugh or at least grin, he'd cry. Andy had no more saved his life, he thought, than his marriage—to the detriment of the one he had orchestrated the other. Now both were going badly and Andy's return only heightened Matt's anxiety.

"He was there when I needed him, Son. If that's saving my life, then I'll accept that logic." He tossed aside a stone from the pitcher's mound, mumbling, "Life's nothing but a shitload of myths and half-truths." Given the double life he led, he was confident with that conclusion.

"Tell me about it, Dad. About getting shot up. How come you don't display your medals?" His fascination with combat annoyed Matt, though not as much as the exalted status that Andrew enjoyed in his son's eyes.

"War isn't what you think." Matt's thoughts flashed back to Eddie and their life as trench rats. "You've been watching too many Hollywood movies. There's nothing romantic about it. *Nothing,* do you hear?"

Robert's chin dropped. All he wanted was to place his father on a pedestal, to look up to his deeds instead of his faults—to revere the soldier and not the war he fought in.

"Gee, I just thought that maybe you'd tell me …"

"Forget all that war story stuff. It's ancient history. Besides, we lost!" I lost, he thought, as his vision of Eddie returned. "Now, let's zero in on baseball. Your coach says if you work harder he'll give you a shot at the mound."

"I'm kinda happy in the outfield, and besides …"

"You're a second-string center fielder, Son. You can do better …

much better. All you've got to do is practice, practice, practice. Now let's hit it! Enough with the chin music."

Matt cursed through his teeth at the emasculate influences his son had to overcome, then he stepped atop the mound and hurled the ball. As he loosened up, he kept thinking about how Faith had muddled his boy's priorities. With each pitch he scrutinized Robert's stature. Beneath that underdeveloped exterior was a budding man … maybe one ripe for a college coach to recruit. Matt knew, though, that for Robert to blossom he'd have to step out of Faith's smothering shadow.

"I'm gonna start winging some fastballs. Get ready now."

The ball slapped the boy's glove. Matt wound up and fired another with a grunt. Pain etched Robert's face, but Matt couldn't see it. He was too busy wrestling with the notion that Robert could be all that his father wanted if only they spent more time together. Abandoning his business travel, though, would mean going straight. Matt knew—God knew—he'd tried to turn away from the gay life, but he couldn't make the cut. Like Robert, Matt was a second-stringer, a benchwarmer, when heterosexual play was the contest. Angrily he uncoiled his arm, and Robert ducked the threat.

"Come on, Rob! Get with the program! If you spent less time with your sister and more with your buddies …"

"But I don't have any buddies, Dad. At least none that wanna play ball."

"Maybe if you weren't so damn pussy-whipped," Matt muttered, shaking his head.

Perspiration formed on Matt's brow as he rocketed the ball with more and more resolve. It didn't hurt his aim that he'd painted an imaginary target on Robert's chest, with Faith's face as its bull's-eye. Smack went Robert's mitt, and he flung the glove from his beet-red hand and began to wail.

"Wimp!" groused Matt.

೮೨

That night, sulking over Andy's return and Faith's clout over Robert, Matt drank a snout full of beer. It had been months since he'd felt so sorry for himself. The house was quiet, the hour late, and Julie had taken a sedative. He had punished Faith before and she'd said nothing, so each time he felt more emboldened, more justified in his cause. She had drawn first blood, he reasoned, by spiriting Robert off to effeminate worlds. So for that offense against his son's manhood he'd spirit her, like a hawk would its prey, into his own vengeful world.

The floorboards creaked under Matt's weight. Pausing outside Faith's bedroom he let go a throaty burp that he muffled in his T-shirt. It watered his eyes and burned his nostrils, but he still turned the doorknob with the aplomb of a second-story man. The night was warm, and the air seemed moist with her deep breathing. He stood beside her bed, examining the lines that the sheets traced along her scissored legs. The moonlight illuminated her glistening hair, while faint, crescent-shaped shadows, formed by her prominent cheekbones, were cast below her eyelashes. He grinned and knelt, cupping his palm over her mouth. She woke with a start, her eyes flooded with fear. He admonished her to keep quiet, smiling at the command he had over her.

He had long ago explained his demented logic to her—and she had nodded her understanding, to the extent a nine-year-old could comprehend—and as the years passed she came to accept his violations as a father's right of eminent domain. She believed that any resistance on her part would bring instant retribution. Matt had warned her that any accusations would be vehemently denied, and that he'd abandon her mother and spirit Robert away. Faith was too childlike, too intimidated by his saber rattling, to fight back.

In Faith's mind, it was better to surrender her body than to uphold her dignity at the expense of losing Robert. To that end, she lost her virginity and her self-respect to ensure her brother's love. Had Robert known, he'd have struck his father down with his own hand. Instead, he was perplexed by Faith's mood swings and wondered what he could've done to upset her.

Matt left her room as quietly as he had entered, once more having taken something that wasn't his. To him, Faith was a consumable item—no deposit or return to be paid. The wound he inflicted on her psyche was deeper now—his satisfaction at playing teacher and disciplinarian was momentarily quenched—but he wouldn't relent in his abuse until he broke her hold over Robert.

છ

Many nights, Faith woke up sweating and breathing fast. Her dreams should've been filled with a sixteen-year-old's benign anxieties, but instead they were nightmares of bewildering dimensions. The emotional glue holding her together was her brother's love, and their closeness to one another was never lost on Matt. Wisdom states that it takes two to tangle, but in an incestuous relationship it takes only one—the strength of the predator overpowering its prey. So it was between Faith and Matt, and those around them were oblivious to the horror.

Julie sensed that something beyond mere surface tension—or an unhealthy rivalry for Robert's attention—was at play between Faith and Matt. As mother and daughter, however, they didn't have in-depth exchanges; cursory chats were the extent of their communications. Either Julie was too busy or Faith too moody for the circuit to close and the information to flow. When Julie was receptive to a dialogue, Faith was detached; when Faith was ready to open a door, Julie was closing one. The two seldom shared the same wavelength, and Matt was the beneficiary of their incommunicable ways. But there was another dimension at play, known only to Julie.

Julie's unwillingness to resurrect her sordid childhood had tempered, if not quenched, her suspicions concerning Matt and Faith. Her callow years harbored a dark secret that she refused to share—even with Andy and his Church-installed powers of reconciliation—or to accept. Some things possessed the power to evoke primal fear, and to fall under their spell was to risk one's sanity. For Julie to disclose to anyone that her father had sexually abused her as a child was one of those things; it was an admission that she was broken goods, broken beyond repair. She couldn't jettison her belief that she was both the victim and the instigator of the abuse. No logic justified her dualistic thinking, but then logic could not explain the humiliation and trauma she had suffered. She was helpless to heal her emotional wounds and had swept them into the deepest recesses of her mind. Like Matt's selective memory of Nam, Julie, too, locked away memories that had the capability to destroy her mental stability. Denial had become her only refuge.

Only once did Julie tell another of her abuse. In telling Dan, her first husband, she thought the truth would set her free, but it set loose a demon in him that she was helpless to suppress. He wanted her all to himself, but when he realized he could never enjoy that ownership—either physically or emotionally—he snapped. From that day forth she became the focus of his anger. Dan tried to reconcile her disclosure in his mind, but he was too hurt by her revelation and too easily distracted by the anti-war movement to remain at her side. In time, he went from verbal to physical abuse. When he crossed that line, Julie snapped and sent him packing.

Her soulful letters to Andy while he was in Nam avoided this ugly dimension of her marriage. Refusing to risk another man's rejection, she painted her estrangement from Dan with a broad brush. When Matt reentered her life she was determined to erase her childhood memories and start anew—determined to erect a wall that would forever encase her unclean past. It didn't occur to her that telling Dan had, in fact, freed her from a marriage doomed to failure. The cause-and-effect relation that she drew between telling the truth and suffering its consequences—at least in the matter of her sexual abuse as a child—was something she'd never willingly experience again.

So neither Andy nor Matt was aware of the cross she bore. Just as Matt harbored a secret life, a secret past, so Julie sequestered the shards of her childhood. It's speculation how Matt would have reacted to the news that Julie's father had abused her, but knowing her despair might have convinced Matt to spare Faith the same fate. By cloaking her past, however, Julie tempted history to repeat itself. If Andy had known about her dark side—as he did of Matt's homosexual leanings—he would have abandoned his matchmaking ways. Even as a priest, he accepted that miracles were in short supply. Andy, however, knew precious little of what these two had endured and was overly confident of his ability to mediate on their behalves. So he blissfully orchestrated their union, never realizing that it would ensure their undoing.

Though Andy loved Julie, and would have married her had the Church not been there first, he wouldn't renounce his vows to have her. He knew it was a sin to want her, and he knew he committed a sin with her that winter's night in 1967, but so long as he didn't repeat that error he felt he could continue in his vocation. To that end, Andrew had

171

encouraged their marriage. The real sin was that he did it for his own survival, rather than to improve Matt and Julie's lot in life.

Julie's concealed baggage proved to be quicksand for Faith. For Julie to step forward and ask Faith "the question"—to suggest for an instant that she had suspicions—was to run headlong into a pain that would result in her own immolation. Julie was resolutely incapable of believing the worst; incapable of hurling herself into the fray between Faith and her stepfather. So her daughter was left with no one but Robert.

છ

"Look, I don't care if he misses Mass ... and as far as his homework goes, he can do that Monday morning," argued Matt.

"Why is this baseball game so important?" retorted Julie. "Just watch it on TV! Tape it if you have to, but I think Robert should do his schoolwork and assist Father Andy at Mass."

Matt, wet and sweaty from having washed the car, rolled his eyes and left the kitchen. He'd come inside to ask Robert to help him wax the car, thinking of the joint venture as a tried and true technique to bond with his son. In those hours spent polishing and chatting, a kinship, transcending man and steel, could be forged—or so Matt hoped. He ended up tackling the task alone as Robert, overhearing his parent's dispute, had slipped out to go fishing. The irony was that Robert had planned to ask his dad to join him at his favorite fishin' hole.

Julie sat alone at the bay window, a long-stem glass of wine in hand, to observe the bustle of Main Street. She enjoyed white wine, as Andy did altar wine, and in troubled times she would station herself like a window sentry. Through this portal her world looked less imposing and, thanks to the wine, less focused. It was akin to looking in a carnival mirror, but seeing only a felicitous image of herself and not the distorted world that surrounded her. Had she seen her real situation—her real self—she'd have shattered the mirror, adding years to her already unlucky existence.

Seeing Robert return, Julie bellowed, "Matt, tell Rob to stow his fishing gear and get scrubbed for confession."

172

She steadied herself, having finished a half bottle of Bianco, then tugged her gleaming hair back and cinched its tie. Lines had formed just above her blushed cheeks, and a shallow crow's-foot confirmed her passage into middle age. She was careful in her grooming, careful of what she ate, careful to avoid the sun, and careful to maintain her figure. Alcohol and stress, though, had taken a toll. Stately she was, like a tall ship whose sails were unfurled and full before the wind, but on close examination one could see the cracks in her main mask and the wrinkle in her hull plates from life's pounding waves.

"Why spill your guts to Andy again? You made the pilgrimage just last week."

"That's between God and me. You'd never understand."

"Have it your way, but Robert should stay home. You have him so hog-tied with religion that he'd never think a dirty thought ... let alone do the dirty deed."

"It's just like you to think that way. There's more out there than sex that can corrupt him. Temptations ... evils ... they're everywhere. You read the paper, you watch the news."

"Look, I was fourteen once. Trust me, he has nothing to tell Andy or the Almighty ... if there's a difference between the two," he added under his breath.

"It wouldn't hurt, you know, if Rob did have a little romance in his life. Isn't junior high when a boy's fancy turns to girls? Sports, sports, sports! Isn't there anything else for him to pursue?"

"Now wait a minute! Athletics is a good character builder."

"Oh, nonsense. A boy his age should have the friendship of a girl. At least be acquainted with one. He doesn't have to be a Don Juan, but he could show some interest in the opposite sex. Didn't you at his age?"

Matt pursed his lips. At fourteen he'd already surrendered to the gay side. "That wine is clouding your vision, sweetheart. Open your eyes. He already has a love interest."

"What are you talking about? If he was seeing someone, I'd know it."

"For God's sake, woman, if it was a snake it would bite you. Can't you see? He's enthralled with his sister. Enchanted it would seem. She's got her hooks in him so deep that ..."

173

"That's enough! If you didn't have Faith to belittle you'd dream up some other …" Seeing the children approach, she cut herself short.

The room was afire with their parent's discontent, and the kids sensed it instantly. When Faith saw the empty goblet in her mother's hand and the glare in her father's eye, she curled her lip. *Why couldn't they stop bickering and put their kids' interests first?* she thought. *Better yet, why couldn't she and Robert just escape to a peaceful island?* Beside Faith stood Robert, the unwitting pawn in his parent's dispute—the chess piece certain to decide the match.

"Now, Rob, which is it going to be?" asked Julie, the wine slowing her speech. He was confused by her question, and it showed.

"What your mom is asking, Son, is whether you want to help me finish waxing the car or go to confession with her. More to the point, whether you want to go to the Pirate's game tomorrow or stay home and serve Mass. That's a no-brainer, huh?"

They'd left him no graceful retreat. He looked to Faith, and she rolled her eyes. Robert stammered, then sheepishly responded, "I'll go with what the majority thinks."

Incredulous, Matt opened his mouth to speak, but Faith leaped in. "Well, it's definitely confession and church for me. What do you say, Robbie?" No matter that she hadn't attended either in months, if entering the confines of that dreaded confessional would thwart Matt, then it was worth it.

"I guess I'll stay home then," uttered Rob with a shrug. "We can go to a game another …"

"You've got to be joking! You'd rather be with these two?" Matt glared in turn at each one of the three. Robert and Faith lowered their heads while Julie thrust her shoulders back and stood tall.

"Oh, for God's sake, quit taunting them, Matt. Just go and wax your silly car and invite a coworker to the game."

The three slowly converged, circling the wagons, as Matt stood stone-faced. His head was pounding, and his eyes squinted from the shooting pains. Exasperated, he lowered his mental fists and left the room.

As Julie backed the station wagon down the driveway, the kids watched Matt swirl the buffing cloth over the hood of his car, stopping only to take a long gulp from a sweaty beer can. He never looked at them.

"Fuck 'em!" he hissed.

❧

"Bless me, Father, for I have sinned. It's been one week since my last confession. My sins are ..."

Andy immediately recognized Julie's voice, the curtain between them concealing the alcohol on her breath. There was something alluring, yet forbidden, about her 'fessing up. At times he felt embarrassed listening to her tales, but as long as Matt was his self-appointed ward, Andy would press his ear to Julie's emotional rail.

Andy had forged life's rivers of uncertainties and wandered the deserts of loneliness that celibacy demanded, all to ensure his arrival at the Garrison family doorstep. In his mind, it was altogether fitting that he be privy to the family's inner workings. How else, he asked himself, could he minister to their needs? He had planted their seed fifteen years ago on the barren Khe Sanh plateau and now he wanted to revel in the shade of their flowering limbs. A blight, however, was wilting the leaves and shriveling the fruit. To gather a harvest he'd have to prune the deadwood. *But where should he start?* he asked himself.

Andy absolved Julie of her sins, attentive more to her tone than the content. She regretted not being there for Robert and Faith during their formative years—whether in pursuit of a social cause or a failed career, she had rendered them latchkey children. She bemoaned her schism with Matt, but justified it by labeling him as a disciplinarian who favored one child over the other. Julie felt her mission in life was to buffer the children from him. Yet she refused to ask Faith what form her stepfather's resentment took. She chose to pigeonhole Matt's behavioral traits, deluding herself into thinking that the whole of his conduct was less than the sum of its parts.

While Julie was in his confessional, Andy never asked the tough questions that might unmask her culpability ... that might cause her to abandon her weekly updates. He never quizzed her about her drinking or the impropriety of their own alliance. He ignored, almost with an air of insouciance, her desire to be with him instead of Matt. What Andy didn't know was that she routinely held him up to the kids as a role model, as a figure more attuned to fatherhood than their own dad. He didn't see that he himself was the vine, the blight, that was choking the Garrison family tree.

During Julie's confession the children stayed in the shadows, ostensibly preparing for their reconciliation with God. Faith, however, was cynical of the rite and those who administered it. Who was he, she asked, to give her absolution? Though she ached to tell someone of Matt's sexual abuse, she felt certain that no adult could be trusted. Disclosing her dark secret would mean losing Robert. She sighed. Her only solace was that Matt ignored her whenever he could monopolize Robert.

Faith was willing to loosen her ties to Robert so long as Eric, her new flame, was there to comfort her. He and Robert gave her life meaning. Her brother was a confidant for all but her most troubling secret, while Eric was her crutch against a teenager's insecurities. He was there to listen to her needs and, in turn, she cared for his. A young man's persona was to be virile and fearless, and Faith helped Eric satisfy those instincts without sharing his bed—a virtuous behavior, she reasoned, and one that didn't require a confession.

As Robert knelt beside Faith, he knew nothing of her trials. He just wanted his parents to stop bickering—to stop making him the center of their battles—and to put a halt to his sister's slip from his grasp. Surely, he thought, these weren't sins. Robert's nature was to be noncombative, to cling to his Sunday schooling that the meek would inherit the earth. Displaying such meekness, he reasoned, should never condemn him to hell.

Julie exited the confessional and lit a votive candle, then knelt in the front pew to recite her prayers of penance.

"You better go in, Sis, before Mom sees you."

"No."

"What do you mean?" he whispered. "Mom expects you to go to confession. You said you would."

"Well, I changed my mind. Why should you or I have to open up to Father Patterson? He's just like every other adult. All they do is snoop into your life and then tell you what to do."

"Yeah, but …"

"No buts about it, Robbie. How do you know he won't blab what you confessed to Mom?"

As the door to the confessional opened the children crouched, hidden from Andy's view by the aid of a pipe organ that adorned the rear of the church. Andy moved up the side aisle, past the first seven Stations of the Cross, his eyes fixed on Julie's penitent pose. Her silky hair was draped over one shoulder and hung between her breasts, while her forehead lay cradled in her palms. He knelt beside her, before the statue of the Blessed Mother, and placed his hand at the small of her back. He couldn't help noticing that her hair had the same color and repose as the Virgin's image.

Faith scowled at Andy's display of affection and grabbed Robert's hand. "Come on, we're going." She guided him through the vestibule, jerking his arm when he reached for the holy water font. Once clear of the church she persuaded him to accompany her to the creek. It was there, along the north bank of Oil Creek, that they had their hideaway—a hollow amongst the trees and shrubs that sheltered a small pond. With slabs of shale for benches and water bugs, frogs, and toads for companions, they could enjoy solitude and the company of each other. Here, under nature's green canopy, they were free to compare thoughts and to catalog their dreams.

ಬ

"I'm sorry that you and Matt are at odds."

He shifted his hand to her shoulder then caressed her earlobe, which was graced by a simple gold ring. His breath fanned the loose strands of her hair as he shifted closer to her.

"Please, Andrew! The children."

"What?"

"They're with me. You just heard their confessions. Remember?"

"What are you talking about? Neither of them made a confession."

Julie abruptly stood up and scanned the church, like a Field Marshal atop a tank turret, then walked the aisles. When her search had failed she returned to Andy's side and sighed.

177

"I can't believe they took off. I don't understand what's gotten into Faith. She's bent on defying grownups—and now she's got Robert doing it."

"It's in a teenager's blood to be defiant. You know that. It's you I'm more worried about—really, about you and Matt. There must be a solution to this impasse."

Her soft hand gripped his. Intermittently, as he made his points, he squeezed her fingers and thumbed their painted nails. With her, he could take on any form that her emotional state desired. Temperament and business travel had combined to make Matt the black sheep, his frequent absences an easy target for her ridicule. Andy's dilemma was whether to stand by or intervene. In shielding Julie from Matt, in becoming her protector, he knew he'd seek the right that went with the responsibility: the right of passage into her bed. *Should I lunge?* he asked himself. *Will a safety net catch me if my timing is off or her grip unsure?* To cross the Rubicon and take Julie once again was the paradisiacal vision he had wrestled with for months… and her weekly confessions only magnified his inner struggle.

Julie understood Andrew as she, too, had been leading a celibate life. Her relationship with Matt, like Andy's with the Church, had fallen into disrepair. Andy need only ask, she thought, and she'd grovel at his feet. Man had instituted the law that bound this priest to a brideless marriage, so if a man broke that law, she reasoned, then he should answer only to another man. No God would cast him into hell for having broken that man-made law … no God, she felt, should ask that their love be held forever in limbo. *If only he'd ask,* she thought to herself.

∞

Robbie kissed her on the cheek. Their sibling love seemed boundless. Lying outstretched on the warm rock, he hoped that their journey together into adulthood would not diminish their bond. It was natural that Robert wanted her undivided affections. At his tender age, he lived only for the day. He was blissfully unaware that there were other men in her life. Some of them came to hold her hand and gaze into her hazel eyes, some to flirt and dream of kissing her, while one

178

came by night to destroy her dignity. She was prey for men, young and old, and Robert was oblivious to them all.

ॐ

Matt floored his maroon sedan up Interstate-79, annoyed that insects were plastering its freshly waxed finish. He had spent the day alone, watching his Pittsburgh Pirates take it on the chin. His belly was full of beer and hot dogs and his mind with anger toward Faith. "The bitch should've kept her mouth shut," he grumbled. "She had no call to butt in … no right taking Robert away from me like that." When he arrived home he saw that the station wagon was gone, then he remembered that Julie's Bible study group met on Sunday evenings. He gulped the last beer in the ice chest, then relieved himself down the garage floor drain. The sun was just setting, and his fatigue from the heat and being behind the wheel had taken their toll.

"Anybody home?" he yelled. He halted at the kitchen sink, belched loudly, then took a couple of aspirin. He hollered once more, again hearing no response, then he started up the stairs … that was before he noticed Faith's foot, nails painted, dangling from behind the hallway door. She was on the phone, whispering. Matt abruptly turned upon her.

"Where's your mother and brother?" he bellowed, swaying.

Startled, Faith clamped her hand over the receiver. "Mom's at church, and Rob is doing homework at a friend's house." She lifted her palm from the mouthpiece to mutter something.

Matt grinned. His urge to retire was suddenly usurped by the urge to get even. He continued up the stairs, to Faith's relief, then quietly descended the back stairway. He wanted to know who held her attentions, to know the chink in her emotional armor. He knew this wasn't a girlfriend on the line, and her closing remark and long-distance kiss confirmed his suspicion that she and her caller had enjoyed more than hand-holding strolls through Burgress Park.

"Who were you gaga over just now?" Matt asked sternly, emerging from the shadows.

Faith jumped and looked warily into his glassy stare. "Just a friend."

He burped. "I'd say by your good-bye that he's more than a friend, young lady."

Faith detested his spying. "I don't see why I can't have a private conversation."

"Conversation? Sounded more like two dogs in heat. Why don't you do a striptease the next time you're talking to him? Or maybe he's already seen that." She bit down hard on her lip.

"Eric is a gentleman. He just likes to flirt. I don't see why my friendships have to concern you."

"Because this is the Eighty's, daughter. Remember? People like to put their actions where their mouths are, especially if it feels good. From what I just heard, I'd say you've been seeing plenty of action. And Eric must feel good about that. Don't forget, your business is *always* my business!"

She frowned. It was pointless to argue. Any objection would be overruled. He had tried her case before a jury of one and made his decision. "I've got homework to do," she uttered and moved toward the landing, then she took the steps by two. Matt wasn't far behind. She closed her bedroom door and stood behind it, but he pushed violently against it. She stumbled backward and fell on her bed.

"I'm not finished, girl. And don't storm away from me like that!"

He paused to take in the wall posters, along with the cutesy trinkets and beads that adorned her dressers. She'd papered the walls in a bold floral pattern, and her pink bedspread, frilly pillowcases, and cluttered vanity signaled her ascent into womanhood, her cosmetics producing a perfumed lair.

"I don't like it when you manipulate Robert."

"What are you talking about?"

"I'm talking about that little shenanigan you pulled to get him to blow off our baseball outing. And don't give me that shit that he's a free spirit."

"You're just jealous that he chose Mom and me over you. Any freshman psych major could see that."

His eyes narrowed, and she knew she'd lit his fuse. Now it was just a fretful countdown before the explosion. There was no taking back the words and she was too frightened to expand on their truths. Matt focused first on the hamster cage and the rodent running tirelessly on its wheel, then he saw Robert's class portrait angled toward her pillow. Squinting, Matt read the inscription "I love you, Sis." He suddenly felt the weight of his own confinement—how Faith had jailed him … like she had her hamster.

"So, you think I'm jealous? Well, you might be right. But I'm not here to get mad about it. I'm here to get even."

He sprang forward and leaned on her frame. She resisted, but his grip tightened. He tugged at her tie-dye top and yanked her bra free. She squirmed, while Shamrock growled and barked. Even he knew something was wrong but, like her, he was helpless.

"So, you've even turned the dog against me. Silly mutt!" He kicked the animal, sending it howling from the room. Then he reached out to turn Robert's photo face down and to extinguish her bed light. He didn't want to see her, nor give her any comfort in seeing her brother.

As quickly as the contest started it was over. Matt emerged triumphant, and, while she lay motionless, he collected his clothes. Her face was expressionless, her eyes fixed in a thousand-yard stare. He shook her forcefully and turned her head so her eyes would meet his. For a moment, her thoughts were of Eric galloping toward her atop a white steed. Finally, her glassy pupils gave way to a focused look.

"Keep your mouth shut. Say one word and I'll have you thrown into a nut house. Nobody will believe a thing you say. Nobody! Try to hurt me and you know who I'll take away."

Matt held up Robert's picture, then dropped it beside her pillow. She clutched it and he chuckled, then growled at the dog. Within minutes he was in bed, snoring. His self-denial—that well-oiled escape mechanism that he'd used since Nam—was serving him well.

Matt woke with a mild hangover and noticed that Julie's bed was unruffled. He comforted himself with the proposition that had she known of his crime she'd have killed him in his sleep. He lay in bed, rubbing his eyes and scratching himself as he monitored the quiet. Anxiety etched a furrow above his brow and his jaw muscles tightened when he heard Julie enter Faith's room. Their words were muted, indiscernible. Matt knew he'd overreacted the night before, but Faith's behavior had brought back detestable memories of his stepsister, Janice. She'd hurt him so badly—scuttling his relationship with his father—that Matt wanted only to lash out at Faith, whom he saw as

181

Janice's contemporary.

"Hope you feel better soon, Hon. I'll call school and let them know you're sick. Get some rest now. I'll fix you breakfast when you come down." Julie could see that Faith was aloof and, had she looked closer, she would have seen Matt's underwear lying beside her bed.

At hearing Julie's words, a smile crossed Matt's lips. He'd spun the revolver's cylinder, pulled the trigger, and once more had beaten the odds. If Faith was intimidated enough to remain silent, then she might finally distance herself from Robert. That triumphant vision was all the pumping up that Matt needed to ready himself for his scheduled business trip. With gusto, he bid Julie and Robert an uxorious farewell, pecking Julie on the cheek and sandwiching the boy's hand in his with a hearty two-fisted handshake. In three days time he'd return, then his ascension into fatherhood could begin without further interference from Faith.

ℴ

"Faith. Faith, honey. It's time you ate something. I don't want you taking root up there."

Julie's call to Faith to rejoin the living was not the first. She had been moping about since her father departed, and neither her mother nor brother could capture her attentions. She was quick, though, to answer the phone so Julie reasoned she was well—just held in the grip of a moody menstrual cycle. Still, it was vexing for Julie. It wasn't like her daughter to be indifferent when Robert was vying for her interest.

Faith put her pen down and cradled her head. Her diary entry had been long, its narrative her sole relief valve. It chronicled her suffering, not only at the hands of her stepfather but from the peer pressure of dating. To read her journal was to hear her conscience, to hear her conscience was to know her hurt, and to know her hurt was to understand her hell—a hell she would share with no one but her guardian angel.

Tonight her diary account spoke of Eric. Like most young men, his fantasies were launched by glandular commands. Women might feign headaches to thwart men, but Eric complained that he had them because his "manhood" was unfulfilled. Faith understood Eric's

182

craving, but not her father's. The one was complimentary, the other grotesque. She caved into the one out of fear, to the other she held out in the hope that he was Mr. Right.

Julie characterized her daughter's behavior as being typical for a teenager. Nothing suggested a sinister agenda. No evidence of drugs, alcohol, or promiscuity. She seemed a good girl, though understandably perplexed by youthful insecurities. Julie recalled that as a teenager she had traveled that same windy road. Her contemplative powers, though, were too immersed in the spiritual world—and with the priest who served it up regularly on her plate—to see Faith's rocky road. And any key that might unlock her past had long since been discarded.

All Robert knew was that something was dragging his sister away, and he couldn't stop it. Adrift in a sea of confusion, he had no buoy to anchor his spirits. Unlike Matt, who hated his two stepsisters, Robert truly loved his. Faith had never caused him pain or anxiety … until now—and for that he took the blame. He was determined to uncover the source of her melancholy or to exhaust himself, like a salmon swimming upstream to spawn, in trying.

"Mom, how come Faith is always in her room? All she does is listen to music and talk on the phone."

"Sometimes that's the way girls are, Robert. Remember what I told you about women and their monthly cycles?"

"Yeah, but it's worse than ever. Are you sure, Mom?"

"She's also discovered boys. Trust me. I was sixteen once myself."

"But why can't she …?"

"It'll have to keep," Julie stammered as she rushed to primp in the hallway mirror. "I've got a Parish Council meeting, and I don't want to be late."

Unsatisfied with his mother's explanation, Robert went to Faith's bedroom to search for the diary he knew she kept. Yet once in her room, he couldn't bring himself to violate her space. To read the journal was to see her dark side and, like his mother, Robert refused to probe. So he bolted from the house and headed to the business district to peer through the pizza shop window. Beyond the large pane and the garlic-laced aroma, he hoped to sight Faith. She frequented the shop with Eric, but not today. His concern heightened, fearful that she might be alone with her troubled thoughts.

He made for the creek and their chapel amongst the cattails and pussy willows. As he navigated the bank, he stooped to snatch a crayfish. When he entered the vaulted clearing his sister was perched atop her customary rock. He lowered the crayfish into the shallow pool and sat beside her to catch his breath. She flung a pebble into the still water and they watched as the ripples fanned outward, then he inched his hand over to hers and cupped it firmly.

"I hope you weren't following me."

"Don't be mad, Sis. When I couldn't find you at the pizza shop, I figured you might be here. I guess … I was worried about you."

She smiled and squeezed his hand. She knew she'd been ignoring him, but her thoughts were simply overcrowded, near paralysis. To tell him of Matt's abuse was impossible. Even if sworn to secrecy through some mystical rite, Robert would eventually breakdown. But she knew she couldn't shoo him away empty-handed. He had come to comfort her, and to give him no hint of her pain, to let him think that he'd only scratched the surface, would lead him to dig deeper. She wanted him as a companion, not as a relentless sleuth.

"You're kind to worry about me, Robbie. Things have been pretty tough lately."

"I sort of figured that, Sis. I mean, you've been awful quiet, you know. Besides, I don't believe everything Mom says." Faith looked up, her forehead furrowed.

"What do you mean?"

"You see, Mom says it's just one of those girl things. You know … your period. But I think it's more. Lots more."

"Nice to see she's given this a lot of thought. You know, Rob, adults can be ridiculously shallow. Can't they see beyond their own noses?" Her red nose, Faith wanted to say, as she thought of her mother's drinking.

"Well, Dad sure can't figure out what I want. Only what he wants seems to count."

His statement plunged like a dagger into Faith's consciousness. *Only what he wants. What he wants. His wants!* That ugly truth wormed through her mind, boring deeper with each silent refrain. She shook her head wildly, as though a bee had lighted on her nose.

"But I get sick and tired of the peer pressure, too."

"Are you talking about Eric?"

"And my classmates. They want things that I don't want to give."
She hoped he wouldn't ask any specifics.

"Hold out for what you believe in, Faith. Don't let anyone tell you
what to do. Not grownups or kids … nobody. OK? I get fed up, too,
with all the crap that people throw my way. Nobody cares what you or
I want. Not Dad, not Mom, not our friends. Nobody."

Robert was impassioned—inflamed—driven by the accumulated
hurts that he and his sister had suffered. She had struck a responsive
cord, unleashing a coiled spring within him, and he rapid-fired his
indignation.

"How come we get hassled? We don't ask others to live our lives,
just to help us out a little along the way. And what do they do? They
dump on us. On you and me, Sis! I'm sick of it. I can't stomach another
person wanting me to be something I'm not. I wanna look after my
needs … and yours. And nobody, I tell you, is going to stop me!" His
arms flailed as he spoke, his teeth often clenched.

She was surprised by his ferocity. His resentment was refreshing,
and she understood it completely. To her amazement he lambasted
Father Andy and, for the first time, questioned their mother's
relationship with the priest. Again and again Faith nodded in agreement
to his claims, her silence fueling his fiery oration. His criticisms were
like a blazing machine gun, its barrel red-hot from the nonstop volley.
Every adult was suspect, every classmate untrustworthy, every person
save his sister was to be doubted. Slowly, like a runner who'd
completed a grueling marathon, he regained his composure. Robert,
though, wanted an outward sign that would cement their sibling bond.
A simple celebration of their love—something less than marriage but
more than a kiss—was what this wide-eyed boy of fourteen wanted.

"Sis, I want you to pledge to me like I've done to you." Uncertainty
crossed her face, and she squinted with a mild frown.

"You know I agree with everything you said. It's just you and me.
To hell with everyone else!"

"Then let's seal that promise by becoming blood brothers. You
know, like Indians did in the Old West."

"Uh, gee, Rob … I don't know. Seems barbaric. Can't you just
accept my word?"

185

He lowered his head. The whole idea seemed silly to Faith but nothing else would mollify him. She hastily reasoned, though, that if she could forfeit her body to her father, then she could certainly consent to her brother's benign request. Suddenly, the idea became romantic. It had a simplicity that transcended the calculated affections shown by adults. *Oh, why not?* she concluded.

"OK, little brother, but it better not hurt."

Robert's eyes sparkled as he took the penknife from his pocket and exposed the blade. Faith winced at its gleaming edge but said nothing. He gently clasped her hand and turned it palm side up. The creases lining the hollow of her soft palm were paper thin, her lifeline deep and long. With a flourish, he brought the knife's edge to bear on the heel just below her wrist. He guided the blade into her skin, and blood oozed to the surface. She was fascinated by the swelling bead and how it shimmered. Immediately he cut himself, then took his hand and pressed it to hers. With their palms clasped tightly, they raised their hands high as though in prayer, blood trickling down their young wrists.

They rose from their kneeling position, and she licked the wound and pressed her finger over the shallow incision. Though she had been willing to suffer her hardships alone, she could never deny him the satisfaction of coming to her aid.

"See, Sis? That wasn't so bad. It's the only way we can share our pain. Now we're officially blood relations. Nothing Dad says or does can come between us. He can call you my half-sister, but to me you're my blood sister. We'll share our pain and our gain."

Chapter 13

What will I do if he wants to make love? I can't lose him. Those thoughts plagued Faith as Eric snuggled beside her, his fingers twirling her silky hair. He'd been patient, but time and again she had rebuffed him. He was special in her eyes and had ignited a flame the others hadn't. She wanted to keep him, but the flame was flickering. A wisp of chill air might extinguish it.

She thought she could handle suitors her own age, but their methods were almost as debasing as her father's—only their motivations differed. Eventually she came to see all men except Eric as predators. She dreaded the time when he'd discover that she wasn't a virgin, wasn't the pristine flower with petals still intact that he'd want to marry. In idolizing Eric, she ignored her male classmates who had gone before him. Had she removed her blinders, she'd have seen them marching at his flanks, cheering him on to the same victory they had enjoyed.

"Ah, this movie sucks. What are we gonna do until the second feature?"

Eric knew that the first feature was a bust, and he hoped he could capitalize on it. He couldn't stand another necking session without consummation. He needed, wanted, and expected more, and he was frustrated with masturbating to his fantasies. From what his buddies said, there was no reason for his desires to go unmet.

Faith said nothing, but she knew what was being asked of her.

"Here, Honey, have a swallow of this. It'll warm your insides."

Not wanting to disappoint him, Faith took a drink from the flask. The whiskey stung her tongue and burned her throat. She passed the leather-sheathed canteen back, and he took a swig.

"Here, try this. It's smooth." He handed her a lighted joint, proud of its tight wrap. She'd tried marijuana before, but its unpredictable high left her wary. To please him, though, she took a deep drag, then clouded the pickup's cabin as she coughed and hacked. They passed the cigarette back and forth, and soon Faith was reeling.

"Whoa, this is heavy," she said with a twinge of apprehension.

Eric smiled, thankful he'd spent his money wisely. They both felt as though they were floating about the cab, their conversation leaping from one silly thought to the next. Eric claimed he was having an out-of-body experience and chuckled incessantly, drooling. Faith's head was a tabernacle of good and bad perceptions, but this high was unleashing the bad. She kept thinking of how she'd abandoned Robert to avoid her stepfather's wrath, how she'd cast off his line and set him adrift. *Why,* she asked herself, *couldn't Robbie just enjoy his freedom?* The why became apparent when her introspection shifted to her parents behavior. It upset her that Matt was monopolizing Robert, but her success at halting his abuse was too welcome for her to focus on Robert's needs. As for her mother … Faith saw her as a lush who'd given her heart to Andy and her soul to the Church … as someone who answered problems with platitudes and biblical lore—leaving her only Eric to cling to.

He kissed her on the ear—his words a welcome respite from her unwelcome thoughts—and she leaned into his advance. "I've waited so long for you. You're all the woman I've ever wanted." His hands caressed her, his breath warming her earlobe. Finally, she unzipped his trousers, then stroked him with the same passion his tongue did her mouth. Suddenly he was on top of her.

"I've never done this before," she uttered, hair clinging to her moist forehead.

"I love you, Faith," he murmured as his thrusts accelerated and his embrace tightened.

Repeating that refrain he climaxed, his body shuddering. She hoped that what had eluded her with the others would come true with Eric, but Matt's ghost left her unresponsive and Eric was too ecstatic to notice that she didn't share his bliss. His conquest was fulfilled. He had "gotten in her shorts" as his buddies predicted, and he, like them, soon boasted of the feat. Faith had again been devalued, a pawn to gratify a man.

ॐ

Eric took her a few more times, found her enthusiasm wanting, and abandoned her. He had become her Judas, a Janus-faced lover who helped to hasten her fall. Faith soon felt that without a lover, no matter how shallow his motives, she had nothing. So she gave herself to any man who would utter, "I love you." She lacked the moral compass needed to navigate her Bermuda Triangle of emotions. Her family knew something was amiss but, because of their own distractions, each refused to enter into her world.

Matt was busy reveling in his hard-fought victory to overcome Faith's hold on Robert. His scorched-earth game plan had worked, and he was too busy floating in a limpid pool of contentment to see the mud Faith was wallowing in. His knack for denial ensured he'd never acknowledge his role in destroying her self-esteem.

Julie was so consumed with her religious revival that she had lost sight of Faith's earthly survival. In her world of biblical allusions and a vengeful God, she was unwilling to intervene—unwilling to question providence. Like Matt, she exercised her own form of denial. Her axiom was "Let God's will be done" and if His wrath fell upon Faith, then she viewed it as her penance for having been an unfit mother.

Robert, meanwhile, was too centered on being a father's boy and obtaining the car keys to make the detour into his big sister's world. In growing apart physically and socially, they had also grown apart in spirit and emotion. He had become one-dimensional, seemingly incapable of showering affection on more than one family member at a time. It was a desolate situation for Faith, but a necessary one if Matt was to be kept out of her life.

ಶಿ

"I don't see why she can't stay home," protested Julie. "Every night she's out, her lips and eyes painted like a harlot's." Matt looked to the heavens and shook his head.

"For Christ's sake, she's eighteen! Lighten up, the girl is an adult."

"It ought to concern both of us when our daughter comes home smelling of beer and cigarettes. And have you seen those skirts she wears?"

"Sure, I'd rather she didn't smoke. But if she can't see the evils of smoking through my experience then she'll never catch on. And let's face it, if she can't see the evils of drinking through your experience, then ..."

"That's enough! I enjoy an occasional wine, but I'm no lush!" She nearly spilled her wineglass as she lifted herself from her bay window rocker.

"Yeah, yeah. I'm the perfect father and you're the perfect mother. Ward and June Cleaver, right? So why are we having this conversation? If we were so squared away, Faith would be entering a convent and Robert the seminary. Well, I've got news for you—neither of them is headed down the yellow brick road."

"But you're her father! Isn't it your place to protect her from men? To shield her from their lustful ways?" She blotted out a flashback of her own father, steadfastly refusing to cross the mental bridge that linked these two generations of molesters.

Matt scowled. "OK, let's see if I've got this straight. You can drink yourself into a stupor, hang around Andy like some groupie, recite hollow prayers morning, noon, and night, and then piously write off your role as mother of the house ... and all because you spill your guts in the confessional each week? You've pickled your brain, woman."

"That's preposterous! Don't blame your failings on me. Where were you when the kids and I needed you? You and your silly business trips. You abandoned us as surely as Pilate did Jesus ... like Peter did Christ ... like the Prodigal Son did his father. You've conveniently washed your hands of the whole mess and now you're going to stand by while your daughter is crucified."

"Can the biblical crap." Her mention of the Prodigal Son escaped him. Had it registered, he'd have lambasted her for an allusion he knew was of Andy's making. "Everything you think, say, or do has to have some scriptural overtone. Talk English, will ya? Why can't you just admit that you've been a piss-poor mother?"

"You're mean-spirited! Here I am pleading ... begging ... that you do something for our daughter. And ..." She began crying and moved toward the kitchen.

Throughout their argument, Robert had been sitting on the second floor landing, shaking his head in disgust.

"Well, I'll tell you one thing. I don't give a rat's ass what Faith does.

She can camp out on a street corner with a mattress strapped to her back for all I care—she's Dan's seed … and a bad one at that! You should've been more discriminating about who you slept with."

"You're no better than Satan for talking like that."

"Yeah, yeah. Color me black and you white. And don't forget the horns, pitchfork, and spiked tail. Oh, and paint a pair of wings on your backside 'cause you'll need 'em where you're going. What a crock! Wake up, will ya?"

"Lord willing, I'm going to heaven … because you've surely been my earthly penance. God won't martyr me by forcing me to spend an eternity with you."

"You've lost it, woman. Why don't you run along now to Andy and confess all your rinky-dink sins? I know the real you, and there's no penance suitable for your offenses."

They parted, their schism unbridgeable, while Robert slipped out and made for the creek. He needed a place to reflect. It upset him terribly that Matt would not accept Faith. Then and there, he decided that he could no longer be a silent witness to his sister's fall. He had tried the rough-and-tumble world his father demanded, even breaking his leg playing JV football. He had ransomed his soul for his driver's license, the car keys that gave him access to his buddies, and the chance at basking in some fatherly adulation. Instead of feeling good about it, though, he felt their father/son relationship was the root cause for his sister's decline. While he knelt prayerfully in their hideaway, Robert reaffirmed his earlier blood oath to Faith, then he fell asleep. He had become increasingly lethargic; his dad chastised him a day earlier for dogging it during a baseball tryout. He'd be a senior in the fall and he wanted to stay with his team—even if he was a second-stringer—but he felt so physically washed out that he wasn't sure he'd make the cut.

The following day Matt left town on business. Characteristically, neither parent could find time for Faith's emotional needs—they were too busy being the problem, too busy blaming one another for the family's problems. Robert wanted to leap into this void, but, instead, he landed in bed. Doctor Golden, the family physician, found his lymph glands swollen and his throat inflamed and declared him a victim of mononucleosis. Matt was disappointed that his son wouldn't be ready for spring baseball, but content knowing he'd been sidelined by the "kissing disease." *Surely,* he thought, *I've raised a stud after all.*

&

"What do you mean, Robert was 'admitted for observation'? What is Golden telling you?" Matt was alarmed; not the sort of news a parent wanted to hear, particularly when away from home and the messenger was the parish pastor.

"Julie asked me to call you, Matt. You know how excitable she can be." It was vintage Julie to enlist Andy whenever she didn't want to talk to Matt.

"Forget that," Matt retorted. "He looked fine when I left. I thought he was on the mend."

"Everyone's surprised. Nobody thought he'd get pneumonia."

"Pneumonia! What's going on here, Andy?"

"It's just a temporary setback. He'll be coming home soon."

Andy tried to sound upbeat. He'd seen men perish in combat, but Robert's threat, the bullet he was trying to dodge, seemed different. Springtime was a period of renewal, a time to shed nature's gray and don a colorful and vibrant spirit—to Andy's way of thinking, a time to wear Joseph's Cloak of Many Colors and rejoice in life. Instead, Robert was bedridden, gaunt, and wearing a bleached white hospital gown. As the Pharaoh had summoned Joseph, so Julie now summoned Andrew to interpret her dream about Robert. To him, though, there was nothing in her dark premonitions that coincided with what a merciful God should have in store for a boy. Andy's optimism, however, wasn't shared by the intern assigned to Robert's case.

Peter Martin, a recent med school grad, had an uncomfortable suspicion concerning Robert's ailment. He had toyed with doing his internship and residency in Philadelphia, but his dream of being a country doctor led him to the corridors of Titusville Memorial. He enjoyed his training but found his colleagues woefully uninformed about sexually transmitted diseases—understandable, he reasoned, in an oasis so far removed from the decay of the big cities.

"Nurse, order an enzyme-linked immunosorbent assay for the Garrison boy."

192

"But Doctor Martin, that's for detecting AIDS. Is that … that what you suspect?"

"Just want to eliminate all the variables. Come on, work with me here."

"But we'll have to send the specimen to Erie for analysis."

"I understand, so let's get it done stat." He smiled in a comical fashion to defuse her obvious concern. He didn't want any wild rumors to erupt among the nurses.

"No doubt I'm all wet, but I want to cover the bases. And say nothing to the boy, Nurse. I hate false alarms."

When the results came back positive, Doctor Martin had the test repeated. Like the captain of a crippled vessel, he had to confirm the severity of the torpedo's damage before giving the irrevocable order to abandon ship. When the second test authenticated the first, Martin ordered a Western Blot Test. When it, too, came back positive he knew his hunch was correct: Robert was HIV positive. When informed of the diagnosis, Doctor Golden, in disbelief, asked a battery of skeptical questions, but soon deferred to the industrious intern's training and accepted the verdict. Unlike Martin, however, who was clinical and detached, Golden was emotional and involved. He was dumbfounded at how the lad could have contracted the virus, but one thing he was certain of: this savvy intern would be there to help him break the horrific news to Robert's family.

Robert's health ebbed and flowed in the days preceding the doctor's diagnosis. Slowly, he overcame the opportunistic infection that had triggered his pneumonia. His family visited him regularly, Andy diligently including him in his daily rounds, while Matt postponed his business travels to be at his side. Late on an overcast Thursday afternoon, Doctor Golden ushered the family into a consultation room. The somber look on the faces of Doctors Martin and Golden only fueled Matt's runaway imagination.

"Matt, Julie … uh, Faith, we've asked you in to discuss Robert's condition," said Golden in a fatherly manner. "I believe you've all met Doctor Peter Martin. He's been assisting me with Robert's treatment." They nodded in unison, Faith adding an admiring grin, for she enjoyed Peter's engaging conversation. "Robert's immediate condition has improved, and I expect to release him shortly, but …"

"What do you mean by, 'immediate condition'?" interrupted Matt.

"Well, that's why we're here. Robert's pneumonia is more a symptom than the actual problem." Golden was tiptoeing. He knew the ice was thin where Matt was concerned.

"I don't understand. Whaddaya saying?" Matt shifted to the edge of his seat, his hands clasping the armrests.

"Let Doctor Golden finish," said Julie. She, too, had inched forward in her seat.

"What Doctor Golden is intimating, Mr. Garrison," interjected Martin in a businesslike tone, "is that your son has tested positive for antibodies to the AIDS virus. Please ... Mr. Garrison, sit ... sit back down," sputtered the youthful intern, his hands waving as though warding off an attacker. "I understand your alarm, but I'm not finished. Please!"

Terror and confusion were etched on the family's faces, Matt's eyes like saucers.

"When Robert didn't respond to normal medications, I had his blood screened using the HTLV-III/LAV antibody test. I've studied the virus, and Robert had many of the classic symptoms."

"But how could he have AIDS?!" blurted Matt. "He's not a drug user or a ... a ... homosexual. There's no way!" Golden had moved from center stage to take up a position behind Julie.

"Please! Let me finish. You need—we need—to have the whole story before anyone jumps to conclusions." Martin subconsciously rested his hand on Faith's forearm. She was trembling.

"A positive antibody test can mean many things. It could mean that he's immune to HTLV-III/LAV ... or that he's healthy but a carrier of the virus ... or that he's well today but could later develop overt AIDS. And, lastly, the results could be a false positive. That is, he might not have been exposed to the virus, but something in his blood specimen reacted with the test system to cause a positive result."

"That must be it!" blurted Julie, a twinge of relief in her eyes.

Matt sat still, shaking his head as he ran his fingers through his hair.

"We don't know that," Martin said. "I realize this is all terribly confusing, but there's so much we don't know about the virus."

"Yes, but what about the obvious, Doctor," was Matt's rejoinder. "What if he truly has AIDS?"

"Oh, nonsense, Matt." Julie was almost hysterical. "It's just a simple mix-up ... something haywire in the test results. I can't believe our little Robert ... our baby ... has AIDS. He's ... he's too innocent to ..." She wept and Golden rested his hands on her shoulders.

"It's premature to make that assumption, Mr. Garrison," said Martin. "He's on the mend right now, and we'll continue to observe him closely, but if we confirm he's HIV positive, then ..."

Faith broke down. She hadn't sobbed so forcefully since Eric betrayed her. Martin slid closer toward her, and she rested her head on his shoulder. He put his arm around her, feeling clumsy as her consoler, but since her parents offered her no comfort he felt compelled to fill the void. Matt abruptly left the room, stone-faced, giving only a furtive glance at Julie. He hesitated as he passed Robert's room, then quickened his pace. His head was spinning, his stomach churning.

"Does Robert know?" Julie asked Martin as she blew her nose.

"Yes, Mrs. Garrison. I told him a half-hour ago, though I doubt it sank in. I need more time with him. This may sound harsh, but I'd like you not to see him just now. I owe him the professional courtesy of answering his questions before his family descends on him."

Julie nodded and let Doctor Golden's hand slip through hers. Her eyes remained fixed on the tile floor, never peering up at Faith. Martin squeezed Faith's hand and rose, then motioned that he was returning to Robert's room. Faith stood on tiptoes to whisper in his ear, pleading to accompany him. He reluctantly consented, hoping that Julie wouldn't notice his favoritism.

Oxygen tubes protruded from Robert's nostrils and looped around his head like the reins of a horse. Faith, relieved to see that he was breathing comfortably, stepped forward to clasp his flaccid forearm. He smiled, then withdrew when he saw Martin.

"He told you. Huh, Sis?"

"Yes, Robbie. It's horrible! It's got to be some kind of monstrous mistake. There's no way it ..." She shuddered, bawling as though she were standing over his freshly covered grave. Martin feared her hysterics would rob him of a meaningful exchange with Robert, so he clutched Faith by the shoulders and muttered into her ear. Tears streaming, she nodded and left the room. Doctor Golden entered, and he and Martin turned their attention to Robert.

195

"Don't worry. She'll get over it. My sister's tough. Real tough!" His claim was convincing, and the doctors admired how much he loved her.

"How about you, Rob? How are you taking it? Has it sunk in yet?" asked Doctor Martin. A calm had descended over Robert—less because he understood his situation than because his years with Matt and Julie had fostered a fatalistic outlook.

"I know what you're talking about, Doc. At least I think I do. I mean, I've heard about it on the news, but why hasn't someone discovered a cure?"

"I wish I could tell you there is one, but the medical world is stumped," said Martin.

"But I don't know how I caught it. That's what confuses me. I don't even know anybody who knows someone who has it."

The boy's innocence only fueled Martin's frustration. Yet if there was a truth to be told that might shed some light, he wanted to ferret it out. Robert knew he couldn't contract it from a kiss, a handshake, or a toilet seat and had said as much to Martin, who respected his intelligence and treated him like an adult.

"Lots of things—we call them behavioral patterns or high-risk practices—can cause someone to test HIV positive. It's prevalent among bisexuals and gay men, along with intravenous drug users who share needles. Then there are heterosexual partners of AIDS carriers, infants born to mothers who've tested positive for HIV or AIDS, and hemophiliacs or others who need blood transfusions. Beyond that, there aren't any other ways to contract the virus."

As Robert listened to Martin his bewilderment mounted. He fit none of those categories. He found girls attractive, but had never ventured beyond pecking one on the cheek, and the thought of having sex with a guy repulsed him—"Gross me out!" he exclaimed to the doctors. Nothing answered their burning question, nothing lifted the burden of proof from their shoulders. Suddenly—excitedly—Robert remembered his leg injury—the fracture he'd suffered while playing JV football the previous year.

"I've got it, Doctor Martin! I know how I must've caught it!"

Both doctors leaned forward, as though an insider stock market tip was about to be revealed.

"Go on. Tell us, Robert," said the intern, his interests whetted. Golden stood bobbing his head, like a chicken pecking at an ear of corn.

"Last fall I busted my leg in a football game. We were playing a high school in Erie, and I landed at the bottom of a pileup. I was screaming bloody murder for everyone to get off me, and then I heard the bone crack, just like in the movie *King Kong* when he breaks the Tyrannosaur's jaw. Next thing I knew they were carrying me off on a stretcher. It was a compound fracture. You know, one where the bone sticks out through the skin." He pointed toward his left shin.

"I bet it hurt plenty," said Martin. Both doctors nodded and Robert grimaced.

"Well, I passed out in the ambulance, and I lost enough blood that they gave me a transfusion." Quiet satisfaction crossed Robert's blanched face. The doctors looked wistfully at one another, the younger scissoring his lower jaw in thought. Then he whispered to the older, who responded with a frown. The intern knew that receiving contaminated blood under such circumstances was remote.

"Well, Rob, we'll certainly look into it. In the meantime, keep thinking about the other possibilities I mentioned. Even if it's something you're embarrassed about. OK? Will you do that for us?"

Robert, looking disappointed, signaled his consent with a dip of his pimply chin.

"How about taking a nap now? I'll be back later," Martin said with a fatherly inflection.

Following the consultation, Julie moved swiftly to the hospital chapel where she knelt, hands tightly clasped, to offer a litany of prayers. Her petitions were rapid—polished as though endlessly rehearsed—yet she felt empty. Down deep, where instincts take hold and cognitive thinking ends, she knew her son had AIDS. In her martyred mindset, it was part of a larger punishment—God's way of cleansing the family of their Original Sin. A sin for which she accepted ownership, just as she accepted her childhood molestation as being preordained.

As the Rosary beads slid through her fingertips, Julie cataloged her contributions to the family's sin. She knew she had come between God and man by her pernicious relationship with Andy. It was a sin against the Lord and mankind—against God because she had intervened, like a homewrecker, in His marriage to Andy; against man because she had stolen the sanctity of their holy man. She had shorn Andy's mane as Delilah had Samson's, leaving him powerless to fulfill his priestly vows.

A smile of contentment crossed her lips, then she admonished herself. Less than a fortnight had passed since she and Andy had made love. The Parish Council meeting they attended that evening had been long, and Andrew's tensions were high. Julie didn't leave home intending to sleep with him, but Matt was out of town and the children were preoccupied. Events and emotions unfolded in a way she found impossible to foresee or to control. She had promised herself that she would not backslide, but when he looked at her during the meeting she felt his stress and the need to ease his yoke.

It was the only time they'd made love in the rectory. Though it was his home, Andy knew that to use the rectory for carnal pursuits was an affront to the parishioners who paid for its upkeep. That night, however, was different; that night he was angry over the demands of his job and feeling sorry for himself. It proved convenient, almost satisfying, for him to spite his congregation by seeking the comfort of her embrace. He talked to her of leaving the priesthood, of escaping the confines of its celibate lifestyle, but Julie had heard it before and was not taken in—just being in his arms and away from Matt was reward enough for her. To encourage him to abandon his vows seemed certain to anger the Lord. She chose, instead, to see herself as doing the Lord's work by giving Andy the emotional refuge he needed to carry on with his ministry. She was content to remain in the wings—being there for him when he needed her—even if she did have to struggle to characterize her role as being his benefactor and not his concubine. Any public display of their affections, though, would surely destroy the fragile balancing act that typified their affair.

Not until the morning after the Council meeting, when Julie had departed through the pantry entranceway, did Andy realize his blunder. In the midst of celebrating the daily morning Mass, he inexplicably paused while consecrating the host. It was as though his mind had gone blank; the words he'd spoken so many times before suddenly failing to flow. A vision of Julie's naked body lying beside his flooded his thoughts. He remembered every curve, every mole, every heave of her chest and beat of her heart as he nested his head in her breasts. It was several seconds before he regained his composure, before his dream slammed headlong into his consciousness. The elderly congregation present—the daily faithful—couldn't help but notice his preoccupation, but they were too forgiving, too unassuming, to suspect anything other than simple fatigue. From that awkward moment forward, Andy vowed to steer clear of Julie's temptation. It was a vow he wrestled with daily.

As Julie knelt in the hospital chapel she made an oath to God, as Delilah once had, to make amends for her sinful ways. She pledged, under the pain of mortal sin, to end her affair with Andy—to douse the fires of their love and scatter the ashes. She knew he was a vessel of the Lord, a missionary in a land of sinners, and that she had squandered him for herself. Her challenge now was to undo that wrong and return him to the Lord's fold. She had contributed to the Alpha and Omega of his priesthood, and if it took the death of her son on Abraham's altar to rectify that sin then she would accept it. "God's will be done," she proclaimed, her palms prayerfully clasped.

When Doctor Martin rejoined Faith, her eyes were swollen. Like her mother, she was grieving: for Robert because she loved him unconditionally, for herself because she'd lost her brother's confidence. For years he'd confided in her, but now she felt he had experimented with his sexuality and had kept it a secret from her. His dark side had somehow wrestled him to the ground, and Robbie hadn't given her a chance to rattle her saber in his defense. She scolded herself, chastising the way she'd become a plaything for men instead of a playmate to Robert.

"You know him better than your parents," Martin uttered to Faith … a perceptive indictment. "How do you think he contracted the virus?"

"I've been mulling this over and over, but I keep coming to the same conclusion." She cupped her face in her hands, and he moved to comfort her. His first priority was to solve this medical conundrum, but consoling Faith was a welcome side effect.

"Tell me, Faith? There's got to be a logical answer."

"Logical to you maybe, but only a heartbreak to me. All it can mean is that he's gay. His classmates would taunt him because he's … well … you know, sort of wimpy. But I ignored it. Now, looking back, it's the only explanation that makes sense."

"What about IV drug use? Or sex with a woman?"

She bristled at the first suggestion. "No way, Peter! I can call you that … can't I?" He nodded and she continued. "He won't even take aspirin. And he's definitely not a ladies' man. No, the more I think about it, Robbie must've been with another man. I dread my father coming to that conclusion. Believe me, it'll blow his mind."

She cringed at the vision of Robert being violated by a man and earnestly hoped that he hadn't been forced into having sex. No sooner had she formed that thought than his reason for not confiding in her darted into her path. Just as she had kept Matt's outrages a secret, Rob had seen fit to conceal his from her. Each kept silent, she theorized, for the sake of the other: Faith, to avoid losing her brother; Robert, to shield her from embarrassment and ridicule. *God,* she thought to herself, *how could I have been so oblivious to his plight?*

That same afternoon, Matt returned from the hospital to a vacant house. Everywhere he turned, his focus on Robert only became keener. His presence lurked beyond every door, was displayed on every shelf, or stared back at him from picture frames and trophy cases. Robert may not have met Matt's many expectations, but he was no failure. Every reminder begged Matt to see the good and not the bad in his son.

Scholastically his boy was superior, emotionally he was mature beyond his years, but physically he couldn't make the cut. Regrettably, the latter had been the myopic yardstick by which Matt had measured him. It was a high jump bar that he continually raised and that Robert continually toppled. His boy was an out-of-shape Goliath pitted against a microscopic but determined David, and Matt knew how the contest would end.

Matt had hours to ponder Robert's condition, hours to cry, hours to blame others for his son's demise, but mostly hours to wrestle with why his son was gay. There was no other explanation in his mind. Matt felt certain, though, that Robert hadn't followed in his dad's footsteps—that he hadn't poisoned and corrupted Robert's sexuality as his father did his a generation before. Like a genie released from a lamp, Matt could command his guilt to kneel down to his perceived innocence. Why, he asked himself repeatedly, had his son surrendered to the enemy side, to the side Matt so badly wanted him to avoid? His answer—both self-serving and self-defeating—was to blame Julie and Faith.

Father Andy learned of Robert's condition that same night, first from Julie and then from Matt. He was shocked when told by Julie and reacted with spontaneous prayers—a reaction he carried over for an encore with Matt. He knew Matt wanted to be the messenger, a role he'd staked out for himself since their turbulent times in Nam, so Andy didn't disappoint him. It wasn't enough for Matt, though, that Andy see the bandages. No, Andy had to see the blood flow and probe the wounds; nothing else would satisfy his "Doubting Thomas" ways. By the time Matt got to him, though, Andy, with coaching from Julie, had already determined the probable cause for the family's tragedy—and Matt figured prominently in their finger-pointing.

Robert left the hospital that same week. Though he'd lost weight, his health had improved. What he'd hoped would be a triumphant return home, however, became a wake. He'd already accepted his lot, having cleared the hurdles of shock, denial, and anger, so it confounded him that he, as the victim, was more tolerant of his prognosis than the others. Robert saw it as a personal defeat, not as a collective evil that would shred the fabric of his family. For him it was almost a badge of honor, for he was sure he'd contracted the virus doing his father's bidding on the football field—like a gladiator whose duty it was to die in the arena. He simply wasn't prepared for his father's self-centered agony or his mother and sister's syrupy doting.

Robert's football injury and blood transfusion—a credible alibi—figured prominently in the family's thoughts. What better way to accept or explain the situation than to frame it as an act of God … as a heavenly fireball that had randomly landed in the lap of this middle-class family? The hospital's confirmation that the blood was not infected, however, ruptured their ground-hugging balloon ride. Their hearts were now as empty as the balloon they had clung to.

Matt was a pressure cooker ready to explode. He ran the gamut from feeling sorry for Robert to feeling sorry for Julie to feeling sorry for himself. Once his needle was stuck on himself, there was no throttling his denial. He could feel sorrow for the others, but for Faith, like his stepsister, Janice, he had only contempt. She became the focal point of his blame and his silent discourses for revenge. Matt was determined to stone her, and not once did it occur to him that he was living in a glass house. That was the stuff of which his blind rage was made.

Matt refused to draw a link between his lifestyle and Robert's perceived homosexuality. To accept that connection was to admit that history was repeating itself—that this father of the Eighty's was a worse failure than his father of the Fifty's. What goes around never came around in Matt's mind, leaving his head firmly planted in the proverbial sand. That was the cornerstone of Matt's denial, and he honed it to a razor's edge in the days following Robert's diagnosis.

Not unexpectedly, Matt hit the road. Away, he could displace himself and live the gay life. He began to seek other men in a monstrous display of self-gratification that any observer would've concluded was a death wish—a free-fall into self-immolation without a parachute. For Matt to indiscriminately take lovers was a clear proclamation that he wanted to join in his own son's fate.

ॐ

It was the morning of Matt's departure to Schenectady for the Powertrain meeting. In the days preceding, he hadn't felt well. He attributed his fatigue to the toll Robert's illness had been taking, which diminished his appetite and left him a chilled and sweaty mess from his ghoulish nightmares. Watching his son decline, along with the family's campaign to keep his medical condition a secret, was proving oppressive. He slept poorly the night before, awakening to a war party of women.

"It's time we talked, Matt," said Julie, her voice resolute.

He peered up from his coffee. In a short while he'd be on the road to the Erie airport. *So why,* he asked himself, *can't they just leave me alone?*

"Can't it wait? I'm leaving soon."

"That's of your choosing. I think your traveling days should be over."

"Look, when you bring home the paycheck then I'll agree. Until then, just deal with my being on the road. OK?"

"What I can't deal with is your behavior toward Robert. I don't understand why you've deserted him … why you've turned your back on him." She softened her tone, hoping to ignite an ember of compassion.

"Don't lay that rap on me," Matt said thumbing his chest. "I didn't give him AIDS, and I sure as hell didn't lead him down the garden path, like Miss Priss here." He motioned wildly toward Faith. "Why are you here, anyway? Aren't you supposed to be at work?"

Julie planted her feet and tightened her jaw muscles. "Don't change the subject. We came to discuss Robert. It's time you ended this pity party. He hasn't been to school in three weeks, and you haven't spent an hour of that time with him. What's gotten into you?"

"I thought you two would've put your starry-eyed heads together by now and come up with the answer." Neither woman said a word. "Well, I'll spell it out. I can't stand that he's gay. OK? Now I've said it! That's what's been eating me ... and it ought to be eating you, too!" The pain in his eyes was real, the break in his voice a measure of his anguish.

"All you care about is the inconvenience he's caused you. 'Poor Matt' ... you might have to endure some embarrassment ... or even ridicule. So what? That's your son lying up there. How can you be so goddamn callous?!"

Matt looked up. She and Faith stood like two pillars, balancing atop their shoulders a mountain of revulsion for him and an ocean of compassion for Robert.

"I hope you'll see Andy today," he said. "Heaven help you if you don't confess your sinful language, not to mention your sinful thoughts toward me."

"It's just like you to belittle me. All I asked was that you show a little humanity ... a little humility. And you can't even fill those tiny shoes. It sickens me to be in your company."

Faith's eyes opened wide. She thought for sure he'd spring to his feet, but he sat motionless. A hot flash was ripping through his body, his ears ringing, and he couldn't muster the wit to blunt her spitfire temperament.

Finally, he said, "Well, you know how you can remedy that." And he jerked his head in the direction of the front door.

Julie stormed from the kitchen to find Robert, but he'd already made his escape to his creekside hideaway ... he couldn't deal with another shouting match. The men in my house are oil and water, Julie lamented as she sat slumped over on the corner of Robert's bed. She wanted to enlist Andy to help undo the impasse, but she was fearful of reopening that door. Instead, she wept bitterly.

"Why don't you chase after your mother? After all, being in my company must make you sick, too. I can tell you one thing," he trumpeted, "being in yours makes me wanna puke."

"Try looking in the mirror sometime," retorted Faith.

"No, you take a hard look into that mirror and ask it who's the fairest of them all. You know what you'll hear? It ain't you, bitch! You shattered that mirror long ago, and ever since this family has had nothing but bad luck."

He sat defiantly. Hate begat hate. It was their only bond.

"Cat got your tongue? Let me take a chapter from your mother's favorite book and cast you as the leading lady. Only this is no 'Once-upon-a-time' fairy tale. You see, there was this troublesome girl whose father asked her not to eat the fruit from his tree of goodwill. Well, one day she disobeyed her father and plucked the fruit from that tree and forced her little brother to eat it. You see, she thought she could just take whatever she wanted. So her father rightfully decided to punish her. He took away his goodwill, then his love, and finally," Matt roared, "her virginity. And now this meddlesome bitch is doomed to slither on her belly forever. You remember this story, right?"

Faith was silent, incredulous. He rose and pushed his chair aside. As he moved closer the coffee on his breath invaded her nostrils. In her eyes, he was the serpent.

"Nothing you said is true."

"Maybe you've forgotten, my little empty-headed stepdaughter, but I took your virginity from you ... and I can take whatever more I want."

She backpedaled, then stood flatfooted. "No! There's nothing left for you to take ... do you hear ... nothing!"

Enough, he thought, and raised his hand. She stiffened, but just as his glare turned to stone a car horn, like a klaxon, blew long and loud. Matt snapped out of his trance and peered outside. He signaled to the driver, a coworker who'd offered to drive him to Erie, then collected his bags. "We'll finish this when I get back. Call me in Schenectady if Robert has any problems," he demanded, lifting his bags with a grunt, then he slammed the door like the gate of a cellblock.

For the moment she was free of him, released from her cell to the prison yard. Her world was as menacing as the lighted towers, armed guards, and razor wire of a maximum-security penitentiary. For her, though, there was no escape or pardon, only the reality that her brother was on Death Row.

Chapter 14

"I'm glad you're home, Mr. Garrison," said Doctor Martin. "Robert has been asking for you." Martin stood at the foot of Robert's bed, thumbing through his charts.

Matt was tired, his trip to Powertrain had taken a heavy toll. His son had been asleep since before he arrived, waking only briefly to enjoy a caress from his dad, then waking again to confirm that it wasn't a dream. It was a sound repose, made all the more restful since he and his father had made their peace. It was a reconciliation comprised of gestures and touch, more than of words, but each understood what the other was thinking.

Martin motioned for Matt to follow him to a corner of the sunlit room. "I won't mince words, Mr. Garrison. Robert's condition is deteriorating. He has fluid buildup on his left lung, his blood pressure is high, and his lymph nodes are enlarged. You can see for yourself how labored his breathing is."

"Yeah, but you can give him oxygen and antibiotics, right? Won't that make a difference?" The intern showed no sign of agreeing. "There's more to this, isn't there, Doc?"

"Yes. Simply put, he's lost the will to live. I can insert tubes and administer all the antibiotics known to man, but that'll do no good unless he wants to recover."

Matt gazed out the window to the park below, where kids were chasing one another around the blockhouse. Up the ladder and down the slide, up the monkey bars and down the fire pole. Up and down. Up and down. The tempo of life, as Matt saw it. Robert's health had deposited Matt with a thud at the bottom of life's slide; his chin quivered as he looked at the young doctor, then at Robert's withered body.

"We can transfer him to Pittsburgh, Mr. Garrison. There's an excellent facility there that can offer him specialized AIDS care."

Matt stared to a point distant in both time and place … to where he'd seen men dying … to where he'd smelled and touched their flesh … to where he'd seen heroic efforts to patch them together when their bodies were in shambles. He would never forget their cries for loved ones. To die alone was Matt's worse fear, and he couldn't allow Robert to face that empty end.

"No, Doc. Strange surroundings and people will only hasten his slide. If he lives, let it be by your hand and my prayers—if he dies, let it be in the arms of his family."

Peter Martin solemnly nodded. Something had changed in this man, the intern concluded, and none too soon, for he knew that Robert wouldn't leave the hospital again. Matt's outward appearance had changed too, disturbingly so to the young doctor. He was haggard, almost cadaverous, and Martin knew he was in the company of a broken man. As a medical professional, Martin had to offer the option of transferring Robert, but he was relieved when Matt rejected the idea—not only for his patient but because it meant that he'd have more time to spend in Faith's company.

On the third day of his hospital stay, Robert suffered with shortness of breath and profuse sweating. Martin consulted a classmate in New York City, and both agreed the symptoms were those of Pneumocystis carinii pneumonia, a common cause of AIDS deaths. Chest X-rays revealed a bilateral infiltrate—haziness on the film—but the bronchoscopy proved damning. Robert's lung tissue contained the Pneumocystis carinii parasite, and Martin started an intravenous antibiotic regimen of trimethoprim/sulfamethoxazole. Robert's anxiety grew over his labored breathing, but short of inducing paralysis or using a ventilator the doctors could offer him no relief.

Robert's family grimly accepted the news, each having prepared themselves differently. Julie relied on her Bible for strength, while Matt relied on a small collection of medical journals. Each gave their reader an answer for what plagued Robert—one spiritual, the other organic. Each was their user's life jacket in a sea where swelling anxieties were as vicious as a shark attack. Not unexpectedly, Faith chose to rely on Peter Martin, who did nothing to discourage her.

Late on the fourth day, the doctors summoned the family. Martin also invited Andy, as he knew the news he was about to deliver would need spiritual tempering. Robert's condition had worsened, and Martin proposed using a ventilator. Doing so, however, meant the insertion of an endotracheal tube, which would prevent Robert from speaking. Once inserted, the intern knew that removing this life-support device could create a legal concern. When Doctor Martin suggested the procedure to Matt, he made certain that Andy was in earshot. Martin knew these two men—these two survivors of Khe Sanh—would be the decision-makers.

Matt and Andy felt that to die speechless was to die alone. Death was a communion with the living, and transmitting one's thoughts through words was sacrosanct. Not even Homeric feats of the medical profession, no matter how well meaning, should impede that cardinal need. Andy prevailed on Julie to agree, and the doctors, when informed of the decision, were philosophical. Though the patient's biological needs were their first concern, they agreed that in Robert's twilight hours his emotional needs should take precedence. So the deathwatch began. In a few hours, Robert would cross the narrow divide between suffering and redemption.

"Smoke, Andy?" Matt asked, lifting a pack from his pocket.

His chain-smoking partner removed one and peered into the chilly darkness. It was early morning and, for those whose task it is to wait, the night was truly darkest before the dawn. Some bright spots, some moments of levity, however, illuminated their anxious hours. They exchanged thoughts, and, through the nicotine haze, they buried their differences. The emotion of Robert's imminent death had peeled away their hardened defenses. It was a vigil reminiscent of their night spent together in Andy's hooch, only this time Matt's wounds weren't physical. Like that night eighteen years earlier, each relied on the other for strength, and each awaited the flutter of wings that would signal the arrival of the Angel of Death.

Suddenly a "Code-Blue" crackled over the intensive care wing. Matt and Andy stiffened. Like the klaxon's alert to incoming, the alarm set their hearts to leaping and their blood to rushing. Martin quickly appeared to tell them that the code was for another ... then he scuttled their relief by informing them that the beginning of the end was near for Robert. The news burrowed deep into their consciousness. These aging warriors butted their cigarettes, stoically gazed at one another, then rejoined Julie and Faith.

Matt stood alone, focused on Robert. Father Andy soon asked that they join hands, and they formed a horseshoe shape about his bed, with Matt between Julie and Andy. If ever Matt wanted Andy's prayers to succeed, it was now; if ever he wanted his cup to runneth over, it was now; if ever he wanted Julie to evoke the power of the Almighty, it was now. Matt was like a conduit between these two devout people, and their petitions surged through him to electrify his thoughts.

Robert lay motionless, enclosed in an oxygen tent—his color not unlike the sheets he was swaddled in. They stepped back as Andy administered Last Rites, as though he needed elbowroom to wrestle with the demons trying to take Robert away. The oxygen prevented lighting the ceremonial candle, but the oil of the sick placed on the boy's palms and the supplications that filled the air were offered with profound sincerity. As Andy had done numerous times in his two decades as the Church's shepherd, he blessed the dying. The many souls he had prepared for this journey shared a single vision: to behold their Maker and be judged worthy to sit at His banquet table.

While Robert lay still, his one hand clasped by Andy and the other caressed by Faith, his body let go a slight tremor and his chest a momentary heave. He passed away, never uttering a word, never opening his eyes, never embracing the sunshine that brought warmth to the living and hope to the dying. He died inside a clear plastic tent, not unlike the fish bowl existence his life had taken on.

They let go of his pale hands, and Andy lifted the plastic to expose the body—to release his soul toward heaven. Matt's lips were compressed to a fine line, his forehead furrowed, as tears streamed down his cheeks. Peter comforted Faith, while Julie knelt beside Andy and held his hand. Matt retreated to the window overlooking the park, where he focused on the children below. He beamed his silent message to their parents, who sat passively by on benches: Let them be the focus of your thoughts, words, and deeds, he implored, for, as he so keenly knew, they might soon become the focus of their pain.

Andy moved about, embracing Julie, consoling Faith, and thanking the weary Peter Martin for his marathon watch and care. He then joined Matt in the sun's rays, where their long shadows were cast across Robert's body. They gazed out the window to the scene of laughter and play below and, for an instant, Andy felt the joy of the living.

"Another time, another place, and that could've been you and Julie down there. It's hard to make sense of it all. He was here ... now he's gone. What I do know is that what remains ... all that we've really got to cling to, old buddy, are our memories ... and the feelings we have for him in our hearts. Let them be good ones, Matt. Never ones that turn you from the joy that he brought us all."

Matt squeezed the hand that Andy extended, then turned back toward the window. Words seemed so inept at communicating the pain. Andy knew that in another time, in another place, his love for Julie might have created a son—he could've been the mourning father, he thought, and that ashen youth, his son. As Andrew withdrew, he scanned the harvest of what he had sown. *Was anybody saved,* he asked himself, *or was it all bad seed?* Examining this family of the living dead, he left thinking that he'd done more to kill than he had to heal.

℘

Faith knew her brother wanted his teammates to be his pallbearers, so she appealed to the captain of the baseball team. Several players volunteered, tastefully displaying no enthusiasm for the solemn duty. They were an odd collection of adolescence, and not a one owned a suit that fit. The same could be said of Robert, who was dressed in one of Matt's business suits along with a flashy tie he was fond of sporting. Entwined in his short, waxy fingers, next to the Rosary that Andy had given him, was his tattered ball cap. He'd worn that beanie during many a sweaty ball game and practice, so Matt decided he shouldn't leave without it.

Faith stood stoically beside Robert throughout the viewing hours and the parish vigil that followed. She politely nodded to each well-wisher, holding back a frown when classmates who'd challenged his sexuality approached—even though she'd reluctantly come to accept that their jeers were valid. When the coffin was sealed, she sat in the front pew of Saint Titus Church where Father Andrew would celebrate the funeral Mass.

Incense perfumed the air and the female soloist, accompanied by the organist, heightened the climate of sorrow. Andy's eulogy spoke of a youth ravaged by AIDS, by an evil that preyed on the innocent as well as the guilty. He never speculated about its origin or suggested that it was a punitive measure for Robert's lifestyle. Instead, he spoke of Robert as a lamb led to slaughter; of his family and friends as those who'd shepherded him through life's challenges; of Robert being scourged and nailed to a cross fashioned by a decadent society. It was Andy at his finest, his most convincing—if not his most hypocritical.

Rain was threatening as the hearse pulled away. The funeral procession to the Cemetery of Saint Catharine of Sienna followed a short and well-traveled route. A golf course was in view, its patrons stroking and putting away, oblivious to the passing mourners. Each was in search of a hole in the ground, one marked by a pennant the other by a headstone. A funeral entourage was a common sight along this roadway, and only a glance was cast its way as the gray-flagged caravan of sedans rolled by.

Evergreens and shade trees adorned Robert's resting place. His plot was adjacent to the sculptured religious stone that marked the gravesite of Julie's parents. The weathered stones of Robert's neighbors, some towering obelisks with surnames etched deep, stood at attention. The funeral party waited in the green limousine as the pallbearers positioned the coffin above the vault. The flowers from the funeral home had been strategically placed around the platform to conceal the dark hole beneath it that would become Robert's final repose. The tent flaps rustled wildly, snapping in the brisk wind as the mourners huddled within the canvas cocoon.

Andy included in the Rite of Committal the 23rd Psalm. He had offered other intercessions, but his farewell hosanna was David's Psalm, and he recited it without the benefit of a text:

The Lord is my Shepherd; I shall not want. He maketh me to lie down in green pastures; he leadeth me beside the still waters ... Yea, though I walk through the valley of the shadow of death, I will fear no evil: for thou art with me ... Thou preparest a table before me in the presence of mine enemies; thou anointest my head with oil; my cup runneth over ....

His diction was flawless, his pace measured, and his tone reflective. Every eye was misty, every throat swollen, every ear attuned to his tribute.

Hidden amongst the mourners was a former classmate of Faith's who'd been infatuated with her for years. Though captivated by her beauty, he had been careful not to cross the murky divide between curiosity and stalking. Still, his peculiar mannerisms had, on occasion, driven Faith to angry outbursts. This shadowy admirer—who marched blissfully to an obscure drummer—inched his way to within earshot of Faith. After Andy concluded the rite and those gathered were bidding farewell with a sprinkle of holy water, this gnome whispered the message to Faith that Stacy Richards had AIDS. As stealthily as he appeared he disappeared, leaving Faith no opportunity to challenge him. Her mind, however, immediately engaged the threat, its fangs sinking deep into her consciousness. Within seconds she was agitated. To bury a brother fallen to AIDS was bad enough, but to learn that she'd made love to a man with the virus was terrifying.

Suddenly the crush of people became oppressive and Faith struggled to burst free, losing her heel to the soft earth as she raced for the limo. Every eye saw her, every ear heard her sobs, but no one came to her aid. Even Peter Martin, who stood in the wings, didn't weigh in to assist her or retrieve the slipper. Everyone conveniently, if not innocently, surmised that she was overwhelmed with grief. Only her wannabe suitor knew the truth, and he laughed so hard at her frenzied exodus that his tears helped him masquerade as a mourner.

The Garrisons opted to have no wake. They had no answers for the curious, because they had no answers for themselves. Instead, they withdrew to their Main Street bunker. It was a retreat, a retrograde as a Marine would call it, but a necessary evil for a family stripped of their flak jackets and shell-shocked by fate's volley. It was a futile maneuver, however, as the rumor mill shifted into high gear, and not once did its cylinders misfire in spite of their absent faces.

Speculation about Robert was rampant. It was an oddity bordering on freakishness for a member of this tiny community to be stricken with AIDS. That was a big city blight, they judgmentally concluded, where its news would've scarcely received notice. In Titusville, however, it was the focus for days. Only the knowledge that Robert had been reclusive tempered their fears. Few believed he was heterosexual or used IV drugs, so that led them—as it had Faith and Matt—to conclude that he was homosexual. Once they knew their daughters were safe, and because they couldn't conceive of their sons being gay,

213

the brouhaha over Robert's death dissipated. The panicked villagers returned to their homes, convinced that no Frankenstein had threatened their children.

&

Faith took shelter in her room, writing in her diary. She had much to work out. Without Robert, the chains that bound her to home were broken. She began to envision herself leaving Titusville to start anew, but one question remained unanswered: was the virus coursing through her veins? To have a prayer of starting life over, she had to resolve that fear.

Peter Martin lifted the receiver and was surprised to hear Faith's voice, and even more taken aback when she asked him to lunch. Ever since the funeral he'd wanted to go to her, but he was unsure of himself. An intern's oppressive work schedule was his convenient ball and chain, but at her invitation he swiftly rearranged his calendar. The following afternoon they met in the pizza shop.

"Did you know I was at the cemetery that afternoon?" His question caused Faith to blush.

"No, I didn't. That was kind of you. Then … I guess you saw my hysterics?"

"Why be embarrassed? Even in the brief time I knew Robert, I came to like and admire him."

"That's sweet, Peter. But … there was more to my outburst than Robert's burial. That's why I asked you here today." Her manner was mysterious, and he reached across the café table to clasp her hand. "I was devastated by his death … I still am … but it's what someone said to me that day that rattled me so."

"Why would anyone want to upset you more? That's malicious!" he said sternly.

"I don't know how to say this, Peter, because it's more in the line of a confession, but I haven't anyone else to turn to … to talk to."

He squirmed, then said, "What about Pastor Patterson? He could…"

"No, I couldn't go to him with something like this." She shifted in her seat, then looked into his searching eyes. "You see, I was told at the gravesite that an old boyfriend of mine has AIDS."

"That's bizarre. Could this be linked in anyway to Robert? I mean…"

"No. Not a chance. Stacy … that's his name … is many things," she said in an almost complimentary tone, "but he's not gay. Besides, I doubt that Robert even knew him."

"Why, then, did the news that he had AIDS upset you so badly?" Peter knew the answer, her anxious eyes told him.

"Well, I slept with him … several times." She frowned and pursed her lips, embarrassed at her disclosure and frightened of its ramifications.

Peter set his soda down and squeezed her palms. He was determined that she not suffer another day of unrest—and, to satisfy his own interests, to find out if she had become an untouchable. His shameless and manipulative side emerged, however, as he sought to fuel his fantasies of her. It was an abuse of her confidence … but her self-confessed unholy past had toppled her from the pedestal that he had placed her on.

"Have you considered, Faith, that heterosexual transmission of the virus can be problematical?"

"What do you mean?"

"Vaginal sex can be an inhospitable setting for the virus. After all, it's a fragile strain that simple soap and water can destroy."

"So you're saying I may not have to worry?" He could see relief flood her face, and she lifted her eyes toward heaven.

"No, that's not what I meant. Certain types of sexual activity are friendlier to the virus than others. For example, anal sex."

She lowered her eyes to the tabletop and slowly exhaled. Faith's sexual practices were conventional, but if a lover whispered the proper inducements …

"I did that with Stacy. God, this is embarrassing. I thought I loved him, Peter, I … I really and truly did." She sighed.

Peter's fantasy was escalating with each heave of her chest and blink of her tastefully shaded eyelids.

"I'm not here to stand in judgment, Faith, so you needn't feel embarrassed." She smiled, and he promised to arrange for her blood work that afternoon.

After the blood samples were taken, Faith sought the solitude of her creekside hideaway. It boggled her mind that she could be a carrier, that she could've passed along the virus to those she'd made love to after Stacy, but those recriminations paled when she suddenly remembered that she and Robert had commingled their blood. In a flash, she made the link between that innocent bond and the AIDS that swallowed him. Her mind reeled, and she started to hyperventilate. Like a passenger aboard a runaway train, she panicked, her body trembling. She wanted desperately to leap free of her speeding emotions, but nothing could ease her anguish. She rose, legs wobbly, and scanned the rusting train trestle that spanned Oil Creek. Then she examined the rocks beneath it. *Only a few paces,* she thought, *separated her from that fall. Only a few moments separated her from telling Robert that she was sorry.* She took two steps then collapsed, vomiting violently into the tiny pool that she and her brother had stocked with crayfish, tadpoles, and minnows. Seconds later, she passed out.

Later that week, when Peter Martin informed her of the blood test results, Faith felt hopelessly alone. His manner on the phone was clinical, detached, and he signed off with the banal recommendation that she call an AIDS hotline in Pittsburgh. In his eyes she was a spent commodity, first soiled and now spoiled, a diamond in the rough that would shatter and blind its cutter at the first plunge of his mallet.

Julie was restless as she lay in bed, something gnawing at her subconscious. A short while earlier Faith had brushed past her, a look of utter desolation in her eyes. Julie rose and reached into the medicine cabinet for her prescription sedatives, but the bottle was empty. She paused, thinking Matt had taken some, then dismissed the notion—alcohol was his preferred opiate. *Was Faith using the pills?* she wondered. *If so, then why were they all gone?* She dropped the vial and raced into her daughter's bedroom.

ଚ

The emergency room staff labored over Faith's body. After summoning the ambulance, Julie had frantically called Andy and he met her in the Emergency Room. He tried to contact Matt at his motel, but the calls went unanswered, though not unheard. He had been clinging to his pillow and sweaty bed sheets, feverish for hours. His throat was raw and his cough dry and persistent. He told himself it was a nasty bout of bronchitis, but the white patches in his mouth and the purple blotches on his skin said otherwise.

Faith had compounded the effects of her drug overdose with alcohol, but the ER staff purged her stomach and saturated it with charcoal to absorb the poisons. She lay semiconscious, a ventilator and a full-time nurse her watchdogs, while Julie sat nearby clutching the envelope that Faith had placed on her nightstand. To open it and read Faith's explanation was more than Julie could handle. She reasoned that if she left it unopened—left the demons in Faith's mind to reside in its unread print—then her plan for self-destruction would be thwarted.

Matt had struggled through the night with his own demons, only to be loudly awakened by the desk clerk at Andy's insistence. Andy had stationed himself beside a phone in the hospital lounge to await Matt's call, while Julie, preferring a conversation with the Almighty, knelt in the hospital chapel to thank the Lord for sparing Faith. Andy, though, was troubled by Matt's speech. He didn't need to look into Matt's eyes or smell his breath to be alarmed. The two had spoken before when Matt was hung-over, but something peculiar was buried in Matt's voice. Smokers, drinkers, and comrades-in-arms possess an uncanny communion of thoughts—a hidden affinity for each other's emotions. Andy, however, wasn't prepared for Matt's indifference toward Faith's attempted suicide—it was as though he was tired of life itself.

"She's off the ventilator, Father," uttered Martin. "You can talk with her, but please be brief."

Doctor Martin had come on duty at seven a.m. and nearly vomited when told of Faith's suicide attempt. He scrutinized his behavior toward her, wondering what he could've said or done differently. The blunt manner in which he had informed Faith, however, seemed justified. In his pragmatic mind, his approach served not only to advise her of her medical condition but to announce that what she had to offer him was unwanted currency. A country doctor he was not.

"Thanks, Doc. Let me be the one to tell her mother the good news. But first … I want a moment alone with Faith."

"Listen closely to her, Father. There's a lot on her mind."

With that understatement Martin departed, thankful he didn't have to see Julie for fear of what Faith may have told her about his phone-side manner. He was moving swiftly out of their lives, distancing himself from the explosion he felt sure was coming. He knew when to fold and when to hold—with Faith as a player, the stakes were too high to even play.

"I'm so very pleased you're still with us, Faith. You gave us all a nasty scare. It isn't time for you to leave. We need you."

"Nobody needs me, Father," she answered in a raspy voice. "I wish God had just let me die."

"Don't say that. Please! Each of us is special in His eyes."

"Don't kid yourself. Only the givers like Robert are special. I'm just a taker … someone who destroys others. We'd all be better off if I were dead."

"I won't accept that. How could you destroy a life when you've barely started your own?"

"You wouldn't say that if you knew that I killed Robert. I'm like a black widow. As soon as I'm done mating I kill my partner." Andy raised his brow, confused.

"You're not making sense. What are you trying to say?"

"I took a lover, then I killed my brother. One gave me the bug, then I passed it along to the other. All I'm capable of giving is pain and suffering. Now tell me, Father, why wouldn't the Lord want to rid the planet of me?"

"Light a candle, Faith, don't curse the darkness. Help me! Are you saying that you have the virus, too?" His face paled at her nod, his tongue partially exposed.

"That's right, Pastor. That's my confession. The first and last one you'll hear from me. I've broken nearly every one of God's commandants, even His fifth, so how could I possibly be saved?" She struggled to raise her head, her throat raw from the ventilator tube, and asked for a drink. Andy lifted her head, its hair matted and stringy, and placed a cup of water to her lips. He then stroked her forearm, careful to avoid the IV tubes, and dabbed her forehead with a moist towel.

"Please. No more riddles. Why exactly did you try to kill yourself?" He felt sure that in her cryptic language could be found the emotional needle long hidden in this family's haystack. He had to find it, though, before the stack burned to the ground.

"This is as straightforward as I can say it, Father. I've been diagnosed as HIV positive, and Robert and I were blood brothers ... blood siblings, if you like. Now you figure out the rest."

His emotions went from amazement ... to horror ... to nausea. "My God. But couldn't Robert have given it to you?"

"Nice try, Father, but I made love to Stacy Richards before Robert and I shared our blood. And now Stacy is dying of AIDS."

"You can't blame yourself for Robert's death. You couldn't have known."

"Tell that to him, Father. Tell Robbie it was all an accident."

"You have to tell your parents. Their world is upside-down, and only you can right it."

"No! I told you this was my first and last confession. If you want them to know, you tell them. Forget your vow of silence." Faith, however, had one condition to impose. "I may have beat you to the punch, though, Father. I left a note. If Mom read it, then she knows everything. If she didn't, then get the note back to me and say nothing about Robert."

There was so much more she could've added, but she refused. *Why traumatize Mother further?* she reasoned. Faith found herself wishing that she had let her father rape her that afternoon he returned from Powertrain. Instead of threatening him with a knife, she could've infected him with the virus. *What better way to get even?* she thought. For once, his grin could've been answered by her own more devilish one.

Father Andrew accepted her condition, pleased at half a loaf instead of none, and kissed her good-bye. Moments later he knelt beside Julie in the chapel and asked for Faith's note, explaining with a smile that she wanted him to return it. Julie greeted the news that her daughter was awake with tears of joy. Andy, however, was disappointed to see that the envelope's seal was unbroken. He hugged Julie, encouraging her to go to Faith, then he departed with the promise to visit the house that evening.

৪৩

Late that same afternoon Matt returned from a business trip, avoiding any stop at the hospital. He was gaunt, diarrhea and the sweats having depleted him. When Andy arrived at the Garrison's back door that evening he saw a sink full of dishes, the kitchen table a mess, and the lights dimmed. It was not like Julie to neglect housework—she was fastidious to a fault—so the disarray confirmed Andy's suspicion that she was stressed to the point of breakdown. *How,* he wondered, *could she manage the news that Faith was HIV positive?* He knocked, and the door was opened to him.

"Matt. Julie. Good seeing you under a flag of truce." His comment met with stony stares.

"Beer, Padre?" Matt asked.

"This isn't a social call." Neither spoke, so he continued. "Faith and I talked today, and I now understand much of what she's going through … and has been through." He looked directly at Matt, who stared back anxiously into Andy's eyes … he could tell, though, that Andy knew nothing of Faith's abuse. Andy, for all his polish, had never cultivated a poker face.

"No doubt she yammered about how her old man mistreats her. She never misses an opportunity to snipe at me. The girl is a flake and ought to be …"

"That's enough!" blurted Julie. You've got no cause to kick her when she's down. Haven't you figured out yet that you're a big part of her troubles?"

"Look, you two, I didn't come here to referee. Your daughter tried to take her life today, and now she's got little else to look forward to but sessions with a shrink and more suffering. So, can it! I'm here for her benefit, not yours."

"What do you mean 'more suffering'?" shot back Julie. She had quietly—resolutely—vowed to restore Faith's self-image and persuade her to attend college, so Andy's comment alarmed her.

"That's why I'm here, people. Something beyond Robert's death led her to attempt suicide, and she wanted me to tell you. It's a sorry state of affairs when a child can't talk to her own parents."

Julie felt hurt, scolded, but Matt said, "Out with it. What pack of lies and half-truths has she got you believing?"

220

"Think what you like, but this 'lie' is backed up by a doctor's report."

"Never mind him, Andrew. Please, tell us!"

He cleared his throat, glanced at Matt, then looked with apprehension at Julie. "Faith is HIV positive, too."

Julie dropped to her knees, precisely the stance she was so accustomed to, her eyes searching the heavens. Matt stood silent, brooding, his mind racing.

"How? How could this be happening?" she gasped. "Could ... could she somehow have gotten it from her own brother?"

"From what I can tell, all she got from Robert was much-needed love." To amplify that point, Andy sorely wanted to disclose their blood bond, but he had promised Faith to hold his tongue. Either way, he knew Julie's heart was breaking. "She apparently contracted it from a former boyfriend. A fellow named Stacy Richards. She had her blood work done on the QT, under Doctor Martin's supervision, and she learned of the results yesterday. The rest you know."

"God have mercy on her soul," muttered Julie. "I've got to go to her. She can't be alone at a time like this."

"Yeah, you do that. Get off your kneeler there and rush to her side. Never mind that she got the damn virus sleeping around. I told you she was a tramp. Now you see ..."

"For God's sake, leave it be, Matt! You should *both* go to her ... *both* make your peace. She desperately needs to know you *both* care."

"Well, count me out, old buddy. I'm no hypocrite. If she's got nothing better to do than peddle herself to every Tom, Dick, and Harry, then ..."

Julie leaped up and shouted in his face, "Shut up, do you hear me? Shut up, you fool!"

"Ah, go fuck yourself. I'm fed up with your pompous bullshit. Take her, Padre, and her slut daughter, too. I've had enough of them to last me a hundred lifetimes." Matt barreled up the stairs, while Julie and Andy hurried to be at Faith's bedside.

Matt paced aimlessly about Robert's room, cradling a matted teddy bear. *Could Robert's curse be Faith's curse and now his?* he wondered. Was it possible that lightning had struck so many times in one place? Matt was too confused to remember when he'd last punished Faith—*was it before or after she'd dated Stacy?* he asked himself. Timing was everything, but his mind wasn't working and his emotions were on overload.

Matt sobbed as he viewed the pennants and sports posters covering Robert's walls. It was out of love for his dad that he had hung them. His beloved books, comics, and stamp collections—the things Robert really cherished—had been stashed, like a chipmunk's hoard of winter nuts, beneath his bed. Without warning, a violent coughing spasm gripped Matt and he vomited. Something horrible was shadowing him, and the news of Faith's ailment made it imperative that he find out if the fruit that had fallen to the ground was rising up to choke the limbs that had given it life.

Chapter 15

Before Faith's discharge from the hospital, Matt fabricated a reason for leaving town. He wanted to get away from his family and his job, away from the scrutiny he felt was mounting. His enmity, though, like a ball and chain, had kept him from visiting Faith. He was too preoccupied with his own failing health to show an interest, even an insincere one, in the person he thought had caused his decline.

In requesting blood tests, Matt said nothing to alarm Doctor Golden. It was, however, a needless cover-up. The elderly physician, upon seeing him, would have ordered the blood work regardless of his family history. Matt had planned his absence well, only Golden—shackled to a doctor/patient relationship—knew the real purpose for his travel. Matt arrived at the Erie lab, where an expedited blood analysis confirmed his suspicions. Like his son and now his stepdaughter, he tested positive for HIV. Unlike Faith, though, his condition had deteriorated into AIDS.

Since his return from Schenectady, Matt knew something was wrong. He chose, however, to focus on his son's needs. Now he wanted his own health moved to center stage. Matt had never been health conscious or one to practice preventive medicine. Rather than engage in self-evaluation or New Year's resolutions, he'd just fire up his well-oiled engine of mental displacement and give himself a clean bill of health. Being diagnosed with the virus, however, had poured sand into that self-serving machine.

For years, Matt closed his mind to what brought discomfort and flung it wide open to what brought pleasure—that is, unless he could blame that discomfort on his stepdaughter. When Matt felt wronged by Faith, he was a one-man grand jury, and she was arraigned and punished for every offense, real or imagined. Small wonder, then, that Matt accepted his AIDS with a mix of satisfaction and hate—satisfaction at thinking he'd infected Mike and his goon squad, hate at thinking he'd contracted it from Faith. Each was its own brand of justice: those who'd raped him and his confidant-turned-Judas deserved it, while Matt's offense against Faith was punishable only by a contagion intrinsic to the act. The punishment had to fit the crime, and Matt took a morbid interest in seeing this axiom played out.

The pieces were fitting together rapidly, like the virus that was consuming his body. While in Erie, he drove by the unassuming flat that he and Julie had rented in 1968 after their whirlwind courtship and wedding. Their love nest was a place for him to put aside Vietnam and be a spouse and father, a place for Julie to hope that Matt would supplant her love for Andy. He was shocked then to see that their house of dreams had been boarded up, choked by a tangle of weeds and vines, and unfit for occupancy. It was an eyesore in need of razing.

His need to reminisce led him to visit Saint Peter's Cathedral, which he and Julie had attended and where Faith had been baptized. Its architecture held them spellbound—Julie for the spiritualism she gathered from its Royal Bavarian stained-glass images and life-sized statues, Matt for its vaulted ceilings, white Carrara marble Reredos, granite columns, and handcrafted woodwork. He scaled the Cathedral steps, blessed himself at the holy water font, then sat behind a three-column pillar. From there he watched as a handful of the faithful entered and exited the confessional. He wrestled with going in—to test the waters of a sacrament he'd avoided for twenty years—but the elderly priest soon departed, leaving Matt to sit and take stock of the rainbow of colors that bathed the altar.

Left without a confessor, Matt knelt at the altar's apron and repented his sins. He'd come to recognize, though not understand, how his hatred for his stepsister, Janice, had been transferred to Faith. He saw that his insecurities had worked to drive Robert into Faith's arms and how his own self-delusions had disabled his conscience and robbed him of humility. He saw, with disgust, the ugly mosaic that his life had become and he asked the Lord to help him salvage something ... anything. Before leaving, he lit a votive candle and vowed to make a proper reconciliation when he returned to Titusville.

Once home, Matt was contacted by Doctor Golden and urged to have his blood work redone, but he refused. So Golden then insisted on informing Julie immediately. Terrorized by the tribunal that Julie, Faith, and Andy would convene upon hearing such news, Matt pledged to tell her himself. He convincingly argued that as Julie's spouse he should break the news, defusing the doctor's anxiety by disclosing that they hadn't made love in years. Golden, though, put a timetable on holding his tongue, so Matt knew his doomsday clock was ticking.

Late that same afternoon, Matt journeyed to Saint Titus Church to make a proper confession. Too weary to walk, he drove instead, steeling himself along the way. Now, with Father Andy on vacation, was the time to unload his guilt. For Matt to expect that Andy could hold his tongue when entrusted with information that could set Faith free was to ask him to be party to the jailing. He knew he could never enlist Andy as a turnkey, especially if Julie or Faith was the one being held prisoner.

"Bless me, Father, for I have sinned. It's been years … many years … since my last confession. My sins are …"

Matt's voice pierced the thin veil that separated malefactor from benefactor; only words could pass between them. Eye contact, though permissible for the rite, was unacceptable to Matt. His objective was to get right with the Lord, not to publicly reveal himself and his homosexuality. The Sacrament of Reconciliation was a time-honored ritual of the blind leading the blind—where blind faith could beget blind forgiveness.

Matt's voice, timid and wavering, was immediately recognized by the priest, who knew this was a momentous event. He knew, too, that Matt had timed this visit precisely to avoid him. Having abruptly postponed his vacation so he could attend the funeral Mass of a fellow priest, Andy now sat alertly behind the curtain. For years Matt had steered clear of the confessional, but now that he had made a leap of faith Andy wanted to catch him. Confessing his sins, Andy reasoned, might be just what the Garrison family needed. To that end, Andy decided to mask his voice.

"I don't know where to start. So much has happened … and none of it good."

"Yes?" Andy muttered. He knew his inflection would be credible, so long as Matt thought he was a visiting priest.

"Well, I've been drinking a lot … and it makes me do stupid things. Things that hurt others."

"Uh-huh."

"You see, I'm a," he sighed and took a deep breath, "… a homosexual. I've tried, God knows I've tried, but … but I can't go straight. It's not that I find women unattractive. It's just that … ah, it's all so confusing. I just know I need other men, and that I'm powerless to stop."

Matt waited for a perceptive response from the father figure behind the curtain, but nothing happened. No bolt of lightning, no Angel of God descending on a cloud, no awesome display of radiant light flooding the confessional. Nothing save a grunt from Andy greeted the secret he'd guarded so closely all his adult life.

Andy mulled over Matt's words, recalling his morphine-induced confession that night at Khe Sanh after they'd patched his wounds and awaited the arrival of the medevac chopper. He recalled Matt's anguish as he told how his stepsister had caught him in the backseat of a car with a male classmate. It didn't startle Andy to hear today what Matt wouldn't openly admit then—what Eddie's farewell letter had plainly disclosed. It suddenly became apparent to Andy that just because he had wrestled his own sexuality over to the straight world was no assurance that Matt could do the same. Smoke, mirrors, and self-denial couldn't disguise what God had ordained.

Andy's matchmaking had failed miserably. He had naively thought he could entice Matt to abandon one stimulant for another, but instead, Matt embraced the one while only dabbling in the other. No marriage could sustain itself with a husband lukewarm to his vows; no marriage could endure when a husband needed more than one mate.

"Please … go on."

"Well, I've been living two lives—two lies. I've used every trick possible to take this secret to the grave. I've never told this to anyone else." Matt shifted in his seat and cleared his throat.

"Uh-huh," responded Andy in the same unrecognizable tone.

Matt wanted a give and take, a dialogue, with his confessor, but he soon realized he'd have to settle for just jettisoning the cross he'd carried since his youth.

"There's more, Father. For years I've fought with my wife. I tried to be loving and affectionate, but nothing worked. She and I are forever butting heads."

"I see." It upset Andy that what he had desired, Matt had let slip through his fingers.

"I don't think you do, Padre. I mean, at times I wanted to choke the life out of her. To crush her skull like a ripe melon between my palms."

"Why?" Andy asked, incredulous.

"Because I think she's been having an affair. I've never caught them, but a husband knows when his wife loves another. It's bad enough when there's another man, but when that man is a priest ... it's an ... an abomination." Matt's voice was heavy with emotion. He'd never vented this suspicion before, and certainly not to someone in Andy's fraternity. Matt wanted to rip down the veil separating them and shout his defiance of the whole breed, but he was too mortified to show himself.

Andy sat upright, as though the point of a knife was at his back. He felt sure that Matt knew nothing. He'd been so discreet, so tight-lipped, so careful not to draw attention to their love. Not once had Julie entered the rectory while he was alone, not once had he entered her home via the back door, not once had they entered a motel at the same time, not once had they been seen together at anything but a church activity—and never had they displayed the overt eye contact that might betray them. Except for that one night in the rectory, discretion had been the hallmark of their amour.

Andy squirmed. He wanted to defend himself, to say he was only there because Matt wasn't, but something told him this confession wasn't over. Both men were sinners—and against the same family—but this wasn't Andy's hour to repent. So he wiped his moist brow, relaxed his taut muscles, and remounted the horse that had just thrown him.

"You probably think I'm making this up, that I get my kicks by telling priests that my wife is in love with one of them. Well, you're the first one I've told. I can't even confront my wife, let alone the priest. It's crazy, but I love him." His voice trailed to a whisper.

"Please. Forgive them. Forgive him." Andy's voice broke.

"Easier said than done. There's more, Padre. Let me tell you the real reason I came today."

Matt's mouth was dry, his speech rapid. Andy leaned into the veil that separated them. His mind was racing. *What could be left unsaid?*

"I came to tell you … actually to tell the Lord … that I've …" he took a deep audible breath. "I've abused my stepdaughter. I forced her … several times … to have sex with me. Ever since she was a child … and now I hate myself. Do you hear me? I hate myself!" Matt cupped his face with his palms and sobbed, his body shuddering. Without warning, a spasm of coughing and hacking enveloped him—as though he was choking on his own words.

Andy hesitated, frightened to step out, but Matt's gagging and gurgling so alarmed him that he bounded from behind the curtain. Matt was sweating profusely, his face red and eyes bulging. Seeing Andy, he momentarily stood, staggered, then collapsed in the corner, staring blankly as though he'd seen his Maker. Not since Nam had Andrew seen a man in such a trance. His genuine concern for Matt's well-being, however, soon was transformed into a bubbling rage as he watched him cower.

"How could you, man? How could you rape your own daughter?"

"Why are you … what are you … you doing here? I thought …"

"You thought another priest would be here … that you could dodge me and dump on him. Well, it's me, all right, and you've given me an earful. The Almighty—not fate—brought us together today. How could you violate your own daughter's body? What were you thinking? What was going through your head?"

Matt lay helpless. All he wanted was divine forgiveness. Instead, Andy pummeled him with judgments. Matt accepted the blistering tirade as part of his penance. He was too weak, too confused—his mind ravaged by AIDS—to respond. So Andy made use of the silence to bore in, to plunge and twist the blade he felt sure couldn't cut both ways.

"And all this time Julie trusted you … I trusted you! Faith had nothing but love in her, and you drove it out. Thank God that Robert died not knowing how you tortured her. Even when she told me why she had tried to kill herself, she never mentioned you. You carried her to that ledge and then forced her to jump. Damn you, Garrison!"

"But … but …"

"But what? All she cared about was her brother. She worried herself sick … to the point of attempting suicide … because she thought that their innocent and loving blood brother bond had given him the virus.

Not once did she hint that you were torturing her or …" Andy abruptly stopped, his tortured face filling with apprehension when he realized he'd broken his vow of silence to Faith. Matt's wild-eyed look began to frighten him. Something said had strummed his emotional chord to the breaking point.

"Blood brothers? You mean they shared their blood?" He clamped his eyelids shut. "No, sweet Jesus, no!" Matt trembled, repeating the plea, his voice cracking. He sprang to his feet and ran like a madman, stumbling, groping for the hardwood pews as he raced out, while Andy stood, hunched over in the confessional doorway.

&

Matt sat quietly in his den. He had wandered through Burgess Park as though shell-shocked, mindlessly flinging pebbles into the still pond, until nightfall prodded him homeward. No matter which way he turned he was in a cave, darkness within and darkness without. In minute detail he'd pieced together how, through Faith's hand, he had destroyed his son and wrongfully accused him of being gay. Stacy Richards hadn't infected Faith. Instead, he had contracted the virus from her. Nothing would diminish Matt's sense of guilt and no truth, save one, could set him free.

Matt squinted as he peered down the barrel of the revolver, the rifling catching the light. He could see the dome-headed round that rested in the cylinder. He knew that only an instant separated him from liberation. In Nam he had lived in terror of a bullet crashing through his skull. He'd seen combat up close and knew that he'd never hear the one that got him. He'd hear it now, he thought; both bullet and sound would travel as one. Only a squeeze of his finger and the agony would end; only a pang of pain and he'd be with Robert. Millions before him had done it and millions would follow. Even at this instant, others as tortured as he—fathers who had trampled their own seed—were preparing to die. He wouldn't be alone in his final moment, he thought.

He read aloud from the Gospel of Luke, but for this Prodigal Son there was no homecoming to enjoy or feast to be celebrated. He turned, instead, to Mark 9:43, and read the verse that would free him from his hell:

229

If your hand is your difficulty, cut it off! Better for you to enter life maimed than to keep both hands and enter Gehenna, with its unquenchable fire. If your foot is your undoing, cut it off! Better for you to enter life crippled than to be thrown into Gehenna with both feet. If your eye is your downfall, tear it out! Better for you to enter the kingdom of God with one eye than to be thrown with both eyes into Gehenna, where 'the worm dies not and the fire is never extinguished.'

Matt had to remove the demon that resided in his mind, to tear out the evil that had crippled his power to reason.

He pressed the cool muzzle to his temple and released the safety, then whispered, "If your mind is your difficulty, destroy it!" He repeated the words as he curled his index finger around the slim trigger, his hand steady. His salvation lay before him, and he welcomed it with a firm grip of the gun handle. *Just a little more squeeze,* he thought, *just a little more pressure, just a little more . . .* The shot rang out, his neck snapped, and his head crashed to the desktop. Robert's photo was pinched between his thumb and forefinger as the blood erupted from the wound.

Faith sat up in bed, startled by the report. She couldn't tell a gunshot from a firecracker, but she knew the blast had come from within the house. Her mother was out, so she tiptoed down the staircase, her bare feet brushing the carpet with each reluctant step. Her head was cocked, ready for any sound, and her breathing shallow. Shamrock scratched and growled at the den door, digging at the carpet as though a bone was beneath it. She knocked, then slowly turned the doorknob and peered in. Upon seeing her father's body and smelling the spent gunpowder, she screamed. Shamrock leaped atop his master's desk and sniffed his shattered head, whining. Faith haltingly entered, terrified of what she'd see. Matt's mouth hung open, a trickle of blood mixed with saliva pooled below his ashen lips, his eyeballs glazed as though wrapped in clear plastic. She looked long at the dark hole made by the bullet's entry, its rim a bluish hue. His hair was mussed from the muzzle blast, and she watched with horror as the puddle of blood swelled beneath his head.

She stepped back, running her fingers through her hair. There was no note on the desk, only Robert's bloodstained photo and his teddy bear sitting atop the Bible. At Matt's side was the walnut-handled revolver, his finger still curled around its trigger. She circled the desk, coaching herself to call the police, when her anger suddenly got in the way. *Why did he get to escape?* she asked. *Why, on the eve of her announcement that she was leaving town, had he taken center stage?* Nothing made sense to her … nothing seemed fair.

She felt empty, void. Why no message of regret for having tormented her? *Why leave without speaking your mind, without saying your peace?* she wondered. He had taken so much from her already, why hadn't he killed her, too? Either way, she was a dead woman. She didn't know what to feel toward him. *Was he a coward to be scorned or a freak to be pitied?* Had she deserted him as she had Robert—one to die by his own hand, the other by her bloodied palm? *Some good,* she kept telling herself, *had to be a part of Matt's make-up.* No one, she reasoned, could be totally barren—devoid of a grain of sand that when trapped in life's oyster would yield a pearl.

She soon sighed, her search futile. She went to the phone to call Father Andrew. He should be the first to know, she thought, for her mother would surely turn to him for comfort.

Chapter 16

Andy lowered his head and dropped his arm, the telephone receiver tumbling to the floor … along with his heart. He couldn't believe Matt was dead, or deny that he, himself, was a party to the tragedy.

Andy flushed the toilet a second time; he hadn't vomited so violently in years. His stomach muscles ached from contracting, but this news, so hot on the heels of Matt's tortured confession, left him powerless to hold back the nausea. If only he'd held his temper, his tongue. If only he'd left the judgments to the Almighty. He had lashed out at Matt like an irate father would a back-talking son. Now, in an instant, Matt ended Andy's speculation about how his marriage would end. Father Andrew was instrumental in creating and now slaying this monster, and there was no pleading innocent to his failed experiment. He had assumed he could care for Julie and still serve his priestly vocation by corralling Matt—the black sheep—to coexist with the white to the betterment of all. It was vainglorious folly.

Faith, as instructed by Andy, contacted the police. With little time to reach Julie before the authorities, Andy hastily put on his cleric shirt and collar and rinsed his mouth. His throat and nose were raw from the upheaval, but he sprinted to the social hall where he saw Julie talking with a friend. He stood, panting, hidden in the shadow of a huge maple, while a valley breeze whipped up the dust created by a summer drought. Andy's impatience grew as she continued chatting with her companion. Finally, she was free of her and Andy made his move.

"Julie! Over here."

"What? Well, aren't we out late? It's past your bedtime, Pastor." *Our bedtime!* she thought. She would've shared his bed, liberated as she was by the heat and the wine, but his stern look defused her amorous mood.

"Something's happened," said Andy in a hushed tone.

"Not Faith again? She's all right, isn't she?!"

"No. I mean … yes! She's fine. But …"

"For God's sake! What is it?"

"It's Matt. He's gone and ... and ..." The disbelief in his eyes guided her like a lantern.

"He killed himself, didn't he? That's it, isn't it?"

"May God have mercy on his soul ... on mine. Yes, he shot himself. I don't know what to say." His shoulders drooped and he glanced at the ground.

She looked up, and the moon illuminated her pale skin, her nostrils like black beads on a wedding gown. Then she rested her face in her palms, as though serving her head on a platter.

"You don't need to say any more, Andrew. I think I knew it would come to this. There was a time when we might've worked through our problems, but Robert's death ... and now Faith's ..." She collapsed, and he carried her to her car. Her body was frail and, for once, he embraced her with no concerns for who might be watching. He had done his share to whip up this ill wind, and now he wanted desperately to shield her from the ensuing storm.

"I'll take you home," he whispered, trying to comfort her.

He whisked her down Main Street, slowing his sedan for the flashing lights and curiosity seekers gathering outside the Garrison house. He pulled into the driveway, the police chief waving him on, and they entered through the kitchen door—where they froze at the sight of Matt's shrouded body being wheeled toward the foyer. The chief, who had reentered through the front door, directed the paramedics to halt the gurney, then he spoke in a subdued tone to the medical examiner before approaching the stone-faced couple.

"I'm terribly sorry, Mrs. Garrison," said the chief. Andy's facial expressions alerted him to that fact that she knew what had happened. "I wish Matt hadn't done this."

The chief's sorrow was genuine, as his son had been Robert's teammate. The chief and Matt had spoken often, exchanging their hopes, dreams, and fears for their teenage boys.

"I want to see him, chief," said Julie.

Both men hesitated. Their instincts were to protect her, but it was her house, her spouse ... and her nightmare. The chief lifted the sheet, and Julie turned away. Slowly she looked back and muttered something indiscernible, as though speaking to Matt's hovering spirit. She stroked his ashen cheek with the back of her hand, then gently placed the sheet over his face.

"He was clutching this when your daughter found him." The chief handed the photo of Robert to Julie and added, "There was no note—nothing in the den, on his person, or in your bedroom. He died of a single, self-inflicted gunshot wound to the head, and that's how the coroner's report will read."

"I want to see the den."

"I'd like to discourage you, ma'am. There's still cleaning up to do and …"

"I understand your concern, chief. But it's something I need to do."

The chief nodded, and Andy escorted her to the mahogany desk that Matt had refinished after learning that he was being considered for a promotion. He bubbled with excitement and had decorated the den with the expectation that he would use it for pampering his clients. He had added woodcarvings, sports trophies, and conversation pieces to ease the chill a stranger might feel. It was his hideaway, his refuge, and to those who knew him it was a snapshot of the business success that had eluded him.

Matt's boss, Ron Evans, had dangled the plum of a promotion after Matt's trip to Powertrain. It was rumored that Matt was in line for a marketing position, but when the doors to the smoke-filled room closed and the department heads began deliberating, Matt came up short. Evans had seen to that. In his mind, to improve Matt's lot was to diminish his own. He had skillfully sown seeds of doubt, orchestrating the consensus that Matt wasn't the right fit for the job. Matt accepted the disappointing news with grace, as Robert's passing had already knocked the fight out of him.

Julie shuddered at seeing the crimson pool atop Matt's desk, while Andy focused only on Robert's teddy bear and the Bible resting beneath it. He wondered if Matt had taken comfort from The Word before pulling the trigger. Faith had been flitting about the den, observing the postmortem with detachment, when Julie motioned her over.

"I'm sorry, baby. No child should have to see this." Julie hugged her to her bosom.

"Not now, Mother," was her wooden rebuff and she pulled away.

"But, Faith, can't we …?"

"Let her go now, Julie. It can keep awhile longer. She has to grieve in her own way."

Flustered, she accepted Andy's judgment and moved to her observation post beside the bay window. Andy drew the shades low and she sat and rocked. He brought her a glass of white wine and she sipped it slowly, just wetting her lips with each tilt of the rocker, while the strobe lights on the emergency vehicles cast eerie shapes on the window blinds. Matt's body was soon en route to the morgue while Chief Hamilton remained to ask a few routine questions. He then repeated his condolences and left. Darkness again descended on the neighborhood.

"I want Matt to be buried quickly, Andrew. No visiting hours … and definitely no wake."

"Yes, but don't you think …?"

"I know you think funerals are for the living, but look around. Do you see anyone alive here? A wax museum has more life!"

"Whatever you say," he offered in a dejected voice. "I'll talk with Director Farley. I suppose he'll understand." I just wish I did, Andy thought.

"And be sure Farley uses a simple metal casket. Matt hated to see good hardwood go to rot."

Andy nodded and pursed his lips. He wanted to hug her, but, like her daughter, she had assumed a mechanical air. Not until the business of burying Matt was complete would she lower her guard.

"Run along now. I'll be fine, Father. I'm sure there are others in need of your attention. We're not the only parishioners hurting tonight." She was too upset with Faith's behavior to even recognize that Andy needed consoling, too.

&

Andy kept visualizing the Bible resting atop Matt's desk. So after leaving Julie's side, he detoured to the den and opened it to the page where the red ribbon was tucked. There before him was Luke's account of the Prodigal Son. Had the parable he had used twenty years earlier to taunt Matt somehow come back to push him over the edge? Andy knew that Matt would never enjoy the Prodigal Son's rebirth, that he'd given up on life because he had no father to return to. Andy, who'd unknowingly played that fatherly role all these years, had stripped from Matt what little dignity he had left. God Almighty, he thought, I should've stayed behind the curtain and said nothing.

Andrew paced the rectory study like a sentry into the early morning hours. He'd be celebrating Mass soon, but his mind was as far away from that uplifting event as it was from understanding Matt's desperate act. Matt had scorned those in Nam who resorted to self-inflicted wounds, labeling them cowards. He'd once said that suicide was the epitome of selfishness. "So what had changed?" Andy wondered aloud.

He knew he'd blundered badly during Matt's confession—it was wrong, no matter how justified his motives, to have confronted him in that way. Andy tried to mitigate his own guilt over Matt's death; after all, he reasoned, no one could drag around an ankle weight such as Matt's without wanting to hack off his own foot. Yet Andy felt there was a deeper motive—one beyond his learning of Matt's abuse of Faith—that triggered the suicide. During Robert's twilight hours, Matt spoke to Andy of his fear that his son might die alone. So for Matt to perish alone, by his own hand, was a profound statement of despair.

He replayed the confession over and over, freeze-framing each moment. Matt was busy revealing, while Andy was concealing. They were at opposite ends of the spectrum, while converging like missiles on the same point. Both sought peace of mind for Matt, but all that swiftly changed when Andy disclosed that the kids were blood brothers. Andy dwelled on that one point ... for hours.

Could it be possible? Did Matt somehow realize that Faith gave Robert the virus? If so, why would that piece of information cause him to snap? Unless . . . ? It suddenly began to make sense to Andy: Faith must've contracted the virus from her father, not Stacy. If so, then Matt must've known that he was infected, too. "God Almighty!" he exclaimed aloud. "He killed his own son!"

Andy now realized that Faith was being held captive for a crime she didn't commit. Matt had forced her to walk the plank blindfolded, but to his horror she had landed squarely on Robert. No wonder she tried to kill herself. "Dammit!" he thundered. How could he release her and still honor his vows as a priest? Though inexcusable to have attacked

Matt in the confessional, it was unforgivable, even after his death, to compound the error by violating the rite's confidentiality.

&

"The Medical Examiner agrees, Father, that no autopsy is necessary. Given Mrs. Garrison's wishes for a hasty burial, it would be a cruel and unnecessary evil to transport the body to Pittsburgh for examination."

Andy listened intently to Doctor Golden. He'd have to act now if he was to confirm his suspicions. "This is awkward for me, Doctor, and I'm prayerful you won't take it wrong. But I'd like you to remove a blood sample from Matt before his body is released to the funeral home."

The doctor looked askance. "For God's sake, Father, why?"

"Please, I know this is irregular but I've got an alarming notion—call it a divinely inspired premonition—that Matt was HIV positive. It sounds farfetched, but if I can prove it, I believe I can help this family cope with its tragedies. Trust me."

"It's not that I don't trust you, Father. I'm sure your motives are honorable. It's just that I'm at a loss to understand how that information would benefit Julie and Faith. Regardless, and I don't think I'm breaching any confidences here, I can tell you unequivocally that Matt had AIDS." Golden made the disclosure because he believed that Matt, as he had promised, told Julie of his diagnosis. Now, as he looked at Father Andy's face, a man he knew to be Julie's confidant, he wasn't so sure. "Undoubtedly she told you that he tested positive. I mean, Julie knows, right?"

"Why do you say that?"

"Well, your notion that Matt had AIDS must be based on something she said."

"No. Not at all."

"Then why would you make such a request, Father?" he asked with a befuddled look on his face. Golden suddenly realized that Matt might have killed himself rather than tell Julie of his condition.

"Look, Doc, I can't disclose my source. This may sound silly, especially since Matt is dead, but I'm under a vow of silence. Try to understand."

"I do. We doctors have a similar code. I just wish I understood how this information could help now. Unless, of course, you suspect he had sexual contact with others and ..."

"Look, you've been very helpful, Doctor. Forget I ever asked for the blood sample. Let's move his body to Farley's Funeral Home ASAP so we can get on with healing this family."

"All well and good by me, Father. But now I'm concerned ... very concerned ... that Julie doesn't know that her husband had AIDS. Nothing you've said indicates that Matt told her, even though he suspected the worst for weeks before it was confirmed. He stubbornly refused, however, to tell me how he contracted it. What an incredible situation that three family members should all be infected! It's mind-boggling. I'll have to meet with Mrs. Garrison tomorrow."

"Hold up, please. Let me tell her in my own way. It's unorthodox, I know, but I think I can do it in a less traumatic manner. Trust me. Damn, there I go again with that sales pitch."

"That's OK, but don't foot-drag, Father. We have an obligation to her. I've got to finish my rounds now. Take care and please don't delay."

Doctor Golden left him standing at the chapel entrance. Andrew, having unraveled all the loose ends, knotted his knapsack filled with deliverance. He knew, however, that if he slashed the knot and the secrets spilled out prematurely, then he would unleash his own destruction. He had to bring Julie and Faith back into the fold, but without disclosing Matt's tortured confession.

 භ

To satisfy Andy's pleas, Julie agreed to abbreviated visiting hours provided he'd keep his eulogy and gravesite service short. Faith, as she had done with Robert, hovered close by her father's casket. To onlookers it was a loyal gesture from a beloved daughter; to Julie, and particularly Andy, it was an inexplicable posture. Andy was left thinking that she wanted the last word—that well-wishers' petitions would be negated when her wrath spewed forth as the coffin was sealed.

Before the casket was closed, Andy tucked inside it the combat boot that he'd kept for so many years—since that March morning in 1968 when Corpsman Suscheck gave his life to help medevac Matt to safety. For all those years it had served to remind him of himself—its battered appearance was his spirit before finding Matt, the shine he later applied a testament to his priestly rebirth. His love for Julie, however, led him to fail Matt as well as the symbolism he'd attached to the boot. It seemed only fitting, then, that they be buried together.

The father's funeral procession followed the same route as his son's. When the small group of mourners gathered about Matt's coffin they couldn't help but trod the earth atop Robert. Two months had passed since the boy's burial, yet the mound had no green. Andy, as he had promised to Julie, paid brief homage to Matt. He knew the man's faults better than any living being, yet he respected him for the homosexual cross he had borne, for the marriage of convenience he had endured, and for the trials he suffered in Nam. No tributes, however, flowed that steamy August morning and Andrew abruptly concluded with the 23rd Psalm.

"Let's go home, baby," Julie said, nudging Faith gently, but she remained kneeling at her brother's grave. She was swamped by life's turbulent waters, which had swept away her brother and father and were now threatening her. She dreaded the prospect of wasting away in her mother's presence. She wanted anonymity, and that meant breaking her ties to this valley.

"I don't want to. There's nothing there for me."

"I'm there, honey. And Father Andy is, too. And ..."

"Oh, great! Now you two can carry on with total immunity."

"What are you saying?"

"I'm talking about you and your lover there." She pointed accusingly at Andy. "Did you think I didn't know? Do you think Robert didn't? And what about Dad? How could you do that to him? Chasing after a priest. The whole thing is ... is ... unbelievable. You're both warped."

Andy turned away. It was bad enough when he thought only Matt knew.

"You don't know what you're saying. You'll feel better after ..."

"I don't plan on being around long enough to feel better, and that's not because of the virus. I'm leaving this town. This weekend! I'll find someplace, anyplace, but I'm not living another week in that house. Certainly not around you two lovebirds." She stabbed her finger at each of them.

"You can't be serious. Oh, honey, please, try to understand. Now is the time to mend fences. You're just frightened and upset. Put this craziness aside and ..."

"You don't get it, do you, Mom? I'm dead serious ... certainly dead either way. I'm not wasting what little time I've got left watching you console yourself from a church pew. And I'm sure as shit not listening to that pompous ass over there," she was practically shouting, "tell his faithful to lead a holy life. You two are hypocrites!" She rose and marched quickly past the limousine and down the gravel lane.

"Stop her, Andy! Talk to her. She'll listen. Please!"

"No. Not now."

"But, Andy!"

"No, I said. She's angry and rightfully so. We've betrayed her and our vows." Andy felt stripped of his dignity. He wanted to spout off—about Matt's anguish, Faith's abuse, and Robert's death—but the timing was all wrong. To woo this pair back to life, he had to have them center stage and himself in the shadows.

"I'm so ashamed. I can't believe she knew about us ... that Robert knew. I feel dirty."

Andy knew how destructive it could be to lead two lives, especially after seeing what it had done to Matt. There was no more room for self-deception. Certainly, no more deceiving Julie with the lie that he'd renounce his vows and marry her. Enough was enough, he thought. It was time he returned to God, his Father and Shepherd.

"For once, we have to be honest with one another, Julie. There's no place in this world for a couple like us. We're a mismatched pair, two left boots, whose callings are mutually exclusive ... if not mutually destructive. This isn't college or the Sixty's. Our rebellious ways have to end. Look at the destruction we've caused. Christ said that whoever exalts himself shall be humbled ... that whoever humbles himself shall be exalted. That sums up our past, but it can, if we let it, also describe our futures."

"I don't know what I was thinking," said Julie, "or if was I thinking. I knew our love could come to no good. But I couldn't stop myself. I love you, Andrew. I've never stopped loving you since that night we first made love." What she couldn't bring herself to tell him, though, was that Faith was the product of that night—that Andrew, not Dan, was the father of her daughter.

As she walked toward the limo, negotiating the tombstones, Andy could see that she'd lost the spring in her step, that she held herself less upright than before. The weight of life's trials, along with the gray that streaked her temples, heralded a change in her direction. Andy could still see Faith in the distance, her stride brisk. He watched as two generations marched off before him: one younger and bolder, the other older and wiser. He owed them a debt of gratitude for having let him enter their lives, but instead, he had paid them back with ruin.

৪০

When Father Andy visited Julie the next evening she pointed anxiously to the luggage in the foyer. She had pleaded with Faith to reconsider—to give it one more chance—but she was determined to leave home.

"Look, Andrew, she's packed and ready to go. Nothing I say makes a difference. Nothing! I can't let her go off to die in some strange place. You understand, so why can't she?"

"I've been praying that you could turn her around. She needs us for the tough times ahead." *Especially since they hadn't been there for the tough times before,* he thought.

"I know. I know. I've been praying, too."

"There's something you need to know, Julie. Something that Matt was supposed to tell you but didn't. Doc Golden would've told you himself, but I asked him not to." Andrew walked toward the bay window and Julie followed, frowning.

"It's bad news, isn't it?"

He stopped cold. Could she handle it? Yet he had no right to withhold knowledge of her destiny. He'd asked to be the messenger, and now he had to deliver. "I don't know how to say this, so I'll give it to you straight out." He took a deep breath. "Shortly before he died, Matt was diagnosed with AIDS. Apparently, he …"

"What? That's impossible!" Her voice was strained, her eyes a mix of confusion and terror.

"It's true, Julie." He stepped closer. "I only wish it weren't."

"How? How could this happen? How could we be so cursed?" Her voice trailed off, a look of bewilderment enveloping her. She plopped down in her rocker and wept. It was the final dab of glue she needed to cement her belief that the Almighty had ordained it all.

"It's you I'm worried about. He was your husband ... your mate. If he carried the virus, then you might be infected too." He and Matt had shared the same lover, the same meal, and he couldn't help but wonder whether they were destined now to share the same fate, the same poison.

"Don't worry, Andrew. I haven't been intimate with Matt in years. When our love for each other blossomed I lost any desire for Matt. And he lost his for me long ago."

"You still need to be examined. That's the least you should ..."

"Yes, yes. I understand all that. But how did he contract it? What sort of life was he leading?"

"I've had doubts since Nam, but I've never voiced them. I just ... never wanted to accept them."

"What do you mean? What sort of doubts? Matt wasn't a drug user. I'd have known that. Was it another woman?" Andy stared blankly, noncommittal. "Are you saying ... no ... he was gay? Is that it? Is it?" Andy nodded. "God, did I really know so little about him?"

Andy was prepared to produce Eddie's farewell letter, though he feared for how it would reflect on his own judgment. He considered burying the note alongside Suscheck's boot, but he kept it to ward off any skeptics. He didn't need it, though, because Julie suddenly remembered the cache of sexually explicit magazines she had discovered in Matt's dresser some years earlier. She was offended by their graphic photos of men and women in homosexual acts, and wanted to quiz him, but their marriage was already strained. So for the kid's sake, she chose not to tip their unstable canoe. Now she saw the connection between that discovery and Andy's disclosure.

Andy felt he had negotiated this first hurdle without a fall, but to reach the finish line Julie had to link Matt's AIDS to Robert's death ...

243

and Andy refused to erect that bridge. He couldn't betray the dead for the living and still remain a priest.

"You've got to tell Faith about Matt," declared Andy.

"What possible good can come of it? Why have her worrying about my health, too?"

"You've got to trust me. I know I've been an unholy priest, but on this matter I feel very strongly … I feel guided by the Lord's hand. Please, tell her? Don't let her leave without exposing this skeleton."

Julie's mind was on overload. She knew it was Andy's love that had shielded her from the virus that had taken her son … and would eventually take her daughter, too. She had to show trust, to somehow reinforce his shattered self-esteem, but if Faith spun out of control, Julie knew she'd follow suit.

"All right, Father, into your hands I commend my soul. God help us both if you're wrong."

"Amen," he answered.

ɞ

Twice the following morning Julie had been on the verge of telling Faith about Matt, but each time she shrank from the challenge. Faith may not have admired him, Julie reasoned, but blackening his memory seemed distasteful and unnecessary.

Faith rebuffed her mother's last-ditch arguments for remaining home, certain that by living in Chicago with her former classmate she could start life anew. Andy had no intention of accompanying them to the bus depot, but Julie pleaded for his support and he caved in. He was upset that she had said nothing to Faith about Matt and worried, too, that Faith still might not make the connection once told. Whenever Julie beckoned, however, he couldn't refuse. So he hastily shuffled his schedule, and now found himself buckled in, aching for a cigarette; aching to know if today this family could begin to heal.

Faith was quiet. Julie and Andrew exchanged few words during the forty-mile drive to the bus station in Erie. Both were concerned that any conversation, however trite, would re-ignite Faith's anger. Neither wanted her farewell to be on a bitter note. After arriving at the congested terminal, Andy unloaded the car while the women went to the ticket counter. He hadn't seen a bus depot in years, and the seedy-looking travelers reminded him of the inhospitable world Faith was about to enter.

"Father, can you load those bags?" Faith waved her ticket aloft as she made the request. Andrew was sporting his dog collar and cleric shirt, leaving those who were watching to think he couldn't possibly be her father. They, like Andy, had no knowledge of the conception that occurred when he had succumbed to her mother's advances during that rowdy winter break in '67.

Julie fidgeted and Andy knew she was under intense strain. As he stowed the luggage in the belly of the idling bus, he prayed that Julie would open up, that she'd lance the boil festering in Faith's conscience.

"Is there nothing we can say? Won't you please reconsider?"

"No, Father Patterson. My mind's made up. After all, I'm not joining the Peace Corps to work in deepest, darkest Africa. I'll only be a day's drive away."

"Yes, but will you keep in touch, baby? You know I'll be worried sick if you don't …"

"We've been through all this, Mom. I'm a big girl now, remember? I'm not going to hide from you or check in every day. I want a fresh start, but I can't do that if I have to reconnect with my past everyday. Now please, don't get all fussed up again."

"Your mother and I are only worried about you. You'll be taking a real leap in cultures. Out of the valley and into the jungle, so to speak."

"Well, it's kind of you to think that way. And I know you mean it. But rest easy, I'll manage. I've had to deal with tougher challenges just living on Main Street." She looked directly at Andrew, then gave her mother a hug and a kiss.

"I think there's one more challenge your mother wants to hurl your way." He held up his index finger to accent his point.

Faith turned with an air of puzzlement, almost annoyance. The driver was making his final inspection of the bus and looked anxious for her to board.

"Mom? There's nothing that'll change my mind."

"Go ahead, Julie, it's time." He stood behind her, resting his hand on her shoulder.

"Mom, you look like you've seen a ghost."

Andy whispered in Julie's ear. Faith's eyes were riveted on her mother, whose anxiety was etched deep on her brow. The driver, unhappy with the delay, requested that she board.

"Please, Mom. Out with it."

Faith began backpedaling to appease the driver, which gave Julie the impetus to act. She took a swallow to clear her throat, then blurted out, "Your father … God rest his soul, had AIDS. That's why we think he took his life."

Faith stepped down from the bus's stairway and stood frozen. Julie looked down, then up, and then to Andy. Faith quickly grasped the significance of the news, quickly merged the past with the present, and just as quickly saw her guilt in a changing light. Her eyes opened wide and her lips trembled. "It wasn't me. I didn't do it, Mama. It wasn't my fault … he didn't die because of me."

"Now, now, baby. You didn't have anything to do with your father's death." *There's no linking them,* Julie told herself, convinced that God had ordained it all.

"Don't you see, Mom? I couldn't have done it! It wasn't my fault after all." She clasped her palm over her mouth and nose, crying uncontrollably.

Julie stared sternly at Andy. He knew her consternation would turn to scorn if she didn't see the wisdom in having told Faith the news.

"Go on, Julie. Tell her everything," he implored. "For the love of God, do it now."

"There's more, baby. Your father … may God have mercy on him … was … a homosexual. All this time and I didn't have a clue. That's what was killing him, honey. He caught the virus from another man. All those years he traveled … and I thought it was just for business." Her words trailed off as she contemplated with disbelief his enigmatic life.

"Can't you see, Mom? He gave it to me!" Faith repeated the claim as she wept.

"For God's sake, Andrew, what's she talking about? I told you she wasn't ready …"

"Let it go, Faith. Let the truth set you free. Let it set your mother free."

Faith stepped forward, then crumpled into her mother's arms. The driver moved to assist her, but Father Andy, his collar a badge of authority, motioned him off. Andy eased Faith onto a nearby bench then signaled the driver to open up the cargo bay. Quickly they removed her bags, then Andrew told him to shove off. The driver muttered a word of encouragement to Faith, then boarded. In moments the lumbering bus, diesel exhaust choking, roared from the curb.

"What is it, baby? You can tell your mother. Please, help me to understand." Julie's face was squarely in Faith's.

"Mom," she replied, her eyes taking on a distant stare, "I've never known how to say this. But Daddy ... Daddy ..."

"Abused you, child? Stole your very heart and soul."

Faith looked up to see tears streaming down her mother's cheeks.

"Again and again he raped me, Mama! I don't know why ... honest ... but he just did. He told me if I said anything he'd take Robert away."

Julie cradled her, rocking gently to and fro. *How could I have neglected her so?* Her hypnotic stare signaled a reopening of the childhood wound she so long ago had sealed in her subconscious.

"I'm so terribly ... terribly sorry. I let you down, baby. I should never have let him into your life. Never!"

Her words stung Andrew. He was ashamed of the subterfuge he'd used to bring Julie and Matt together—yet he still had no inkling that Julie, like Faith, had been abused as a child. He set aside his guilt, though, to refocus on his goal. He had brought the three of them together as a family and now that their mutual thorn had been removed, it was time to reunite mother and daughter.

"But there's more, isn't there, Faith?"

They both looked up at Andy. Julie was spent, incredulous that anything was left to be said, while Andy prayed that Faith would come to realize that her father was Robert's killer.

"Go on, tell her how you and Robert cemented your love. Remember? Down by the creek ... in your little hideaway."

A redemptive aura enveloped Faith, and she turned, almost beaming, to her mother. "Robbie and I were blood brothers, Mom. It seemed so innocent at the time. I didn't want to do it, but ... but he insisted. Do you see now, Mom?" She was exhilarated, almost excited.

"Dad gave me the virus and I gave it to Robbie that day beside the creek."

"God bless him. He must've known. That must be why he killed himself." She looked to Andrew and said, "That's it. Isn't it? May God forgive him. The suffering he must have gone through." Julie had no reserve. She sat, hollow-eyed.

"Come on, Mama, let's go home."

ৡ

Julie closed the door to the confessional and knelt. She asked him to open the curtain so she could see his face, so he could see hers and know the sincerity in her words.

"Bless me, Father, for I have sinned. I've sinned with you and against both God and man. I've led you astray and in doing so led my family and myself from His commandants. I ask the Lord to forgive my sins and help me to never stray again."

Andy responded by asking for her forgiveness, and she gave it without hesitation. As the Apostle Paul had proclaimed to the Romans, Andy now said to her: "If we live according to the flesh, we will die; but if by the spirit we put to death the evil deeds of the body, we will live." She lowered her head.

Like ships in a fog, they had abruptly altered course. The sea of misguided dreams that they'd traveled had revealed its jagged reefs. They weren't pilots—events had proven them helpless to navigate safely in such hazardous waters. Stay together and they would sink; veer from their collision course and they might both find a friendly harbor. To God they pledged they would be moored, and never again would they cast off their lines.

It had all become so clear to Andy. His self-deceptions and misconceptions had vanished. He felt as though he was atop a mountain, only now no fog or low-flying clouds obscured his vision. He could see the convoluted path he had followed, and up ahead to the narrow straightaway he wanted to tread. It was a welcome panorama, one devoid of conflict and anxiety. He had only to follow his conscience, he thought, to follow the covenant that he had made with God a score of years before.

ಬ

Andy, palms clasped, bowed low toward the altar and to the tabernacle that adorned it. He'd listened intently to the Scripture readings: it was Saint Matthew at his best, at his most perceptive. The seeds, so the parable went, had been sown, some to fall on good earth and others on rocky soil. Weeds had grown in amongst the wheat, but not until harvest time could the wheat be freed of the strangling weeds, one to be burned, the other collected and stored. It was a fitting allegory to the gospel that Pastor Andrew had chosen. From the lectern he scanned the congregation gathered before him this warm September Sunday morning. Only a handful were strangers, but in amongst this flock stood a mother and daughter who had not gone hand-in-hand under God's roof in years. It was the Godsend he'd prayed for, the fulfillment of his vision for the Garrison women.

He looked on with admiration as they held hands, clasping his palms together and raising them like a prizefighter. They smiled at his tribute, and he knew the reward that awaited them for having mended their schism. He opened the Lectionary to a passage from Luke, then raised the microphone closer to his lips. He had taunted Matt with the story of the Prodigal Son, and many had suffered for his arrogance. Today, instead, he looked to Luke for healing and for an affirmation of the two women standing before him and God.

He adjusted his bifocals and lifted the leather-bound book to see its words. He was anxious to bare his soul and to recount the parable that defined his life. His chest heaved and his voice cracked. He paused, cleared his throat, and delivered the verse with a conviction he'd not thought possible:

...What man having a hundred sheep, and losing one of them, does not leave the ninety-nine in the desert, and go after that which is lost, until he finds it? And when he has found it, he lays it upon his shoulders rejoicing. And on coming home he calls together his friends and neighbors, saying to them, 'Rejoice with me, because I have found my sheep that was lost.' I say to you that even so, there will be joy in heaven over one sinner who repents, more than over the ninety-nine just who have no need of repentance.